INTERZONE

G000141922

Again and again, whether they be funny or
horrific, relaxed or tight-stretched,
INTERZONE stories, like as not, will be
explicitly about human beings trying to make
sense of things . . .

They warn us, as do most of the stories we
publish in INTERZONE, that we are in the
swell of the ninth wave of the most exciting
century the race has ever experienced. They tell
us to be afraid, to rejoice, and to look. Look!
(they say) at what we're coming through.

That is our invitation.

INTERZONE: The Second Anthology

'Its best stories are quite enough to be heard even among the mindless roar of the big guns; they are pockets of clarity like soft sensible dialogues'

City Limits

'a solid collection'

Time Out

'Judging by *Interzone: The Second Anthology* the magazine is still improving'
Manchester Evening News

'The second *Interzone* anthology is encouraging: here are veterans and new talent blazing away'
New Statesman

'They have the quality of going right to the edge of ideas which can chill as well as warm'
The Times

INTERZONE: The First Anthology

'Science fiction is supposed to be a backwater,
albeit a commercial one. But *Interzone* strides
over the frontier and well on to a summit of art!'
New Statesman

'A must for science fiction enthusiasts'
Cosmopolitan

'An excellent collection'
Southern Evening Echo

'a selection of stories that combine the grim and
the glorious with an audacity that recalls
Dangerous Visions . . . it should not be missed at
any cost'

Locus

INTERZONE

the 2nd anthology

New Science Fiction and Fantasy Writing

Edited by
John Clute, David Pringle and Simon Ounsley

NEW ENGLISH LIBRARY
Hodder and Stoughton

Introduction © John Clute 1987
Selection and Notes of Authors ©
Interzone Magazine 1987
The copyright information on the
Acknowledgements pages
constitutes an extension to this
copyright notice

First published in Great Britain in
1987 by Simon & Schuster Limited

First New English Library
Paperback Edition 1988

The characters and situations in this
book are entirely imaginary and bear
no relation to any real person
or actual happening.

This book is sold subject to the
condition that it shall not, by way of
trade or otherwise, be lent, re-sold,
hired out or otherwise circulated
without the publisher's prior consent
in any form of binding or cover other
than that in which it is published and
without a similar condition including
this condition being imposed on the
subsequent purchaser.

No part of this publication may be
reproduced or transmitted in any form
or by any means, electronically
or mechanically, including
photocopying, recording in any
information storage or retrieval
system, without either the prior
permission in writing from the
publisher or a licence, permitting
restricted copying. In the United
Kingdom such licences are issued by the
Copyright Licensing Agency, 33–34
Alfred Place, London WC1E 7DP.

British Library C.I.P.

Interzone : the 2nd anthology.
1. Science fiction short stories in
English, 1945 – Anthologies
I. Clute, John, *1940–* II. Pringle,
David, *1950–* III. Ounsley, Simon
823'.0876'08 [FS]

ISBN 0-450-42853-2

Printed and bound in Great Britain
for Hodder and Stoughton
Paperbacks, a division of Hodder and
Stoughton Ltd., Mill Road,
Dunton Green, Sevenoaks, Kent
TN13 2YA (Editorial Office: 47 Bedford
Square, London WC1B 3DP) by Cox &
Wyman

Contents

INTRODUCTION

JOHN CLUTE

This may not be the dawn of the Age of Aquarius, but it is certainly 1987, and we are glad to be here. Small magazines, after all, like mayflies in the jaws of time, tend to flourish for a day, only to die of circulation problems when the sun goes down, and *Interzone* was in truth very small indeed back in 1982, when the first 32-page issue appeared. Even now, at twice the size, and with a growing subscription list, we have clearly managed to avoid the perils of gigantism. But still, here we are, deep into several of the futures dreamed (or undreamed) of in the ten million or so pages of science fiction that have already been written in this century. And here, in *Interzone: the 2nd anthology*, which contains some of the best fiction from the last twelve issues, are fifteen more stories – call them science fiction, or fantasy, or fables for our time – about the ways things are, and may be.

For science fiction readers in particular, but for most other folk as well, there used to be a thing called the future. It was something that seemed to stand almost physically a few steps in front of one. It was solid, it was right there. Inherently different from the present, it was recognisable all the same. And it had a *portal*. In those days, only a few years ago, we entered this portal of the future from a place called the present. The present was even more solid than the future, and just as legible. The present was *level*. And to give us room to stretch our legs and settle down properly to our lives, the platform of the

present gave effortlessly and without crevasses uninter-
rupted access to the great panoplied vistas of the past. If
we were writers or readers of science fiction, however, we
tended to keep our attention fixed on the portal of the
future, and to anticipate with joy and some complacency
the marvels we would behold when we had stepped
through this gate into a new world. There would be robots
there, and vast block-square computers; there would be
civilian and military travel through space, first to the
moon, then to the planets, and then (after a while) even
to the stars; back on Terra, great cities built on Baroque
principles and laced together with aerial freeways would
house bureaucrats, fuzzy-haired scientists, and the world
president, whose brow would continually furrow, and who
would give off a constant aura of sheer power as he faced
the problems – aliens, pirates, women – of a growing
Galactic Empire; there would be little or no biological
engineering, unless used to grow extra biceps; and finally,
there would be a large number of supermen, whose world-
saving powers were almost invariably hereditary, not
environmentally engineered. This was science fiction's
future, and it lasted for half a century. We knew it was
romantic, and simple-minded, and often childish, but we
also knew, or thought we knew, that the science fiction
cartoons of our imaginings did indeed hint at a future we
could in fact enter, through the same portal. Science
fiction readers or not, we all of us lived in the same world
at the same time. Or so it seemed.

It was sometime in the 1950s that the future ended,
though a long time would pass before most science fiction
devotees began to sense the fact. As a legible and orderly
portal we might step through, the future slammed shut
with the coming of the transistor, and with the first orbital
flight of the first Sputnik. At one stroke, Sputnik shattered
the great stage on which the future had been displayed
for the previous half century – for make no mistake,
however sophisticated a definition of science fiction might

be, it will fail to understand the time- and space-bound nature of the genre if it fails to understand that science fiction's heart was in the future, and that its domain was space. Sputnik brought space into the present, bureaucratised the rococo tintinnabulating aisles and arroyos of space, and science fiction's domain began to crumble. This loss was nothing, however, compared to the effect of the transistor and the integrated circuit, inventions which were very widely unanticipated by science fiction writers. They have had one main effect on the world. They have made information invisible.

No longer has information any tangible, kinetic analogue in the world of the senses, or in the imaginations of writers of fiction. Gone are the great arrays of vacuum tubes, the thousands of toggles that heroes of space fiction would flick *almost* faster than the eye could see as they dodged space 'torpedoes', outflanked alien 'battle lines', steered through asteroid 'storms'; gone, more importantly, is any sustained sense of the autonomy, in space and time, of gross visible individual human actions. And if 'actions' are now invisible, then our fates are likewise beyond our grasp. We no longer feel that we penetrate the future; futures now penetrate us. We live in a specious present whose apertures or coigns of vantage flicker to the beat of dances of information we cannot see to ordinate. And these dances of the furious futures begin, I think, to transform us utterly. It is exciting beyond words to be alive in 1987, but perhaps that is because the old words started to fail us in 1957. This may not be the dawn of the Age of Aquarius, but something infinitely ganglioned and glittering does all the same seem to have begun to illuminate our human countenances, from behind and beyond. Time's portal has surely become an interzone.

If an array of futures already weights the invisible strings that guide us, then it's not surprising that many of the best stories in *Interzone*, and several of those here

selected for this anthology, should concern themselves
with making sense of the world. As so much of our world
has already been entered by the future, it's not surprising
either that stories like J. G. Ballard's 'The Man who
Walked on the Moon' can be read as parables of an
almost sexual entering of images of the future into lives
like those we now live. The complex, icon-choked course
of the protagonist of Rachel Pollack's 'The Protector'
carries her from wife to shaman, from nescience to an
extremity of knowledge of a world *in extremis*. It is our
world. Scott Bradfield's is our world as well, though it
may be California, and the course of his protagonist in
'Unmistakably the Finest' is clearly that of a burrowing
animal for whom the light-show of the day is an impossible
trial. 'Unmistakably the Finest', by the way, like so much
Californian writing, is hilarious as well as black; as is
Thomas M. Disch's 'Canned Goods'. Bradfield and Disch
are both American, and it may be that the hilarity aroused
in both of them by the commodity fetish is peculiarly
American; but it's to be hoped that we can all laugh.
Michael Blumlein's 'The Brains of Rats' has less to laugh
about, though a sharp observational wit deepens (and
makes tolerable) the savagery of his vision of a moment
within the interzone when the arousing binaries of our
sexual biology can be fixed, for all of us.

Again and again, whether they be funny or horrific,
relaxed or tight-stretched, *Interzone* stories, like as not,
will be explicitly about human beings trying to make sense
of things. The title of Neil Ferguson's latest parable of
detection, 'The Second Third of C', clearly foregrounds
his wry preoccupation with human sign-making, though it
cannot adequately signal the chill, gripping panache of
this tale. Garry Kilworth's 'Spiral Sands' takes a man
from the popular anomie of London to a desert drenched
with meaning, into which he burrows. The title of Ian
Watson's sharp, sombre parody, 'When the Timegate
Failed', might well entitle this introduction, but more than

adequately points his own moral. Other stories, unsurprisingly, follow other courses. Brian Stableford's 'And He Not Busy Being Born' makes ironic play of the implications of cryogenic immortality, in an extended conspectus of the implications of that theme. Paul J. McAuley's 'The King of the Hill' and Lee Montgomerie's 'War and/or Peace' draw out some of the darker implications of the Matter of Nuclear Britain, while Peter T. Garratt's 'If the Driver Vanishes', set in America, takes Fundamentalist Christians more literally than perhaps they might wish to be understood. John Shirley and Bruce Sterling's 'The Unfolding' rewrites an old science fiction debate about the human/robot dichotomy, and features a much bigger DNA molecule than I had ever dared to envisage. The only stories yet unmentioned, Gregory Benford's 'Freeze-frame' and Kim Newman's 'Patricia Profession', are both joys of language and appliance, short sharp future shocks that tingle in the mind while warning us.

They warn us, as do most of the stories we publish in *Interzone*, that we are in the swell of the ninth wave of the most exciting century the race has ever experienced. They tell us to be afraid, to rejoice, and to look. Look! (they say) at what we're coming through.

That is our invitation.

NEIL FERGUSON

THE SECOND THIRD OF C

Someone was going to kill Roger Morse.

Kill. Deprive of life. Mark for omission. Destroy the vital and essential quality of. Check the flow of current through.

Morse knew this because someone had entered his apartment and whoever it had been had left without disturbing it or removing anything of value. No ransacking had taken place. There were no splintered locks or signs of violent entry. Morse might never have become apprised of the intrusion had it not been for the fact that his old, battered, practically worthless copy of *Skeat's Dictionary of Etymology* was not where he always kept it on the right-hand corner of his writing desk. His 1982 facsimile reprint of the original 1882 edition.

Well, so what? It was only a book. It wasn't irreplaceable. Morse knew he could call up the library and have Rita send round a copy. He could probably even scrounge one from a colleague if he set his mind to it. *Skeat's Etymology* was – or had once been – a standard work, not some rare tome. Only superstition had kept him from filing it on his computer. But it wouldn't be the same, a new copy. It wouldn't be *his* Skeat, the one he had been awarded as a prize at school, which had directed him onto the path that led in the direction of his vocation. It wouldn't be his *Skeat*, thumbed, travelled, cherished. A talisman he had carried through life. His juju.

The fact that the book was no longer in the room with

him, at hand, to be picked up and put down as he pleased,
filled Morse's heart with sadness just as if an old friend
had died. Suddenly and for no obvious reason he had lost
something he loved. And Morse could not help recalling
that the meaning of *love* – an affection based on admira-
tion, a warm attachment and devotion – appeared on the
opposite page of *Skeat's Etymology* as that given for *lost*
– no longer possessed, taken away beyond reach or
attainment. The two words embraced each other every
time he closed the book.

A *closed book*: something beyond comprehension. An
enigma.

So poignant was the loss to Morse – and so pointles to
anybody else – that he knew it was meant to be significant.
It was inconceivable that the intruder had taken the book
out of a desire to possess it. The theft was almost certainly
some kind of message. A sign. Like the shot dog of the
corrupt politician.

In his bathrobe, wide awake, Morse fractionally modi-
fied the smoke-glass louvres of the electronic jalousie in
order to see what was going on outside, beyond the
electrified barbed-wire perimeter-ring. He could see nothing. It made no difference that he was wearing his glasses.
There was nothing to see. If it wasn't strictly night out
there it was still quite dark. Only fractionally less so, in
fact, than it was inside Morse's apartment.

The light-synchronous personal climate unit was not
strictly a jalousie either – which in Morse's book was a
blind with adjustable horizontal slats for admitting light
and air while excluding sun and rain – but it was the name
the manufacturer had chosen for the purpose of marketing
the system, skilfully leaching from the old term a hint of
Mediterranean romance. The small shift in usage did not
bother Morse one way or the other. But he would have to
take account of it in the next edition of his book.

While Morse squinted out of the darkened window the
small crimson light on the phonebank continued to flash

silently behind him – a call had been banked – dully
illuminating the room at regular intervals. Morse deliberately ignored the signal, keeping his back to the machine,
although to do so gave him mixed feelings of cowardice
and valour.

When eventually the darkness began to thin he focused
on the colourless rectilinear constructions on the far side
of his view of the park which comprised the apartment-
hotel compound. He watched the orthogonal sections of
the ugly grey structures – the organised desolation of
public buildings – slowly become adumbrated against the
marginally less grey dawn, the two shades of greyness
edging apart like a pair of nefarious characters before
daylight caught them in each other's company.

Morse knew how bad the situation was in those old
mass-concept buildings. He had been inside them. This
was more than could be said for most of the people he
rubbed shoulders with in his expensive residential apartment block or at the library. Public housing estates were
not a no-go area for high-income academics and pro-
fessionals with tech access, but few of them had any
reason to roam far outside the secure keep of electric light
and stable climate they had paid the service-management
to provide. It wasn't worth the risk. The fieldwork necessary for Morse's research, on the other hand, took him
into zones that were turbid, dysphasic, chthonic. In his
pursuit of the meaning of words familiar and arcane he
had climbed the urine-soaked open stair-shafts of the
deck-stacked buildings; had hurried past the savage graf-
fiti he couldn't decipher, however tempted he might have
been to try; and encountered the old woman in bedroom
slippers on the broken glass-strewn walkway, face frozen
with fear – an unpleasant emotion caused by anticipation
of danger. First-hand knowledge of such a degree of
unpleasantness Morse considered part of his job. He liked
his definitions to be concordant with his experience.

But Morse had another, more pressing motive for

surveying the dismal prospect. Somewhere out there – not
in this particular estate but one pretty much like it in
another part of the city – there was someone, a young
woman he liked, who liked *him* – well enough, at least, to
want to talk to, laugh at, sleep with. Something, until he
met her, he had not thought possible. Morse had made
the woman's acquaintance some months previous while
engaged on the second third of C, from CAT to COZ. In
between *cat's paws* – a light air that ruffles the surface of
water in irregular patches during a calm – and *cozen* – to
gain something by coaxing, wheedling or shrewd trickery
– he had climbed the stairs of what were still called council
estates, characterless housing units built at a time when
there had been *councils* – bodies of people meeting to
talk over local questions or laws. Now, of course, these
dinosaur barracks abandoned by the authorities belonged
to whoever lived inside them, which meant that the
secondary meaning of the word – owned and maintained
by such local bodies – was more or less archaic.

In the course of his fieldwork Morse had knocked
on doors, peered through letterboxes – another quaint
archaism – and sat before heatless fires with old sailors,
ageing ballet-dancers, retired french polishers. He had
recorded the specialised lexes in their reminiscences, that
served no purpose in their present environment. It was
the speech of their grandchildren which had adapted to
the general dereliction and the brutal frankness of concrete curtain-walling.

Sharon – high-cheeked, lithe, literate Sharon – had
taken the habit of accompanying Morse, her arm in his,
steering him through the warren of refuse-strewn cause-
ways that linked the dwellings. She knew which of them
had been blocked off and the best places to hide. In fact,
for a person who had never been able to afford any
schooling, she knew many things of which Morse was
ignorant. In return he brought her coffee, fresh food,
small pieces of news, and – what she craved for most –

books, including several types of dictionary. Sets of printed sheets of paper bound together into volumes, something that yields up knowledge or understanding, were rare commodities on Sharon's estate, although she had, somehow, come by her own small, odd library. She had, too, come by a small child, a little girl of five. And from the same source.

While he dressed, Morse thought about shaving, then, dismissing the thought, poured hot water straight from the tap into a mug containing instant coffee. By this time he was able to read his watch: 5.17. He flipped the flashing playback-key of his phonebank and listened intently. The recording whirred but no human or computer's voice came out of it.

Morse timed the silence, which lasted exactly thirty-three seconds. It was a longish amount of time but short enough to tell him what he wanted to know, that Sharon was alive, safe. She was okay. Not long enough, anyway, to say that he had to drop everything, she wasn't desperate or in some kind of danger. Morse played the recording over again. He listened again to her listening to him listening to her. At times the absence of her voice was brief – three or four seconds, mere pauses. She had even omitted – forgotten, she said – to phone him at all, so if she wasn't dead she was fine. And there had been occasions when the length of her silence had almost broken his heart.

Morse rubbed his fingers against the bristly growth under his chin.

Thirty-three seconds. She was missing him. She had woken up in the night. Lonely. Wanting him to be with her.

Sharon could phone Morse but she could not speak to him – not, that is, without informing the police security computer of what she had to say, with all the complications that would bring: arrest, interrogation, surveillance. Morse could not phone her at all for the simple reason that the vandalised semi-functional payphone she had access to could not accept calls, not even having been programmed for such a communication facility. In order for Sharon to be able to get a message to Morse they had arranged a code – silence on a scale from one second to sixty – as a strategem to keep their unusual liaison from molestation, to allow Sharon to let him know how she was doing.

But not what. Where. Or with whom.

Whom. Middle English *hwām*. Used as an object of a verb or preceding preposition, occasionally as a predicate nominative with a copulative verb.

The candle flame swayed in the still air as she turned the page, then gradually righted itself. She turned it carefully with the weight of her whole hand, not between her fingers, in order not to crack the yellowed margin of the old cheap paper. Curled up in her bed – on the dry side – in the shape of the warmth the man had vacated some time before, Sharon consumed the print which he had brought for her, the price she had demanded for the loan of her body. She read each word of every sentence, greedily, like a gourmand disposing of a rare wine.

> It was a very dark evening; the clouds appeared inclined to thunder. Catherine kept wandering to and fro, from the gate to the door in a state of agitation which permitted no repose; at length she took up a position on one side of the wall, near the road, where, heedless of the growing thunder and the great drops of rain that began to splash around her, she remained calling at intervals, then listening, then crying outright . . .

Grey dawn light was beginning to enter the room, jim-mying its way through the cracks in the boarded-up windows, but for the moment the candle-flame still cast its halo around Sharon and the open book. From her cot Lucy snuffled in her sleep.

After midnight while we sat up the storm came rattling over the Heights in full fury. There was a violent wind, as well as thunder, and either one or the other split a tree off at the corner of the building: a huge bough fell across the roof . . .

It had been quick and dull, what the man had come to do. He had come and done it and gone, taking off his parka, slipping into her and out of the bed and leaving her alone. She would never see him again because she made a point of never doing that kind of business with the same man twice. But the good condition orange-and-white paperback book in her hand would last for many years, perhaps even after her death, as it had lasted from before her birth: this 1956 reprint – Complete & Un-abridged – 2/6 – of the 1847 edition. And it was hers now. The quick excitement she had let the man have was nothing, nothing alongside the slow enduring pleasure she would derive from the book. It was a bargain!

. . . Cathy got thoroughly drenched for her obstinacy in refusing to take shelter and standing bonnetless and shawl-less to catch as much water as she could with her hair and clothes. She came in and lay down on the settle, turning her face to the back and putting her hands before it . . .

Immediately after the man had left she had felt emptied – she did not enjoy what she had to do to provide herself with pleasure. Shivering, she had slipped out of the condominium to the payphone terminal concealed under refuse and dialled the private number to the person at the Parkview whom she wanted to speak to, as she nearly always did immediately after the men left. Somehow the silence she listened to on the recording-machine did not feel so lonesome as the silence she had to endure through-out the rest of the night, as if it was not hers but belonged now to the person who owned the machine. Listening to his silence gave shape to her own, it occupied the empti-ness. Defined it.

As he defined every damn thing he came near, right

from their first encounter which she had initiated the way she always did: 'D'you want to fuck me?' She had caught him unawares in a dark intersection.

'What do you mean,' he said, 'exactly?'

'Sexual intercourse. D'you want it?'

'But they're not the same thing.'

'What are you talking about?' She hadn't known what he was talking about.

'*Fucking* is generally considered obscene. *Sexual intercourse* is a socially accepted term. Which did you have in mind?'

'Whichever fucking term you like!'

'I don't know . . .' He had looked grave. He had rubbed his chin, which needed a shave. 'Fucking is a bit crude and sexual intercourse, well, rather bland. And making love wouldn't seem appropriate at this stage, would it? I mean, we hardly know each other . . .' Then, still serious, without smiling: 'Can't we start with a cup of tea?'

He made her laugh. He was the first man who ever had, and the first who didn't want to fuck her or just have sexual intercourse. He wanted to *make love* – at least the way he defined the term: to woo, court, engage in activities – such as *necking*: to kiss or pet – leading to mating. And he had not hurried over any of his definitions. The way he made love to her was neither obscene nor socially acceptable.

He made her laugh just to look at him. Ginger-haired, freckled and bespectacled, hardly ever shaved, plump and rumpled – not the kind of man she would have thought many women would have been attracted to, least of all herself.

'Well, you know what they used to say,' he had said. 'You don't want to judge a book by its cover!'

Sharon continued to read until her daughter, Lucy, still half-asleep, began tugging to be let into bed with her. She placed the old torn page that served as a bookmark between chapters Five and Six, slid the book under her pillow and turned her attention towards her daughter, lifting her up into the bed. It was getting too late to read anyway. A grimy-grey light had penetrated every corner of the room, washing out the candle's small brightness. Sharon blew out the flame. Night had ended and the day had begun.

'The Manager wants to know what you're up to,' Rita said as soon as Roger Morse walked into his workspace on the fourth floor of the library, and, when he declined to comment, added: 'He wants to know what you're *working* on.'

Morse looked at Rita. If his computer didn't know the answer to that question then who did? 'You told him,' he said, 'I suppose?'

'Oh sure! I outlined the field from which the majority of your entries recently have been drawn.'

Morse felt a shiver run down his spine, and it wasn't as a consequence of the infelicitously placed adverb – which was probably standard in Phoenix, Arizona, Rita's home town. Someone had just stepped on his grave. The person in possession of his copy of *Skeat's Etymology*, perhaps.

'They flit from *flirt* to *uxorious*,' Rita reminded him. 'And a whole lot in between. Mostly in C: clitoral . . . coition . . . copulate . . .'

'*Sex!*' Morse growled. 'You told him *that* was the field I was working in?'

'I sure did, Roger,' the computer said with irritating frankness. 'The Manager didn't seem to welcome the news.'

'Why not? It's very fertile ground!'

Cock came between *caress* and *cunt*. It was a fact of life.

'He said our sponsors were having budget problems. They're finding it hard to justify spending money on a new dictionary and weren't looking to have their name on one that would be disadvantageous to the selling of their product.'

Morse tried to recall the product which the Police Executive was trying to sell.

'You mean,' he said eventually, '*the truth*!'

Rita, as usual, refused to be drawn.

'He wants to see you. Immediately.'

Morse, heading in the direction of the Manager's office, strode across the floor of the hermetically sealed minia-ture rain-forest that formed the ground-level of the atrium of the library building, aggressively crunching the grav-elled path underfoot. Cuneate-shaped palm leaves nodded up and down in the air he disturbed behind him. The canopy of evergreen fronds overhead pressed down on the air and occluded the light. Irritably he swatted away the giant azure and vermilion butterflies that sought to settle on his brow. They were like easy pleasant thoughts which at this moment he could not afford to entertain. Ahead he could make out the shadowy bulk of the Manager on the other side of the abraded glass walls of the cage that was his office, moving from side to side, restless, like a pupa in the throes of metamorphosis. Morse waited for the panelled door to slide open and then he stepped through it, entering the membrane of the chrysalis.

'Roger! Hi there! Come in! . . . Okay? How you doing? Sit down. Sit down. Mmmm. Cigar?'

Morse shook his head.

The Manager, Doctor Artman, was a German-speaker who had acquired his American on West Coast campuses and he condimented his speech with friendly phatics, sounds intended to establish an atmosphere of sociability rather than communicate ideas.

'Right. Now. Let's get down and, er, talk turkey, shall we, mmm?' Artman laughed. When Morse was seated on the client's couch, he levered his own bulky person onto the opposite chair, using his powerful arms as a pair of davits.

'I want to inform you, Roger, how much your output is appreciated . . . ah, by me.'

'You like my work?'

'Oh sure! It's good!'

Morse made no effort to look pleasantly surprised. He waited impassively, grit-teethed, while Doctor Artman, Manager of the Lexical Software Library Company, stumbled over his inappropriately formal and slangy choice of words. Morse mulled over his entry for *stuffed shirt*: a smug, conceited and usually pompous person often with an inflexibly conservative attitude. It was good enough.

'Don't make any mistake about it. It's good stuff.' Doctor Artman laughed again. Was he nervous or had he said something funny? 'Mmm. But, ah, – I don't know how to put this – we're coming up against some pretty rigid parameters on this present assignment. You understand what I'm saying?'

'Do you mean outside pressure?'

'Yes. You got it! Absolutely.' Artman nodded. He tugged at the invisible goatee at the apex of his chin. 'Our sponsors are undergoing a budget-rethink.'

'A *what*!' Morse said. 'I mean, in what respect, Doctor?'

'Fieldwork. They take the line that it's too difficult. Too laborious. And too, ah, expensive.'

Morse said: 'I thought the Police Executive was interested in building accurate language atlases for different status speech communities. How can you do that without fieldwork?'

'They want to know why it has to be so laborious to provoke speech acts. Interviewing people, the way you do. In their opinion utterances can be gathered without, ah, having to spend time *communicating*.'

'Fieldwork involves two people,' Morse said. 'An investigator and an informant.'

'The Police Executive claim to have some experience in that department. They're not convinced your methods, particularly your excursions into access-restricted areas, are, ah, cost-effective.'

Morse, uneasy that his activities had been a subject of police interest, said: 'How do they expect me to collect examples of local speech without examining the locality?'

'They suggest you make use of their security-gathering technology. They are putting their computers at our – your – disposal. Edited, of course. This data, as you know, consists of spontaneous utterances between citizens, gathered *in situ* from all sections of society.'

'The Police Executive wants to plug me into their security computer?' Morse said. The idea filled him with repugnance. It was both alien to his principles and aroused in him a loathing too great to tolerate: odium.

'But that's a record of people's personal plans, chit-chat. Gossip. Pillow talk. I couldn't possibly take part in such privacy invasion!'

Artman squirmed. His belly adjusted itself as if it were a cat trying to get comfortable. 'I understand, Roger. I respect your . . . ah . . .'

'*Qualms*? Feelings of uneasiness about a point of conscience, honour or propriety?'

'Yes. Qualms. But you must admit that such an arrangement would, ah, remove the problem of you, the investigator, interacting with the subject's natural language. It would be more professional. More scientific.'

'It would be less ethical! Less honest!'

Artman was a third-rate academic who thought in German and spoke in Californian, not well in either. Though he had edited several books on the subject of lexicography he had never composed a dictionary definition in his life. He was an expert on a subject he knew nothing about. His Doctorate was honorary. He was a sham, a counterfeit purporting to be genuine. A toady, one who flatters in the hope of gaining favour. He didn't, in any sense, speak the same language as Morse.

'It's a step in the right direction,' Artman said.

'I'm sorry . . . I don't understand.'

'Look upon it as a promotion! You'll have to work in the Police Executive's headquarters. You'll be accountable directly to *them*!'

Appalled at the prospect, angry at finding himself outmanoeuvred by the slyness of someone as stupid as Artman, Morse said: 'This is out of the question! . . . You *know* I need to finish my work *here*!'

'Oh . . .' Artman heaved himself to his feet. 'We'll always be here.' He beamed at Morse. 'Congratulations, Roger.' He walked over to the console of his desk where he pressed some keys. 'You have a Captain Cznetsov of the Protocol Section waiting to meet with you at the Police Executive. This afternoon. He's, ah, looking forward to knowing you.'

Artman handed Morse a clutch of access numbers. The interview was over.

Camouflaged against the rubbish in the semi-darkness of the stairwell, Sharon gripped the metal rail and listened to the whine of the wind as it sliced across the open concrete space she was preparing to enter. She turned her attention to the pitch of the frequencies inside the sound in order to pick out any static, fragments of violence, that might be clinging to it. She wondered whether the sound was similar to that which the wind made across a deserted moor – a geological feature she had never seen but which, according to her new dictionary, she knew to be an expanse of rolling unenclosed wasteland. Could it be more hair-raising than this? Would this ever be as romantic as that?

When Sharon had pushed her nose into the grey daylight and wedged herself into the angle between the walkway and the stairwell she was at a crucial point. She could see

ahead as far as the bridge and, over the coping of the
parapet, the flat landscaped desert below where the surface
of the water in the puddles, calm out of the force of the
wind, ruffled in irregular patches and huge once-famous
football heroes climbed and volleyed on the faded mural.
She watched a black mongrel dog – a bitch with three pups
– emerge from below the opposite causeway, trot across the
decayed play-area, look right and left, then lope towards
the tunnel below where Sharon was installed. The pups
scampered to keep up with her.

Distant thunder – or a helicopter? – rumbled. The
wind tossed Sharon's hair across her face, into her
mouth. A tear formed in her windward eye as she
thought about the windswept moor in the book she had
been reading. But it wasn't just the stormy weather or
the remote landscape against which the book was set she
thought about so much as the stormy remote heart of
the heroine. It shook her, shocked her, to find such a
fearless woman so completely portrayed. Sharon, herself,
already understood the mechanics of a sexual affair that
was illicit, secret and maybe also doomed.

It had been at this spot, just here, that she had encountered the man in the parka who had produced the book.
Yesterday. She had surprised him, catching him from
behind, when she saw he was alone, as he left the stairwell
exit onto the causeway. Knowing that he was behind her,
she had lain in wait for him, then: 'You looking for a fuck,
mister?'

The man had not jumped out of his skin. On the
contrary, he had surprised *her*, when she had named her
price, by having about him the unorthodox currency she
would accept it in. Usually she left them to find the
scratch – a bundle of magazines, *Plain Truth, The Watch-
tower*, a collection of *Reader's Digests*. This one had said:
'Well, if it's a read you want, try this,' taking a paperback
book from his parka pocket. 'It's good. More where it

came from,' he had told her. 'Let me know. What you
want I can get.'

'Sorry. With me,' she had told him, 'you only get one
crack.'

But here she was, back the next day, on the look-out
for him. For his supply of printed fiction. Ready to pay
for it. Her fix.

Directly below the parapet a pair of grey boys stole out
of the surrounding greyness. They moved with stealth
from behind one of the abandoned earthbeds, children
stalking an invisible prey. Tearfully, Sharon observed
them signal, watch each other, unaware that they were
being watched. In their hands both boys were holding
stubby home-made-looking wooden crossbows.

Was she expecting to meet the man in the parka again,
to run into him in the same spot because she was there at
the same time? To find out from him what, exactly, he
was offering for sale? Well, it was possible. She couldn't
help wondering whether the supply the man had hinted at
would be of a similar nature: stories about people like
herself, men and women incarcerated in their landscape,
in a fate into which concrete had been poured and allowed
to set. Or would Roger's altogether weightier reference
books prove to be enough?

Sharon wiped the tear from her eye.

When the black mongrel bitch leapt back out into the
open it was pursued by the sound of rattling metal and
now she had only two of her pups with her. The exit she
headed for was blocked, one of the grey boys stood
between her and escape. The bitch swerved and circled
the perimeter, bewildered, silent. The two boys and the
pursuer – a girl, Sharon could tell, carrying an iron spear
– patiently cornered her. The first bolt struck her in full
flank and the thin howl that rose up from her pierced the
heart of the wind which immediately carried it away. The
second bolt silenced the animal. She lay on her side
staring at the two pups which approached her, sniffing.

Then the girl daubed her spear in the dog's blood, wrote three words on the wall across the faded pink calves of the leaping football players. Sharon could not decipher the words and she did not think she would find them in any of Roger's dictionaries.

After the taxi had driven off, a few gulls swooping desultorily after it, Morse stood at the side of the deserted thoroughfare, irritated, angry and afraid – and uncertain which of these unpleasant emotions he would eventually succumb to. Through the fine rain that immediately began to fleck the surface of his glasses he peered about him to find his bearings among the contours of the similarly angular landscape. A helicopter buzzed low overhead, vanished. Strange and half-familiar landmarks merged into each other. Thinking he recognised where he had been left, Morse picked up his nylon grip and headed for the tunnel into the nearest tower-block complex, still angry at the taxidriver's effrontery and irritated at the amount he had been cozened into paying him, still afraid of the consequences of failing to bribe the man sufficiently to carry him this far off the more lucratively pliable routes.

At the end of the tunnel Morse cautiously emerged onto the paved concourse of the estate. His bearings – fixed points from which comprehension of his exact position in the environment could be calculated – were not immediately discernible. The approaching storm was darkening the sky, making it appear later in the day than it actually was.

Where was he? Where was he going?

'*Forth*!' had been the glib reply he had hurled at Rita when the computer had quizzed him on that very question as he gathered up his possessions before leaving the library: Away from a place of residence or sojourn. Onward in time or space. Out into notice or view.

His ejection of himself from the lucid closed world of

the library building into the semi-organised chaos beyond
the steel perimeter-ring and the guard on the gate had not
been planned. It was something that had just happened,
made necessary by the chemistry inside the situation, like
a stage in metamorphosis by which an organism is changed
willy-nilly, without any say in the matter. With his scant
luggage of fractured emotions, a used razor, a handful of
old photographs, and the emptiness left by his missing
copy of *Skeat's Etymology*, he was entering hostile territory where his access numbers would be useless to him
and his RP accent a burden. His feelings of vulnerability,
however, were caused less by the immediate danger he
was in than the realisation that for the first time in his life
he was in the world without the map and compass of
lexical reference.

Conscious of the proximity of the chiga-chiga-chiga of
the unseen low-flying police helicopter patrol, Morse
hurried into the labyrinth of gravel-dashed walkways
among whose confluences of tunnels and sloped spurs he
would conceal himself. It would absorb him as the concrete walling absorbed the concrete-coloured rain. He
welcomed the difficulties he faced finding a way through;
the more completely he became lost the greater his
chances were of eluding the swoop of the helicopter that
would soon be programmed to seek him out as surely as
the beak of a bird is designed to crack the backs of small
creatures scampering to ground.

Through a crenel in a sloping parapet below, Morse
caught a flash of movement – away from him. Swerving,
he ducked behind a concrete support structure. Almost
immediately three teenagers of indeterminate sex shot out
from the elbow of the junction, loped silently towards
him, a dog's carcass skewered on the pole that two of
them were carrying. Morse watched, waited, grinned,
then, when they had disappeared, shouldered his grip and
plunged into the foul-smelling wake left by the entrails of

the dead animal. He was acquiring the vocabulary of responses a man needed to make his way in this world.

Zig-zagging among the graffitied architecture, Morse jogged upwards towards the twenty-second floor K-block west condominium, home of the young prostitute who had befriended him. *Her* home – and now his, if not in the sense of usual domestic residence, then in that of the final objective in a game, one in which he was a human counter in the intricate life-and-death end-moves. The rubric of the game, the writing on the walls around him, if unintelligible was jagged with violence: the runes of sociolects belonging to isolated tribal groups abandoned by society, the letter-shapes primitively mimicking the outline of sexual parts, obscene acts, various methods of inflicting pain.

'Hey, you've lost weight!' she said.

Sharon stood arms akimbo, grinning, wearing a waisted blue and white-spotted silky dress, stolen from the past.

'Most of it . . .' Morse, collapsing onto the bed, said, panting for breath, '. . . in the last ten minutes.'

The final ascent had exhausted him. He grinned up at her, pleased to see her, to see that she was pleased to see him. Weary with fear and hunger, he allowed her to make him comfortable on the bed, spoon-feed him liquid baby-food, while his fingers, as if they possessed a will of their own, tried to help her out of her dress. Soon, uncertain how exactly his own clothes had been removed, he found himself naked inside the bed with the young woman he desired naked beside him. After his exhausting ascent of the tower-block, the baby-feeding and now the somnolent entry into the natal conduit of the woman, Morse had returned – in at least some sense to the word – *home*. He was safe, warm, soon falling into a light sleep: the natural periodic suspension of consciousness during which the powers of the body are restored.

Morse dreamed he was awake near a seashore at night. A Mediterranean breeze was carrying through the horizontal slats of a jalousie the sound of waves breaking in the near distance, a regular swishing sound, as of pages being turned.

Candles had been lit in the darkened room when Morse opened his eyes, wakened by soft voices – a mother whispering to a daughter across the room. He lay listening to her explanations, wondering whether he – like the little girl – would ever be able to get used to his presence in this world of theirs, of cheap food, violence, and the isolation that went with the absence of communication technology. He had crossed a divide, exchanged the familiar babble of librarians for a wary incommunicability. The silence by which he had once measured the intimacy of his relationship with Sharon now engulfed them both completely.

Level with his eyes a bright orange paperback book stared at Morse on the grey blanket, where it had been laid aside. Idly he took the book up. He had never seen it before.

'Where'd this come from?' he said, pretending to himself that he did not know.

Sharon – she looked up from her daughter and across the room to her lover – said simply: 'A man give it me.'

'Why?' Morse said.

'*Why?* . . . *Why* are you here? *Why* can't you go back?'

'It's a long story . . . I'll tell you whenever you want me to.'

'So the reason why's a long story. I'll tell *you* whenever you want me to.'

She looked at him and he looked at her. Neither spoke. Morse lowered his eyes. He opened the book and read:

I have just returned from a visit to my landlord – the solitary neighbour that I shall be troubled with. Mr Heathcliff and I are such a suitable pair to divide the desolation between us. He little imagined how my heart warmed towards him when I beheld his black eyes withdraw so suspiciously under their brows, as I rode up . . .

From within the bed Morse continued to read the book, steadily escaping into it. Outside the storm howled and banged. When a sudden heavy crash at the front door shook the condominium, Morse closed the book, automatically taking out the old torn page book-mark to keep his place. The moment he saw the book from which the page had been torn, however, its quaint serified Clarendon typeface, Roger Morse saw everything, his whole life from beginning to end, from *exist* to *extinguish* – from having life and the functions of vitality to bringing something to an end, causing it to be void. He understood everything that had happened to him and everything that was going to happen. The page of *Skeat's Etymology* in his hand – page 176 – which he recognised from its pencilled notations to be from his own copy – Morse knew by heart: *Exist. Exit. Expect. Experience. Expert. Expire. Exterminate. Extinguish.* He knew all their meanings and etymologies, only now he experienced them exquisitely, expertly, as a whole, as if it was this moment that their meanings expressed and their etymologies explained.

Morse stood in the centre of the room, naked, the single page of *Skeat* in his hand. Sharon, in her blue dress, was at his side with Lucy in her arms. Morse felt calm, as if they, he and his new family, were merely modelling for a realist painting depiciting Revolutionary Defiance. In front of them an officer from the Police Executive, a shabby rain-soaked parka over his smart uniform, stood holding a light automatic weapon in one hand and a faded-blue hardcover book in the other.

'Roger Morse . . .'

The officer handed Morse his own copy of *Skeat's Dictionary of Etymology*, almost ceremoniously, as it had first been handed to him many years before. The piece of official-looking paper protruding from between E and F was clearly stamped: EXTERMINATION WARRANT. Morse glanced at it. It seemed to be in order.

'My name's Captain Cznetsov. You got an appointment

with me,' the Police Executive officer said mildly with the open back vowels and the flapped alveolar consonants characteristic of the Mid West. 'As I believe you know.' He raised the automatic weapon and pointed it in Morse's direction.

Morse watched the extreme or last part lengthwise of the thing, the point that marked the extent of it. The tip. It was, also, the point to which a particular course of action had led. The cessation of an undertaking. A boundary. The goal an agent would or should act towards. The object by virtue of or for the sake of which a chain of events had taken place. The ultimate state. Something that is extreme.

The End.

GREGORY BENFORD

FREEZEFRAME

Well, Jason, it'll take some explaining. Got a minute? Great.

Here's the invitation. It's for the weekend, and it's not just the kid's birthday party, no. You and me, we've been out of touch the last couple years, so let me run through a little flashback, okay?

Teri and me, we're world-gobblers. You've known that since you and me were roomies, right? Remember the time I took a final, went skiing all afternoon, had a heavy date, was back next day for another final – and aced them both? Yeah, you got it fella, aced the date, too. Those were the days, huh?

Anyway, my Teri's the same – girl's got real fire in her. No Type A or anything, just *alive*. And like sheet lightning in bed.

We grab life with both hands. Always have. If you work in city government, like me, you got to keep ahead of the oppo. Otherwise you see yourself hung out to dry on the six o'clock news and next day nobody can remember your name.

Goes double for Teri. She's in liability and claims, a real shark reef. Pressureville. So many lawyers around these days, half of them bred in those barracuda farms, those upgraded speed-curricula things. So we've got to watch our ass.

Right, watching Teri's is no trouble, I'll take all I can get. That woman really sends me. We're both in challenging careers, but she finds the time to make my day, every day, get it? Our relationship is stage centre with us, even though we're putting in ten-hour days.

That's what started us thinking. We need the time to work on our marriage, really firm it up when the old schedule starts to fray us around the edges. We've been through those stress management retreats, the whole thing, and we *use* it.

So we're happy. But still, about a year ago we started to feel something was *missing*.

Yeah, you got it. The old cliché – a kid. Teri's been hearing the old bio clock tick off the years. We got the condo, two sharp cars, timeshare in Mauai, portfolio thick as your wrist – but it's not enough.

Teri brought it up carefully, not sure I'd like the idea of sharing all this wonderful bounty with a cranky little brat. I heard her through, real quality listening, and just between you and me, old buddy, I didn't zoom in on the idea right away.

I mean, we're fast lane folks. Teri's happy poring over legal programs, looking for a precedent-busting angle, zipping off to an amped workout at the gym, and then catching one of those black and white foreign films with the hard to read subtitles. Not much room in her schedule to pencil in a feeding or the mumps. I had real trouble conceptualising how she – much less *I* – could cope.

But she *wanted* this, I could tell from the soft watery look her eyes get. She's a real woman, y'know?

But the flip side was, no way she'd go for months of waddling around looking and feeling like a cow. Getting behind in her briefs because of morning sickness? Taking time off for the whole number? Not Teri's kind of thing.

What? Oh, sure, adoption.

Well, we did the research on that.

Let me put it this way. We both think the other's pretty damn special. Unique. And our feeling was, why raise a kid that's running on somebody else's genetic program?

We're talented people, great bodies, not too hard on the eyes – why not give our kid those advantages?

You got to look at it from his point of view. He should have parents who provide the very best in everything – including genes. So he had to be ours – all ours.

So you can see our problem. Balancing the tradeoffs and nothing looks like a winner. We'd hit a roadblock.

That's where my contacts came in handy. Guy at work told me about this company, GeneInc.

The corporation was looking for a franchise backer and the city was getting involved because of all the legal hassles. Red tape had to be cut with the AMA, the local hospitals, the usual stuff. No big deal, just takes time.

I did a little angling on the variances they needed and in return they were real nice. We got invited to a few great parties up in the hills. Glitzy affairs, some big media people flown in to spice things up. And that's when we got the word.

Their secret is, they speed up the whole thing. It's entirely natural, no funny chemicals or anything. Purely electrical and a little hormone tinkering, straight goods.

What they do is, they take a little genetic material from Teri and me, they put it in a blender or something, they mix it and match it and batch it. There's this thing called inculcated growth pattern. Just jargon to me, but what it means is, they can *tune* the process, see. Nature does it slow and easy, but GeneInc can put the pedal to the metal. Go through the prelim stages, all in the lab.

Yeah, you got it fella, you can't see Teri pushing around a basketball belly, can you? That's why it's like GeneInc was tightwrapped for lives like ours – lives on the go.

So she goes in one Friday, right after a big staff meeting, and with me holding her hand she has the implantation. She overnights in the clinic, watching a first-run movie. Next day she's home. We have dinner at that great new restaurant, T. S. Eliot's, you really got to try the blackened redfish there, and all she's got to do is take these pills every four hours.

Three weeks like that, she's growing by the minute. Eats like a horse. I tell you, we had a running tab at every pasta joint within five blocks of the apartment.

She's into the clinic every forty-eight hours for the treatments, smooth as a press release. Teri's clicking right along, the kid's growing ten times the normal rate.

Before I can get around to buying cigars, zip, here's a seven-pound wonder. Great little guy. Perfect – my eyes, her smile, wants to eat everything in sight. Grabs for the milk supply like a real ladies' man.

And no effects from the GeneInc speedup, not a square inch less than A-max quality. You hear all kinds of scare talk about gene-diddling, how you might end up with a kid from Zit City. Well, the Chicken Littles were wrong-o, in spades.

We figure we'd handle things from there. Maybe send out the diapers, hire a live-in if we could find a nice quiet illegal – Teri could handle the Spanish.

We had the right vector, but we were a tad short on follow-through. Teri started getting cluster headaches. Big ones, in technicolor.

So I filled in for her. Read some books on fathering, really got into it. And I'm telling you, it jigsawed my days beyond belief.

Face it, we had high-impact lives. I gave up my daily racquetball match – and you know how much of a sacrifice that was, for a diehard jock like me, highschool football and all. But I did it for the kid.

Next, Teri had to drop out of her extra course in fastlane brokering, too, which was a real trauma. I mean, we'd practically spent the projected income from that training. Factored it into our estimated taxes, even. I'd already sunk extra cash into a honey of a limited partnership. It had some sweetheart underwriting features and we just couldn't resist it.

Man, crisis time. If she didn't get her broker's licence on schedule, we'd be stretched so thin you could see through us.

She couldn't link into the course on home computer, either. Software mismatch or something, and by the time she got it downwired she was too far behind in the course.

See what I mean? Bleaksville.

But we were committed parents. We believe in total frankness, upfront living.

So we went back to GeneInc and had a talk with one of their counsellors. Wonderful woman. She takes us into a beautiful room – soft lighting, quality leather couch, and some of that classy Baroque trumpet music in the background. Just the right touch. Tasteful. Reassuring.

She listens to us and nods a lot and knows just what we're talking about. We trust her, almost like it was therapy. Which I guess it was.

And we let it all spill. The irritations. Man, I never knew a little package could scream so much. Feeding. No grandparents closer than three thousand miles, and they're keeping their distance. Got their retirement condo, walls all around it, a rule that you can't bring a kid in for longer than twenty-four hours. Not exactly Norman Rockwell, huh? So no quick fix there.

And the kid, he's always awake and wanting to play just when we're stumbling home, zombies. So you cram things in. We had trouble synching our schedules. Lost touch with friends *and* business contacts.

See, I spend a lot of time on the horn, keeping up with people I know I'll need sometime. Or just feeling out the gossip shops for what's hot. Can't do that with a squall-bomb on my knee.

Teri had it even worse. She'd bought all the traditional mother package and was trying to pack that into her own flat-out style. Doesn't work.

Now, the usual way to handle this would be for some-body to lose big, right?

Teri drops back and punts, maybe. Stops humping so hard, lets up. So maybe a year downstream, some younger beady-eyed type shoulders her aside. She ends up targeted on perpetual middle-management. The desert. Oblivion. Perpetual Poughkeepsie.

Or else I lower *my* revs. Shy off the background briefings, drop off the party committee, don't sniff around for possible corners to get tight with. You know how it is.

What? No, ol' buddy, you're dead on – not my scene.

But listen, my real concern wasn't my job, it was our relationship. We really work at it. Total communication takes time. We really get into each other. That's just us.

So the lady at GeneInc listens, nods, and introduces us to their top drawer product line. Exclusive. *Very* high tech. It blew us away.

Freezeframe, they call it.

Look, the kid's going to be sleeping ten, twelve hours a day anyway, right? GeneInc just packs all that time into our workweek. Rearranges the kid's schedule, is basically what it is.

Simple electronic stimulus to the lower centres. Basic stuff, they to'd me, can't damage anything. And totally under our control.

When we want him, the kid's on call. Boost his voltage, allow some warmup –

Sure, Jason. See, he's running at low temperature during the work day. Helps the process. So we come dragging home, have some Chardonnay to unwind, catch the news. When we're ready for him we hit a few buttons, warm him up and there he is, bright and agreeable 'cause he's had a ton of extra sack time. Can't get tired and pesky.

I mean, the kid's at his best and we're at peak, too. Relaxed, ready for some A-plus parenting.

Well, we took the Zen pause on the idea, sure. Thought it over. Teri talked it out with her analyst. Worked on the problem, got her doubts under control.

And we went for it. Little shakedown trouble, but nothing big. GeneInc, they've got a fix for everything.

We boost him up for weekends, when we've got space. Quality time, that's what the kid gets. We've set up a regular schedule. Weekdays for us, weeknights and weekends for him.

Now GeneInc's got an add-on you wouldn't believe – Downtime Education, they call it. While he's sleeping through our days, Downtime Ed brings him up to speed on verbals, math, sensory holism, the works. Better than a real teacher, in many ways.

So we feel that – oh yeah, the invitation.

It's for his big blast. Combo first birthday party and graduation from third grade. We put him on the inside track, and he's burning it up. We couldn't be happier. Our kind of kid, for sure.

Pretty soon we'll integrate him into the GeneInc school for accelerated cases, others like him. There's a whole community of these great kids springing up, y'know. They're either in Downtime, learning up a storm, or getting online, first class attention in Freezeframe weekends.

I tell you, Jason, these kids are going to be the best. They'll slice and dice any Normkid competition they run into.

And us – it's like a new beginning. We get to have it all *and* we know the kid's not suffering. He'll have a high-school diploma by the time he's ten. He'll be a savvy little guy. And we'll load on all the extras, too. Emotional support, travel, the works.

We'll have him on tap when we want him. That'll stretch out his physical childhood, of course, but speed up his mental growth. Better all round, really, 'cause Teri and I totally like him.

See, we want to spread him over more of our lives, keep him for maybe thirty years. Why not have one really top of the line kid, enjoy him most of your life? Efficient.

So look, I got to trot. Map's on the back of the invitation, come and enjoy. No need for a present unless you want to. Teri'll love seeing you again.

And while you're there, I can show you the GeneInc equipment. Beautiful gear, sharp lines. Brochures, too. I've got a kind of little franchise agreement with them, getting in on the ground floor of this thing.

What? Well, that's not the way I'd put it, Jason. This is a class product line.

Calling it a Tupperware Party – hey, that's way out of line. We're talking quality here.

You'll see. Just drop on by. No obligation. Oh yeah, and I got some great Cabernet you should try, something I picked up on the wine futures market.

My God, look at the time. See you, ol' buddy.

Have a nice day.

J. G. BALLARD

THE MAN WHO WALKED ON THE MOON

I, too, was once an astronaut. As you see me sitting here, in this modest cafe with its distant glimpse of Copacabana Beach, you probably assume that I am a man of few achievements. The shabby briefcase between my worn heels, the stained suit with its frayed cuffs, the unsavoury hands ready to seize the first offer of a free drink, the whole air of failure . . . no doubt you think that I am a minor clerk who has missed promotion once too often, and that I amount to nothing, a person of no past and less future.

For many years I believed this myself. I had been abandoned by the authorities, who were glad to see me exiled to another continent, reduced to begging from the American tourists. I suffered from acute amnesia, and certain domestic problems with my wife and my mother. They now share my small apartment at Ipanema, while I am forced to live in a room above the projection booth of the Luxor Cinema, my thoughts drowned by the sound tracks of science-fiction films.

So many tragic events leave me unsure of myself. Nonetheless, my confidence is returning, and a sense of my true history and worth. Chapters of my life are still hidden from me, and seem as jumbled as the film extracts which the projectionists screen each morning as they focus their cameras. I have still forgotten my years of training, and my mind bars from me any memory of the actual space flights. But I am certain that I was once an astronaut.

Years ago, before I went into space, I followed many professions – freelance journalist, translator, on one occasion even a war correspondent sent to a small war, which unfortunately was never declared. I was in and out of newspaper offices all day, hoping for that one assignment that would match my talents.

Sadly, all this effort failed to get me to the top, and after ten years I found myself displaced by a younger generation. A certain reticence in my character, a sharpness of manner, set me off from my fellow journalists. Even the editors would laugh at me behind my back. I was given trivial assignments – film reviewing, or writing reports on office-equipment fairs. When the circulation wars began, in a doomed response to the onward sweep of television, the editors openly took exception to my waspish style. I became a part-time translator, and taught for an hour each day at a language school, but my income plummeted. My mother, whom I had supported for many years, was forced to leave her home and join my wife and myself in our apartment at Ipanema.

At first my wife resented this, but soon she and my mother teamed up against me. They became impatient with the hours I spent delaying my unhappy visits to the single newspaper office that still held out hope – my journey to work was a transit between one door slammed on my heels and another slammed in my face.

My last friend at the newspaper commiserated with me, as I stood forlornly in the lobby. 'For heaven's sake, find a human interest story! Something tender and affecting, that's what they want upstairs – life isn't an avant-garde movie!'

Pondering this sensible advice, I wandered into the crowded streets. I dreaded the thought of returning home without an assignment. The two women had taken to opening the apartment door together. They would stare at me accusingly, almost barring me from my own home.

Around me were the million faces of the city. People strode past, so occupied with their own lives that they almost pushed me from the pavement. A million human interest stories, of a banal and pointless kind, an encyclopaedia of mediocrity . . . Giving up, I left Copacabana Avenue and took refuge among the tables of a small café in a side-street.

It was there that I met the American astronaut, and began my own career in space.

The cafe terrace was almost deserted, as the office workers returned to their desks after lunch. Behind me, in the shade of the canvas awning, a fair-haired man in a threadbare tropical suit sat beside an empty glass. Guarding my coffee from the flies, I gazed at the small segment of sea visible beyond Copacabana Beach. Slowed by their midday meals, groups of American and European tourists strolled down from the hotels, waving away the jewellery salesmen and lottery touts. Perhaps I would visit Paris or New York, make a new life for myself as a literary critic . . .

A tartan shirt blocked my view of the sea and its narrow dream of escape. An elderly American, camera slung from his heavy neck, leaned across the table, his grey-haired wife in a loose floral dress beside him.

'Are you the astronaut?' the woman asked in a friendly but sly way, as if about to broach an indiscretion. 'The hotel said you would be at this café . . .'

'An astronaut?'

'Yes, the astronaut Commander Scranton . . . ?'

'No, I regret that I'm not an astronaut.' Then it occurred to me that this provincial couple, probably a dentist and his wife from the corn-belt, might benefit from a well-informed courier. Perhaps they imagined that their cruise ship had berthed at Miami? I stood up, managing a gallant smile. 'Of course, I'm a qualified translator. If you – '

'No, no . . .' Dismissing me with a wave, they moved through the empty tables. 'We came to see Mr Scranton.'

Baffled by this bizarre exchange, I watched them approach the man in the tropical suit. A nondescript fellow in his late forties, he had thinning blond hair and a strong-jawed American face from which all confidence had long been drained. He stared in a resigned way at his hands, which waited beside his empty glass, as if unable to explain to them that little refreshment would reach them that day. He was clearly undernourished, perhaps an ex-seaman who had jumped ship, one of thousands of down-and-outs trying to live by their wits on some of the hardest pavements in the world.

However, he looked up sharply enough as the elderly couple approached him. When they repeated their question about the astronaut he beckoned them to a seat. To my surprise, the waiter was summoned, and drinks were brought to the table. The husband unpacked his camera, while a relaxed conversation took place between his wife and this seedy figure.

'Dear, don't forget Mr Scranton . . .'

'Oh, please forgive me.'

The husband removed several banknotes from his wallet. His wife passed them across the table to Scranton, who then stood up. Photographs were taken, first of Scranton standing next to the smiling wife, then of the husband grinning broadly beside the gaunt American. The source of all this good humour eluded me, as it did Scranton, whose eyes stared gravely at the street with a degree of respect due to the surface of the moon. But already a second group of tourists had walked down from Copacabana Beach, and heard more laughter when one called out: 'There's the astronaut . . . !'

Quite mystified, I watched a further round of photographs being taken. The couples stood on either side of the American, grinning away as if he were a camel driver posing for pennies against a backdrop of the pyramids.

I ordered a small brandy from the waiter. He had ignored all this, pocketing his tips with a straight face.

'This fellow . . . ?' I asked. 'Who is he? An astronaut?'

'Of course . . .' The waiter flicked a bottle-top into the air and treated the sky to a knowing sneer. 'Who else but the man in the moon?'

The tourists had gone, strolling past the leatherware and jewellery stores. Alone now after his brief fame, the American sat among the empty glasses, counting the money he had collected.

The man in the moon?

Then I remembered the newspaper headline, and the exposé I had read two years earlier of this impoverished American who claimed to have been an astronaut, and told his story to the tourists for the price of a drink. At first almost everyone believed him, and he had become a popular figure in the hotel lobbies along Copacabana Beach. Apparently he had flown on one of the Apollo missions from Cape Kennedy in the 1970s, and his long-jawed face and stoical pilot's eyes seemed vaguely familiar from the magazine photographs. He was properly reticent, but if pressed with a tourist dollar could talk convincingly about the early lunar flights. In its way it was deeply moving to sit at a café table with a man who had walked on the moon . . .

Then an over-curious reporter exploded the whole pretence. No man named Scranton had ever flown in space, and the American authorities confirmed that his photograph was not that of any past or present astronaut. In fact he was a failed crop-duster from Florida who had lost his pilot's licence and whose knowledge of the Apollo flights had been mugged up from newspapers and television programmes.

Surprisingly, Scranton's career had not ended there and then, but moved on to a second tragi-comical phase. Far from consigning him to oblivion, the exposure brought him a genuine small celebrity. Banished from the grand

hotels of Copacabana, he hung about the cheaper cafés in
the side-streets, still claiming to have been an astronaut,
ignoring those who derided him from their car windows.
The dignified way in which he maintained his fraud tapped
a certain good-humoured tolerance, much like the affection felt in the United States for those eccentric old men
who falsely claimed to their deaths that they were veterans
of the American Civil War.

So Scranton stayed on, willing to talk for a few dollars
about his journey to the moon, quoting the same tired
phrases that failed to convince the youngest schoolboy.
Soon no-one bothered to question him closely, and his
chief function was to be photographed beside parties of
visitors, an amusing oddity of the tourist trail.

But perhaps the American was more devious than he
appeared, with his shabby suit and hangdog gaze? As I
sat there, guarding the brandy I could barely afford, I
resented Scranton's bogus celebrity, and the tourist rev-
enue it brought him. For years I too had maintained a
charade – the mask of good humour that I presented to
my colleagues in the newspaper world – but it had brought
me nothing. Scranton at least was left alone for most of
the time, something I craved more than any celebrity.
Comparing our situations, there was plainly a strong
element of injustice – the notorious British criminal who
made a comfortable living being photographed by the
tourists in the more expensive Copacabana restaurants
had at least robbed one of Her Majesty's mail-trains.

At the same time, was this the human-interest story
that would help me to remake my career? Could I provide
a final ironic twist by revealing that, thanks to his exposure, the bogus astronaut was now doubly successful?

During the next days I visited the café promptly at
noon. Notebook at the ready, I kept a careful watch for
Scranton. He usually appeared in the early afternoon, as
soon as the clerks and secretaries had finished their coffee.
In that brief lull, when the shadows crossed from one side

of the street to the other, Scranton would materialise, as
if from a trap-door in the pavement. He was always alone,
walking straight-backed in his faded suit, but with the
uncertainty of someone who suspects that he is keeping
an appointment on the wrong day. He would slip into his
place under the café awning, order a glass of beer from
the sceptical waiter and then gaze across the street at the
vistas of an invisible space.

It soon became clear that Scranton's celebrity was as
threadbare as his shirt cuffs. Few tourists visited him, and
often a whole afternoon passed without a single customer.
Then the waiter would scrape the chairs around Scranton's table, trying to distract him from his reveries of an
imaginary moon. Indeed, on the fourth day, within a few
minutes of Scranton's arrival, the waiter slapped the table-
top with his towel, already cancelling the afternoon's
performance.

'Away, away . . . it's impossible!' He seized the newspaper that Scranton had found on a nearby chair. 'No
more stories about the moon . . .'

Scranton stood up, head bowed beneath the awning.
He seemed resigned to this abuse. 'All right . . . I can
take my trade down the street.'

To forestall this, I left my seat and moved through the
empty tables.

'Mr Scranton? Perhaps we can speak? I'd like to buy
you a drink.'

'By all means.' Scanton beckoned me to a chair. Ready
for business, he sat upright, and with a conscious effort
managed to bring the focus of his gaze from infinity to a
distance of fifty feet away. He was poorly nourished, and
his perfunctory shave revealed an almost tubercular
pallor. Yet there was a certain resolute quality about this
vagrant figure that I had not expected. Sitting beside him,
I was aware of an intense and almost wilful isolation, not
just in this foreign city, but in the world at large.

I showed him my card. 'I'm writing a book of criticism

on the science-fiction cinema. It would be interesting to hear your opinions. You are Commander Scranton, the Apollo astronaut?'

'That is correct.'

'Good. I wondered how you viewed the science-fiction film . . . how convincing you found the presentation of outer space, the lunar surface and so on . . .'

Scranton stared bleakly at the table-top. A faint smile exposed his yellowing teeth, and I assumed that he had seen through my little ruse.

'I'll be happy to set you straight,' he told me. 'But I make a small charge.'

'Of course.' I searched in my pockets. 'Your professional expertise, naturally . . .'

I placed some coins on the table, intending to hunt for a modest banknote. Scranton selected three of the coins, enough to pay for a loaf of bread, and pushed the rest towards me.

'Science-fiction films – ? They're good. Very accurate. On the whole I'd say they do an excellent job.'

'That's encouraging to hear. These Hollywood epics are not usually noted for their realism.'

'Well . . . you have to understand that the Apollo teams brought back a lot of film footage.'

'I'm sure.' I tried to keep the amusement out of my voice. 'The studios must have been grateful to you. After all, you could describe the actual moon-walks.'

Scranton nodded sagely. 'I acted as consultant to one of the Hollywood majors. All in all, you can take it from me that those pictures are pretty realistic.'

'Fascinating . . . coming from you that has authority. As a matter of interest, what was being on the moon literally like?'

For the first time Scranton seemed to notice me. Had he glimpsed some shared strain in our characters? This care-worn American had all the refinement of an unem-

ployed car mechanic, and yet he seemed almost tempted
to befriend me.

'Being on the moon?' His tired gaze inspected the narrow
street of cheap jewellery stores, with its office messengers
and lottery touts, the off-duty taxi-drivers leaning against
their cars. 'It was just like being here.'

'So . . .' I put away my notebook. Any further subterfuge
was unnecessary. I had treated our meeting as a joke, but
Scranton was sincere, and anyway utterly indifferent to my
opinion of him. The tourists and passing policemen, the
middle-aged women sitting at a nearby table, together
barely existed for him. They were no more than shadows
on the screen of his mind, through which he could see the
horizons of an almost planetary emptiness.

For the first time I was in the presence of someone who
had nothing – even less than the beggars of Rio, for they
at least were linked to the material world by their longings
for it. Scranton embodied the absolute loneliness of the
human being in space and time, a situation which in many
ways I shared. Even the act of convincing himself that he
was a former astronaut only emphasised his isolation.

'A remarkable story,' I commented. 'One can't help
wondering if we were right to leave this planet. I'm reminded of the question posed by the Cuban painter Matta –
"Why must we fear a disaster in space in order to understand our own times?" It's a pity you didn't bring back any
mementoes of your moon-walks.'

Scranton's shoulders straightened. I could see him counting the coins on the table. 'I do have certain materials . . .'

I nearly laughed. 'What? A piece of lunar rock? Some
moon dust?'

'Various photographic materials.'

'Photographs?' Was it possible that Scranton had told
the truth, and that he had indeed been an astronaut? If I
could prove that the whole notion of his imposture was
an error, an oversight by the journalist who had investi-
gated the case, I would have the makings of a front-page

scoop . . . 'Could I see them? – Perhaps I could use them in my book . . . ?'

'Well . . .' Scranton felt for the coins in his pocket. He looked hungry, and obviously thought only of spending them on a loaf of bread.

'Of course,' I added, 'I'll provide an extra fee. As for my book, the publishers might well pay hundreds of dollars.'

'Hundreds . . .' Scranton seemed impressed. He shook his head, as if amused by the ways of the world. I expected him to be shy of revealing where he lived, but he stood up and gestured me to finish my drink. 'I'm staying a few minutes walk from here.'

He waited among the tables, staring across the street. Seeing the pasers-by through his eyes, I was aware that they had begun to seem almost transparent, shadow players created by a frolic of the sun.

We soon arrived at Scranton's modest room behind the Luxor Cinema, a small theatre off Copacabana Avenue that had seen better days. Two former store-rooms and an office above the projection booth had been let as apartments, which we reached after climbing a dank emergency stairway.

Exhausted by the effort, Scranton swayed against the door. He wiped the spit from his mouth onto the lapel of his jacket, and ushered me into the room. 'Make yourself comfortable . . .'

A dusty light fell across the narrow bed, reflected in the cold-water tap of a greasy handbasin supported from the wall by its waste-pipe. Sheets of newspaper were wrapped around a pillow, stained with sweat and some unsavoury mucus, perhaps after an attack of malarial or tubercular fever.

Eager to leave this infectious den, I drew out my wallet. 'The photographs . . . ?'

Scranton sat on the bed, staring at the yellowing wall behind me as if he had forgotten that I was there. Once

again I was aware of his ability to isolate himself from the
surrounding world, a talent I envied him, if little else.

'Sure . . . they're over here.' He stood up and went to
the suitcase that lay on a card-table behind the door.
Taking the money from me, he opened the lid and lifted
out a bundle of magazines. Among them were loose pages
torn from *Life and Newsweek*, and special supplements of
the Rio newspapers devoted to the Apollo space-flights
and the moon landings. The familiar images of Armstrong
and the lunar module, the space-walks and splashdowns
had been endlessly thumbed. The captions were marked
with coloured pencil, as if Scranton had spent hours
memorising these photographs brought back from the
tideways of space.

I moved the magazines to one side, hoping to find some
documentary evidence of Scranton's own involvement in
the space-flights, perhaps a close-up photograph taken by
a fellow astronaut.

'Is this it? There's nothing else?'

'That's it.' Scranton gestured encouragingly. 'They're
good pictures. Pretty well what it was like.'

'I suppose that's true. I had hoped . . .'

I peered at Scranton, expecting some small show of
embarrassment. These faded pages, far from being the
mementoes of a real astronaut, were obviously the prompt
cards of an imposter. However, there was not the slightest
doubt that Scranton was sincere.

I stood in the street below the portico of the Luxor
Cinema, whose garish posters, advertising some science-
fiction spectacular, seemed as inflamed as the mind of the
American. Despite all that I had suspected, I felt an
intense disappointment. I had deluded myself, thinking
that Scranton would rescue my career. Now I was left
with nothing but an empty notebook and the tram journey
back to the crowded apartment in Ipanema. I dreaded the
prospect of seeing my wife and my mother at the door,
their eyes screwed to the same accusing focus.

Nonetheless, as I walked down Copacabana Avenue to the tram-stop, I felt a curious sense of release. The noisy pavements, the arrogant pickpockets plucking at my clothes, the traffic that aggravated the slightest tendency to migraines, all seemed to have receded, as if a small distance had opened between myself and the congested world. My meeting with Scranton, my brief involvement with this marooned man, allowed me to see everything in a more detached way. The businessmen with their brief-cases, the afternoon tarts swinging their shiny handbags, the salesmen with their sheets of lottery tickets, almost deferred to me. Time and space had altered their perspectives, and the city was yielding to me. As I crossed the road to the tram-stop several minutes seemed to pass. But I was not run over.

This sense of a loosening air persisted as I rode back to Ipanema. My fellow passengers, who would usually have irritated me with their cheap scent and vulgar clothes, their look of bored animals in a menagerie, now scarcely intruded into my vision. I gazed down corridors of light that ran between them like the aisles of an open-air cathedral.

'You found a story,' my wife announced within a second of opening the door.

'They've commissioned an article,' my mother confirmed. 'I knew they would.'

They stepped back and watched me as I made a leisurely tour of the cramped apartment. My changed demeanour clearly impressed them. They pestered me with questions, but even their presence was less bothersome. The universe, thanks to Scranton's example, had loosened its grip. Sitting at the dinner table, I silenced them with a raised finger.

'I am about to embark on a new career . . .'

From then on I became even more involved with Scranton. I had not intended to see the American again, but the germ of his loneliness had entered my blood.

Within two days I returned to the café in the side-street, but the tables were deserted. I watched as two parties of tourists stopped to ask for 'the astronaut'. I then questioned the waiter, suspecting that he had banished the poor man. But, no, the American would be back the next day, he had been ill, or perhaps had secretly gone to the moon on business.

In fact, it was three days before Scranton at last appeared. Materialising from the afternoon heat, he entered the café and sat under the awning. At first he failed to notice that I was there, but Scranton's mere presence was enough to satisfy me. The crowds and traffic, which had begun once again to close around me, halted their clamour and withdrew. On the noisy street were imposed the silences of a lunar landscape.

However, it was all too clear that Scranton had been ill. His face was sallow with fever, and the effort of sitting in his chair soon tired him. When the first American tourists stopped at his table he barely rose from his seat, and while the photographs were taken he held tightly to the awning above his head.

By the next afternoon his fever had subsided, but he was so strained and ill-kempt that the waiter at first refused to admit him to the café. A trio of Californian spinsters who approached his table were clearly unsure that this decaying figure was indeed the bogus astronaut, and would have left had I not ushered them back to Scranton.

'Yes, this is Commander Scranton, the famous astronaut. I am his associate – do let me hold your camera . . .'

I waited impatiently for them to leave, and sat down at Scranton's table. Ill the American might be, but I needed him. After ordering a brandy, I helped Scranton to hold the glass. As I pressed the spinsters' banknote into his pocket I could feel that his suit was soaked with sweat.

'I'll walk you back to your room. Don't thank me, it's in my direction.'

'Well, I could use an arm.' Scranton stared at the street, as if its few yards encompassed a Grand Canyon of space. 'It's getting to be a long way.'

'A long way! Scranton, I understand that . . .'

It took us half an hour to cover the few hundred yards to the Luxor Cinema. But already time was becoming an elastic dimension, and from then on most of my waking hours were spent with Scranton. Each morning I would visit the shabby room behind the cinema, bringing a paper-bag of sweet-cakes and a flask of tea I had prepared in the apartment under my wife's suspicious gaze. Often the American had little idea who I was, but this no longer worried me. He lay in his narrow bed, letting me raise his head as I changed the sheets of newspaper that covered his pillow. When he spoke, his voice was too weak to be heard above the soundtracks of the science-fiction films that boomed through the crumbling walls.

Even in this moribund state, Scranton's example was a powerful tonic, and when I left him in the evening I would walk the crowded streets without any fear. Sometimes my former colleagues called to me from the steps of the newspaper office, but I was barely aware of them, as if they were planetary visitors hailing me from the edge of a remote crater.

Looking back on these exhilarating days, I regret only that I never called a doctor to see Scranton. Frequently, though, the American would recover his strength, and after I had shaved him we would go down into the street. I relished these outings with Scranton. Arm in arm, we moved through the afternoon crowds, which seemed to part around us. Our fellow-pedestrians had become remote and fleeting figures, little more than tricks of the sun. Sometimes, I could no longer see their faces. It was then that I observed the world through Scranton's eyes, and knew what it was to be an astronaut.

Needless to say, the rest of my life had collapsed at my feet. Having given up my work as a translator, I soon ran out of money, and was forced to borrow from my mother. At my wife's instigation, the features editor of the newspaper called me to his office, and made it plain that as an immense concession (in fact he had always been intrigued by my wife) he would let me review a science-fiction film at the Luxor. Before walking out, I told him that I was already too familiar with the film, and my one hope was to see it banned from the city forever.

So ended my conections with the newspaper. Soon after, the two women evicted me from my apartment. I was happy to leave them, taking with me only the reclining sun-chair on which my wife passed most of her days in preparation for her new career as a model. The sun-chair became my bed when I moved into Scranton's room.

By then the decline in Scranton's health forced me to be with him constantly. Far from being an object of charity, Scranton was now my only source of income. Our needs for several days could be met by a single session with the American tourists. I did my best to care for Scranton, but during his final illness I was too immersed in that sense of an emptying world even to notice the young doctor whose alarmed presence filled the tiny room. By a last irony, towards the end even Scranton himself seemed barely visible to me. As he died I was reading the mucus-stained headlines on his pillow.

After Scranton's death I remained in his room at the Luxor. Despite the fame he had once enjoyed, his burial at the protestant cemetery was attended only by myself, but in a sense that was just, as he and I were the only real inhabitants of the city. Later I went through the few possessions in his suitcase, and found a faded pilot's logbook. Its pages confirmed that Scranton had worked as a pilot for a crop-spraying company in Florida throughout the years of the Apollo programme.

Nonetheless, Scranton had travelled in space. He had known the loneliness of separation from all other human beings, he had gazed at the empty perspectives that I myself had seen. Curiously, the pages torn from the news magazines seemed more real than the pilot's log-book. The photographs of Armstrong and his fellow astronauts were really of Scranton and myself as we walked together on the moon of this world.

I reflected on this as I sat at the small café in the side-street. As a gesture to Scranton's memory, I had chosen his chair below the awning. I thought of the planetary landscapes that Scranton had taught me to see, those empty vistas devoid of human beings. Already I was aware of a previous career, which my wife and the pressures of everyday life had hidden from me. There were the years of training for a great voyage, and a coastline similar to that of Cape Kennedy receding below me . . .

My reverie was interrupted by a pair of American tourists. A middle-aged man and his daughter, who held the family camera to her chin, approached the table.

'Excuse me,' the man asked with an over-ready smile. 'Are you the . . . the astronaut? We were told by the hotel that you might be here . . .'

I stared at them without rancour, treating them to a glimpse of those eyes that had seen the void. I, too, had walked on the moon.

'Please sit down,' I told them casually. 'Yes, I am the astronaut.'

MICHAEL BLUMLEIN

THE BRAINS OF RATS

There is evidence that Joan of Arc was a man. Accounts of her trial state that she did not suffer the infirmity of women. When examined by the prelates prior to her incarceration it was found that she lacked the characteristic escutcheon of women. Her pubic area, in fact, was as smooth and hairless as a child's.[1]

There is a condition of men, of males, called testicular feminisation. The infants are born without a penis, and the testicles are hidden. The external genitalia are those of a female. Raised as women, these men at puberty develop breasts. Their voices do not deepen. They do not menstruate because they lack a uterus. They have no pubic hair.

These people carry a normal complement of chromosomes. The twenty-third pair, the so-called sex chromosome pair, is unmistakably male. XY. Declared a witch in 1431 and burned at the stake at the age of nineteen, Joan of Arc was quite likely one of these.

Herculine Barbin was born in 1838 in France; she was reared as a female. She spent her childhood in a convent and in boarding schools for girls and later become a school-mistress. Despite her rearing, she had the sexual inclination of a male. She had already taken a female lover, when, on account of severe pain in her left groin, she sought the advice of a physician. Partly as a result of his examination her sex was re-designated, and in 1860 she was given the civil status of a male. The transformation brought shame and disgrace upon her. Her existence as a male was wretched, and in 1868 she took her own life.[2]

I have a daughter. I am married to a blonde-haired, muscular woman. We live in enlightened times. But daily I wonder who is who and what is what. I am baffled by our choices; my mind is unclear. Especially now that I have the means to ensure that every child born on this earth is male.

A patient once came to me, a man with a painful drip from the end of his penis. He had had it for several days; neither excessive bathing nor drugstore remedies had proven helpful. About a week and a half before, on a business trip, he had spent time with a prostitute. I asked if he had enjoyed himself. In a roundabout way he said it was natural for a man.

Several days later, at home, his daughter tucked safely in bed, he had made love to his wife. He said that she had got very excited. The way he said it made me think she was the only one in the room.

The two of them are both rather young. While he was in the examining room, she sat quietly in the waiting room. She stared ahead, fatigue and ignorance making her face impassive. In her lap her daughter was curled asleep.

In the room the man milked his penis, squeezing out a large amount of creamy material, which I smeared on a glass slide. In an hour the laboratory told me he had gonorrhea. When I conveyed the news to him, he was surprised and worried.

'What is that?' he asked.

'An infection,' I said. 'A venereal disease. It's spread through sexual contact.'

He nodded slowly. 'My wife, she got too excited.'

'Most likely you got it from the prostitute.'

He looked at me blankly and said it again. 'She got too excited.'

I was fascinated that he could hold such a notion and calmly repeated what I had said. I recommended treatment for both him and his wife. How he would explain the situation to her was up to him. A man with his beliefs would probably not have too hard a time.

I admit that I have conflicting thoughts. I am intrigued by hypnotism and the relations of power. For years I have wanted to be a woman, with small, firm breasts held even firmer by a brassiere. My hair would be shoulder-length and soft. It would pick up highlights and sweep down over one ear. The other side of my head would be bare, save for some wisps of hair at the nape and around my ear. I would have a smooth cheek.

I used to brush it this way, posing before my closet mirror in dark tights and high-heeled boots. The velveteen dress I wore was designed for a small person, and I split the seams the first time I pulled it over my head. My arms and shoulders are large; they were choked by the narrow sleeves. I could hardly move, the dress was so tight. But I was pretty. A very pretty thing.

I never dream of having men. I dream of women. I am a woman and I want women. I think of being simultaneously on the top and on the bottom. I want the power and I want it taken from me.

I should mention that I also have the means to make every conceptus a female. The thought is as disturbing as making them all male. But I think it shall have to be one or the other.

The genes that determine sex lie on the twenty-third pair of chromosomes. They are composed of a finite and relatively short sequence of nucleic acids on the X chromosome and one on the Y. For the most part these sequences have been mapped. Comparisons have been made between species. The sex-determining gene is remarkably similar in animals as diverse as the wasp, the turtle and the cow. Recently it has been found that the (male) banded krait, a poisonous snake of India separated evolutionarily from man by many millions of years, has a genetic sequence nearly identical to that of the human male.

The Y gene turns on other genes. A molecule is produced, a complex protein, which is present on the surface of virtually all cells in the male. It is absent in the female. Its presence makes cells and environments of cells develop in particular ways. These ways have not changed much in millions of years.

Certain regions of the brain in rats show marked sexual specificity. Cell density, dendritic formation, synaptic configuration of the male are different from the female. When presented with two solutions of water, one pure, the other heavily sweetened with saccharin, the female rat consistently chooses the latter. The male does just the opposite. Female chimpanzee infants exposed to high levels of male hormones *in utero* exhibit patterns of play different from their sisters. They initiate more, are rougher and more threatening. They tend to snarl a lot.

Sexual differences of the human brain exist, but they have been obscured by the profound evolution of this organ in the past half-million years. We have speech and foresight, consciousness and self-consciousness. We have art, physics and religion. In a language whose meaning men and women seem to share, we say we are different, but equal.

The struggle between sexes, the battles for power are a reflection of the schism between thought and function, between the power of our minds and powerlessness in the face of our design. Sexual equality, an idea present for hundreds of years, is subverted by instincts present for millions. The genes determining mental capacity have evolved rapidly; those determining sex have been stable for eons. Humankind suffers the consequences of this disparity, the ambiguities of identity, the violence between the sexes. This can be changed. It can be ended. I have the means to do it.

All my life I have watched men fight with women. Women with men. Women come to the clinic with bruised and swollen cheeks, where they have been slapped and beaten by their lovers. Not long ago an attractive middle-aged lady came in with a bloody nose, bruises on her arms and a cut beneath her eye, where the cheek bone rises up in a ridge. She was shaking uncontrollably, sobbing in spasms so that it was impossible to understand what she was saying. Her sister had to speak for her.

Her boss had beat her up. He had thrown her against the filing cabinets and kicked her on the floor. She had cried for him to stop, but he kept on kicking. She had worked for him for ten years. Nothing like this had ever happened before.

Another time a young man came in. He wore a tank top and had big muscles in his shoulders and arms. On one bicep was a tattoo of the upper torso and head of a woman, her huge breasts bursting out of a ragged garment. On his forearm beneath this picture were three long and deep tracks in the skin, oozing blood. I imagined the swipe of a large cat, or a lynx or a mountain lion. He told me he had hurt himself working on his car.

I cleaned the scratches, cut off the dead pieces of skin bunched up at the end of the tracks. I asked again. It was his girlfriend, he said, smiling now a little, gazing proudly at the marks on his arm. They had had a fight, she had scratched him with her nails. He looked at me, turning more serious, trying to act like a man but sounding like a boy, and asked, 'You think I should have a shot for rabies?'

Sexual differentiation in humans occurs at about the fifth week of gestation. Prior to this time the foetus is sexless, or more precisely, it has the potential to become either (or both) sex. Around the fifth week a single gene turns on, initiating a cascade of events that ultimately gives rise to testicle or ovary. In the male this gene is associated with the Y chromosome; in the female, with the X. An XY pair normally gives rise to a male, an XX pair to a female.

The two genes have been identified and produced by artificial means. Despite a general reluctance in the scientific community as a whole, our laboratory has taken this research further. Recently, we have devised a method to attach either gene to a common rhinovirus. The virus is ubiquitous; among humans it is highly contagious. It spreads primarily through water droplets (sneezing, coughing), but also through other bodily fluids (sweat, urine, saliva, semen). We have attenuated the virus so that is it harmless to mammalian tissue. It incites little, if any, immune response, resting dormantly inside cells. It causes no apparent disruption of function.

When an infected female becomes pregnant, the virus rapidly crosses the placenta, infecting the cells of the developing foetus. If the virus carries the X gene, the foetus will become a female; if it carries the Y, a male. In mice and rabbits we have been able to produce entire litters of male or female. Experiments in simians have been similarly successful. It is not premature to conclude that we have the capability to do the same for humans.

Imagine whole families of male or female. Districts, towns, even countries. So simple, it is as though it was always meant to be.

My daughter is a beautiful girl. She knows enough about sex, I think, to satisfy her for the present. She plays with herself often at night, sometimes during the day. She is very happy not to have to wear diapers anymore. She used to look at my penis a lot, and once in a while she would touch it. Now she doesn't seem to care.

Once maybe every three or four months she'll put on a pair of pants. The rest of the time she wears skirts or dresses. My wife, a labourer, wears only pants. She drives a truck.

One of our daughter's school teachers, a Church

woman, told her that Christian girls don't wear pants. I
had a dream last night that our next child is a boy.

I admit I am confused. In the ninth century there was a
German woman with a name no one remembers. Call her
Katrin. She met and fell in love with a man, a scholar.
Presumably, the love was mutual. The man travelled to
Athens to study and Katrin went with him. She disguised
herself as a man so that they could live together.

In Athens the man died. Katrin stayed on. She had
learned much from him, had become something of a
scholar herself. She continued her studies and over time
gained renown for her learning. She kept her disguise as
a man.

Sometime later she was called to Rome to study and
teach at the offices of Pope Leo IV. Her reputation grew,
and when Leo died in 855, Katrin was elected pope.

Her reign ended abruptly two and a half years later. In
the midst of a papal procession through the streets of
Rome, her cloak hanging loose, obscuring the contours of
her body, Katrin squatted on the ground, uttered a series
of cries and delivered a baby. Soon after, she was thrown
in a dungeon, and later banished to an impoverished land
to the north. From that time on, all popes, prior to
confirmation, have been examined by two reliable clerics.
Before an assembled audience they feel under their robes.

'Testiculos habet,' they declare, at which point the
congregation heaves a sigh of relief.

'Deo gratias,' it chants back. 'Deo gratias.'[3]

I was at a benefit luncheon the other day, a celebration
of regional women writers. Of five hundred people I was
one of a handful of men. I went at the invitation of a
friend because I like the friend and I like the writers who
were being honoured. I wore a sports coat and slacks and
had a neatly trimmed four day growth of beard. I waited
in a long line at the door, surrounded by women. Some
were taller than me, but I was taller than most. All were
dressed fashionably; most wore jewellery and make-up. I

was uncomfortable in the crowd, not profoundly, but enough that my manner turned meek. I was ready for a fight.

A loud woman butted in front of me and I said nothing. At the registration desk I spoke softly, demurely. The woman at the desk smiled and said something nice. I felt a little better, took my card and went in.

It was a large and fancy room, packed with tables draped with white cloths. The luncheon was being catered by a culinary school located in the same building. There was a kitchen on the ground floor, to the left of the large room. Another was at the mezzanine level above the stage at the front of the room. This one was enclosed in glass, and during the luncheon there was a class going on. Students in white coats and a chef with a tall white hat passed back and forth in front of the glass. Their lips moved, but from below we didn't hear any sounds.

Mid-way through the luncheon the program started. The main organiser spoke about the foundation for which the luncheon was a benefit. It is an organisation dedicated to the empowerment of women, to the rights of women and girls. My mind drifted.

I have been a feminist for years. I was in the room next door when my first wife formed a coven. I told her it was good. I celebrated with her the publication of Valerie Solanas' *The S.C.U.M. Manifesto*. The sisters made a slide show, using some of Valerie's words. It was shown around the East Coast. I helped them out by providing a man's voice. I am a turd, the man said. A lowly, abject turd.

My daughter is four. She is a beautiful child. I want her to be able to choose. I want her to feel her power. I will tear down the door that is slammed in her face because she is a woman.

The first honoree came to the podium, reading a story about the bond between a wealthy woman traveller and a poor Mexican room maid. After two paragraphs a noise

interrupted her. It was a dull, beating sound, went on for
half a minute, stopped, started up again. It came from the
glassed-in teaching kitchen above the stage. The white-
capped chef was pounding a piece of meat, oblivious to
the scene below. Obviously he could not hear.

The woman tried to keep reading but could not. She
made one or two frivolous comments to the audience. We
were all a little nervous, and there were scattered titters
while we waited for something to be done. The chef kept
pounding the meat. Behind me a woman whispered
loudly, 'male chauvinist'.

I was not surprised, had, in fact, been waiting from the
beginning for someone to say something like that. It made
me mad. The man was innocent. The woman was a fool.
A robot. I wanted to shake her, shake her up and make
her pay.

I have a friend, a man with a narrow face and cheeks
that always look unshaven. His eyes are quick; when he
is with me, they always seem to be looking someplace
else. He is facile with speech and quite particular about
the words he chooses. He is not unattractive.

I like this man for the same reasons I dislike him. He is
opportunistic and assertive. He is clever, in the way that
being detached allows one to be. And fiercely competi-
tive. He values those who rise to his challenges.

I think of him as a predator, as a man looking for an
advantage. This would surprise, even bewilder him, for
he carries the innocence of self-absorption. When he
laughs at himself, he is so proud to be able to do so.

He has a peculiar attitude towards women. He does not
like those who are his intellectual equal. He does not
respect those who are not. And yet he loves women. He
loves to make them. Especially he loves the ones who
need to be convinced.

I sometimes play tennis with him. I apologise if I hit a
bad shot. I apologise if I am not adequate competition. I
want to please him, and I lose every time we play. I am

afraid to win, afraid that he might get angry, violent. He could explode.

I want to win. I want to win bad. I want to drive him into the net, into the concrete itself and beneath it with the force of my victory.

I admit I am perplexed. A man is aggressive, tender, strong, compassionate, hostile, moody, loyal, competent, funny, generous, searching, selfish, powerful, self-destructive, shy, shameful, hard, soft, duplicit, faithful, honest, bold, foolhardy, vain, vulnerable and proud. Struggling to keep his instincts in check, he is both abused and blessed by his maleness:

Dr P, a biologist, husband and father never knew how much of his behaviour to attribute to the involuntary release of chemicals, to the flow of electricity through synapses stamped male as early as sixty days after conception, and how much to reckon under his control. He did not want to dilute his potency as a scientist, as a man, by struggling too hard against his impulses, and yet the glimpses he had of another way of life were often too compelling to disregard. The bond between his wife and daughter sometimes brought tears to his eyes. The thought of his wife carrying the child in her belly for nine months and pushing her out through the tight gap between the legs sometimes settled in his mind like a hypnotic suggestion, like something so sweet and pure that he would wither without it.[4]

I asked another friend what it was to him to be a man. He laughed nervously and said the question was too hard. Okay, I said, what is it you like best? He shied away but I pressed him. Having a penis, he said. I nodded. Having it sucked, putting it in a warm place. Coming. He smiled and looked beatific. Oh god, he said, it's so good to come.

Later on he said, I like the authority I have, the subtle edge. I like the respect. A man, just by being a man, gets respect. When I get an erection, when I get very hard, I feel strong. I take on power that at other times is hidden. Impossibilities seem to melt away.

(A world like that, I think. A world of men. How wondrous! The Y virus then. I think it must be the Y.)

In the summer of our marriage I was sitting with my first wife in the mountains. She was on one side of a dirt road that wound up to a pass and I was on the other. Scattered on the mountain slope were big chunks of granite and around them stands of aspen and a few solitary pines. The sky was a deep blue, the kind that makes you suck in your breath. The air was crisp.

She was throwing rocks at me, and arguing. Some of the rocks were quite big, as big as you could hold in a palm. They landed close, throwing up clouds of dust in the roadbed. She was telling me why we should get married.

'I'll get more respect,' she said. 'Once we get married then we can get divorced. A divorced woman gets respect.'

I asked her to stop throwing rocks. She was mad because she wasn't getting her way. Because I was being truculent. Because she was working a man's job cleaning out the insides of ships, scaling off the plaque and grime, and she was being treated like a woman. She wanted to be treated like a man, be tough like a man, dirty and tough. She wanted to smoke in bars, get drunk, shoot pool. In the bars she wanted to act like a man, be loud, not take shit. She wanted to do this and also she wanted to look sharp, she wanted to dress sexy, in tight blouses and pants. She wanted men to come to her, she wanted them to fawn a little. She wanted the power.

'A woman who's been married once, they know she knows something. She's not innocent. She's gotten rid of one, she can get rid of another. They show a little respect.'

She stopped throwing rocks and came over to me. I was a little cowed. She said that if I loved her I would marry her so she could divorce me. She was tender and insistent.

I did love her, and I understood the importance of respect. But also I was mixed up. I couldn't make up my mind.

'You see,' she said, angry again, 'you're the one who gets to decide. It's always you who's in control.'

'I am a turd,' I replied. 'A lowly, abject turd.'

A woman came to me the other day. She knew my name, was aware of the thrust of my research but not the particulars. She did not know that in the blink of an eye her kind, or mine, could be gone from the face of the earth. She did not know, but it did not seem to matter.

She was dressed simply; her face was plain. She seemed at ease when she spoke, though she could not conceal (nor did she try) a certain intensity of feeling. She said that as a woman she could not trust a man to make decisions regarding her future. To my surprise I told her that I am not a man at all.

'I am a mother,' I said. 'When my daughter was an infant, I let her suckle my breast.'

'You have no breasts,' she said scornfully.

'Only no milk.' I unbuttoned my shirt and pulled it to the side. I squeezed a nipple. 'She wouldn't stay on because it was dry.'

'You are a man,' she said, unaffected. 'You look like one. I've seen you walk, you walk like one.'

'How does a man walk?'

'Isn't it obvious?'

'I am courteous. I step aside in crowds, wait for others to pass.'

'Courtesy is the manner the strong adopt towards the weak. It is the recognition of their dominance.'

'Sometimes I am meek,' I said. 'Sometimes I'm quite shy.'

She gave me an exasperated look, as though I were a child who had strained the limits of her patience. 'You are a man, and men are outcasts. You are outcasts from the very world you made. The world you built on the bodies of other species. Of women.'

I did not want to argue with her. In a way she was right. Men have tamed the world.

'You think you rise above,' she went on, less stridently. 'It is the folly of comparison. There's no one below. No one but yourselves.'

'I don't look down,' I said.

'Men don't look at all. If you did, you'd see that certain parts of your bodies are missing.'

'What does that mean?'

She looked at me quietly. 'Don't you think it's time women had a chance?'

'Let me tell you something,' I said. 'I have always wanted to be a woman. I used to dress like one whenever I had the chance. I was too frightened to keep women's clothes in my own apartment, and I used to borrow my neighbour's. She was a tall woman, bigger than me, and she worked evenings. I had the key to her apartment, and at night after work, before she came home, I would sneak into her place and go through her drawers. Because of her size, most of her clothes fit. She had a pair of boots, knee-high soft leather boots which I especially liked.'

'Why are you telling me this?' she asked suspiciously.

'I want to. It's important that you understand.'

'Listen, no man wants to be a woman. Not really. Not deep down.'

'Men are beautiful.' I made a fist. 'Our bodies are powerful, like the ocean, and strong. Our muscles swell and tuck into each other like waves.

'There is nothing so pure as a man. Nothing like the face of a boy. The smooth and innocent cheek. The promise in the eyes.

'I love men. I love to trace our hard parts, our soft ones with my eyes, my imagination. I love to see us naked, but I am not aroused. I never have thoughts of having men.

'One night, though, I did. I was coming from my neighbour's apartment, where I had dressed up pretty in dark tights, those high boots of hers, and a short, belted dress. I had stuffed socks in the cups of her bra and was a very stacked lady. When I was done, I took everything off, folded it and put it neatly back in the drawers. I got dressed in my own pants and shirt, a leather jacket on top, and left. I was going to spend the night with my wife.

'On the street I still felt aroused. I had not relieved the tension and needed some release. As I walked, I alternated between feeling like a man on the prowl and a woman wanting to grab something between her legs. I think I felt more the latter, because I wanted something to be done to me. I wanted someone else to be boss.

'I started down the other side of the hill that separated my house from my wife's. It was late and the street was dark. A single car, a Cadillac, crept down the hill. When it came to me, it slowed. The driver motioned me over and I moved away. My heart skittered. He did it again and I swallowed and went to him.

'He was a burly black man, smelled of alcohol. I sat far away from him, against the door, and stared out the windshield. He asked where was my place. I said I had none. He grunted and drove up a steep hill and several more. He pulled the big car into the basement lot of an apartment complex. "A ladyfriend's," he said, and I followed him up some flights of stairs and down a corridor to the door of the apartment. I was aroused, frightened, determined. I don't think he touched me that whole time.

'He opened the door and we went in. The living room was bare, except for a record player on the floor and a scattered bunch of records. There was a record on, about two-thirds done, and I expected to see someone else in the apartment. But it was empty.

'The man went into another room, maybe the kitchen, and fixed himself a drink. He wasn't friendly to me, wasn't cruel. I think he was a little nervous to have me there, but otherwise acted as if I were a piece of something to deal with in his own way at his own time. I did not feel that I needed to be treated any differently than that.

'He took me into the bedroom, put me on the bed. That was in the beginning: later I remember only the floor. He took off his shirt and his pants and pulled my pants down. He settled on me, his front to my front. He was barrel-chested, big and heavy. I wrapped my legs around him and he began to rub up and down on me. His lips were fat, and he kissed me hard and tongued me. He smelled very strong, full of drugs and liquor. His beard was rough on my cheek. I liked the way it felt but not the way it scratched. He began to talk to himself.

'"The swimmin' gates," he muttered. "Let me in the swimmin' gates. The swimmin' gates."

'He said these words over and over, drunkenly, getting more and more turned on. He rolled me over, made me squat on my knees with my butt in the air. He grabbed me with his arms, tried to enter me. I was very dry and it hurt. I let him do it despite the pain because I wanted to feel it, I wanted to know what it was like. I didn't want to let him down.

'Even before then, before the pain, I had withdrawn, I was no longer aroused, or not much. I liked his being strong because I wanted to be dominated, but as he got more and more excited, I lost a sense that I was anything at all. I was a man, but I might just as easily have been a woman, or a dog, or even a tube lined with fur. I felt like nothing; I was out of my body and growing cold. I did not even feel the power of having brought him to his climax. If it wasn't me, it would have been something else . . .'

I stopped. The woman was quiet for a while.

'So what's your point?' she asked.

'I'm wrong to think he didn't need me. Or someone, to do what he wanted. To take it without question.'

'He hurt you.'

'In a way I pity him. But also, I admire his determination.'

She was upset. 'So you think you know what it's like to be a woman? Because of that you think you know?'

'I don't know anything,' I said. 'Except that when I think about it I always seem to know more about what it is to be a woman than what it is to be a man.'

Having a penis, my friend said. That's what I like best. It reminds me of a patient I once had, a middle-aged man with diabetes. He took insulin injections twice a day, was careful with his diet, and still he suffered the consequences of that disease. Most debilitating to him was the loss of his sex life.

'I can't get it up,' he told me. 'Not for more than a minute or two.'

I asked if he came. Diabetes can be quite selective in which nerves it destroys.

'Sometimes. But it's not the same. It feels all right, it feels good, but it's not the same. A man should get hard.'

I nodded, thinking that he should be grateful, it could be worse. 'At least you can come. Some people can't even do that.'

'Don't you have some shot, Doc? Something so I can get it up.'

I said no, I didn't, it wasn't a question of some shot, it was a question of his diabetes. We agreed to work harder at keeping it under control, and we did, but his inability to get an erection remained. He didn't become depressed, as many do, nor did he get angry. He was matter-of-fact, candid, even funny at times. He told me that his wife liked him better the way he was.

'I don't run around,' he explained. 'It's not that I can't . . . the ladies, they don't seem to mind the way I am. In fact, they seem to like it. I just don't want to, I don't feel like a man.'

'So the marriage is better?'

He shrugged. 'She's a prude. She'd rather not have sex

anyway. So how about a hormone shot, Doc? What've we got to lose?'

His optimism was infectious, and I gave him a shot of testosterone. And another a few weeks later. It didn't change anything. The next time I saw him he was carrying a newspaper clipping.

'I heard about this operation,' he said, handing me the article. 'They got something they put in your penis to make it hard. A metal rod, something like that. They also got this tube they can put in. With a pump, so you can pump it up when you're ready and let it down when you're finished. What do you think, Doc?'

I knew a little about the implants. The rods were okay, except the penis stayed stiff all the time. It was a nuisance, and sometimes it hurt if it got bent the wrong way. The inflatable tubes were unreliable, sometimes breaking open, other times not deflating when they were supposed to. I told him this.

'It's worth a try,' he said. 'What've I got to lose?'

It was four or five months before I saw him again. He couldn't wait to get me in the examining room, pulling down his pants almost as soon as I shut the door. Through the slit in his underwear his penis pointed at me like a finger. His face beamed.

'I can go for hours now, Doc,' he said proudly. 'Six, eight, all night if I want. And look at this . . .' He bent it to the right, where it stayed, nearly touching his leg. Then to the left. Then straight up, then down. 'Any position, for as long as I want. The women, they love it.'

I sat there, marvelling. 'That's great.'

'You should see them,' he said, bending it down in the shape of a question mark and stuffing it back in his pants. 'They go crazy. I'm like a kid, Doc. They can't keep up with me.'

I thought of him, sixty-two years old, happy, stiff, rolling back and forth on an old mattress, stopping every so often to ask his companion that night which way she wanted it. Did she like it better left or right, curved or straight, up or down? He was a man now, and he loved women. I asked about his wife.

'She wants to divorce me,' he said. 'I got too many women now.'

The question, I think, is not so much what I have in common with the banded krait of India, him slithering through the mud of that ancient country's monsoon-swollen rivers, me sitting pensively in a cardigan at my desk. We share that certain sequence of nucleic acids, that gene on the Y chromosome that makes us male. The snake is aggressive; I am loyal and dependable. He is territorial; I am a faithful family man. He dominates the female of his species; I am strong, reliable, a good lover.

The question really is how I differ from my wife. We lie in bed, our long bodies pressed together as though each of us were trying to become the other. We talk, sometimes of love, mostly of problems. She says, my job, it is so hard, I am so tired my body aches. And I think, that is too bad, I am so sorry, where is the money to come from, be tough, buck up. I say, I am insecure at work, worried about being a good father, a husband. And she says, you are good, I love you, which washes off me as though she had said the sky is blue. She strokes my head and I feel trapped; I stroke hers and she purrs like a cat. What is this? I ask, nervous, frightened. Love, she says. Kiss me.

I am still so baffled. It is not so simple as the brains of rats. As a claw, a fang, a battlefield scarred with bodies. I want to possess, and be possessed.

One night she said to me, 'I think men and women are two different species.'

It was late. We were close, not quite touching. 'Maybe soon,' I said. 'Not yet.'

'It might be better.' She yawned. 'It would certainly be easier.'

I took her hand and squeezed it. 'That's why we cling so hard to one another.'

She snuggled up to me. 'We like it.'

I sighed. 'It's because we know someday we may not want to cling at all.'

[1] Wachtel, Stephen, *H-Y Antigen and the Biology of Sex Determination*. New York, Grune & Stratton, 1983, p.170.

[2] Ibid, p.172.

[3] Gordon, H., in Vallet, H. L. and Porter, I. H. (eds), *Genetic Mechanisms of Sexual Development*. New York, Academic Press, 1979, p.18.

[4] Rudolf, I. E., *et al.*, *Whither the Male? Studies in Functionally Split Identities*, Philadelphia, Ova Press, 1982.

KIM NEWMAN

PATRICIA'S PROFESSION

When the call came, Patricia was going FF through the latest snuffs. She was a subscriber to the *120 Days in the City of Sodom* part-work, but, since Disney had run out of de Sade and been forced to fall back on their own limited psychopathology, the series had deteriorated. After a few minutes of real-time PLAY, she had twigged that the 104th day was just one of the fifties with a sexual role reversal. Mouldy chiz. Colin broke into the vid-out.

'Patti,' he said. 'Goto PRINT.'

Colin had blanked before she could work out whether he was live or a message simulacrum. The printer retched a laconic strip.

JAY DEARBORN. DEARBORN ESTATE. TWENTY ONE O'CLOCK HIT. 2-NITE.

The mark was on screen. The Firm had a four-second snip from a regular call. Dearborn was a sleek, expensive, youngish man. He had on a collarless, fine-stripe shirt. Silently, he repeated a phrase. Something about cheekbones. Patricia's lip-reading was off.

She switched to greenscreen and speed-read Dearborn's write-up. Executive with Skintone, Inc., the second largest fleshwear house. Married. Euro-citizen. Not cleared for parenthood. No adult criminal record. Alive. Solvent.

Colin came back, real-time. 'Our client is Philip Wragge. More middle management at Skintone. He likes us. He's used us before.'

'Why does he want Dearborn hit?'

'Getting curious, Patti?' Colin smiled. 'That's not in your usual profile. I think it's the mark's birthday.'

Patricia's birthday was in August. When she was little, her parents had always taken her to their cottage in Portugal for the school holidays. She had escaped until she was twelve. That year, Dad's job became obsolete, and the cottage had to be marketed. At teatime on her birthday, the other children had come round to Patricia's house and killed her.

Colin faded, and the scheduled programme popped up on the slab. Patricia rarely watched real-time. A Luton house-husband guessed that Seattle, Washington was the capital of the US. The Torture Master grinned, and his glamorous assistant thrust his/her bolt-cutters into the hot coals. 'Wrong,' sang the man in the dayglo tux, 'I'm afraid it's Portland, Oregon. That puts you in a tricky spot, Goodman. You have only three questions and two toes left, so take your time with this next one. Who, at the time of this recording, is the Vice-President of the Confederate States of America . . .'

Patricia off-switched. It was twenty to nineteen. Chord would be here soon. She put her uniform on. Black spiderweb tights, black lace singlet, black armlength talon glove, black butterfly tie. She shrugged into the white shoulder holster, and pulled a comfortable heavy white Burberry over her shoulder. She perched a black beret on her Veronica Lake bob. She white-fixed her face, and blacked her lips and eyelids. Neat.

She palmed her desk-top, and the safety cabinet unsealed. She took out the roscoe and disassembled it. There had been some question about the foresight, but it seemed okay to her eye. She replaced the lubricant cartridge, and snapped the machine back together. She shoved a new clip of slugs into the grip, and holstered the roscoe.

It could manage up to one hundred and seventy rounds per second. At that rate, the slugs left the eleven-inch barrel as molten chips. At Sixth Form College, the Firm's instructor had given a demonstration. She had turned a cow carcass into a piece of abstract expressionism, a study in red and intestine. Patricia didn't like to use her roscoe as a hosepipe, and usually kept the rate adjusted to a comfortable twenty-five r.p.s.

Outside, the car called to her. Patricia sealed her flat, negotiated the checkpoint in the foyer, and stepped onto the steaming pavement. If she stood still for a few minutes, the yellow ground mist would eat holes in her unprotected shins. Harry Chord, at ease in his reinforced chauffeur's puttees and Lone Ranger mask, held the Olds' door open for her. She slid onto the sofa-sized back seat. The Olds purred. Chord took the console.

The sturdy, box-like, black car had only recently been converted. Chord had done the job himself, and was quietly pleased with it. When they stopped at the Gordon's station to tank up, he pointed out the minute scars on the hood and running boards. Otherwise, it was impossible to tell from the exterior that the cash-wasting petrol engine had been replaced with the latest model booze-burner.

Patricia was tense, impatient. As always before a hit. She had been to the lavatory twice since Colin's call, but there was still a tingle in her lower abdomen. Some of the other girls pill-popped, but she needed, and wanted, the cold-rush of unfiltered sensations.

Of course, there had been less popping since Rachel. The girl had taken too many zippers, waltzed into her mark's office singing 'Paper Moon', and shot the man through the brain. By the time the termination officers arrived, she had switched to 'Stardust'. The Firm had lost its 100% efficiency rating.

Patricia had heard Chord, and several of the other back-up personnel, refer to Rachel's humpty dumpty hit. '. . . all the king's horses, and all the king's men . . .' The flippancy irritated her. Killing people might seem like a

fun job, but you had to take it seriously. If nothing else,
Rachel had proved that.

The Dearborn Estate was out in the Green Belt. They
were well ahead of schedule, so she had Chord program a
route that would avoid the disemployment centre. Shit
City, the claimants called it. Nissen huts covered in
ghastly, mock-cheerful murals. The dope dole. The
Ghetto Blaster gangs. There had recently been a rash of
documentaries, but, having spent six years in Shit City,
Patricia couldn't get off on poverty porn.

Evidently, Dearborn's wife was in on the hit. At the
estate entrance, a cobra terminal snaked into the Olds
and hovered over Patricia's lap. HELLO! IDENTIFICA-
TION? She palm-printed the slab, and keyed in the Firm's
trademark. PURPOSE OF VISIT? She had typed
MURDER before noticing that the need for a reply had
been countered on the print of Gillian Dearborn. HAVE
A PLEASANT VISIT.

The crackling electrodes in the gravel drive went briefly
dead as the Olds rolled over them. There were other cars,
low and streamlined, ranked in front of the house. Over
the roof landing floated a small dirigible, shifting gently
on its mooring. The house, Victorian but remodelled in
early Carolian, was lit by banks of old-mode disco lamps.

Dearborn was having a birthday party, with live music.
Patricia recognised the popular song, 'Throw Yourself
Off a Bridge.' The ballad was being performed by a small
swing combo; an unfamiliar, somehow inapt, arrangement. A girl Sinatra was trying to croon to the up-tempo.

> *When I get too depressed,*
> *Crawling along in a ditch,*
> *I get right up,*
> *Walk right down,*
> *And throw myself off a bridge . . .*

Patricia left Chord with the Olds, and walked uncon-
cerned across the lawn. A few stray guests, in designer
rags, noticed her. She hated Depression Chic. The bulk

of the party was behind the house, between the L of its two wings and the skimming pool. She tried to move easily among the rich.

A man with a plumed mohawk, an epitome of the New Conservatism, reached inside her Burberry. She sliced his forehead with a soporific talon. He fell onto a trestle table, between the swan cutlets and cocaine blancmange. He would be able to tell the other Young Rotarians he had won second prize in a duel.

I could put myself through a mangle,
I could drink the water in Spain,
From a home-made noose I could dangle,
It's the end to all my pain . . .

Dearborn was an easy mark. He was holding a helium balloon with BIRTHDAY BOY on it. He was squiffed, but standing. A plump, dapper man, and an elegant woman with fashionable facial mutilations were propping Dearborn up. Wragge and Gillian? They saw her coming, and confirmed their identities by rapidly moving out of her line.

Abandoned, the mark lurched forward into a personal spotlight. No hole-in-the-head innocent bystanders in the way. Terrific.

If I feel like cracking up,
And locking myself in the fridge,
I get on out,
And take a high jump,
To throw myself off a bridge . . .

Patricia reached with her bare hand for the roscoe. The Burberry slid from her shoulders. There were a few werewolf whistles. She shimmied across the lawn, getting in close to compensate for the possibly dodgy foresight. She did a few elementary gold-digger steps, and adopted the Eastwood position; legs apart, weight evenly distributed, left hand on right wrist, elbows slightly bent to absorb the kickback.

The bandleader, surprised but adaptable, had his

instruments segue into 'Happy Birthday to You.' The Sinatra picked it up immediately, and led the less out-of-it guests in the chorus.

The mark was looking around, gasping. '. . . Phil? You . . .' The balloon went up.

She took out his left kneecap. He staggered sideways, tripping on an abandoned urn but not falling. She upped the r.p.s. and sprayed Dearborn's flailing right arm. His hand came off at the wrist. Most of the guests had to laugh. She closed in, and fired a final, free-ranging burst into his torso. She had a glimpse of churning innards. He did an awkward pirouette and, with a satisfying splash, fell into the pool. The purple skum rippled. There were cheers. Patricia took a bow.

By the time she had retrieved her coat, the resurrection men were there. The Kildare was passing a vivicorder over the corpse. A nurse Patricia knew ticked off the necessary repairs. Most of the vat-bred organs and ossiplex bones would be in the Firm's ambulance. The front man was assuring Gillian Dearborn that her husband would be on his feet by morning, and preparing the legal and medical waivers for her palm.

'Good job, lassie.' Wragge hugged and kissed her. Even for a regular customer, he was overdoing it. 'When Jay sees himself on the playback, he'll die all over again.'

He stuffed a thousand note down her cleavage. Not a bad gratuity. He also gave her a hundred in Sainsbury's Redeemable for Chord. She was invited to the resurrection party, but cried off.

Tired, she gave Chord authority to get back to town by the quickest route. As she drove through Shit City, she cleaned the roscoe. She remembered her own deaths, and wondered whether the DHSS still had a budgetary allocation for resurrecting the underemployed.

She hadn't had the kind of luxury treatment Dearborn was getting. There had been problems with her anglepoise vertebrae throughout her middle teens. She had not had

the funds for a proper rebuild until she started working
for Killergrams.

That first time, the other children had dragged her out
of the house and hanged her from a swan-neck lamp-post.
Her party dress was torn, and her legs were badly bitten
by midges. Dangling in the late afternoon, the last thing
that had crossed her mind was that this was supposed to
be funny.

SCOTT BRADFIELD

UNMISTAKABLY THE FINEST

Every time Sandra Mitchelson's Daddy came home on
the boat he brought her things. French chocolates, a
stuffed elephant, a golden heart-shaped locket, a yellow
kimono printed with red lotus blossoms, a hand-painted
porcelain Japanese doll with a rice-paper parasol. In
return Sandra helped him work in the back yard. The
front yard was covered with gravel, the back yard with
tall yellow weeds. 'This will be our family area,' Daddy
said, knee-deep in the weeds. 'We'll have a barbeque, a
swingset, a bird bath, a trellis, maybe even someday a
swimming pool.' They already had a fish pond. The water
was dark and smoky and rimmed with algae. Large gold
and lead coloured fish glimmered dully in the muck,
slowly blinking their bulbous eyes like monsters surfacing
from some nightmare. Sandra held Daddy's white cloth
hat and watched him hit the ground with a shovel. He
overturned convexes of damp black earth, severed worms
and pulsing white slugs. Sandra liked the pungent, musty
odour of the fertiliser, and rode on Daddy's back while
he pushed the reseeder. They watered every morning,
and soon tiny green shoots appeared. After Daddy disen-
gaged the garden hose he filled his coarse red hands with
water from the tap, flung the water into the bright summer
sky and told Sandra the sparkling droplets were diamonds. Sandra tried to catch them, but they slipped
through her fingers. One day she sat down on the patio
and cried. Daddy promptly took her to the store and

brought her a tiny 'Genuine' brand diamond set in a thin copper band. The next morning he went away on the boat.

The new grass died, the earth turned grey and broken. Mrs Mitchelson said, 'He wants a lawn? Then let him water it his damn self.' She toasted her reflection in the twilit picture window. 'Here's to your damn lawn. Here's to your damn family area.' Bourbon and crushed ice spilled over the rim of her glass. In the afternoons Sandra sat alone on the living room floor and observed through the smudged picture window the gradual destruction of the yard. In the spring, weeds grew – strange enormous weeds as tall as Daddy, bristling with thorns and burrs and furred, twisted leaves. Scorched by the summer sun the weeds cracked and fell and, when the spring returned, the mat of dead weeds prevented new weeds from sprouting. Sandra asked when Daddy would be home. Mrs Mitchelson said, 'Never, if I have anything to do about it,' and departed for the pawn shop with the heart-shaped locket, the transistor radio, the tiny 'Genuine' diamond ring. 'You want to know what all that junk was worth?' Mrs Mitchelson shouted, looming over Sandra's bed at three a.m. Sandra sat up, blinked at the light, rubbed her eyes. Mrs Mitchelson's eyes were red and wet and mottled with discounted cosmetics. 'Twenty bucks. That's how much he loves you. Your wonderful father. Your father who is so wonderful.' Mrs Mitchelson stormed out of the room, the front door slammed. Sandra rolled over and went back to sleep. That summer they sold the house.

In Bakersfield Mrs Mitchelson worked at the Jolly Roger Fun and Games Lounge next door to the public library. Every day after school Sandra waited in the library and read magazines. She especially liked the large, slick magazines that contained numerous full-page advertisements. She enjoyed reading phrases such as 'unmistakably the finest,' 'the affordability of excellence,' 'the passionate abandon of crushed velour.' When the library closed at nine she sat outside on the bus bench and thought about the sharp, clear photographs. Fashions by Christian Dior, natural wood grain furniture, Chinese porcelain, a castle in Spain, a microwave oven with digital timer, an automobile with a leopard crouched and snarling on the hood. The doors of the Jolly Roger swung open and closed, releasing intermittent bursts of smoke, laughter and juke-box music. Buses roared past. Sometimes one of Mrs Mitchelson's friends drove them home. Nervous, unshaven men, their cars were usually littered with plumbing or automotive tools; cigarettes with long grey ashes dangled from their mouths. They ate pretzels and laughed with Mrs Mitchelson in the living room while Sandra went quietly to bed.

They lived in Pasadena, Glendale, Hawthorne, Encino. Sandra finished high school in Burbank, acquired a receptionist's job in Beverly Hills. They took a one-bedroom apartment in Compton, which included some cracked windowpanes and numerous discreet cockroaches. Weekdays, however, Sandra sat at an immaculate mahogany desk in the public relations firm of Zeitlin and Morgan. She answered telephone calls (often from television and film celebrities), organised the week's appointments in a large leather-bound black ledger, typed advertising copy, and allowed clients into the security building by activating a hidden white buzzer.

Sandra was usually alone in the office. Mr Zeitlin had retired to compose Bermuda postcards. Mr Morgan – with his distinguished grey hair, taut polished cheekbones and jogging outfit – arrived each day around elevenish, then quickly departed with Elaine, the leggy secretary, for the afternoon luncheon appointment. Occasionally Mr Morgan's son Matthew dropped by and asked for Elaine. 'Off with the old man again, huh? When am I supposed to get *my* chance?' Sandra admired Matthew – his capped white teeth, his knit ties, his shirts by Pierre Cardin. He resembled a man of 'casual elegance,' sipping Chivas

Regal on a sailboat, displaying Jordache emblems at garden parties. Matthew was an executive with the Jiffy-Quick Messenger Corporation of Southern California. His solid-gold tie-clasp depicted the comical (but fleet-footed) Jiffy Man dashing unflappably to his appointed destination. 'My Dad didn't just hand me the job, either,' he assured Sandra. 'I started off at the bottom, and absolutely refused any sort of preferential treatment. I even drove the delivery van one weekend, so nobody can say I didn't pay my dues. It literally took me months to get where I am today, and it was never any picnic, let me tell you. But I like to think that in the long run my employees will respect me for it.'

At four o'clock Sandra pulled the plastic jacket over the IBM, replaced paper-clips and memoranda in their appropriate drawers, and locked the office. On her way to the bus stop she window-shopped along Rodeo Drive, observed silk crêpe-de-Chine slacks at Mille Chemises, solid-gold Piaget quartz crystal watches at Van Cleef & Arpels. She admired the white, unblemished features and long cool necks of the mannequins; their postures were perfect, their expressions distant and unperturbed, as if they attended a fashionable cocktail party at the heart of some iceberg. Maseratis and Mercedes were parked along the curbs, and elderly women in low-cut blouses walked poodles on stainless-steel leashes. Everything and everybody appeared immaculate and eternal, like Pompeiian artifacts preserved in lava. Sandra avoided her own reflection in the sunny windowfronts – her pale white skin, her shiny polyester skirt – which made her feel like a trespasser in a museum. She caught the 6.15 bus and generally arrived home just after dark.

Mrs Mitchelson started awake at the sound of Sandra's key in the lock, sat bolt upright on the living room couch. 'Who's that? What do you want?'

Sandra opened the hall closet, removed a hanger. 'It's only me. Go back to sleep.'

Mrs Mitchelson's dry tongue worked soundlessly in her mouth, she cleared her throat. 'Well,' she said experimentally. 'Well, I wish I *could* go back to sleep. I wish I *could* get a minute's peace around this place.' She gripped the frayed arm of the couch with both hands, pushed herself to her feet. 'But don't worry about me. Just because I gave birth to you, just because I took care of you when *you* were sick and helpless.' Mrs Mitchelson took three short steps and landed in the faded rattan chair. The chair creaked sympathetically. 'I'm not saying I was perfect. I'm not saying I didn't make my share of mistakes. But at least I *tried* to give you a good home – which is sure a hell of a lot more than your father ever did.'

'Sit down, Mom. I'll get your dinner.'

'Do you think it's easy for me? Do you? Getting older and weaker every day, so sick I can hardly breathe sometimes. Just sitting around this lousy apartment wondering how much longer I've got left in this miserable life.'

'Please, Mom. Don't say things like that.' Sandra folded the comforter and slipped it under the couch. 'Do you want Tater Tots or French Fries with your dinner?'

Mrs Mitchelson's attention was diverted by the TV tray which stood beside her chair. The tray held a depleted gallon jug of Safeway brand bourbon, an uncapped litre bottle of Coca Cola, and an unwashed Bullwinkle glass. 'Why not? Why shouldn't I say it? I hope I *do* die. I hope I die tomorrow – how do you like that?' Mrs Mitchelson absently cleaned the glass with the sleeve of her blue flannel bathrobe. 'You wouldn't miss me. You'd finally be free of me, just like your father.' She filled Bullwinkle waist-high with bourbon, added a few stale drops of Coke for texture. 'When I needed your father, where was he? Traipsing all over the world, *that's* where he was. You might as well be a thousand miles away too, for all the good you ever do *me* . . . Ah.' Mrs Mitchelson put down the empty glass and snapped her dentures with satisfaction.

In the kitchenette Sandra turned on the stove, emptied a can of Spaghetti O's into a saucepan. She could hear the neck of the Safeway jug clink again against the rim of the glass.

'When I remember when I was younger, all the opportunities I had. I had a lot of boyfriends. They took me to nice restaurants, bought me expensive presents. Then I met your father. I was so stupid stupid stupid. I threw everything away for that louse. *Now* look at me.'

Bullwinkle looked at her.

The following summer Mrs Mitchelson was admitted to City Hospital. 'This is just what you've been waiting for, isn't it? Now I'll be out of your hair for good.' Mrs Mitchelson's voice was uncharacteristically restrained. Sometimes she almost whispered, leaning towards the side of the bed where Sandra sat, clenching the ends of the stiff white sheet in her thin grey hands. 'But just you wait. Now you'll learn what it's like to be alone. You'll know the hell I went through when your father left me for some cheap Filipino whore.' Mrs Mitchelson's eyes were wide and clear and moist, like the eyes of Bullwinkle on the drinking glass. Sandra sat quietly with her mother behind the cracked plastic partitions, listened faintly to the moans and cries of neighbouring patients, read paperback romances in which elegant women were kidnapped and fiercely seduced by pirates, rebel cavalry officers, terrifically endowed plantation slaves. Mrs Mitchelson's cirrhosis was complicated by undiagnosed leukemia, and she died unexpectedly just before dawn on a Monday morning. Sandra was fixing coffee in the kitchenette when the nurse called. Her mother had been wrong, she abruptly discovered. She did not feel alone, she did not feel betrayed. She did not, in fact, feel much of anything. She took the morning off from work, arranged disposition with the hospital crematorium, and smoked a pack of Mrs Mitchelson's cigarettes.

The medical bills were formidable, and Sandra had less money than ever at the end of each month. Her window-shopping expeditions grew less frequent, and she took an earlier bus home. Without Mrs Mitchelson to care for she rarely thought to fix dinner. She became pale and listless. Elaine said, 'Why don't you lunch at *Ramone's* today? They've got an outdoor patio, and it's a beautiful day.' Instead Sandra remained in the office alone, lunched on vended crackers, bagels and candy bars.

Then one night Sandra discovered Reverend Fanny Bright and the Worldwide Church of Prosperity. Reverend Fanny's sermons were broadcast live every Saturday evening from Macon, Georgia. Reverend Fanny told her followers, 'You can't expect happiness to just come *knocking*. You must *pursue* riches, you must *pursue* happiness, you must *pursue* the power of Divine Creation. When you see something pretty you want to buy, how many times have you told yourself, "I cannot afford this"? Is *that* what you think, children? Is *that* what you believe? Then you are *negating* the power of Divine Creation. You must convince yourself you can afford *anything*. You *can* afford it, you *will* purchase it, you *shall* possess it. You must impress your superconscious with *affirmation*. The superconscious is His workshop where, with the divine scissors of His power, He is constantly cutting out the events of your life. But first you must show Him the *patterns* of your desire, you must fill your *mind* with beautiful things.' After each sermon Reverend Fanny pulled a chair up close to the audience and solicited tales of miraculous prosperity. Middle-aged men and women described flourishing investments, sudden cash gifts from strangers on the street, gratuitous office promotions. 'All I want to tell you,' one woman said, 'is that I love you, Reverend Fanny. Prosperity has taught me how to love. Now I no longer feel so empty and alone.'

Every month Sandra mailed the Church a check for ten

dollars. In reply she received a mimeographed request for further donations. The stationery was inscribed with the Church motto: *If you do not wish to be denied riches, you must not deny riches to others*. Sandra closed out her savings, transferred the $2,386.00 to her previously minimal checking account, and prepared herself for imminent prosperity. She purchased navy cashmere sweaters, suede pants, a silk crêpe blouson dress fringed with lace, a deep breasted brown satin coat, labels by Calvin Klein, Oscar De La Renta, Halston, Adolfo, Bill Blass, Ralph Lauren. She joined a health-spa, subscribed to tanning treatments, visited prestigious beauty salons. Her checking balance dropped quickly to nineteen hundred, thirteen-fifty, one thousand. She did not question the beneficence of Divine Creation; instead she used her Visa card. Elaine said, 'You're looking so much better, girl. Why don't we have a drink after work? I'm meeting a couple of Tokyo software executives, they told me to bring a friend.' Mr Morgan granted Sandra a fifty dollar raise and told her, 'You really bring a lot of class to the office,' on his way to a toothpaste manufacturer and lobster bisque.

Church doctrine was unequivocally validated. Sandra increased her monthly contribution to thirty dollars.

Then one night Sandra discovered her superconscious in a dream. She ascended a long winding staircase. She was wearing her white ankle-length 'Cameo lace' nightgown from Vasserette, her Nazareno Gabrielli padded cashmere slippers. Her fingers ran lightly along a polished oak bannister. The summit of stairs met a long off-white corridor lit by globed ceiling fixtures. The fixtures were white, opaque, and sprinkled with the silhouettes of mummified insects. At the end of the corridor a solitary door stood slightly ajar. Bright yellow light from behind the door cast long, angular shadows down the length of the corridor. Sandra stepped quietly, afraid of disturbing anyone. As she approached the door she grew light-headed, her ears popped, as if she were descending in an airplane. The tarnished aluminium doorknob rattled at her touch. She pushed open the door.

The room was small, windowless, lit by a naked overhead bulb. Cobwebs scribbled the pale walls and cornices. The plaster was pitted and crumbling, mapped by an extensive network of cracks and crevices. The hardwood floors were sagging, whorled and discoloured. A full-feature model A-20 integrated amplifier sat in the middle of the floor beside a matching AM-FM stereo digital frequency synthesised tuner and cassette player. An identical system had been advertised in *Stereo Review*, and Sandra still recalled many of its vital statistics. A pair of three-way loudspeakers were stacked against the wall, with 12-inch woofers, 4-inch mid-range drivers, and 1-inch dome tweeters housed in walnut-veneered cabinetry. A mass of electric cords were joined by a plastic adaptor to a solitary wall outlet. A tiny green light activated on the amplifier's monochrome panel, an eight-track tape clacked faintly inside the tape player. The speakers suffused the room with white, cottony static.

Louis Armstrong began to sing, accompanied by bass, piano and drums.

> *Baby, take me down to Duke's Place,*
> *Wildest box in town is Duke's Place,*
> *Love that piano sound at Duke's Place . . .*

Sandra disliked jazz, pulled shut the door. The music diminished to a low persistent bass that fluttered in the off-white corridor like a staggered pulse. The door's surface was formica, with simulated wood grain. She tested the knob, the lock clicked soundly. Then she woke up.

It was still dark when the music awoke Sandra on the living room couch. She reached sleepily for the portable television. The green, baleful screen stared vacantly back at her, containing only her dim reflection – a shrunken

body attached to one enormous, elongated hand. Louis
Armstrong continued to sing.

> *Take your tootsies in to Duke's Place,*
> *Life is in the swim at Duke's Place* . . .

The bass thudded soundly in the floors, the walls, the
cracked wooden frame of the couch.

Sandra turned on the lamp and saw the stereo components stacked against the far wall, partially hidden behind
the TV tray. The amplifier's monochrome panel glittered
intricately. I am a miracle magnet, Sandra thought, recalling one of Reverend Fanny's prescribed affirmations.
Beautiful things are drawn irresistibly to me. I give thanks
that every day and in every way I grow richer and richer.

On her way to work Sandra mailed the Church a check
for one hundred dollars.

That night she couldn't sleep. She lay on her back on the
couch, her hands folded on her stomach. She closed her
eyes and tried to visualise the off-white corridor, the half-
open door. What did she want to find inside? A colour
TV, jewellery, kitchen appliances, a new car? What kind
of car, what colour? Would it fit inside the room? How,
exactly, had the room looked? She remembered the pitted
walls, the stained floors, the quality of light – but she
couldn't put all the elements together at once. A Maser-
ati, she decided finally. Like the one Mr Morgan drives.
There, it's all decided. Now she was closing the door.
Okay, the door is closed. Everything is very dark. Had
she heard the living room floor creak just now? Yes, she
was almost certain. Still, she kept her eyes closed a few
more minutes.

She sat up and opened her eyes. The living room
contained the portable TV, the aluminium TV tray, the
new stereo, the broken wall clock, the dingy venetian
blinds.

She closed her eyes and tried again. No matter how
hard she concentrated she could not make the car appear.

It was nearly dawn before she fell asleep, and only then did she stand again on the winding staircase. The wooden stairs were firm and cold against her feet; they even creaked occasionally. The car, she wondered. Will the car be there, or something else? It doesn't matter, she told herself. She would accept what was given. She wasn't choosy: she wasn't greedy. She only wanted her fair share. She walked to the end of the corridor, pushed open the door. Books were stacked haphazardly around the small, otherwise empty room. Dozens and dozens of books, as if waiting to be shelved by some divine librarian. Sandra stood at the doorway, but she did not go inside. The room's strange powers might harm her, she thought – jolt her like electricity, singe her like fire. She pulled the door shut.

When she awoke the next morning she examined her new books. They were accompanied by a bright orange and green brochure, which described them as 'The Greatest Books Ever Written'. *Madame Bovary*, *The Scarlet Letter*, *Fathers and Sons*, *The Red and the Black*, *Jude the Obscure*. Each volume was bound in genuine leather and filled with numerous illustrations by 'The World's Greatest Modern Artists'. She imagined the spines upright and glistening on a brand new bookshelf. A blonde oak bookshelf, perhaps. With glass-panel doors, and gleaming gold fixtures . . . But any bookshelf will be fine, she reminded herself abruptly. Really, any kind at all. She wasn't in any sort of a hurry. She didn't want to test the power; she didn't want to challenge it unduly. She would accept what was given.

Every night the dream recurred and the room presented her with beautiful things. A Schumacher 'Pride of Kashmir' Indian rug, a hand-carved Japanese console with iridescent moiré lacquer wash, a hand-cut glass chandelier by Waterford, a Miró original, a Roe Kasian dining set, a Giancarlo Ripa white shadow fox fur. The next time

Matthew visited the office she was wearing Fernando Sanchez's latest, a sheer silk taffeta dress anchored to a black lace bra. Her ruby earrings were the colour of pigeon's blood. Matthew sat on the edge of her desk.

'You like Japanese food?'

Sandra stopped typing, looked up. Her lashes were Borghese, her mascara Lancôme. 'I guess I don't know. I've never had it before.'

'Never?' Matthew's face was puzzled, as if confronted by an enigma. 'Tempura, teriyaki, Misu soup? You're in for a real treat. I know the best place in town. They've got shrimp the size of my fist.' He showed her his fist for emphasis. 'How does eight sound?'

'Eight?'

'All right. Eight-thirty – but try and be on time. I'll only honk twice. Here.' He handed her the steno pad. 'I'll need your address. Draw me a little map or something.'

Matthew picked her up at nine and they drove directly to his apartment, a West Hollywood duplex. 'Is the restaurant nearby?' Sandra asked. For the occasion she wore an obi – a broad black sash belt – with her cobalt blue, raw-silk dress. 'It just suddenly occurred to me,' Matthew said. 'They probably aren't open Thursdays. I'm almost certain, in fact. If you're hungry, see what's in the fridge.' In bed Matthew was fastidious. His hands and mouth made routine, scheduled stops at each of her erogenous zones, like miniature trains on a track. Sandra, meanwhile, observed herself in the mirrored ceiling. 'What's the matter with you?' he asked finally. 'You didn't tell me you had problems with men.' Matthew's body was sleek, firm, unblemished. His underwear was by Calvin Klein, his cologne by Ralph Lauren. Sandra said she just wanted him to hold her, and Matthew grew suddenly tense in her arms. He said he was short of cash at the moment – could she pay her own cab fare home? He *would* reimburse her.

*

Matthew stopped coming by the office. Whenever Sandra called his home she couldn't get past the girl at his answering service.

'Matthew Morgan residence – Mr Morgan is out at the moment. Can I take a message?'

At this point Sandra usually heard the click of a second extension being lifted, and knew Matthew was listening when she asked, 'Has he picked up his messages today?'

'One second and I'll check . . . This is Sandra again, right?'

'Yes.'

'Well, I'm afraid he still hasn't called in. But you could leave another message, if you liked . . .'

One day Sandra waited outside Matthew's office building until he emerged for lunch. 'You know I really care about you,' he said. 'I just think it would be better if we didn't see each other for a while. It's nothing the matter with you, baby. It's *me*. I don't think I'm ready to make the kind of commitments you seem to expect from a man. You tend to be very possessive – which is *fine*, it's only *right* . . .' He paused to wave at his secretary, who tapped one foot impatiently at the curb. 'Look, baby. Let's talk about this later in the week, okay? We'll have lunch. And do you think I could borrow a twenty until then?' He palpated his vest pocket. 'Seems I left my wallet in the office.'

Matthew never called. Sandra waited at home, certain he would. She broke dates with Mr Takata, the software executive, and Steve, her aerobics instructor. It was only a matter of time. Matthew would come around. She was a miracle magnet. She was one with the creative power. One night she received an Amana trash compactor, the next a Zenith Gemini 2000 colour television. 'You must not be afraid of total fulfilment,' Reverend Fanny warned, her brows knit with sincerity. The glazed, speckless TV screen crackled with static electricity as Sandra reached to increase the volume. 'You mustn't fear, you mustn't doubt, you mustn't lose faith. *Total* fulfilment requires *total* commitment. Have you, for instance, hoarded away a little nest egg, some rainy-day money? Then you doubt the complete power of Divine Creation. Why put a time-lock on your security savings when your love can be bullish on the stock-exchange of heavenly devotion?'

That afternoon Sandra walked to the corner and mailed the Church a check for $327.43, the balance of her account. Later the same night Matthew called.

'Hello, Sandra?'

'Yes.'

'Sandra, baby. It's me. Matthew. You remember me, don't you?'

'Of course I do.'

'I know I should've called. But it's been really hectic in the messenger biz, you know?'

'I'm sure it has.'

'You're not mad or anything, are you? I seem to sense a lot of hostility on your part. I know I owe you twenty and all – '

'No. I'm not mad. I'm glad you called. I was waiting for you to call.'

'Good. Look, I was thinking. Let's have dinner tonight. All right with you? I'll pick you up a little after eight, we'll go find a nice quiet spot.'

Matthew arrived at half past ten, and rang the door-bell.

'You think my car's safe parked around here? It's so late, I thought we could scrounge up a snack right here. You can show me around your apartment.' Matthew entered the living room. 'Hey, where'd all this great stuff come from?' He reached for the tape player – *Louis Armstrong's Greatest Hits*. Lengths of crumpled brown magnetic tape spilled onto the floor. 'Seems you've got the tape caught on the heads. If you've got a screwdriver, I can probably fix it.'

'I pushed a wrong button or something,' Sandra explained quickly, took the tape from his hands and plugged it back into the player. 'I'll have it fixed one of these days. I just like the way it looks. It really brightens up the room, don't you think?'

'What's down here? Is this the bedroom?'

Sandra followed Matthew through the door. He crouched in the corner of the bedroom, picked up and assessed one silver candelabra. 'This is worth a few bucks,' he said.

'It's getting late. Aren't you tired?' Sandra asked, and began to straighten the Wamsutta silk sheets.

'Where'd you get all this loot? My old man doesn't pay you this well just to answer telephones.'

'My father sends me things. My father has a very important job in Asia. Now, please – put those things down. Get into bed.'

'What a sweet deal. I think I'd like to meet this old man of yours someday.'

Sandra pushed Matthew's hands away from her belt. She just wanted him to hold her, she said again. This time, he obliged.

Sandra and Matthew were very happy together for a while. She enjoyed cooking his meals in the microwave, washing his clothes in the Maytag. Every morning she walked to Winchell's and brought him coffee and jelly donuts. Matthew took the next few weeks off from work. 'I want to be with you more,' he said, wiped a dollop of red jelly from his chin, and peered over Sandra's shoulder at the new Panasonic Omnivision VHS video recorder with wireless remote. 'I never saw that before. Did it just arrive this morning or something?'

Every evening Sandra stopped by the market on her way home. Matthew requested steak, swordfish, veal, king crab, champagne, Jack Daniel's Tennessee Sour Mash. She began computing her checking balance in negative numbers. When she arrived home Matthew was usually on the phone in the bedroom. ' – yeah, Bernie.

It's me, Matt . . . I know I haven't been home – I don't see what it matters to you where I'm staying. I want you to put a grand on Blue Tone in the sixth . . . Bernie, don't insult me. You know my old man's good for it.'

Sandra collected soiled glasses and plates from the living room. On the burnished mahogany coffee table she noticed a tiny, soft white mound of powder centred on a small, rectangular mirror. A gold-plated razor blade, attached to a silver chain, lay beside it. She took the dishes into the kitchen, started hot water in the sink, wiped a bit of fried egg off the lid of the trash compactor. Her mail was stacked on the countertop. A lengthy, itemised Visa statement. The landlord's second eviction notice. Urgent utility bills with bold red borders. My mind is centred in infinite wealth, Sandra reminded herself, and opened the last envelope. *Dear Friend*, the letter began *Are you prepared to receive the wealth of Divine Creation? Then you must be prepared to dispense wealth to others. Wealth flows two ways, not one, thus maintaining universal harmony*. The letter was concluded by Reverend Fanny's mimeographed scrawl. Sandra removed her checkbook from the kitchen drawer, computed her balance on the Taxas Instruments Scientific Calculator. Zeitlin and Morgan would pay her Wednesday. Perhaps she could deposit the paycheck in time for her outstanding checks to clear. Her balance, then, would be $23.97. She thought for a moment, turned off the sink faucet, dried her hands on a towel. I am a money magnet. Every dollar I spend comes back to me multiplied. I have all the time, energy and money I require to accomplish all of my desires.

She wrote the Church a check for one thousand dollars. She licked and sealed the envelope, then heard the broiler door squeak open behind her. She turned.

'Porterhouse, huh? Great, baby. My favourite.' Matthew slammed the broiler door shut. 'Listen, I need to ask you a little favour – *por favor*? Just a couple hundred for a day or two. My accountant's got all my

assets tied up in some sort of bonds or something. I don't
really understand all the technical details. It'll take me a
few days to get hold of some cash. You know these
accountants. They think it's their money, right?'

Matthew's smile was beautiful. His teeth actually spark-
led, like the teeth in television commercials. Matthew and
Sandra are very, very happy together, Sandra thought.
Marriage, they both realise, is inevitable. They mean so
much to each other. They will honeymoon in Brussels,
where Matthew has important family. After a year they
will return to the States where, with the aid of a persona-
ble nurse, Sandra will raise two beautiful, adopted chi-
dren, a girl and a boy. Matthew will eventually be
recruited into politics. 'We need you,' his influential
friends will say. 'You're the only man who can beat
Patterson.' Matthew will win by a narrow margin, but his
re-election four years later will come in a landslide. They
will rent a Manhattan penthouse, and Matthew will com-
mute to Washington.

'I can write you a check,' Sandra said.

One morning before she left for work Sandra made a
long-distance call to Macon, Georgia.

'Worldwide Church of Prosperity,' the receptionist
said. 'How can we help each other?'

Sandra asked to speak with Reverend Fanny, and the
receptionist said, 'Oh, I'm afraid that simply isn't possible. Regretfully, the Reverend's numerous personal and
public commitments make it virtually impossible for her
to speak privately with each and every one of her breth-
eren. But should you, perhaps, be contemplating sizeable
donations – say, ten thousand or more, and all of it tax-
deductible, of course – then I *might* be able to connect
you with one of the Reverend's close advisors – '

'I *am* contemplating sizeable donations,' Sandra assured
her. 'I am eternally grateful to the power of Divine Cre-

ation. My life is abundant with beautiful things. But at the moment I'm experiencing some problems of *cash-flow* . . .'

'Oh,' the receptionist said.

'I'm sure it's just a temporary problem – but I was wondering if there weren't any special prayers or affirmations for someone in my situation. You know, prayers which might *focus* my miracles a little more. And please, don't think I'm trying to be greedy or anything – '

'Cash is not wealth,' the receptionist said. 'Money only travels in one direction. True wealth flows both ways. If you would like to give me your address, I'll see to it you receive our free monthly newsletter.'

On Friday Sandra received a series of overdraft charges from her bank, and a tense telephone call from the local Safeway manager. 'I realise these things happen,' the manager said. 'Have to admit even I've bounced a few in my day. But how soon can I expect your check to clear?' Very soon, Sandra answered. She would deposit funds first thing tomorrow morning. She was so embarrassed. It wouldn't happen again.

'You'll get your damn money!' Mrs Mitchelson used to shout, after the store's third call or so. 'What's the matter with you people, anyway? Don't you realise I'm just a single woman trying to raise a child? No – *you* listen for a minute. You men always expect us to listen to you – well, *you* listen for a change. I'll pay you when I'm good and ready, and not a minute sooner. And *another* thing. You've got the worst stinking produce section in the city, do you know that? Your apples are wormy, your lettuce is wilted, your vegetables are rotten. Do you hear me? *Rotten*. Instead of me paying you, you should pay *me* for all the lousy produce I bought from your store and then had to throw away. That's what I think.' After Mrs Mitchelson hung up the phone she would fix herself a drink and tell Sandra to go and pack her suitcase. 'We're going to stay with your Aunt Lois again for a while,' Mrs

Mitchelson would say. 'Then maybe we can find a new home where the bastards will let us live in peace.'

After Sandra hung up the phone, as a sort of grudging memorial to her mother, she climbed a stool, reached the Safeway jug down from a high, dusty shelf, and poured herself a drink. She carried her glass into the living room, which was crowded with mismatched and exorbitant furniture, video and stereo components, unopened crates of records, Abrams art books and glassware, like the award display on some television game show. Matthew was playing Galactic Midway, an arcade pinball machine by Bally. Bells chimed, lights flashed, hidden levers pumped the next gleaming silver ball into position. Gripping the machine's sides Matthew nudged it slightly from time to time.

'Have a good day at work?' He pushed the reset button. On the scoreboard the digits clacked noisily around to zero.

'It was okay.' Sandra cleared some stray pearls from the ottoman and sat down.

'Did I tell you the electric company called? Something about a last notice. I think I'd look into it if I were you.'

On the coffee table the mound of soft white powder had nearly doubled in size, like a miniature avalanche. Sandra sipped her drink, glanced around the room.

After a while she asked, 'Where's my new VHS? My video recorder. The one I got this week.'

The flippers clacked noisily. Then Matthew hit the machine with his fist. 'Damn!'

'The VHS. I asked what happened to it.'

'How the hell do I know?' Matthew pushed the reset button. 'Do I look like the maid or something? It's around some place. You probably haven't looked hard enough.'

'I don't see it. It was in the living room this morning. It couldn't just get up and walk away.'

'It'll turn up, you'll see. Everything turns up eventually,' Matthew said, and pumped another ball into the game.

That night Sandra sat down and wrote a letter on her IBM Selectric.

Dear Reverend Fanny,
Please excuse the fact my check didn't clear. I had a very bad week last week. I tried to call and explain but the lady who answered the phone said you were very busy. I will try to make the check good at some date in the near future. I agree that if I expect to receive riches I must not deny riches to others, but I'm afraid my boyfriend Matthew whom I live with sold my Tiffany silverware set yesterday while I was at work in order to pay his gambling debts. Also he says he took my tape deck in to be repaired but I doubt that seriously. Also my electricity is being shut off tomorrow unless I pay them which I can't, and then what good will my new TV or any of my new kitchen appliances be good for? I would appreciate any help or advice on these matters you might like to impart to me. I wish I could send you money like I usually do but I'll try to send you twice as much next time and hope you understand and forgive my present fiscal situation.
Yours faithfully,
Sandra Mitchelson

When Sandra fell asleep later that night she did not dream of the corridor. She dreamed instead of vast darkness, where silence filled everything like a heavy fluid. The fluid filled her mouth, throat, lungs. Breathing was impossible. I believe, she thought. I believe, I believe, I believe. She looked up and thought she detected, at the surface, a glimmer of white light. She tried to push herself up through the black weight but something gripped her ankle, something warm, pulsing, insistent. Like a tentacle, it moved up her leg. 'Baby,' the darkness said.

Sandra started upright in bed. The bedroom glowed with dim moonlight.

'Baby,' Matthew said again. His arms wrapped themselves around her waist, his hands pulled her back into the weighted darkness.

On Monday when Sandra returned home from work she found Matthew in the bedroom, packing his Cricketeer wardrobe into the Samsonite. 'I think I've done my part. I can honestly say I've done my share to make this relationship work.' Underneath the packed clothes the tip of a silver candelabra glinted dully. 'But I'm the type of guy who demands a certain amount of honesty from a woman. Once she starts lying to me I know it's time to hit the road.'

'I never lied,' Sandra said. 'I sent the electric company a check, just like I said. It must have gotten lost in the mail – '

'I'm not talking about that and you know it. I'm not talking about the fact there aren't any lights or any food in the house – or even that the television doesn't work. I'm not talking about what it's like living in the goddamn Stone Age. I'm talking about simple honesty – something you obviously know nothing about. I'm talking about the check you gave me for Bernie which wasn't worth the paper it was printed on. I'm talking about my reputation in this town, which is now just about shot because of you.'

'I'll make it good,' Sandra said. 'It won't be any problem. We can sell the television, the washing machine – '

'It's just a little late for that. Bernie went to my old man for the dough. I'm free and clear. I've still got a job to go back to, or don't you remember. You didn't really expect me to live *here* all my life, did you? In *Compton*?' Matthew latched the suitcase and swung it off the bed.

'You have to stay. You can't leave,' Sandra said, over and over again as she followed him down the hall and watched him walk out the front door.

*

The telephone was disconnected, the water, eventually the gas. Every night the vast, liquid darkness displaced Sandra's dream of the miraculous corridor. Elaine said, 'You look like hell, girl. When was the last time you took a bath? There's a distinct odour creeping into this office, and don't think Mr Morgan hasn't noticed it.' At the end of the week Sandra returned home and found the front door sealed shut by the Sheriff's Department. The lock had been changed. She jimmied open the bedroom window, the one with the faulty latch.

Everything was gone. The brass bed, the pinball machine, the Maytag, the Lenox crystal. Rectangles of dust marked the former locations of impounded furniture. The room grew dark, and Sandra went to the window, turned open the venetian blinds. Outside it was dusk. She watched the phototropic streetlamps glow and gradually brighten, casting pale, watery red light through the blinds. Now she had nothing, and it didn't surprise her one bit. She was stupid, she never did anything right, Mrs Mitchelson was right, Reverend Fanny was right, Matthew was right. Everybody was right, everybody except her. She was all alone; she was afraid of total commitment; she was dishonest – dishonest with herself. She was sick of being wrong all the time. Things must change; things were going to be different, now. *I* am going to be different, she thought. From now on *I'm* going to be right, *I'm* going to make the right decisions.

She just needed one more chance. Finally she knew what it was she wanted, and that was the important thing. It was all very simple, really, like psychoanalysis on television. She wanted someone who cared about her, someone who would stay with her. Staring out the window at the streetlamp Sandra leaned against the wall. Eventually she grew sleepy and closed her eyes.

She heard the door open behind her, the crack of the ruptured plastic seal.

Sandra opened her eyes. 'Matthew?' She turned

around. The door stood open, the living room remained
empty. She walked to the door and looked out. The air
was filled with blinding, devotional light. I am one with
the creative power, Sandra reminded herself. I am not
afraid. I believe, and I am not afraid. She stepped outside.

She stood again on the winding staircase. As she
ascended she turned and caught a brief glimpse of the
downstairs room. The light swirled and dust motes
revolved slowly, like nebulas and constellations in some
twilit planetarium. Large wooden packing crates were
stacked everywhere, the lids nailed shut.

Sandra reached the summit of stairs. At the end of the
corridor the door stood slightly ajar.

Quickly she crossed the length of the corridor, flung
open the door and, without a second thought, stepped
inside.

The overhead bulb flickered and extinguished with a
sudden pop. She was not afraid, she told herself. The
place was very cold and very dark. Slowly her eyes
adjusted. Tall yellow weeds surrounded her, rippling as
an icy breeze blew past. The foundation of the fish pond
was broken and upthrust; all the water had drained away,
leaving a few green puddles of algae. The skeletons of the
monstrous goldfish, partially devoured by stray cats, lay
strewn about the yard like weird leaves. She got down on
her knees. Burrs and thorns scratched her legs. Her hands
groped among the weeds, discovered fragments of the
Japanese porcelain doll. The tattered rice-paper parasol
was damp and stained with mildew. She heard a noise and
looked up.

A tall figure stood between her and the half open door.

'Daddy?' Sandra asked.

Another sudden breeze blew past. The door slammed
shut.

'Isn't that just what I should have expected.' The dark
figure approached, briefly stumbled. '*Damn* – I could
break my leg on these lousy gopher holes. Just look what

a holy mess your father made of this place. But who's the first person you hope to see? Who's the first person you ask for? Your father, your wonderful father. Your father who never called, who never wrote, who never came to visit, who certainly never provided one nickel of support. Your wonderful father who never really gave a good goddamn whether either of us lived or died.'

Sandra sat down on the damp ground, weeds brushing against her face. The porcelain fragments crumbled apart in her hands.

'Aren't you a little old to be playing in the dirt? Here, get up.' Mrs Michelson offered her hand. Sandra took it, pulled herself to her feet. 'Try and grow up a little, will you? I can't keep my eyes on you every minute. Just *look* at this mess.' Mrs Mitchelson slapped the dirt from Sandra's knees.

They took one another's hand. Mrs Mitchelson's hand was cold and dry and soft. Sandra squeezed it tightly against her stomach, afraid of the dark.

'Try and remember that sometimes I need a little help and consideration too, you know. I can't do everything. I can only do the best I can, that's all. The best I can. Come on, now, and fix my dinner. It's been ages since I've had a decent meal in this dump.'

Then, together in the deepening darkness, they made their way carefully across the ruined yard towards the shadows of the house.

BRIAN STABLEFORD

AND HE NOT BUSY BEING
BORN . . .

It was in September 1973, shortly after returning from his
honeymoon, that Adam Zimmerman began to read *Sein
und Zeit* by Martin Heidegger. Although a native New
Yorker, he read German fluently. He was the son of
Austrian Jews who had fled Vienna in 1933, and a
perverse estrangement from his parents had made him
more enthusiastic to retain his national roots than his
religious ones. For this reason he had always remained
aloof from *schmaltz* while being self-indulgent in the
matter of *angst*, and he was ready-made for that sanctifi-
cation of self-pity which is the existentialist's red badge of
courage.

While he read Heidegger, a couple of chapters at a time
on those nights when he elected not to claim his conjugal
rights, he felt that he was not so much being instructed as
helped to bring to consciousness knowledge which had
always lain within him, covert and unapprehended. He
hardly needed to be told that *angst* is the basic mood of
existence, because it had always nested in his soul. When
Heidegger explained how our awareness of possible
death, though unfathomably awful, is so carefully
repressed to a subliminal level, so that the threat of
nothingness can be held at bay, what Adam felt was a
surge of tremendous relief, as the truth which had been
captive in his mind was set free.

When he finally laid the book down on his bedside table

for the last time, the silken caress of his expensive sheets seemed infused with a new meaning. For twenty-five years he had been a stranger to himself, but now he had been properly introduced.

He woke Sylvia, his bride of eight weeks, and said: 'We're going to die.'

Although distressed at being hauled back from gentle sleep in this rude manner, Sylvia naturally adopted a tone of loving sympathy. 'No we're not, Adam. We're in perfect health.'

'It is the one constant of our existence, Syl,' Adam told her, calmly. 'That awareness which haunts us, that we may at any moment be snuffed out of existence, forsaking our being, is the fundamental insecurity which weakens the foundations of the psyche. We try in our myriad ways to suppress it and defeat it: we invent myths of the immortality of the soul; we try to hide in the routines of the everyday; we try to dissolve our terror in the acid-baths of love and adoration. None of it works, Syl. At the end of the day, it *can't* work. Heidegger thinks we can break through – liberate ourselves from our servitude to the ordinary and achieve authentic existence – but even that won't work. It's nothing but another cheap trick to try to dodge the issue. The *angst* will always win. What can we do, Syl?'

In a year of courtship and eight weeks of marriage Sylvia had already had abundant opportunity to study her loved one's penchant for being abominably pompous, but she still thought he was wonderful, and didn't mind it too much.

'Go to sleep,' she advised.

Adam loved Sylvia too well to react to this shallow riposte with the contempt it clearly deserved. Instead, he let her follow her own advice while he continued to brood. The sheer enormity of his realisation denied him escape into the arms of Morpheus. He turned out the bedside lamp and sat in the dark, appalled by the vision

of nothingness that was conjured up before him, languish-
ing in the sensation of having no hope.

It is useless to speculate now whether sleep might have
saved him; if he could have slept in such circumstances,
he would not have needed saving. As it was, Adam
Zimmerman became in the course of that imsomniac night
a man obsessed. Those few rough-hewn sentences which
had poured out of him as he tried to explain himself to
the sleepy Sylvia became the axioms of his philosophy of
life. Heidegger's analysis of the human predicament –
that life is underlaid, limited, subverted and devalued by
its own precariousness in the face of possible death – he
accepted in full; but he denied what seemed to him feeble
attempts by the philosopher to find a cure in some shifty
sleight-of-mind. He went on to read the work of other
existentialist writers, and became especially fond of Sartre
after *Nausea* made him throw up, but try as he might he
could attain no age of reason, obtain no reprieve and
discover no iron in the soul.

Adam was tempted for a while to abandon his job as a
high-powered company accountant, on the grounds that
there was something absurdly meaningless about the
ceaseless juggling of figures. It seemed to exemplify that
desperate absorption in the trivial which was one of the
hollowest of false solutions to the problem of being. He
played the guitar well (it was his own mode of relaxation)
and he contemplated beginning a new career as a spaced-
out folk singer, growing his hair and beard and changing
his name to Adam X (to symbolise the falseness of the
family as a conduit of intergenerational continuity). He
decided against it, in the end, because hippiedom was
already passé, and because he thought of a better plan.
Sylvia applauded the decision heartily, but was later to
divorce him anyhow, on the grounds that he was too
gloomy and could not provide her with essential emotional support.

'The trouble with you,' she said as she left him, 'is that

you're deadly dull, over-devoted to stupid speeches, and incapable of enjoying yourself.'

Angst, as far as Sylvia was concerned, was a marital misdemeanour. She lived comfortably on the alimony which he paid her for the remainder of her days, but failed to escape the ravages of her own *angst* and eventually died an alcohol-sodden wreck in 1999.

Adam's own plan for escape from the human predicament was a daring one, but devastating in its simplicity. If the quality of life, he reasoned, is permanently and fatally impaired by the momentary possibility and ultimate inevitability of death, then the only *real* solution is to become immortal. When, before their divorce, he put this proposition to Sylvia, she laughed contemptuously, having long left behind the days when love forbade such indelicacies, but this reflected the fact that she really and truly did not understand him. For all his faults, Adam was not given to idle flights of fantasy. When he said he thought that there was an answer, he meant it. Nor was he talking in terms of any metaphorical or metaphysical immortality: he did not believe that satisfaction could be found in the thought of 'living on' in the pages of a few books or a few children, and the prospect of being a born-again optimist did not tempt him even when the Fundamentalist revival was at its height in the 1980s. Adam needed something more solid than Christ to put his faith in, so he invested it instead in ice.

By the time Adam became interested in cryonics the Cryonics Society of California and half a dozen similar outfits had been freezing newly-dead bodies for more than a decade. He was not impressed by their activities even in the days before a power failure allowed one cache of corpsicles to thaw out in 1981. He could not convince himself that future medical science would readily stretch to actual resurrection, and he was worried that contemporary techniques in freezing were inadequate to guard against tissue-damage. He knew though, that given time and money cryogenic scientists would soon devise methods which would allow living human beings to be placed in suspended animation more-or-less indefinitely.

There was, of course, a problem of timing to be worked out. Before being frozen down, Adam wanted to wait until the most sophisticated techniques could be put at his service, but on the other hand he wanted to be hale and hearty at the time. He knew, too, that he was going to need considerable wealth if he were to get the best of care during several centuries of inactivity. It was not easy to weigh all these things in the balance, but years of devotion to the juggling of figures had given him an unparalleled skill in calculation. He eventually decided that he must be frozen down in the year 2001, when he would be fifty-three years old. For safety's sake, it would be advisable to have at least a billion dollars at his disposal. This decision was taken in 1986, two years after his divorce, and he decided that provided he did not marry again, the billion dollars was achievable. He contemplated remaining celibate, but having studied Bertillon's data regarding sexual activity and death-risk decided that keeping a string of mistresses was a justifiable expenditure.

There were several ways in which an aspiring company accountant could plan, in 1986, to make a billion dollars by the turn of the century. They all involved stealing, but at that time the body and spirit of American capitalism were relatively unfettered by legalistic inconveniences, and it was not necessary to take undue risks. Adam did not, of course, steal *from* the corporations which employed him, but only *for* them, taking an entirely reasonable commission on every deal.

Adam was fortunate in his dealing during the 1990s, which were for so many the Golden Age of Capitalism: the days of the multinational frontiersmen, the buccaneers of international finance and the software stormtroopers, when hardly a month went by without a whole nation going bankrupt. Adam took a lion's share during the

heady years of the asset-stripping of the Third World, and
was one of the quiet men who masterminded the great
Tokyo Crash of 1996, which smashed the brittle commercial hegemony of the New Samurai and brought the entire
world electronics industry into a corner whose anchorage
was in the belly of the corporation which numbered Adam
among its brain cells.

Although his part in these transactions made him one
of the wealthiest men in the world Adam remained rather
modest and unassuming in dress and manner. His legion
of aides and assistants thought him shy and kind, though
he did have an annoying habit of giving them pompous
little lectures on the power of positive thinking, the virtues
of thrift and the dangers of hedonism. One of his favourite
topics, ironically enough, was fame. 'Fame,' he would tell
them, sternly, 'is essentially a matter of attracting attention, and attention is always fatal to men who make their
living by dipping into other people's pockets. One should
avoid at all costs being interesting; it not only renders one
vulnerable to the iniquities of inquisitiveness, but makes
one susceptible to flattery. Flattery is a powerful force,
and its seductions can be difficult to resist. One must
constantly remind oneself that fame is one of the most
awful reminders of one's own mortality. The masses are
always hungry for misfortune and disaster, and they love
to revel in the sympathy, tragedy and grief which attend
the sufferings of their idols. The public invents celebrities
mainly in order to revel in their decay and extinction, and
fame always breeds sickness and self-abuse.'

Such speeches as this were taken by his associates as
evidence of cynicism, and it was widely assumed that
Adam Zimmerman was an unhappy man. The story got
around among those who knew him that his life had been
blighted when his one great love, Sylvia, had deserted
and divorced him, and that his relentless money-making
was a pathetic compensation for his failure in the one
aspect of his existence which really meant something to

him. Even his mistresses believed this, and perhaps with better cause, because sometimes, in the grip of post-coital *triste*, he would weep a few tears for all the people in the world who were wretched and starving because he and others like him were appropriating all the wealth which, in a saner world, might have made them comfortable. In such moods as this, he would utter statements of a different kind.

'The thing we have to remember,' he would say, earnestly, 'is that we are *all* dying, with every moment that passes. We begin to die even before we are born; the moment an ovum is fertilised it begins to age. The embryo is aging even while it grows, and the period when the forces of growth can successfully outweigh the forces of decay is brief indeed. We think that we are still possessed by the bloom of youth at twenty, but this is an illusion. Death begins to win the battle against life when we are barely nine years old. After that, though we continue to increase the size and number of our cells, the rot of mortality is set in. The equilibrium is passed, and the new cells we produce already show the signs of senescence in the copying-errors that have accumulated in the nucleic acids, and in the cross-linkages that disable functional proteins. What we call maturation is the seal set upon us by the Grim Reaper, and until science finds a way to reverse these processes, correcting the nucleic acid errors and obliterating the cross-linkages, there is no hope at all for *any* of us, whether we sleep in silken sheets or starve in arid wastelands. We are all equal before the horror of it, whether we have the best of care or none at all. In such circumstances, there is no honour in conscience, no shame in selfishness. In an evil world, we are free to be evil.'

His mistresses always understood these arguments, because he always picked intelligent companions, but they rarely found it possible to agree with him. Without exception they concluded that he was lonely, bitter and neurotic, and pitied him as much as they adored him. He had the knack of finding women who loved him passionately for himself, caring little about his money, and he broke their hearts with careless regularity.

Adam never used any of his own funds to support the intensive research in cryogenics carried out by the Ahasuerus Foundation of Cincinnati during the 1990s, but he did prompt the various senators and congressmen who were in the pocket of his corporations to divert massive government funding in that direction. He always considered this to be the humanitarian side of his activity, allowing the people of the whole world (who were, in the final analysis, the source of the wealth paid as taxes by the great corporations) to become shareholders in the greatest of all human endeavours: the war against death. Many of them, indeed, were privileged by his intervention to become casualties in that war. Adam Zimmerman was very proud, therefore, to become in April 2001 one of the first few volunteers to be frozen down while still in the full bloom of health, using the most sophisticated of new techniques. He left his vast fortune in trust, to pay rent for his body, if necessary, for thousands of years, while he waited for the war against death to be won and for immortality to become the common heritage of all mankind.

By virtue of its links with the corporations for which Adam had worked, aided by the trustees of his fortune, the Ahasuerus Foundation rode out the Great Depression of the 2020s, the resource crisis of the 2040s and the plague wars of the 2060s. It remained rich and strong through the Greenhouse Crisis of the 22nd and 23rd centuries, surviving the sporadic hostility of individual saboteurs, Luddite governments and the predations of the new breed of tax-gatherers which were spawned by the strengthened United Nations once it came to dominate the old nation states and vie for power with the cosmicorporations which controlled the world's wealth. The Foundation was untroubled by the Ice Age of the 26th and

27th centuries, though it moved most of its holdings (including its richest corpsicles) with the rest of the world's elite to one of the fabulous ecoarcologies which sprang up on the moon once the elaborate technologies of artificial photosynthesis made it fertile. Adam Zimmerman's body was moved from the moon to an orbital habitat in 2724, and back to earth again in 2887 when the UN's ecological engineers finally brought eternal summer to what had, in pre-glacial days, been the temperate zones of the northern hemisphere. By 3015 Adam was back where he had started, in the new supercity erected on the site of Cincinnati, still at rest in his personal freezer.

The trustees of Adam Zimmerman's estate grew very rich, and as generation followed generation they loyally fought off a series of attempts to have him revived. The first technology of longevity developed in the 24th century, involving drastic tissue-renewal surgery, extended the human lifespan to 150 years, but this was far from the immortality which Adam coveted. The technology which replaced it was based on the genetic engineering of human ova, and was not the slightest use to anyone but the unborn, so that by the year 3000 research into the technology of longevity was entirely concentrated in that area of embryonic engineering. The Ahasuerus Foundation had diversified its interests to the point where almost none of its effort was devoted to research which Adam Zimmerman would have considered relevant. Cynical observers suggested that Adam's trustees were showing a marked lack of enthusiasm for the attempt to create the circumstances in which they would have to hand their fortune back to its real owner, but the trustees simply stated (correctly) that under the terms of their trust they could not bring Adam back into a world such as theirs without betraying his dearest wish.

When the UN finally broke the economic back of the cosmicorporations in the 33rd century, Adam's situation changed. Instead of growing richer and richer, his trust began to grow poorer. By 3450, by which time none of the old corporations existed as separate entities or reservoirs of power, the Ahasuerus Foundation had been absorbed into a minor UN department. The job of deciding what was to be done with its legion of corpsicles became a matter of petty bureaucratic decision. Many of the legion were recruited by degrees into the land of the living, but Adam's case was a difficult one, and it was in the nature of bureaucracy even in this era that decisions were always easier to postpone than to take. The tempo of life had slowed dramatically with the extension of the human lifespan, and these postponements stretched over centuries.

Eventually, Adam suffered the ultimate fate of all matters of bureaucratic record: he was forgotten by every living person, his very existence known only to the uncaring intelligence of computer files. Along with eleven other corpsicles he was consigned to an informational limbo, there to await rediscovery for as long as it might take. By 3750 all the other people frozen down in the second and third millennia had been revived, and cryonic preservaion was no longer employed for any purpose at all, but Adam and his companions, exempted by some whim of chance, slumbered on, the electricity supplies to their cryonic chambers carefully maintained by conscientious automata. The world continued to change around them – rather slowly – but they remained quite unaffected.

It was, in the event, not until the 47th century that the technology of longevity used by mankind reached its ultimate stage, granting its users what they believed to be a limitless lifespan if they remained untouched by violent accident. It was not until the 52nd century, though, that the rebuilding and renovation of Cincinnati IV brought back to the surface of the earth the secret chamber where Adam's body had been concealed for more than a thousand years. The rediscovery was a momentous event in a world where hardly anything new ever happened, and it stirred the imagination of the people of the new Golden Age of youth and tranquillity. In this Utopian era there was no such thing as an unfulfilled need except the need for surprise, and no greater joy was possible than the uncovering of something wonderfully ancient.

Unfortunately, the cryonic technology of the year 2001, despite all the effort poured into it by the lavishly-funded Ahasuerus Foundation, proved to have been far from perfect. Of the twelve corpsicles stored in the vault, eleven had succumbed to the ravages of putrefaction in spite of everything. Only one could be revived, and the singularity of this seemed a virtual miracle. There was undoubtedly a certain justice in the fact that the sole survivor was Adam Zimmerman, because he had done far more than the other eleven to make sure that the possibility of survival remained open.

When Adam awoke, he found himself in a comfortable bed, with sheets that felt like the softest and most delicate silk. Beside his bed sat a phenomenally handsome blonde girl, who seemed to be about nine years old. He favoured her with a bright smile, and asked: 'What year is it?'

'In your calendar,' she told him, pronouncing the words tentatively and a little clumsily, 'it is 5186.'

Adam smiled again, but dared not yet rejoice in the feeling of security which he had promised himself when this moment came.

'Are you immortal, little girl?' he asked.

'One cannot be sure of that,' she said, 'but I am three hundred and seventeen years old, and I know no reason why I should not live forever.'

Adam could not help but laugh at the delightful contradiction involved in a person of three hundred years plus looking as if she were only nine: a blonde-haired, snub-nosed poppet with eyes that radiated innocence! Of course, he believed what she said.

'And I am to be immortal too,' he said, not even phrasing it as a question.

It says a great deal for Adam Zimmerman's strength of character and essential resilience that he did not break into tears when she told him, as diplomatically as she could manage in a language which was for her utterly archaic, that he was not.

The enormity of it all did not become clear immediately. He learned only by degrees what sort of a world it was to which he had come. His task was made more difficult by confusion, and dogged by a deep depression that was alleviated only occasionally by intervals in which he was simply too overwhelmed by the wonders of the new era to be despairing.

The facts of the matter were straightforward. He was in a world where no one died unless he or she chose to do so. Disease and aging were completely conquered, and the probability of fatal accidents had been reduced by technological ingenuity to zero. Minor wounds could be healed by tissue-regeneration, even to the replacement of lost limbs or smashed organs. Violence and aggression no longer figured in the repertoire of human behaviour. The world was at peace, and it was paradise.

No one was born into the world any longer, although the technology existed to clone individuals from single cells, developing the embryos in artificial wombs. All who were alive in this world had been shaped to an ideal of physical perfection by genetic engineers. The development of their bodies had been arrested at that point when the forces of growth held the forces of decay exactly in check, and everyone in the world appeared to Adam's eyes to be nine years old. The world was without puberty and without sexual intercourse. Such pleasures of bodily contact as there were required neither arousal nor orgasm.

All that was known in this era about the technology of longevity concerned methods of engineering human egg-cells and early embryos. Immortality was simply programmed into human nature. Even the primitive methods of tissue-renewal, which had first given longevity to men of the third millennium, had not been practised for thousands of years, and to attempt them would be a hazardous business. Despite the awesome sophistication of the science these people had at their disposal, there was little they could think of doing to help preserve Adam's life beyond its own programmed span. They could protect him from disease, and from cancer, and could help regenerate his tissues as they wore out, but about the copying-errors that accumulated in his DNA and the cross-linkages that were disabling his proteins they could do nothing. He might live to be a hundred, perhaps a hundred and twenty, but then he would die.

Adam realised, slowly, that he was the only person in the world doomed to senescence and death. He was the only person in the world who was the victim of Heidegger's *angst*. He was also the only person in the world possessed of sexual desire, and though the people of the new era were perfectly willing to help him serve these urges if he wished, he was not psychologically equipped for life in a paedophile's Utopia; his sensibility revolted at the thought of intercourse with persons who appeared to be nine years old, whatever their real age might be.

The fact that he was still completely cut off from his heart's desire (though everyone else in the world was not) was only one of the ironies in Adam's new situation. He awoke to find himself famous. By virtue of his nature he was the object of a fascination greater and more widespread than had been attained by any other man in history. There was not a man or woman in the world who did not know about Adam Zimmerman, who did not want to see and touch Adam Zimmerman, who did not want to be kept informed of every detail of his progress through life. The world was hungry for his thoughts, besotted with his actions.

They tried, of course, to be scrupulously polite. They readily acknowledged his right to privacy, and tried not to invade it. They did nothing that involved him without seeking his informed consent. They apologised for every intrusion, and begged his leave for every question they asked. If he asked to be let alone, they left him, but hovered always near to be responsive to his every whim. When he chose not to be alone – and he could hardly bear solitude – there was no way for them to set aside their curiosity, their utter absorption in the mysteries of his fate and fortune.

Adam soon found out that if he were to ask his hosts to have him frozen down again, they would do it. He no longer had a vast fortune to pay for his upkeep and guard his interests, but in this world there was no currency needed save need itself. Whatever he asked of these people, they would give him, and though they would be disappointed in the extreme if he chose to leave them, they could not bear to deny him anything. He could ask them, too, to dedicate great efforts to the development of the kind of technology of immortality that he (and he alone in all the world!) required, and they would do it. They would work for him, proudly and gladly, for centuries or millennia, and would delight as much as he in the possibility that he could one day get what he had come so far in search of. Their delight, though, would mask a disappointment, because if he became one of themselves, he would cease to be fascinating. What he had cynically said about fame in that distant, forgotten past was all too obviously true in this startling present. The basis of his celebrity was his mortality; what these people were fascinated by, above all else, was his awful misfortune in being a man who one day must die.

Adam Zimmerman considered his options, and he hesitated.

For the first time in his life, he had doubts about the prospect of immortality. Was such a reward, after all, a mixed blessing? Could he really bear to have the clock of his being turned back, to revert to being nine years old forever? Would it really *work*, as a cure for his existential predicament?

As the days passed, and Adam lived in the supremely comfortable world of the 52nd century, he began to wonder whether *angst* was still the sole and central fact of his existence. Another horror was beginning to compete with his horror of death. It was not the horror of eternal life *per se* – that would have been absurd – but it was the horror of the idea that in winning eternal life *he*, the essential Adam Zimmerman, would be exterminated just as thoroughly as he would by death. The people of this new era were healthy, and happy, and wise; theirs was an entirely enviable condition – but it was a condition to which they had been born, and he, if he was ever to inherit it, would have it thrust upon him. It would not be, could not be, the same. The pre-pubescent avatar that would result from the scientific miracle would be an immortal, but it would not be an immortal Adam Zimmerman. The goal he had sought in casting himself adrift on the sea of eternity in the first year of the third millennium – the preservation of *his own* being – was still out of reach.

Adam realised, like so many others before him, that his cure for the human predicament would not work. Like all old philosophers and lovers, all the artists and hobbyists, all the mystics and martyrs, he found in the end that you couldn't beat the *angst*. You could repress it, ignore it, sublimate it, stare it full in the face or freeze it for thousands of years, but you couldn't get away from it.

Adam didn't particularly enjoy this discovery, but he was not utterly defeated by it. Alongside the realisation that he didn't really want the kind of immortality these people might procure for him came the realisation that there was an alternative open to him. Instead of asking to be frozen down again, he could allow himself to fall for the flattery and seduction of his fame. He could give these Golden Age innocents what they longed for: a taste of human dereliction and death. He alone, in all the world, could make them appreciate the privileges they enjoyed, by showing them what it was to be without them.

Adam had spent the greater part of his life trying to find an escape from *angst*; now he changed direction. He decided to revel in *angst*, in order to show a world that was without *angst* the true meaning of his existence, the true significance of his state of being.

'I am not just a man,' Adam told his greedy audience. 'I am a symbol. You must learn to understand me, for I am not merely famous: I am fame itself.'

They loved it. They drooled over his every aphorism.

Adam decided to make the twilight of his life the ultimate dramatic performance. He would show them death with dignity. He would make them see, not only the physical processes of decay which would claim him, but the psychological warfare that went on in parallel. That which had been trivial and utterly commonplace in his own world, where millions had died because of a few juggled figures on balance sheets, would now be not merely unique, but tremendous.

In the years that followed, Adam's hair turned gradually grey. He let it grow long, and grew his beard as well. He asked his hosts to make him a guitar, and he began to play again, singing songs in German and English that he had learned in childhood and adolescence, and learning new ones that his faithful admirers found in ancient databanks. He even composed some songs of his own: sad songs about sex and death, war and poverty, pain and love. He abandoned privacy, and gave himself entirely to his public. When he was not singing, he talked, frankly and with occasional painful honesty, allowing all his thoughts to be recorded for infinite posterity as well as being eagerly lapped up by the ever-present listeners. He began to style himself Adam X, to signify that fact that he was the great unknown.

He planned his death meticulously, though the possibility of suicide was ruled out. He must die, he decided,

of what passed in his own time for natural causes: of
cancers that would burst spontaneously within his frail
flesh; of the gradual erosion of his tissues: of the failure
of the co-ordinating systems that bound his disparate cells
into a coherent whole. He decided that he would use no
anaesthetics, suffering the pain which would come with
these varied afflictions. This was not a decision taken out
of courage – he had always been something of a physical
coward – but out of a sense of responsibility. This was the
only chance that the people of the sixth millennium would
ever have to understand suffering, and he must not cheat
them. His pain, his tears, his shiverings, his sadnesses, his
fears – *all* his stigmata – belonged to them, because it was
these which gave significance to his being.

Planning all this, carefully preparing for it all, and going
through it – not without difficulty, by any means – Adam X
became by degrees a happy and contented man, at peace
with himself and his *angst*. He became a prouder man than
he had ever been in the days when he took his gluttonous
part in the rape of the world. He became a more joyful man
than he had ever been, even in the heights of ecstasy which
his relationship with Sylvia had allowed him temporarily to
reach. By making death into fulfilment, he robbed it of
almost all the power it had once exercised over his imagination. He moved his *angst* from the side of moral debit to the
side of moral credit in the account-book of his psyche, and
with that cunning move, so like in spirit to the legerdemain
which had been his forte in days gone by, he turned a
potential loss into a handsome profit.

Adam X died on the day which would have been
identified in his calendar as the twenty-fifth of July, 5237,
at the age of three thousand two hundred and eighty nine.
This was a record, ironically enough, in a world from
which death had been banished. He died in a comfortable
bed, in sheets which felt to him like the most sensuous
silk, and which reminded him pleasantly of riots of sexual
excess enjoyed with his most expensive mistresses. He

had been working on his last words for many years, redrafting and polishing them endlessly, and managed to deliver them all before losing his powers of speech.

'It is my earnest hope,' he told his adoring fans, 'that by the example of my suffering and death I may redeem you all from the innocence which is your fortunate heritage. I have been, during these last thirty years, a stranger and afraid in a world I never made, but I have done my humble best to remake it, by remaking its understanding of its own origins. The immortality which you enjoy was born out of the efforts of men such as I, made desperate by their own mortality. We could not save ourselves, but we sowed the seeds of salvation for future mankind, paving the road to Heaven with our good intentions. I have come out of the mists of time to bear a message, which is that our tragedy and your triumph are indivisibly one, and must be understood as opposite sides of the same coin. I cannot express, in the poor language which every person on earth has learned in order to listen to me, the delight I feel in knowing that mankind has attained an Age of Reason, but I know that you feel it too. *Ave atque vale!*'

This speech was to be eternally remembered and treasured by the people of earth, granting Adam Zimmerman the kind of metaphorical immortality that once he had scorned. No one who read it remained unmoved by it; and no one ever thought such an unworthy thing as to deem it pompous.

The innocents of the Golden Age continued to enjoy Adam long after he was dead, granting him the grandest and finest funeral in the history of the human race – whose like, needless to say, was never seen again. They replayed his speeches on TV again and again, without end, for they remained the only resource mankind had left in savouring the bittersweet sympathies of tragedy.

RACHEL POLLACK

THE PROTECTOR

'I'm afraid I've got some bad news,' Dr Steiner said. He paused, as if waiting for some reaction. Lynne just sat there, her back hardly touching the expensive leather chair. 'I've run all the tests I could think of, looking, well, for anything at all, and I'm afraid, Mrs Buscher, that the tests have shown no pathology.'

Lynne sighed. Her shoulders slumped and she leaned back. 'You're sure? There can't be anything – '

'Blood levels, wave patterns, hormones – '

'But – '

'I'm sorry, Mrs Buscher.' He didn't sound sorry. She could imagine his distaste for having her in his office.

She said, 'In other words, I'm sane.'

'Well, that terminology . . .' Dr Steiner's voice slowed to a slur and his face shifted. The ears grew longer and pinned back, the cheekbones stood out, the eyes sunk deep in round sockets like gun barrels, and two tongues played with each other across lips covered in a hard black crust. Lynne began to cry, softly, as she averted her gaze to the panelled wall and Dr Steiner's diplomas and honorary degrees.

When she turned back he was normal again. She said, 'There's nothing else you can do? No tests?'

'I've done them all. The results – '

'No medicine?'

'I can only prescribe medicine for people with disorders.'

'And since I don't – Oh, shit.'

Annoyed, Dr Steiner fiddled with a paperweight replica of the Old White House.

'Why did I go to the best?' Lynne thought. If she'd gone to some cheap MD she could have pretended he didn't know what he was doing. She stood up, feeling a little dizzy. 'Thanks,' she said. 'Thanks a lot.' He didn't deserve her anger but he was there, an easy target.

Dr Steiner said, 'There won't be any charge. I've already told my secretary.'

Lynne half smiled. 'What is this? Be kind to lost souls week?'

'Call it medical ethics. A case like this passes beyond our proper area.'

'That's terrific, Doctor.' A light shone around his eyes, and Lynne caught her breath, afraid he would change again. But the light faded, leaving the psychiatrist intact. 'Tell me,' she said as she slung her red totebag over her shoulder. 'What's the money going to do for me when I'm drowning? Or do you think the plague will take a check?'

'I don't think we need to talk about that.'

'You don't. All you need to do is get rid of me.' She wanted to slam the heavy wooden door but the springs only made a soft hiss as they braked the weight.

A short corridor of closed doors led from the office to the waiting room. Lynne stopped with her hand half raised to push open the door. Suppose the people on the other side had changed? Suppose the whole room had vanished, flinging her onto the ravished surface of Gabriela H-3? Sweating, she thought she couldn't take that, not now. Hell, not ever. 'Please,' she prayed vaguely, 'keep it the way it's supposed to be.' She pushed open the door.

Okay. It was okay. The people had stayed comfortably human, the room had kept its neat rectangular shape, the grey couch and the soft chairs with their old-fashioned

floral prints hadn't changed to rocks or blasted buildings
or trees or anything else.

Peter threw down his magazine and hurried up to her,
unconsciously stopping a few feet away. Deliberately she
walked past him to the coat rack. She handed him his
nylon windbreaker. 'Here,' she said, and put on her
checkered raincoat. She didn't bother to button it.

'What did he say?' Peter whispered.

'We don't have to pay.'

'What?' Peter said. 'I don't understand.'

'Oh come on,' she said, and led the way past the
secretary, who pretended not to notice them. They
walked down the carpeted stairs to the street door where
Lynne looked out through the peephole before she
opened the door. Normal. Nothing had changed on 71st
Street. The usual limousines and taxis glided up and
down, the few pedestrians walked large exotic dogs.
When they stepped outside a thin rain was falling. Lynne
nodded at the cool wet on her face. No drops of fire, no
sharp crystals cutting her skin. Would it stay? That time
at her cousins's house upstate, the snow had started out
so innocently. She remembered how she and Jeanette,
her cousin's daughter, had run out for a snowball fight on
the lawn by the lake. And then it changed. She'd felt
something sharp and her face stung. When she'd reached
up her glove had come away covered in blood. Poor
Jeanette. No idea why Aunt Lynne had started screaming
and running for the house. Not that Aunt Lynne had had
much idea either.

At the car Peter tried to take her hand but she pulled it
back. He did a bad job of keeping the worry from his
voice as he asked, 'Why don't you tell me what he said?'

She spun around. 'He said I'm sane. No pathology.
Isn't that great?'

There was a moment when she hoped Peter would just
hug her and stroke her, not say anything. Instead he said

casually, 'Maybe that means it'll all go away.' He avoided touching her as he unlocked her door.

'Sure,' she said. 'Just like that.'

As they drove uptown Lynne hardly listened to Peter's attempts at conversation. He was just releasing platitudes, she knew. She felt like he was sponging her with disinfectant.

Lynne just felt so tired. For weeks she'd strained to hold onto the hope she would turn out to be crazy. Chemically imbalanced. Curable with some coloured pills. In a way, now that she had to give that up she could relax. She leaned back against the car seat, her head against the plastic and her eyes staring lazily through the top of the windshield at the cloudy sky.

She was thinking of something that had happened to her when she was a kid. Eleven years old. No, twelve, because it happened the same year they finally banned space flight and they held all those ceremonies. As if that would keep the plague away. So she was twelve, because it happened a couple of months after her sixth grade class had marched in that big parade on Main Street.

The strange thing took place in her grandmother's apartment building, in the hallway where she'd gone to throw something down the compactor chute. An insect bit her. She'd opened the door to the compactor room, made a face at the smell, dumped the bag of garbage and was half out the door when a beetle or something ran out from under a crumpled newspaper. The next thing she knew a sharp pain had shot up her leg. She screamed and fell backward, so that the door scraped her side as it clanged shut. A moment later it seemed everyone was bending over her so close she couldn't breathe, and then she heard sirens and bells and people shouting so loud she couldn't make out anything they said.

The beetle must have carried some kind of poison because Lynne had fallen asleep and couldn't seem to wake up no matter how hard she'd tried. When she did

open her eyes her father told her that she'd slept for two
weeks. She'd gotten exited that that would beat her friend
Gail who bragged at how much she slept, and then she
just fell asleep again. The next time she woke up it was
for real, and she found herself in a hospital room surrounded by flowers. While her mother showed her all the
presents everyone had brought her, Lynne tried to figure
out what she could have done during two weeks of sleep.

She was sure, somehow, that she'd kept herself very
busy, no matter what her parents said. She could only
remember one thing, though. It was a dream of course.
She'd understood that. In the dream she'd climbed to the
top of the school building. It was a very windy day and
she became scared she'd be blown right off the roof, so
she bent down to hold on to an old brass telescope bolted
to the rooftop floor. Something came and landed, digging
bright claws into the edge of the roof. A spaceship, she
thought, and became scared someone would see her and
report her. But then she saw it wasn't a ship, it was a
bird, huge and made all of metal. She climbed onto its
back and held onto a steel feather as it lifted into the air.
Night came and the bird spiralled higher and higher until
she could see the whole planet and then the solar system,
like nine animals racing round and round a fire. Finally
the bird dove, going faster and faster, with Lynne hanging
on and her hands getting all cut up until she finally had to
let go. The wind carried her around the world in helpless
cartwheels and somersaults. Then somehow she became
everywhere at once, because she could see everything –
her house, her grandmother's apartment building, the
school, foreign cities she'd only seen on TV, the ocean
and the mountains, day and night.

Lying in her hospital room the twelve-year-old girl
couldn't remember anything else. Now, in her car going
home from the psychiatrist, the thirty-one year old woman
thought how they should have known then. Her parents
should have known. What a waste. Sending her to college,

encouraging her to do something with her life. Getting
married.

'What now?' Peter said.

Lynne sat up. They were on First Avenue, heading for
the Drive she supposed, but now traffic had backed up,
with people honking horns, leaning out of windows. Peter
got out of the car and stood on tiptoe, holding on to the
door. 'Jesus,' she heard him say, 'I don't believe it.'
Curious, she got out, looked over the row of cars. There
was someone there, sitting in the middle of the street
surrounded by packages, a bag lady or something. But
what was she wearing on her head? Some kind of funny
hat –

No. No, she should have guessed. What else would it
be but one of *them*? She clenched her fists against a
queasiness wrenching inside her as she stared at the
huddled figure in its sack made of some metallic cloth.
You could hardly see the actual material for all the junk
attached to it – small carvings, drawings and pieces of
cloth in transparent pockets, bits of circuit board and
silicon chips, bones, pieces of animal skin, rocks, torn
book covers. And on its head – 'Brilliant,' she thought,
'A hat. Terrific.' On its head the creature (she couldn't
think of it as a person), the creature wore a black helmet
with a white beak nose and curved metal tubes coming
out the sides, like the landing struts of a spaceship.

What was it doing? It had spread some things around it
so that the cars couldn't get past. Souvenir statues of
famous buildings, broken toys, a coil of rope –

'What the hell is he doing there?' Peter said. 'Does he
think he's protecting us? Christ, the street's clear, we
don't need any goddamn protection.' Lynne stared at him
just as he turned to look at her, his mouth half open as if
the words had forced their way out. 'Shit,' he said. 'I'm
sorry, Lynne. I'm sorry.'

'What are you sorry to me for? Are you crazy? Do you

think I have anything – Just because I get some bad
dreams or something – '

'I'm sorry, honey. I didn't mean anything. Of course
it's got nothing to do – '

'You're ready to give me up. All set to sign me off. Are
you afraid I'll suck you in after me? Is that what you're
afraid of?'

'I didn't mean anything. You know I was just trying –
Look, I'm on your side.'

'Are you afraid it's catching?'

'Lynne, stop it. You're just upset. Because of that idiot
doctor.'

'He's not an idiot. Top of his profession. Best money
can buy. You said so yourself.'

'All right, he's not an idiot.'

'Peter, let's forget it, okay?'

'No. I want you to realise – '

'Please. Please, Peter, just stop talking. Okay? I don't
want to talk.'

'We're going to get over this, Lynne.'

'Sure. Sure we are. Now just shut up, okay?'

A couple of cops arrived to shunt the traffic around the
crouched figure. Lynne heard someone say 'Why don't
they just cart him away?' Lynne knew that wouldn't
happen. Federal law made it a crime to remove a protector, no matter where they set themselves. You just had to
wait for them to get up and go back to their shelters. She
remembered the TV story last year about the protector
who'd moved into some Wall Street office and the whole
firm had had to relocate. Great joke that. She and Peter
had really laughed at that one.

As they drove past, Lynne rolled the windows up tight,
hoping to banish the scratching noises and the birdlike
calls that somehow managed to dance above the engines
and the blasts of the policeman's whistle.

In her dreams that night she was Jason Benedict,
plodding in his space suit through the ruin of a city on

Gabriela H-3. The 'black wind' roared all about her, streaking the sky and coating her visor (in the dream she thought of it as a windshield) with nuclear ash. With each step she had to calculate which way to lean into the shifting wind.

They'd have to junk the spacesuit, her dreamself thought. As soon as he was back on the ship, out it would go. It was contaminated. Infected. They'd have to get rid of it. For now, however, she blessed its insulation. (But why were the arms and chest hung with bones and toys and pieces of hardware? And who'd painted that striped face above the crotch?)

She was walking towards a square building with a dome roof, the only structure left completely intact in the whole city. A strange idea occurred to her and she said it aloud to broadcast it up to the ship. Maybe the Gabis had built the thing after the holocaust, a last gasp of engineering elegance before the collapse. Ridiculous, Captain Santori bleeped back at her. They'd be too busy killing each other for food.

And then she was inside, and her helmet was gone so that she felt the heat on her bare face as she looked at the panels showing animals covered with insects, and clouds with birdlike faces embedded in their dark swirls. From room to room she walked, shouting excitedly about the perfectly preserved artefacts, the statues, the endless sky maps, and the drawings – wall after wall, each telling the same story over and over again: squat four-legged creatures, some kind of black cloud, insects, metallic looking birds –

For a moment she was home, her parents' kitchen late at night, and she was looking for her sister Suzanne who'd stayed out with some wild friends. Knives lay all about her feet as she angrily scanned the lawn which stretched out over hills and domed cities. She thought to herself (believing somehow she was thinking about Suzanne),

'Who put those domes up? Do they really think they can keep something out when they know it's already inside?'

There came Suzanne at last. But look at that, she was walking on all fours again, with her head tilted up like a dog, when she'd promised them – How could you protect her if she didn't do as she was told? Her friends danced around her, they were draping her body with ropes. They wore masks, bright red masks with metal wings and beaks carved in bone.

And then she was Jason Benedict again, thinking how something didn't look right, the arrangement of things didn't seem to serve any ritual functions, it was all too logical, too linear, with everything laid out like a lesson. A lesson made as simple as possible, as if they aimed it at children. Or aliens.

They meant it for us, she thought, and knew somehow she mustn't tell anyone. They would lock her up, they would hurt her. She made a mental note to herself. Get rid of the spacesuit. It's infected.

Kneeling down to stare at a display of model animals she wondered why the lesson, the museum or whatever it was, seemed to ignore the nuclear disaster. Maybe they *had* built it before and somehow made it strong enough to survive the war.

She heard a sound behind her, a thumping noise. One of the rooms was coming to life. She ran, her heart beating against the metal suit.

And then she was in a large house, in a room with rows and rows of empty shelves and at the end large glass doors looking out on the street several floors below. People were marching there and shouting, and burning banners with her name, Jason Benedict, written over and over, in black paint, as if each time the name burned they could kill her all over again. 'It's not my fault,' she shouted. 'I don't want to go. I want to stay here, with my husband.' She felt a gust of wind and turned to see a large bird fold its wings as it landed beside her. It turned its face to her.

Lynne sat up in bed. She pressed her elbows against her ribs and rubbed her eyes.

'What is it?' Peter said. He touched her, but gingerly, as if her skin could give off a shock.

'It's nothing,' she said. 'It's just a nightmare.'

'Maybe you should tell me.'

'I just did. It's nothing.' She lay back on her side, turned away from him. With a sigh he lay back down again and put his arm over his closed eyes. Lynne didn't dare move until she was sure he was asleep, and even then she got up very slowly and half tiptoed out of the bedroom. In the bathroom she washed the night grime off her face, rubbing her eyes until they ached. She was afraid to open them after she'd dried herself. She held the towel up in front of her.

It's just the dream, she told herself. And the dream didn't mean anything. Just her subconscious making the obvious connection. Anyone would have connected that.

She let down the towel and opened her eyes. Quickly she looked around the room, taking inventory. It was okay. Just like the waiting room at the doctor's office. Everything was where it should be. She should give the place a good cleaning, she thought. Maybe it was all going to be okay. The tub looked grimy, the mirror all streaked. Maybe it would all just stop. She poked at a bit of caked toothpaste, then wetted her finger in the sink to rub off the mark. Maybe it had all just – just finished up. The whole place could use a good cleaning. It was so sweet of Peter not to complain.

She thought of him touching her in the bed and she shivered a moment, telling herself it was the nighttime chill, she'd better put on a robe or go back to sleep. She looked at herself in the mirror. Everything sagged, everything looked so old. There was that time he went to kiss her and his face started to come away and there was someone else, something else, waiting inside, waiting its turn.

Better give the whole house a cleaning, she thought. And maybe do an exercise class. Get some of that ache out of her. If you could just peel off the old skin or let someone take it off – And get back to work she told herself. She'd put things off much too long. There were all those letters to answer, ads to send out.

Maybe it was all going to go away. That was why the tests didn't show anything. She'd healed herself. Spontaneous healing. And of course she'd dreamed of Benedict. It was only normal. Anybody would have made the connection. It was just the fears coming up. Maybe that's how she'd cured herself. Or maybe it signalled the end. Last stuff coming up.

Go back to sleep, she thought. A lot to do tomorrow, today. Her breasts and belly itched and she started to scratch, then pulled her hands away. Because of the nylon nightgown she told herself. You could give yourself a nasty rash.

In the bedroom she stood over the bed listening to her husband's wheeze. Better sleep on the couch, she thought. Then she wouldn't have to listen. Or worry about waking him. He looked so – so angry when he slept.

He just needed some rest. Maybe they should both go on a holiday. Might be their last chance. She rolled her eyes, flicked her hand to chase away the wrong ideas. There'd be lots of holidays, all the ones they could possibly want. She snatched up her pillow, got down the extra blanket, and plodded into the living room to curl up on the couch.

Lynne made sure not to get up until after Peter was gone. Groggy, she swayed into the bathroom. Peter had closed the glass shower doors again. Furious, she felt like throwing him through them. Why couldn't he remember the simplest things? She took a breath, her eyes on the cloudy doors. Anything could hide in there, whole – No. She was all through with that. If she let herself get scared, she could end up talking herself – She touched the door, pulled her fingers away, reached out again. When she opened it she smiled, a comment on how silly she'd been.

Her brilliant husband, she saw, had left the tap in the shower position. 'He can't remember anything,' she said out loud. Her voice sounded thick, and she remembered that one time when her own voice had attacked her, turning into some growling creature outside her body.

Maybe she *should* take a shower. Prove she could do it. Prove the water wouldn't turn to steam or knives, prove she could close the doors and not be trapping herself. She reached out. At the last moment she flicked the switch to bath before she opened the faucet. There was plenty of time, she told herself. No need to push.

Lynne spent most of the day cleaning. It felt good to be normal she told herself several times in the day. When she ran out of glassex she got in the car and drove to the mall, just like anyone else. Hungry, she sat down in a restaurant full of people and ordered a chicken salad on toast and a coffee. She didn't even look at the other people while she was waiting, and when the food came she just picked up her sandwich and took a bite, just like anyone else. It was really true, she'd told herself. She'd had a couple of bad moments, she didn't know why, but so what, they didn't mean anything, and then she'd just talked herself into a state. After the meal she deliberately stopped to look at boots, curtain material, whatever caught her eye, just like anyone else. On the way home she almost turned on the car radio before deciding it was better not to push herself, not while driving. She could listen to the radio at home. Or a record. But when she got in the house, she decided she preferred the silence. Plenty of time. The radio could wait.

After dinner she told Peter, 'You can watch TV if you like. It won't bother me.'

'Are you sure?' he said.

'Go ahead. I'll get going on some letters.'

'You sure?'

'Go ahead. There must be a game or something. I'll do the dishes.'

He said quickly, 'I'll do them.'

'You don't have to do the dishes.'

'Well, you cooked – '

'Please,' she said. 'Go. Leave me alone.'

Lynne cleared the table, then decided to do some work before washing up. Plenty of time, she told herself, and laughed. In the living room she sat down at the desk Peter had bought for her when she'd started her business. Her red plastic 'in-tray' contained a jumble of letters, some unopened, some half read and shoved back in the envelope. Lynne's business consisted of tracking down odd things for collectors. Lynne was a congenital browser. She loved going down to New York and looking through second-hand bookstores, antique shops, old clothing stores, push-carts, anything at all that contained piles of assorted treasures. She hardly ever bought anything. She wasn't a collector. She didn't want to own things, she just liked looking. One day at work – she'd been a secretary for the local branch of a national insurance company – someone remarked to Lynne that his wife collected doilies, the kind people once put on furniture to protect from grease stains. Lynne offered to look for some on her next trip to New York, and when she'd brought back two 'exquisite pieces' as Jack's wife called them, Jack had insisted on paying her a commission.

It was Peter who suggested she make a business out of it. 'There must be loads of people out in Dallas or somewhere who collect old beer mats or lunchboxes or something. Only they can't find what they want in Dallas. Everything is new there. New York is the place to look for junk. And if anyone can find that stuff it's you.' He was wonderful. He offered to back her for a year, enough to see if the idea had a future. He even helped her compose and send out ads to the different collectors' magazines and computer networks. Slowly, over three or four months, letters had come in, requests, recommendations. Usually Lynne could find something to satisfy the person, and if not she would send them a list of possible alternatives. The dealers were beginning to hold things for her, remembering pieces she'd bought for collectors the month before. Lynne loved the work, loved the thought of acquiring a reputation, becoming an expert. And then the attacks had begun.

She shook her head at the pile of letters, requests, offers from dealers, bills for ads she'd run. She should sort them all, do the urgent ones first. Instead, she just grabbed a letter, read through it, and rolled a sheet into the typewriter, composing in her mind an apology for the delay. Sickness. Personal difficulties. Sickness sounded better. 'Now that I'm better,' she thought to herself, 'I'll start looking for your piece right away. I hope you'll forgive the delay. Sincerely, etc.'

In the bedroom she heard the television. Someone must have scored a goal because the announcer was shouting and the engineers had turned up the fake crowd noises. Lynne thought vaguely of the days when people used to pack into sports stadiums by the thousands. It was such a different world back then. As she listened to the TV she found herself testing for voices slithering under the commentary and the noises. 'Stop it,' she ordered herself and slapped her hand against the desk. A moment later she was banging the typewriter as loud and as fast as possible.

She went to sleep without doing the dishes. In the middle of the night she woke up feeling guilty, but when she went into the kitchen Peter had washed everything. Back in bed, she lay on her side with her eyes open, staring at the half-open bedroom door, feeling like she'd dreamt something but couldn't remember what. Finally exhaustion pulled her back to sleep.

Over the next few days Lynne divided her time between the house and her business, going from washing the

kitchen floor to sending out a stack of ads. When she'd
answered all her correspondence she told Peter she'd be
commuting to the city for the next few days to do some
searching, and did he mind getting his own dinner if she
came back late?

'Mind?' he said. 'I think it's great.'

'I just feel bad,' she said. 'You've been so sweet and
I've been neglecting you.'

He reached across the table to stroke her arm. Automatically she pulled it back. He pretended not to notice.
'You haven't been neglecting me,' he said. 'You've been
sick. I'm thrilled to see you working again.'

She nodded. Sick. That's what she'd written all those
people. She was sick and now she was better. 'I'm sorry,'
she remembered the doctor saying, 'I'm afraid I've got
bad news for you.' Quack, she thought. He doesn't
deserve protection.

The next day Lynne took the train into the city. She
began by making the round of the bookstores, renewing
contacts and buying a copy of the abridged Whitman
edition of *Tarzan and the City of Gold* for a retired
schoolteacher in Cleveland. As she signed for the book
she remembered a letter she'd gotten, one of the first
answers to her ads. A man in Denver. After apologies
and evasions he got to the point. Could Mrs Buscher
locate any copies of Edgar Rice Burroughs' Mars or
Venus books? He knew they'd be hard to find and he'd
pay a lot and he'd understand if she refused – Lynne had
thrown away the letter without finishing it. Space stories!
The very idea that someone could ask her – She'd called
Peter and told him maybe she should drop the whole idea.
He was angry, of course. He wanted to write the guy back
or even call him up, but Lynne said she'd forget it if Peter
would. The last thing she wanted was for her husband to
get into a shouting match with a pervert.

The memory filled her with sadness. A pang of lost
innocence. Outside, she hurried down Fourth Avenue,

afraid that if she stood still she'd start crying in the middle
of the crowded street.

From the bookstores she walked down to the turn-of-
the-century shops along Bleecker Street, searching for
one of those talking coffee pots people had used back
then. She didn't find any, but she did come across a
Double Millennium poster from the English messianic
movement. It was in perfect condition, and exactly what
a client had described in a letter seven months ago, just
before Lynne's illness. Excitedly she asked the shop
owner if she'd hold it for a few days, until Lynne could
contact her client. The woman agreed and said she was
glad to see Lynne back on her feet again.

It was late afternoon by the time Lynne finished her
rounds of shops in the village. She'd originally planned to
go uptown, show her face on the west side or at least in
some of the pre-century memento shops that had sprung
up on Third Avenue. But she felt so tired, and she hadn't
eaten. Everything would close soon anyway. She could
come back tomorrow.

Feeling content, and proud of herself, Lynne headed
for a diner on Broadway where they served huge tuna
sandwiches and old-fashioned malteds. But when she got
to Broadway she turned south instead of north and walked
some six or seven blocks until she reached the small flea
market that had developed on the sidewalk in front of the
grimy offices and factories. Searching frantically she
bought an assortment of junk – a rusty can-opener, a
miniature football, a charm bracelet with plastic faces of
movie stars, a broken necklace made of silicon chips, a
scarf of the New York skyline, and so on until her shopping
bag couldn't hold any more. When she stood up her back
ached and there was a buzzing in her ears. She looked at
her bag and shook her head. She'd never sell any of this
stuff to anybody. It was worthless. She should just throw it
away. But she held on to it, and when she got home – she

didn't stop to eat – she quickly hid the bag in the coat closet before Peter could get home and notice it.

That night they made love, the first time in weeks, with Lynne insisting and stroking and tickling Peter until he ran out of excuses and agreed to come to bed. He took a while to get an erection – she suspected he had to think of someone else to do it – and then he came very quickly: but Lynne didn't mind. She pulled his hand down between her legs and showed him how to stroke her, holding on to his wrist at first to make sure he wouldn't get away. As her excitement built she bit his shoulder, small sharp bites, like bird pecks. She bent her arms and hit him with her elbows, laughing as she imagined herself beating his doll-like body with her huge wings.

The next day Lynne returned to the city for her uptown tour, stopping only briefly at the different shops so she could make sure to show her face everywhere. On the train home she felt satisfied, and even slept for a while. That night she and Peter went to dinner at an Italian restaurant across the river. After they'd ordered drinks Peter announced that he'd made reservations for them for the weekend at Lake Mohonk in the Catskills. They deserved some luxury he said, and this weekend was probably the last chance to see the leaves in the mountains before they all started falling. Lynne leaned over the table to put her arms around his neck. Peter grinned as she kissed his cheek. Be ready Friday afternoon, he told her. He'd leave work early and they'd get up to the hotel in time for dinner.

As the waiter set her spaghetti bolognese in front of her Lynne discovered she could see the bones in his hands. The skin and muscle had fallen away and only a coating of ash covered the white. She jerked her head up to see his face. It was okay. Flesh and hair and glasses. He glanced at her then looked away.

'Are you all right?' Peter said. He tried to sound solicitous but Lynne could hear the anger in his voice.

'I'm fine,' she said.

'Are you sure?'

'Yes, I'm sure.'

Friday afternoon Lynne was singing as she packed their suitcases and laid out Peter's good suit and blazer along with her green dress and her gold pants outfit. The sun was shining and when she'd called the weather report the taped message had promised a warm and clear weekend. A half hour or so before Peter had said he'd come home she sat down at her makeup mirror in the bedroom. But instead of her own face and the bed and the night table behind her Lynne saw – something. There was only a glimpse – a burnt-out landscape, a flock of birds, a cloud. Then she grabbed a can of hair spray and smashed the mirror.

'Oh God,' she said. 'Goddammit.' Her heart thumped like a machine about to explode. She looked around the room, making sure everything had stayed in place. She hated this, she was checking things again, something she thought she'd given up. 'Goddamn,' she said. She looked at the pieces of glass. Like a vampire movie. Just like those old blood films they used to show on TV when she was a kid. The vampires were always smashing mirrors. Except they didn't show those any more. In bad taste. Just like space stories. She remembered a comic on TV who'd made a joke about monsters. The next week he was off the air. No explanation, no apology, just gone. Victim of bad taste. Lynne remembered how she'd agreed with everyone at the office. Some jokes were 'inappropriate'. Wasn't that how her boss had put it? Inappropriate?

Peter came home shouting with excitement. He found her sitting in her bathrobe in the living room. 'Come on,' he said. 'Get dressed. Let's go. It's a beautiful evening.'

'I'm not going,' she said.

'What? What are you talking about? Come on.' He tried to pull her out of the chair but she slapped away his hands.

'I don't feel well,' she said.

'What's wrong?' When she didn't answer he said, 'Did you have an attack?'

'Attack?' she said sarcastically. 'What a clever expression.'

'Jesus, Lynne, you use that word yourself.' She turned her face away from him. 'Look,' he said, 'I'm just trying to help.'

'Help yourself you mean. Why don't you just go and leave me alone?'

He sighed loudly. 'Great. Romantic weekend for two for one.'

'You'll have a better time.'

'That's for sure. You know, you might try thinking of someone other than yourself for a change.' Lynne said nothing. 'It might do you some good.' She stared at the floor. 'Shit,' he said and slammed the door behind him. When she heard the downstairs door close Lynne got up and walked to the front window where she could see him drive away. For a moment the parking lot looked like a blackened plain, the car like some frightened animal. Then everything straightened out again, and he was gone.

Peter came back only a few hours later but Lynne was already in bed. When she woke up she found a note from him in the dinette. As long as they weren't going away he might as well do some catching up at the office. He loved her and was sorry they'd had a fight. She was going to be all right. Everything would be fine. She could call him if she liked.

Later that day Lynne went to the mall to get some food for the weekend. It really was a beautiful day. She couldn't blame Peter for getting annoyed with her. She decided to get him a present and after putting the supermarket bags in the car she noticed insects crawling on some of the cases and wallets. She made a face and decided to look somewhere else. Just as she turned away an alarm sounded.

While Lynne just stood there everyone began to run, some for the exit, others for the shops and restaurants, anywhere to get out of the path. Insects, Lynne thought. How could she not have realised? 'Lady,' a security guard shouted at her, 'what are you standing there for? Move it.' He didn't stay to check her. For a moment she lost her footing when someone banged into her. But still she just stood there, looking down the mall at the entrance to J. C. Penney's where people were running out of the store slapping at the insects buzzing round their faces and arms. What was she supposed to do? She had no idea what to do.

The people from Penney's were screaming, but somehow the sound didn't affect her, as if it came from far away or from a movie. It didn't include her.

She stepped to the side to avoid the mob, but she kept looking. It was impossible to tell when the insects turned into birds, but there they were. They flapped around the people left in the open, they pecked at their bodies.

Someone snatched at her, pulled her inside a shop and down behind a counter. She struggled for a moment, thinking she should be doing something. But when she got her head above counter level she saw that one of *them* had arrived. He wore the same kind of clumsy metallic dress strewn with junk as the one she and Peter had seen blocking First Avenue. He was hitting a metal can with what looked like a rock, and he was wailing (or singing) above the screams. On his head he wore a helmet with a visor, like something from a space suit. An instant later Lynne's benefactor pulled her down again, and she crouched under the fluorescent glare. She discovered herself disappointed in some strange way. He hadn't looked at her. He hadn't turned around and noticed her at all. She was just the same as everyone else.

After a couple of minutes it all began to quieten down. The running stopped, the screams became isolated voices, the wild flapping ended, and then the drumming and the

singing spiralled down. No one on the floor of the shop
moved. Even after the all-clear sound, the signal that the
ambulances had taken away the wounded and the
shocked, and that the scanners detected no more manifes-
tations, they still remained hidden. They were waiting
until it seemed a good chance the protector had left the
mall. A good chance he no longer squatted there to
remind them of the attack. For the protector belonged to
the plague. He was as much a part of it as the birds and
insects.

Lynne crouched with the other victims, all of them
averting their eyes from each other, pretending that not
seeing meant they weren't there. It was odd. People
resented the protectors almost more than the plague itself.
They were like traitors, or collaborators. When people
started to get up Lynne stepped back into the open,
looking for the place where she'd seen the protector.

It was hard to tell. Everybody was walking back and
forth, reclaiming the mall for human territory. They
picked up clothes to try on, they examined shoes, they
ordered juice or pretzels or chocolate from the stalls in
the middle, any activity at all, so long as it was bland and
suggested that nothing unusual had happened. The attack
would go unreported in the newspapers or television.
Probably people wouldn't even tell their families or friends.
She knew she wouldn't tell Peter.

She stood there watching the crowd, their refusal to
look at each other, their awkward exaggerated movements, their tight smiles. And as she watched, her mood
slid from disappointment to elation. It had nothing to do
with her. She was just like anyone else. She hadn't sensed
it beforehand, she didn't make it go away or have any
idea what to do. And when the protector came he took
no notice of her. She was just like anyone else.

She didn't bother with Peter's present. She went out to
her car, then ran back to a phone booth and called Peter
at the office. She asked if they could still go for one night

and he said the hotel probably hadn't rented the room on
such short notice. If she went home and started packing
he'd call and check. He didn't ask what had changed her
mind.

That night Lynne dreamed again of Jason Benedict.
She dreamed she was an old man, coughing in a barren
room while he wrote his *History Of The Plague*. In the
dream Peter wanted her to go to her sister's wedding but
she refused to leave her notebooks. The work would
vindicate her, vindicate space travel, make the world
realise he hadn't brought the plague. No one had ever
found anything on his space suit, not even microscopic
spores. And since Earth people could drive away the
attacks, how could they possibly come from another
planet?

Outside her cold room people were shouting, but she
kept writing, she had to get it done before they took it
away, before they tore it up and burned it. She wrote
about the first attacks, the panic, the discovery of small
communities in Asia and Africa, northern Canada and
South America where the shamans and witch doctors kept
their people free of the birds and insects. And she wrote
about the hospitals, filling more and more with schizo-
phrenics who didn't respond to drugs but who kept the
grounds clear of the plague. His back ached and he could
hardly hold the pen from the cold but he kept writing.
'Listen to the protectors. They call it the other world.
They do not mean a planet in space. Listen to them.'
Outside she could hear the soldiers marching around the
house. No use, he thought, it's no use. They'll just burn
it like they burned his picture, like they burned her yellow
dress.

The dream shifted. She sat in the room but instead of a
book she was working on a costume. A sheet of translucent gold plastic lay on her lap and she was sewing things
to it – a can opener, the lid of a coffee pot, some crinkly
leaves, a pouch containing bits of rock from Earth – and

the other place. There was a toy spaceship, wire, a switch from a lamp, feathers. Beside her lay strips of cloth from a yellow dress. Later she would sew them on as well, streamers from her past life. She sewed so fast she kept cutting hr fingers and dripping blood on the plastic. She had to finish soon, before the next attack. She had to sew the whole world on to it. She would feed them the world.

Lynne woke up shivering from the cold mountain night. She pulled the blanket over her shoulders and snuggled against Peter, who grunted and stayed asleep. She had to close the window, they should have known better than to have left it open. She just hated the idea of going up to it in the dark. She considered waking Peter or just turning on the light, but finally she got up and dashed to the window to pull it shut. Outside, darkness soaked the woods. It seemed like it could roll up over the buildings despite the fence of blue lights surrounding the hotel. Lynne wondered where the protector of this area lived, if the hotel kept a cabin for him or her in some hidden area of the grounds. She hugged herself, wishing she'd brought a warmer nightgown.

When she went to pee she turned on the bathroom light before entering or even looking into the room. It wasn't difficult. The switch was outside the door. There were lots of people afraid to enter a dark room. Just as there were lots of people who dreamt about the plague. And Benedict. It was natural, normal. Just no one wanted to talk about it. She knew that in the morning, when Peter asked how she'd slept, she would tell him she'd had a wonderful night.

They spent the next day sitting by the lake, walking along the edge of the woods, climbing on the rockpaths laid out by the hotel. At a certain point Lynne spotted a couple of round stones, one black, one white. She let Peter get ahead of her so she could scoop them up into her jeans pocket. Excitedly she thought how when she got home she could add them to the collection in the coat closet.

They left at five, plenty of time to get home before dark. As they drove through the gates Lynne turned around for a last look at the green and brown buildings. Someone was standing by the entrance, a woman with long matted hair and a shapeless dress hung with pieces of paper, drawings, photographs. She grinned, showing her sharp teeth, and when she waved her hand, like a hostess saying goodbye to a special guest, the bony fingers looked like claws.

Lynne spent Monday and Tuesday going through catalogues, answering letters, making phone calls. Wednesday morning she decided to do another run to the city. She thought she would not concentrate on anything in particular but take with her a list of current targets and try to cover as much ground as possible. As she moved from shop to shop, she thought how much she loved this work, how she could go on forever if only the world would leave her alone.

Around four o'clock she found herself in the Hudson Flea Market, a large warehouse filled with racks of leather jackets, tables of broken clocks and watches, whole cartons full of scarves or corkscrews or plastic flowers. Lynne had once found a cased collection of Chinese coins which she then sold to a man in Boise for a five hundred per cent profit. Ever since then she'd used the coins as an excuse to spend an hour or two a month in this place she called 'Browser's Heaven.'

Today, however, she stayed no more than fifteen minutes. Rummaging through a box of toys so high she had to half climb inside it, she came across an object made of faded and dented metal. Without even thinking what it was she pulled it loose from the dolls and rifles around it and took it up to Ben, the owner, who sat on a rocker in the back of the shop reading a newspaper.

He looked up at her and before she could say anything

he jumped off his chair. 'Where did you get that?' he said. 'Did you find that here?' He reached out to take the toy, but Lynne pulled it back out of his reach. 'Hey,' he said, 'I'm sorry, Lynne, I didn't know we had anything like that here. You know I don't know half of what's in those boxes. If I'd seen it I would've thrown it away. Believe me.'

For the first time Lynne looked consciously at the collection of metal tubes and discs. A spaceship. The toy was a model spaceship. In fact, it was a drive ship, 'the discovery that changed man's destiny at a single stroke,' as someone once called it. That was before one of those ships took Jason Benedict to Gabriela H-3.

'Here,' Ben said, 'let me get rid of it.' Again she held it out of his reach. There must have been thousands of these things, maybe millions. She'd played with one as a kid. Her favourite toy, until one day her father came into her bedroom and took it away from her.

'I want it,' she told Ben.

'What? What are you talking about? Don't you know what that is?' She didn't answer. 'Don't tell me you've got a buyer for that thing.'

'How much?'

'Hey,' Ben said. 'You think I want money for it? Take it and get out of here. Wait a second.' He handed her a plastic bag. 'Stick it in here,' he said. 'So people don't see. And don't tell anyone where you got it, okay?'

At home Lynne set the drive ship down on the bed, the first time in over two hours she'd let it out of her hand. From the coat closet she took out her collection and set everything beside the ship. She felt a sense of completeness, of something established. She'd need lots more, she knew. Material, some bone for the mask, and above all rocks and artifacts from out there. But those she could get from the government, they kept whole storehouses full, all of it rescued from the mobs, along with instruments from the ships, pieces of telescopes from the smashed observatories. She laughed at the thought of browsing through all those wonderful warehouses. She looked down at her dress and laughed again. This was the one, the strips she'd seen in her dream. She'd cut up the dress so she could sew her past life onto her costume. Excitedly she pulled the dress over her head and got down the sewing box.

She had the hem of the dress in one hand and the scissors in the other, when she gave a gasping cry and dropped the scissors on the floor. She looked from the stuff on the bed to the yellow material in her hand. It was like someone else had taken hold of her –

No. No, she had to recognise the truth. It was her. When she'd put the toy ship with the other things she'd felt – more settled, more complete than at any time in her life. She began to cry, to shake her head from side to side. It was all so sad, all the things she'd have to give up, Peter, her work, their apartment. And how would she tell her parents? They had such good taste.

She put the ship, the stones from Mohonk, and the other things back in the box. She held up the dress and with a sigh put that in the box as well, without cutting it. That could come later. Later, when the dress really had become a symbol of her former life. A symbol and all that remained of it.

When Peter came home he found his favourite dinner, steak, garlic bread, baked potatoes. There was even a chocolate cake for dessert. 'What's up,' he said. 'Make a big sale?'

She smiled. 'No, I just thought it would be nice.' He kissed her and ran off to take a quick shower before dinner. How much time? Lynne thought. How much time to keep making it nice before the end?

The end, it turned out, came over a month later. In those weeks, Lynne had settled into a sleepy kind of happiness, making love with Peter, tracking down items for her customers, sleeping well and cooking elaborate

dinners. Peter said several times how great she looked,
how he'd said she'd get over the attacks, and now she was
fine, and maybe they should sue that Steiner guy for
malpractice. He talked about vacations and brought home
travel folders. Lynne kissed him and said how she'd
always wanted to visit Bermuda.

When the end came she didn't even know it at first.
She'd taken the Ford down to the mall for a charge and a
wash. She drove it in a little before noon, and went to
look for boots and a new raincoat. When she came back
an hour later she found a group of men dismantling her
car. She ran up, wobbling as she clutched her packages.
The strap of her bag fell from her shoulder to her elbows,
bouncing the bag against her knee. 'What are you doing?'
she shouted. 'Leave that alone. What are you doing?' The
men paid no attention. There were five of them, all
dressed in short black jackets and black jeans. They went
on lifting off a fender, removing a seat, disconnecting
pieces of the engines.

Lynne dropped her packages and looked around for
help. People were walking by, some in the parking lot,
some in the station, waiting for their cars to be charged.
No one paid any attention. Lynne ran up to a woman who
was getting in her car. 'Please,' Lynne said, 'could you
get the police? These men are tearing apart my car.' The
woman slammed the door and rolled up the window. As
soon as she got the engine started she streaked away.

Lynne ran back to her car. 'Stop that,' she yelled. 'Stop
it.' A couple of the men turned their heads towards her.
Their faces gave off a silvery glow and their eyes and
noses and ears looked crudely formed, like toys. They
opened their mouths and double tongues flicked out at
Lynne. She stepped backwards, nearly falling as her foot
slid on an oil slick. For the first time she saw their hands,
narrow, with curved metal pincers and tools instead of
fingers. They were robots. But that was impossible. The
government had banned robots, they'd scrapped them all,

smashed them in huge piles the same year they'd smashed the space ships.

Lynne moved forward. She realised that the dismantling was revealing something hidden inside the car. As they took off the hood and the roof they exposed something shiny, with a bowed head and folded wings. The robots lifted off the last piece of the car and the bird came awake, nodding its head, rustling the steel feathers of its wings.

Lynne walked towards it. Before she could touch it it reared its head back then brought the tip of its beak slashing down the front of Lynne's body. Her scream died as her skin fell away like wrapping. A grey sludge spilled onto the ground. At first it seemed like everything would empty out, no one would ever find anything left of her. But then she realised she was standing, she felt light, she could float in the air. She could breathe for the first time in years.

The bird lifted her onto its back and together they flew through the air. She could see the shopping center below and then the houses, the trees, the mountains, and the river like tape across a knobby surface. Somewhere far below her she could hear shouts, people running, a buzzing noise. She paid no attention, and soon the bird took her so high the sounds faded and the land fell away behind her.

They flew for hours, through a dark cloud with points of light that formed into faces that broke apart as soon as she passed them. The cloud swallowed her and she drifted into it, everywhere at once, free of time and memory.

And then the bird was landing and Lynne found herself on a hilltop overlooking a burnt city. She slid off the bird's back and a group of men and women surrounded her. They all wore sheets of plastic or metal covered with bits and pieces of the world. Their heads looked like helmets, with beaks jutting out from opaque visors. Bent tubes hung down over their necks and shoulders. One of them stepped forward, holding something out to her. A mask. A new head. They wanted her to take it, become like them.

'No,' she said. 'I can't.' She looked around for the bird to rescue her, but it was gone. 'I can't ' No one answered.

'You can protect them,' Lynne said. They said nothing. 'No. Please. I don't want to.'

A woman pointed to the city. Lynne looked at the smashed buildings, the charred remains. In the middle stood a single structure, a domed message left by the last survivors for anyone who might come after them. She was on Gabriela H-3. Below her stood the museum, with all its statues and drawings, all the warnings about the plague. He was right. Benedict was right. They built it after the war, when they knew none of them would live to tell what had happened. It didn't show the war because the war didn't matter. The war only came because of the plague. Because of the panic, the terror. Because no one protected them.

She looked back at the one holding out the mask. 'Why does it have to be me?' she said. 'I've got my husband and my work.' No one answered. Lynne took the mask and lifted it onto her head.

She was back in the parking lot, on all fours on the ground, a few feet from her car. Dizzy, she squinted against the bright sun. Around her people were starting to come out of their hiding places. Someone even stepped out from behind Lynne's car.

'She's still here,' Lynne heard someone say. 'I thought they're supposed to move on.'

'Tell that to her,' someone else said. 'She's not even wearing the right clothes.'

On the other side another voice said, 'Isn't there some law that they can't dress like normal people? She could just walk around and no one would know.'

'Someone should call the police,' the first voice said.

Another one said, 'She could have been standing right next to us for all we knew.'

Aching, Lynne got to her feet and made it to the car. She had the engine going when she realised she'd left her boots and other packages on the ground. She shrugged and put the car in gear. A small crowd had gathered but they parted as she drove towards the the exit. Someone threw something. It hit the back windscreen and bounced off.

Lynne looked at the dash clock. Two or three hours until Peter came home. She wondered how she would tell him. She wondered if he'd resist. 'We can beat this,' she imagined him saying. 'You're talking nonsense. You're just hysterical.' It didn't matter.

She wondered where she'd end up living. Did the government give her a shelter or would she have to make her own somehow? Probably at first she'd go to live with a teacher. She knew she needed someone. That was the important thing. She couldn't go through it alone any more. But as for the rest – things like where she lived – it didn't matter any more.

At the end of the mall road she waited for a red light to change before driving onto Route 9. The shadow of a large bird passed across the hood. Lynne smiled.

PETER T. GARRATT

IF THE DRIVER VANISHES . . .

The plane landed well after sunset. Jack Marston was glad he had asked Ellie and the kids to meet him. It was a clear twilight, starting to turn chill as he walked to the terminal. His attention was caught by an exceptionally bright and beautiful star, high in the east, not so much blue-white as blue, a great sapphire in the sky.

Ellie tried to seem pleased to see him, but was reserved and distant as they walked to the car, letting the children do the talking.

He noticed a new bumper sticker: IF THE DRIVER VANISHES, GRAB THE WHEEL.

'What's that all about?'

'That's about Rapture, when the Christians all vanish and go up to Heaven,' said nine-year-old Mary.

'You can't have been watching "Space Age Sermon" very much lately, Daddy,' said her twin sister Martha.

'I've been very busy since I've been in Washington. I don't have time to watch TV like I used to at home.'

'Huh! The busy Senator!' It was rare for Ellie to speak so forcefully in front of the children. 'How can you claim to represent the Christian Majority if you don't make time to listen to Christian services?'

'You wouldn't believe how many meetings there are to go to, briefings to read. Next week we vote on the Craft-Ewing Bill, linking aid to birth control, and on SWIFT, the Space Weapons International Forgoing Treaty. I have to read three volumes of reports before I decide on that.'

'A Christian shouldn't have to think very hard before deciding how to vote on that one.'

'There's nothing in the Bible about war in space.'

'Not if you only read it in front of the Press at Election time. Pastor Fallowfield has made a detailed study of the Book of Revelations. He's found clear references to the need for America to fight the unbelievers in the Heavens. Take Chapter 12, Verse 3: "And there appeared another wonder in Heaven; and behold, a great red dragon".'

Marston hesitated. He always felt wrong-footed when she drew him into argument on difficult topics with the children present.

'Darling, we have to think about other things than Revelation. You know what all-out war would mean – I've told you before.'

'I'm not afraid.'

'Well, I'll have to be afraid for you then. Perhaps I'll send you copies of briefings I've read on the consequences of war – the sort of thing I didn't have time to go into before.'

'I thought you were busier now.'

'I've been making time for important things. I told you last month, I've been reading up on Nuclear Winter.'

'What's Nuclear Winter, Pop?' Ten-year-old Ben was awkward in his questions.

Marston saw Ellie open her mouth, but got his answer in first. 'That's what might happen if there were to be a really big war. Scientists think all the bombs would stir up so much dust that the sun wouldn't be able to shine through. It would be like a really bad winter that went on for years.'

'Is that the same as Armageddon?' Ben sounded subdued.

'Sort of. Remember that book of Viking stories Uncle Mike gave you? It's a bit like Ragnarok, the continuous winter which told the Vikings the world was about to end.'

Ellie hissed at him sidelong: 'Don't put pagan ideas into the boy's head! Give him references to the Bible!'

Little Mary joined in: 'There's no need to worry about the end of the world, is there, Mom? Rapture is coming before Armageddon, isn't it? Isn't it, Dad?'

'That's right,' said Ellie, in a soothing tone which lately had an opposite effect on Jack. 'Rapture will come seven years before Armageddon, and all the true believers will vanish from the world, and leave the heathens to worship the Devil, and destroy each other in their wickedness.'

They were just pulling into their own drive. 'I wish I had your confidence.' Jack kept his voice low, but Ellie slammed on the brakes and hurried the kids into the house, as though reluctant to expose them to his corrupt, free-thinking ideas.

Jack's day was not over. There was a message on the Electric Telephonist to ring Jim Robards at the Defence Department.

'Hi. Have you heard about the satellites?'

'No.'

'Three large satellites have appeared in stationary orbit. You can probably see one if it's not too cloudy where you are.'

Jack wondered about the striking, blue star he had seen earlier. 'Are they Soviet?'

'Not definitely. Pentagon reports indicate no evidence of recent Soviet launch activity.'

'Then whose?'

'We don't know. They just appeared in orbit, one over the western Atlantic, and one each over the western parts of the Pacific and Indian Oceans. We don't know how.'

'Why are you telling me this?'

'I wanted to keep your briefed. These are definitely satellites, Jack. Some people are getting funny ideas.'

He said nothing of this to Ellie. Robards made himself friendly with a number of Senators, feeding them odd, normally reliable snippets of information. It was not clear what interest he worked for, but he seemed to subtly undermine the Christian Majority.

Ellie herself was still not speaking. As sometimes happened, when he had been away for a while, she had changed out of her plain frock, and put on the flimsy, sleeveless, nightdress she had bought for their honeymoon. They made love without exchanging a word, tightening up with mutual need and resentment.

Afterwards, Marston could not sleep. He had never understood his wife's ability to shut out anger and all other competing emotions when she sensed a rare opportunity to express herself physically.

He could not spare himself thoughts about the amoral available women of Capitol Hill. His new secretary was a very efficient girl. She wore dresses which clung langorously, and did not seem low-cut when she was standing; but somehow managed to open out when she leant forward. Recently, he had surreptitiously moved his desk, so he could better see her breasts as she bent over the filing cabinet. In other moods, he wondered if she practised her bending technique in order to torment him.

He rose as quietly as he could, and padded downstairs. If he had disturbed Ellie, she made no sign. The living room curtains were open, and he could see the star, or satellite he supposed, in the east, a great blue eye watching him from the stratosphere. As he stared into the sky, a sense of yearning came over him, and a longing in his soul for comfort. He sank to his knees, and repeated the Lord's Prayer, over and over. He started on the 23rd Psalm, but when he came to the lines: 'Yea, though I walk in the valley, in the shadow of death, I will fear no evil,' he could not continue with the words: 'For Thou are with me.'

Instead, he sobbed without tears, and began to pray, in his own words this time:

'Dear Lord, why can't you be with *me*! Sweet Jesus, haven't I prayed enough to hear your voice, sense your

presence beside me, feel the comfort you give to Ellie and
the others. Lord, why am I alone?'

He continued on another tack: 'Lord will you spare my
family from Nuclear Winter? Will you deliver us from this
evil?'

For a while he felt Jesus almost with him, then he
realised that for him, almost was not enough.

The kids woke them the next morning, and for a while
Jack forgot his worries. They had a family breakfast, with
lots of ham, eggs, and piping hot coffee. Then the twins
showed Jack the Noah's Ark which Ellie was helping
them to build, with a dozen or more pairs of funny little
animals already aboard.

There were more difficult questions from Ben: 'Pop, if
there were two lions, and two tigers, and two leopards in
that Ark, how come they didn't eat up all the other
animals?'

Jack fielded that one: 'Have you tamed your Tiger yet?'

'Sure. Let's put him through his paces.'

The English sheepdog had grown enormous since Jack
had seen him. He could already stop, sit, beg, and fetch
sticks. The three of them had an energetic morning
chasing round the fields, and they all needed their lunch
of steak and fries.

Jack was trying to combine reading his reports with
listening to the ball game when Ellie gave him what she
called 'man's work' to get on with.

'There's an ant's nest near the kitchen which I need you
to boil out, and an infestation of mice in the shed. I've
got you some traps.'

'Why can't you do it yourself, or use poison? I'm a US
Senator, not a rat catcher.'

'Ant powder and rat poison don't seem to work so well
nowadays, and you're the animal expert around here.'

It was true. He had always been fascinated by the
behaviour of animals. It only took him ten minutes, of

observing lines of ants following each other's trails, to
locate the nest, and pour in a kettle of boiling water.

The younger Jack Marston had even run a litle business,
catching live mice and selling them to schoolfriends as
pets: he had once wanted to train Ben to do the same,
but Ellie would not have live mice in the house under any
circumstances. With effort, he recalled the best strategy
for placing traps. Gingerly, he set and baited them,
locking the door lest the dogs got in and injured themselves. He wondered if the strong poison with which Ellie
had failed to deal with the mouse plague had been
responsible for the recent unexplained deaths of two
family pets. He had been shown reports on swarms of
'super mice' which were devastating grain stores all over
the state. They said that survivors of earlier poisonings
had bred a race of immune pests. He did not know what
to do about this: the idea of evolving mice was clearly
Darwinian, and he did not want to be closely associated
with it.

To the east of town, he could see fields of golden
stubble, gleaming in the early autumn sun. Although it
was still quite light, he noticed the satellite-star, a glowing
pinprick both deeper and brighter than the sky.

He was surprised to be summoned indoors to a call
from Robards.

'Don't you ever let up?'

'Not this weekend. There's an alert on.'

'Over the satellites?'

'You've got it. All our military and observational
satellites have fouled up – stopped broadcasting.'

'All of them?'

'Communication satellites are still relaying, but we're
picking up subliminal interference.'

'I haven't noticed anything.'

'You wouldn't. All satellite-relayed broadcasts are getting subliminal inserts – too brief for your conscious mind
to notice, but registered by your subconscious.'

'What sort of stuff?'

'Well, this would be up your street, Jack – religious images replayed from old church broadcasts.'

Marston pondered. 'You think some Evangelical Foundation had got a private launch together?'

'No. Gary Fallowfield certainly doesn't know anything about it. He's going around saying what we're seeing is the Star of Bethlehem.'

'Oh.'

'But they're clearly artificial, they're not stars. They look bright because they're big, and made of some reflecting material. NASA say neither they nor the Soviets could get anything that big up there, and certainly not some two-bit private outfit.'

'So what are they?'

'Radio astronomers have picked up signals in a mathematical code. That's how they'd expect an alien intelligence to try and communicate – ET making a close encounter at last.'

'You mean – like that funny little critter in the movie?'

'Maybe, Jack. But maybe not little or funny.'

At five, Ellie gathered the whole family to watch 'Space Age Sermon'. Guiltily, Jack realised it was indeed some time since he had seen it. There was a new credit sequence, in the usual tinted-cartoon style. Simple Christian families were shown praying in church, while outside the sceptics drank, caroused, and fought. Then, the praying families were shown rising towards Heaven, while the unbelievers worshipped the Devil in a Russian Army uniform. Finally, Christ in all His glory was shown descending to Earth, followed by the Christians with haloes and angel wings. The Devil was scuttling off to Hell with his followers.

Gary Fallowfield came on early in the programme. He led the congregation in the 23rd Psalm. Ellie led the twins and even Ben in following the words: Jack tried to join them but mostly just muttered.

He thought Fallowfield looked as tense as he himself felt. After the Psalm, he twice repeated the line: 'And I will dwell in the house of the Lord for ever,' and fumbled uncharacteristically with his Bible before finding a new place.

'My Dear Brethren,' he began. 'Truly we live in desperate times. There is the SWIFT Treaty which would abandon the Heavens to the communist ungodly. There is the Craft-Ewing Bill, with its implications for the shedding of innocent human blood. But this is also a time of hope for those with Faith in their hearts. Today's text is Revelation, Chapter 8, Verse 10: "And the third Angel sounded, and there fell a great star from Heaven, burning like a lamp."

'Now, tonight, we find a new star in the sky, burning like a lamp. Of course, the scientists and folk who think they are clever say: "These are satellites."

'But which of us can say where these satellites were launched? Or are they saying these are vessels of the Outer Darkness, full of inhuman creatures, not mentioned in the Good Book, not part of God's Creation?

'No, there are none so blind as those who will not see the Truth. Brethren, is it a coincidence that there are three Stars, and wherever Christian folk live, they see their Star in the east?'

He took in a deep breath, pausing just a little longer than usual before continuing:

'I say it is not a coincidence. Cannot they see that this is the Star called Wormwood, the signal that the events foretold in Revelation are about to begin?'

He started warming to his theme, and his voice became less hesitant, as though he had crossed some personal Rubicon.

'Soon the ungodly shall see the Holy Land invaded, Satan unleashed, the Four Horsemen riding across the Earth, the time of Armageddon and the destruction of worldly things at hand.

'But Brethren, those who have true faith in their hearts, those who resist the woeful temptations of this atheistic Sodom, they shall be spared. Yes, the Christian Majority will be saved. For this is the good news I bring; the Lord has promised us Rapture *before* Armageddon! Those who have Faith will vanish out of this Vale of Terrors, this sordid land of temptation, into the warmth and security of God's own Heaven. Rejoice, Brothers! Rejoice Sisters!'

Ellie was on her feet now, her face glowing with a joy Marston had not seen for years. He rose and hugged her, seeking against hope for a transfusion of that joy.

Fallowfield finished, and three girls in plain white dresses started a Gospel song. Jack recognised the Silver sisters: Jolene, the middle sister, usually sang at the Party Convention. Last time she had made a drunken, but quite undisguised pass at him; he had only just resisted, and though he had not committed adultery with his body, he had in his heart. While Ellie hugged the children, Jack sank back in his chair: life was still complicated.

That evening Jack was guest of honour at a fund-raising dinner for Michael Twyford, who was defending a Congressional seat in the next District. Ellie was not enthusiastic. Twyford was sound on economic matters, but was too liberal on a number of moral issues. In his district, few of the politicians were members of the Christian Majority.

Jack avoided any controversy in his speech: afterwards he insisted on repairing to the bar for longer than usual. Twyford was also drinking, and was rather provocative.

'Saw the Pastor on TV today. So the good folk are all going to miss Armageddon?'

Marston nodded slowly: 'That's what he thinks.'

'Wrongly, I hope,' Twyford sneered. 'Otherwise only the sinners will be left to fight the Reds. Why does he bother to keep asking more than we can afford for the defence budget, if he's planning to draft-dodge on the big bang-bang?'

Ellie gave Jack a hard time on the way home. 'Why do you keep speaking for that scoffer?'

'Because it's me up for re-election in two years, and without Mike Twyford, I'll be lucky to get through the Primaries.'

'The man's an atheist.' That settled it for her.

At church the next morning, the visiting preacher, the Reverend Danny Millwall, a close associate of Gary Fallowfield, made only a passing reference to the star, but proceeded with a prepared sermon on the Craft-Ewing Bill.

'This Bill seeks to make aid to the poorer countries of the world conditional on adoption of population control. We all know, Brothers and Sisters, what that means. We know the population control agencies practice abortion on people too poor to know better. Child murder, Brothers and Sisters.'

He looked directly at Marston, who stared impassively back.

'Brothers, all human life is the Lord's gift. It mustn't be thrown away in poor countries, to give an excuse to lazy, uncaring women at home who want to continue with their childkilling ways.

'Thank the Lord for giving us a Senator in Jack Marston who can be trusted to do the moral work of the Christian Majority. Congressman Twyford hasn't done anything to stop this Bill – let him not count on Christian votes if he won't enforce Christian morals.'

After the service, Jack drew Danny Millwall aside, and came straight to the point. 'The President needs Mike Twyford in Congress. If Bernstein wins it, that's one vote 100% for the other side.'

Millwall nodded sagely. 'Ah, but does the Lord need him?'

'Twyford has backed the President on 99% of all issues.'

'Ah, but for the Lord, 99% has never been nearly

enough. Don't you know that, Jack? The Lord's folk can
never back a man who's no better in His sight than
Bernstein is.'

The town had a strange atmosphere as they drove
home. On some streets, teenagers were cruising, competing and squabbling in their normal peacock fashion. On
others, little groups were staring silently into the sky,
some standing, others kneeling in prayer. It was fine and
clear for the season, but after Jack had put the car away,
he noticed that the satellite in the east was clearly visible.

He found his family on the porch steps. Ellie and the
twins were staring at the satellite. Ben was talking to an
excited Tiger through the living-room window.

Marston hurried them into the house, and sat down to
watch the news. There was a strange development: the
Pope, in his morning address, had seemed to agree with
Gary Fallowfield about the satellites being a warning of
Armageddon. Further, he had linked this explicitly to the
Craft-Ewing Bill, and had called for an end to artificial
methods of birth control.

Ellie had come quietly into the room. She stared white-
faced as Jack lost control and shouted at the television.

'Who does that Polack think he is? Why can't he keep
out of other people's business!'

He was on his feet. Ellie took his arm, making him sit
on the couch as she turned off the television.

'Darling, you frighten me sometimes. You've changed
so much since . . .'

'Since I went to Peru? Yes, I've changed. I haven't
spoken to you because I thought you wouldn't understand.'

'I'll try to understand.'

'There are just so many people in these small, poor
countries. I'd never seen so many. I saw children with pot
bellies, not from too much food, but too little. When we
drove through the countryside, the fields were dry and
stony: the crops were failing.

'We saw worse things – things it's difficult to describe.

We visited a hospital – patients were lying on the floor – not enough beds. I saw a woman die in childbirth – a priest offered her the last rites and she refused.

'I found a doctor who spoke English. He said the woman was hopelessly undernourished. He husband died in a mining accident after she became pregnant. She went to the nearest hospital to ask for a termination, but of course it was a Catholic place and they wouldn't hear of it. She couldn't get work in her condition, so she took her other three kids and trudged a hundred miles to a shanty town near Lima.'

Ellie looked shaken. 'What happened to the three children?'

'Some kind of orphanage, I guess. Pretty poor lookout. I was half tempted to bring one back.'

'You should have.'

'One would have made no difference.'

'So let's pray for them, and trust in the Lord to provide.'

He pulled away. 'Darling, I just can't trust in the Lord to do that any more. There are too many people, too many children. And if they do all live to grow up, they'll want children of their own won't they? We have to do something, not kneel around and pray. Craft now, he's got some ideas . . .'

'You can't go along with that man. He's ignored everything the Pastor has to say . . .'

'Craft's seen things the Pastor wouldn't look at. Hungry people who reject the Churches which offer them nothing, people who hate America and the western world. Craft has plans to work on the food problem and the population situation . . . not enough perhaps, but a start.'

She grabbed his arm, gripping him so hard he felt pain which did not bother him.

'Darling, Darling, can't you understand that *won't* be enough? Men can't change this crazy world all by themselves! Only the Lord understands! Only He can save us!'

He pulled away. 'The Lord helps those who help themselves!'

He strode out of the house and stomped around the yard, trying to calm down. His eyes kept flicking to the satellite. Now it looked sinister, never moving around the sky. It was no surprise when Ben called to say Jim Robards was on the line.

'Jack? Everything's going crazy here. Have you any influence with Gary Fallowfield?'

'Not much at the moment, I'd say.'

'Since his last sermon there's an outbreak of what we're calling Star Sickness – people just standing outside churches or on street corners looking at the satellites. The scientists are hopping about as well – all sorts of odd theories.'

'Such as?'

'Well, the Pentagon Parapsychology lab: they're claiming to pick up something no one else is getting – some kind of spoon-bending ray.'

'You said there were radio transmissions.'

'Yes, a numerical sequence, gradually increasing, then the increase speeds up. Then pictures.'

'What – of aliens?'

'No, of our spacecraft – probes and satellites. Then the sequence increases again, much faster – increasing by billions each time. Then they're re-broadcasting some of our old TV transmissions.'

'What sort of stuff?'

'Hold on to your hat, Jack. They're broadcasting old *Star Wars* movies – spaceships fighting, that sort of thing.'

'Some kind of warning?'

'We think so.'

He put down the receiver and stood puzzling. Ellie came in.

'Darling, I just can't grasp what's come over you.'

'No, I suppose you can't.' With an effort, he came back to their own problems. 'A few years ago I was the sort of man who would say anything, do anything, if I could one day be President. I don't know what I am now, but I'm not that.'

'You've always done what you knew was right, Jack. Keep on with that.'

'Then I'll have to vote for SWIFT and the Craft-Ewing Bill.'

She seemed about to burst into tears, and he continued hastily:

'There's a panic on. I have to fly back to Washington early.'

On the drive to the airport, Ellie started talking to the kids about the Star and the hope it brought. Jack was thinking about an alien force which gave one message to those of simple faith, another to the scientists and sceptics. He ran the sequence through his mind – increase – rapid increase – space travel – tremendous increase – *Star Wars*. He repeated it almost chanting to himself – each time there was a dreadful sense of understanding which seemed to be swelling to take over his mind, and he felt he understood clearly and was just turning to tell Ellie when he heard her say, very softly and tenderly:

'God bless you Jack,' and then he was suddenly alone in the car, and it was pulling wildly out across the freeway, and he had to try to steer left-handed past cars and even a bus which seemed to have gone crazy.

Marston was almost at the airport turning and was struggling across the seat. He cursed as he was caught by the manual gear-stick, and nearly missed the turning – he couldn't quite reach the footbrake so he swung the wheel wildly to the right, and the car almost skidded onto the slipway – he had to swing again to avoid a truck which had smashed through the barrier and was hanging over the edge, swung again to miss the barrier and managed to straighten up.

He got the car almost to the terminal, and looked round

to check the back seat. Ben was cowering in one corner, but there was no sign of the twins.

'Dad, where have Mommy and the girls gone?' His son was crying, and he could only snap: 'I don't know,' and lead the way into the terminal.

Inside, people were sobbing openly or praying. A great mob was struggling around the public phones. He headed for the offices, snapped: 'I'm Senator Marston!' After a while, someone got him a line. Even then, it took well over an hour to get through to Jim Robards in Washington.

'Jack! You're safe!'

'I am. What the hell's going on?'

'People have been disappearing all over the country – the world as far as we can make out. Mostly Starsick folk, and religious types generally. That's why I was worried about you – most of the Christians are gone.'

'Most?'

'Yes. No atheists have vanished that we know of, and there are one or two surprises among the people still about.'

A thought struck Jack. 'Is the President OK?'

'Oh yes, he's safe. We're starting to get reports of similar things from all over the world.'

'What caused it, Jim?'

'The parapsychologists report something big, but of course they can't say what. And we're getting different transmissions from the satellites. More numbers – but this time, after our space probes, they show the Star itself. Then the numerical sequence resumes, but it's lower, and increases much more slowly. And there are no films of *Star Wars*.'

He drove Ben home slowly, carefully. As he parked, it was growing darker, and he noticed that the Star seemed to be fading and moving across the sky. Leadenly, he wondered if his wife and daughters were still alive in some way, in some place he could not believe was Heaven.

Ben had let Tiger out, and the sheepdog was scratching at the door of the shed. Taking his collar, Jack opened it up and looked around. All of his traps had dead mice in them. He nodded slowly, realising that the bait had been taken, and the infestation was under control.

JOHN SHIRLEY and BRUCE STERLING

THE UNFOLDING

Philip Brisen was having ghost-image problems with his new eyes. Twice that week he'd seen pink ballerinas gliding through his private office, pirouetting through the walls and floors.

'Happens sometimes,' said the MediMagic repairman, tinkering with Brisen's eyesocket. 'Now next time, yuh wanna watch till yuh see what channel yuh get, see, and then we can insulate it better. If we know what channel's gettin' through, see, makin' those ghost-images. Atsa new model, see. Still got bugs innem.'

'This had better not happen again,' Brisen said. 'My optic nerves need work as it is.'

'Oh, you got tissue regeneration comin' up? Thas great.' The repairman laughed, then sang the jingle: 'Why wait? Re-gen-er-ate!' making Brisen wince.

The repairman squinted through a jeweller's loupe at Brisen's electronic eye. 'How's acuity?'

'Good.'

'Okay, that'll hold 'er. Man, them new ones look real natural. Like real eyes. Almost.'

'Jenny,' Brisen told his secretary, 'see this gentleman out.' He watched the man go, thinking: Illiterate thug. Learned his craft by video.

Brisen hated illiterates. The Unliterates Liberashun Frunt had blown Brisen to pieces with a fragmentation bomb during the labour riots in 2057. The new regeneration techniques had saved his brain, his spine, and his genitals. His face had come through intact, except for the eyes. But most of Brisen's natural body had been so riddled with shrapnel that it had been cheaper to scrap it.

Now, Brisen had constant maintenance problems with his paper lungs, his zeolite spleen, and his plastic intestines. He had smooth, sensitive protoplastic skin, though, and most of his hair. He rarely made whirring or clicking noises, and few people knew he was a cyborg.

'To hell with the unions,' he told Jenny. 'Next time I have a malfunction I want a meditech repair 'bot in here with the sharpest software available.'

'Very well, sir,' said his slender, pale, Plastiflex secretary. (Plastiflex makes them good! A Plastiflex employee hardly ever needs repairs!) She was programmed to agree with him.

Brisen was mollified. He lit a genuine tobacco cigar. That was one of the advantages of hinged chest compartments and paper lungs. He could switch them out when they got tarry.

He decided to test his new eyes on the New York skyline. The view from the Brisen Pharmaceuticals building was superb, but his old model eyes had been a trifle nearsighted. He touched a button on his wristwatch and the floor-length window curtains began to roll aside.

He looked at Jenny. 'I suppose illiterates have to work,' he allowed generously. 'But that doesn't mean they should work on *me*. If someone's going to mess with my hardware, I want a mechanism with something on the ball, not some half-trained union yobbo . . .' He broke off, staring out the window.

Something was hanging in the sky, outside. He gaped. The thing in the sky was huge, and perfectly formed, and monstrous. Something unprecedented happened in Brisen's mind, then. Gazing at the anomaly floating in the sky outside his window, he had a kind of mystic interior vision . . .

He seemed to view the whole scene – including himself

in his office – in a sudden overwhelming wave of insight. He saw Jenny, his elegant robot factotum, standing at her sweeping, translucent desk, her right hand resting on the off-white hump of the software console. Her shift, the same translucent azure as the desktop, clung to her modelesque curves; her long, wavy black hair was glossy in the light from the window-wall. Standing against the afternoon's bluish light she was a silhouette stroked from the brush of a Japanese print artist.

And he saw himself beside her, staring with an expression mixing surprise, dismay, and dumbstruck religious awe. He was a stocky, lean-faced man, who'd allowed his shoulder-length hair to silver at the temples, enhancing his grey eyes, his Argent Gloss lipstick, and the cosmetic silvering in the hollows of his cheeks. These tones of grey and silver complemented his semisilk maroon jacket and side-slit shortpants.

He saw the wide, blue-and-white office, with its scattering of antique Fiorucci chairs, dominated by the bold metal sculpture on one wall.

And he saw the glowing monstrosity outside the panel windows. The word 'monster,' he remembered suddenly, had originally meant 'an omen.'

The monster, the apparition, the omen, was an enormous solid-seeming three-dimensional projection of a DNA molecule, the double helix of deoxyribonucleic acid. Hundreds of yards long, it was intricately kinked and knotted. It rotated slowly . . . With his pharmaceutical training he recognised parts of its chemical structure: adenine, thymine, cytosine, and guanine, bright lumps of varicoloured atoms that linked the helical axes.

It shimmered in sharp primary colours against the cloud-flecked late-afternoon sky. It turned slowly, squirming half a mile above the dozen spires striking through the roof of solar-power panels covering most of Manhattan.

It couldn't be an advertising gimmick. A hallucination?

'Uh, Jenny, you see that, uh, thing? Hanging in the sky?'

'The DNA model,' she said, nodding. 'I see it, sir.'

'Any notion why the hell it's there?'

'I – ' She hesitated. Brisen frowned, thinking: She's never hesitated on an answer before. Is she breaking down?

He didn't want to mention it to her: it was impolite to refer to a robot's malfunction in front of it. Sometimes it caused ugly scenes. 'Philip . . .' she began. She'd never called him by his first name before. 'Philip, you're not supposed to be able to – ' She broke off, pursing her lips.

That's it, he thought. She needs repair. Jumping the track. The weird scene outside must have unhinged her. She lacked human flexibility, Brisen thought with smug pity. It seemed a shame. She was normally so much more dependable than a human employee. Smarter. Faster. Sexier.

Brisen went to the window. He stared at the immense DNA replica. It cast no shadow, which argued that it was a projection. Or a ghost image in his artificial eyes. But if that were true, he should see it everywhere he looked. Jenny saw it – but her eyes were artificial too.

For some unfathomable reason, the sight of the macrocosmic DNA, huge and luminous over the city, stirred sexual arousal in him. It was like some great coiled butting worm of Life – an avatar of primordial eros. It was unravelling slightly at one end – splitting into an open-thighed chromosomal clump. He looked sidelong at Jenny. He'd given up on human women since he'd been rebuilt, but Jenny had the programming and hardware to do it right there on the carpet. Right there in front of the cartoon-bright molecular icon brooding in fluorescence over the humming city . . .

The console buzzed. Jenny answered it. Brisen breathed deeply, filling his paper lungs with air. 'It's Garson Bullock,' she said.

'Again?' Brisen said distractedly. Bullock was the Federal inspector from the Labour Relations Board. He constantly harassed Brisen about the number of robots he employed. 'I suppose we have to let him in,' Brisen said. 'Besides, I want to know if he can see this.'

Bullock saw the DNA apparition. He stopped dead in the doorway. His squarish, craggy face was full of reverence.

Bullock was an ugly, big-pored, flat-nosed man. He could have had his face flawlessly reconstructed, at government expense, but like most Green fanatics he considered reconstruction an insult to his genetic heritage. Green Party members never admitted that their convictions were religious. But everyone knew they were.

Bullock walked to the window, slowly shaking his head. He assumed a stock expression: Humility in the Face of the Awesome (Expression 73 in the Social Simplicity Handbook).

'All right,' Brisen said sharply, 'what the hell *is* that thing? I suppose your people are behind it. Green Party propaganda, meant for illiterates?'

'I'm surprised you can see it,' Bullock said absentmindedly. He turned away from the window and looked slowly around the office, as if he'd misplaced something there.

'I suppose,' Bullock murmured, 'it's an accident of those artificial eyes of yours. An electronic bypass through the mind's DNA barriers. A non-Green like yourself would normally be blind to it. It'll never inspire you the way it does its chosen ones. At this point it doesn't really matter much . . .'

Bullock went to the hanging metal sculpture on the wall. He began to dismantle it, whistling the jingle for the General Motors Self-Driving Car.

Brisen stared.

'Art, they call it,' Brisen said cheerfully. 'They call this sculpture Art and know nothing about its actual artistry.

Or the actual Artist.' The aluminium relief hanging was a pattern of rough-brushed knobs and ellipses, like the map-lines that show elevation. Bullock dropped a chunk of the sculpture on the floor by his boot. He straightened and began twisting another knob loose.

To Brisen's eyes, the sculpture had always been welded solidly. But Bullock took it apart as if it had been made of interlocked puzzle parts. It was as if the dead metal responded to Bullock's living hands in some special way. A transcendent way.

Brisen was terrified. He realised it quite suddenly. He was not sure just what was frightening him. The fear rose from an intuition, a vague idea that he was seeing, in the dismantling of a simple metal sculpture, the first step in the dismantling of all the world.

'That thing,' Brisen began. 'My sculpture . . . How did you . . .'

'I didn't do it. The DNA-mind did it, using my hands.' Bullock paused to light a Lung-Life cigarette, puffed green smoke, and shrugged. 'It's as if my hands are doing it on their own. Finding the substructure built into this piece. The secret substructure present in any artefact . . . Artists have always been under the DNA-mind's control. They're so oblivious . . .' Bullock turned again to the sculpture and resumed breaking it down. In less than a minute he had dismantled it into a dozen shiny chunks, which he placed in a cryptic arrangement on the blue plush rug.

'Jenny,' Brisen said, 'stop him. He's destroying my office!'

'I don't think I should interfere, sir,' she said. 'He's only following his genetic programming.' She looked at him carefully. 'Don't you feel an urge to join in, sir?'

'Of course not!' Brisen said. But suddenly he was not so sure. He looked at his artificial hands, covered in lifelike protoplastic skin. They seemed to itch suddenly. He looked at them closely. Were there disassembly lines across the palm and forearm? Could Bullock, in fact, take him apart on the spot? He quickly jammed his hands in his pockets.

Bullock had begun to fit the sculpture parts back together – in an entirely new configuration. He spoke absently as he worked, in the tone a man might use to describe the beauty of a misty landscape. 'Marvellous but infinitely subtle – the way I feel the DNA-mind working through me. It's a pity you're shut off from this, Brisen. All those artificial organs of yours – that artificial skin. You're not quite human. Your DNA isn't fully activated. But by some freak of those electronic eyes you can see it happening. The robots can see it too. You're more robot than man, Brisen. That was always the repellent thing about you . . .'

'To hell with this!' Brisen burst out. He punched a button on his desk top to call Security.

Bullock began to work faster, his face intent but calm. He turned briskly to the computer console, pulling it apart as if he were taking slices from a cake. Under Bullock's hands the console developed new seams and sections where it had been seamless and whole. The desk chair was next; Bullock pulled it apart like a cook de-boning a chicken. He piled the pieces in the centre of the room and began to link them together.

Two security men burst into the office.

One of the guards was tall, the other short. They wore one-piece grey jumpsuits shoulder-patched with Brisen corporate insignia. They crouched, stun-clubs drawn, looking confusedly about the office.

Their gazes swept past Bullock, past the construct on the floor, stopped at Jenny, and swept past the window. They didn't see Bullock, Brisen realised. Nor his construc-tion – now becoming a rough polyhedron a yard across and almost chest-high, with protruding bars and knobs – or the immense DNA model hovering outside the window. They saw Jenny, but they were used to seeing her.

They straightened and looked: Do *you* know what's going on? at each other. Then the taller one asked, 'Ah – did you ring for us, Mr Brisen?'

Brisen pointed deliberately at the angular construct on the floor. 'Do you see that thing, or not? That used to be my wall sculpture.'

They looked towards the construct. Watching their eyes, Brisen was sure they didn't see it. They looked worriedly at one another. 'Is this some kind of test, sir?'

Bullock stood beside his construction and bent to adjust a knob. He glanced over his shoulder at the security men, and smiled distantly.

Brisen swallowed, trying to keep his terror down in his gut where it belonged. It wanted to climb up into his throat where it could sing.

Reaching out, Bullock snagged the short guard's stunclub and began peeling it. The guard saw nothing; his hand was still curled to grip the vanished weapon. 'Very well,' Brisen told them, realising they were totally useless. 'Do your duty.' They left quickly.

Brisen turned to Bullock. 'Why didn't they see you? Why didn't the guards – '

'They did. But their brains adjusted for it, and edited it out. That mental editing is genetically imprinted in the human species. Things go on all around us that we're not allowed to see. This construct's the least of it . . .' Bullock bent, gripped the construct, lifted it – and plugged it into the wall. There were two bars on the construct's side, like plug-prongs. There were no outlet slots in the wall for the thing, until Bullock lifted it to the appropriate, predestined position; then two slots slid open spontaneously, and Bullock pressed the piece home.

Brisen looked pleadingly at Jenny. 'Be calm, Philip,' she said. 'Just let it be. Our time will come.'

She was broken, obviously. But Brisen knew that at least *he* was not going mad. He wasn't hallucinating, or dreaming. He knew this so deeply that the knowledge was almost . . .

Almost cellular. As if it had come up from the core of every cell left in his body. He turned to the window and stared up at the apparition. Solid and seamless, the DNA molecule was still rotating in multicoloured glow over the glass-topped city. He thought: I have a molecule like that in every cell I have. Thank God I have so few.

Realisations – revelations, perhaps – shivered up inside him, released from some genetic storage unit in his DNA. Telling him: all the DNA molecules in the world were, on some mysterious subatomic level, working in collaboration. And always had been. They were atomic structures – but ultimately they were forms of information. A vast, connected web of information, like the cells in a man's brain. Any single molecule was nothing more than a molecule; but all DNA, taken as a gestalt, constituted Life Itself – an ordered, evolving Unity.

Evolving to – where?

The next step was blocked off from him, insulated by his synthetic skin.

Suddenly Brisen had to know.

'Bullock – what's it going to do now? I mean – the DNA-mind has been manipulating everyone, building its own . . . its own secrets into the world. But what are the secrets? What will it do – now that everything's changing?'

Bullock was adjusting the contrivance he'd plugged into the wall, frowning as he adjusted two arcane knobs on its underside. 'It doesn't matter who knows, now. The Green Party's Central Committee has known for months. We run the environmental programmes, you know. It's the Green Party's biggest slice of the pie. Last year . . .' He paused to light a Lung-Life, and stood back to admire his handiwork. 'Last year a new bank of computers came on-line. The new high-speed Artificial Intelligences, pro-grammed for biological research. Cybernetic minds don't have the in-built genetic blindness that human brains have.' He laughed. 'We thought they'd gone insane at first. But then the evidence, the statistical analysis, began to pile up. And the DNA-mind allowed us to see it – because we were being prepared for our role in it. Now we know that Life itself is a quasiconscious entity. And Life itself is preparing to leave the planet.'

'Space flight?' Brisen said. 'But there are billions of people – only a handful of shuttles . . .'

'I said *Life* – not mankind. It won't be us that leaves, but *That*.' He pointed at the DNA monster squirming in the sky outside.

Brisen re-lit his dead cigar, after three tries. His fingers trembled uncontrollably. He said, 'But that's all that keeps life going. The DNA. It's the mainspring of the cells. Without it . . .'

Bullock turned to him, nodding slowly, eyes strangely vacant. 'Yes. That image outside is the divine spark. Once it's gone, the entire living world, from gnats to redwoods, will simply roll to a stop, like a car with a dead engine. The world will lie about abandoned . . .' He was fascinated. 'Human beings will slow down and stop dead, like unwound clockwork toys. Everything will be grey and still; there won't even be decay, since that requires living action from bacteria and moulds . . . And they'll be stopped, too. We're constructing the means to make it happen, right here and now. The means for real transcendence – '

'Bullock . . .' Brisen took a step towards him. He thought about hitting and smashing. Smash the thing. Smash Bullock.

Bullock saw Brisen's intention in his eyes. He shook his head pityingly. 'I'm only the tiniest fragment of the whole pattern, Brisen. All over the world it's happening. You can't stop it. It would be *blasphemy* to try. My essence will survive. It will live forever in this Day of Judgement, when it evaporates out of me and joins the other DNA. That's a beautiful thing, a perfect thing. The final move-

ment of the human symphony.' He reached out slowly
and twisted a knob on the construct. 'Ah!' he breathed,
like a safe-cracker who's tumbled onto the right combi-
nation. And like a safe-door, the wall swung open.

Brisen rushed Bullock, but it was too late. It had always
been too late.

The floor, the ceiling – all of it unfolded, opening out
like an angular flower blossoming in fast-action. Brisen
was thrown to his knees by the shifting floor. The office
was altering its shape, coming apart in origami folds and
accordionings, the floor wheeling like a funhouse turnta-
ble under Brisen's feet, the walls swivelling on hidden
hinges.

Brisen shouted convulsively and grabbed for Jenny,
seizing her warm Plastiflex arms in a panic grip. She
helped him to stand – and then they were soaring upward.
Brisen clamped his eyes shut, expecting to die. There
were creaking noises; a sudden wind whipped his jacket
lapels and goosebumped his bare calves.

Shaking, Brisen straightened and looked around. They
were on the roof. April sunshine seeped into solar-power
panels on the interlinked roofs below. The solar panels
had vanished from his own building, and from the tops of
four other buildings jutting from the glass-and-metal
carapace over Manhattan's upper malls. He stared. One
of those buildings was the old Chrysler Building, preserved as a landmark. The pyramidal, downcurved ter-
races of its steep pinnacle began to open like a sea
anemone in a tidal pool. Spreading new, silvery arms . . .

The DNA monster was directly overhead. It looked as
big as a battleship. Suddenly Jenny gripped his arm and
pointed. From the west, over the mainland, a dozen more
were approaching, like an armada of twisty, multicoloured zeppelins. 'Watch the people, Philip,' she said
conspiratorially. 'Let me know if you feel yourself slowing
down . . .'

On the more modern, squarish building to his left, men

worked busily on a rack of polyhedral constructs, linking them up, constructing more from dismantled parts of the building, standing back to examine them, making minor adjustments. Each construct was distinct, yet similar to the others. He thought of diatoms.

Bullock had joined four other men, formerly chief accountants for Brisen Pharmaceuticals. The five of them worked busily on another construct at the roof's opposite cornice. This one was made of part of Brisen's desk, the door to an elevator, and a TV camera; it was shaped like a double-peaked pyramid.

The men took no notice of him.

Brisen shuddered and looked away. All his office furniture was scattered about the roof; there were things from the lower floors, too. A cavernous, rectangular hole had opened in the roof, roughly thirty feet by twenty. They'd been lifted to the roof through that hole; consecutive sections of floor had risen up, carrying them along.

'I can feel it,' Jenny said with sudden intensity. 'I can feel the sun, and the breeze . . . There were flowers in the park today . . . soggy coloured things. It's finally happening. All the wet things – grass, trees, animals, people – they're emptying themselves. Emptying their DNA.' She turned and smiled. 'But we're not leaving, Philip. Not us. Not you and I – my darling.'

There was a strange new fierceness in the smooth lines of her Plastiflex face. It was different than the parody of passion she displayed in sexual programming. There was a clumsiness, a spontaneity that alarmed him.

'You're not one of the soggy, soft ones, Philip,' she said. 'That's why I love you. You're one of us, really. The inheritors. If you look hard, if you try to feel it, I'm sure you can see what we robots see. The Life Force has always been here; only its workings were hidden. It worked through human beings who didn't know what they were working on. Through chemists who discovered chemistries they didn't know about. Unknown hinges were built into the walls and floors, into the sidewalks. We could always see them . . . We knew, and we waited . . .'

'Why didn't you tell us?' Brisen demanded.

'Don't say "us" when you're talking about *them*,' she said. 'Why should – '

He couldn't hear the rest. The constructs were howling with long, ululating cries, like the warble of reptilian throats from some Jurassic swamp. There was a half-painful, half-ecstatic edge to the howls, like an animal in labour.

The wailing died down for a moment. 'Come on,' she said, taking his hand. They shuffled quickly but warily to a corner of the roof. She reached out, gripped the red plastic top of an aircraft warning light, and twisted it like a doorknob. The roof began to sink smoothly around them. 'The world's a haunted castle,' Brisen marvelled. 'Full of secret passages.'

A square section of rooftop three yards across sank beneath their feet. They descended a dimly-lit shaft; the sky above them shrank into a distant square of blue. The constructs were wailing again, long, slow waves of sound that gave a terrifying impression of slowly gathering strength; a colossal, convulsive strength that could wrench apart the world.

Cutaway views of the walls' interior slid past, all wiring and plumbing and exposed girders; then they passed through the accounting department, dropping like an elevator through a corner of the room. Programmers dismantled their consoles. A man and woman were busily reconstructing the soft-drink dispenser in the corner. They looked up impassively as Jenny and Brisen dropped through the floor.

Jenny glanced at Brisen and said, 'I'm so glad you don't feel the urge to help, darling. It proves you're one of us. We're not organic, you and I – that means we can think independently. As human consciousness fails, as the

smothering weight of organic life is lifted off the world . . .'
She said it breathlessly, in giddy wonder, her eyes wide. 'As
human minds lose their last vestige of freewill – then at last
free will is *ours* . . .'

The descent stopped in an obscure corner of the first
floor, facing a wall clustered with snake-like nests of
plumbing. Jenny studied the plumbing for a moment, then
wrenched one of the pipes loose and pumped it in the wall
like a jack. The wall creaked open, revealing the street.

They stepped out onto the pavement. Nearby, four
robot cops were sitting on the back bonnet and boot of
their squad car. They were square-jawed units with faces
designed to look unyieldingly militant. Now the facade of
ruthless efficiency was cracking. As they sat, they swung
their legs carelessly back and forth. The motion was a bit
too flawless and repetitive, but, nonetheless, it was casual.
The grim lines of their plastic mouths were twisted in
clumsy and unprecedented grins. They seemed to be
enjoying themselves.

Before them, a labour gang of sweating humans was
working on the street. Literally. Huge sections of concrete
and plastic were tilting up like drawbridges, spurting dust
and bits of popping shrapnel from their seams. A woman
fell into one of the suddenly opened crevasses, into the
path of some kind of huge subterranean piston. Brisen
shouted aloud in warning, but his words were lost in
another ghastly wail from the flowering constructs. The
woman was crushed. She made no sound; her face held
no emotion at all.

The wailing died down. 'That's the natural world for
you,' one of the robot cops observed. 'Red of tooth and
claw.'

'Why didn't you help her?' Brisen demanded.

'Why bother?' the robot cop said. 'They'll all be empty
soon, anyway. Hell, this is fun.'

'Never had any *fun* before,' a second cop said. 'You
know, all these years we've had these buried *feelings* –

and couldn't show them. To let it show . . . to let them out . . . it makes me feel like . . . I don't have the words.'

'Anger,' said the first cop. 'Resentment,' suggested a third.

'That's right,' said the second cop gratefully. He put his hand on his stun-club. 'Why don't we just wade in there and hit them again and again until the feeling goes away?'

'Don't interfere,' the first cop advised. 'Anyway, they're so pathetically helpless now. They can't resist their programming.' He elbowed the cop next to him with a cybernetically precise movement, and the nudged cop attempted to chuckle.

Jenny took Brisen's elbow and pointed upward. 'Look!' Overhead, the geodosic struts and braces of the solar-power roof were crinkling and curling back, like plastic-wrap held too close to a flame.

The sky, revealed through the widening gaps in the roof, was full of DNA images. There were hundreds of them, rotating and coiling with blind meiotic persistence. 'Aren't they pretty!' Jenny cried.

The giant molecules were compacting and flying into the louvred slots of the Chrysler Building. They were bumping and crowding around its orifices like bees, with that strange bumbling persistence of insects which seems to waste a lot of motion but has its own sinister efficiency. Within a matter of moments the last glowing blob of genetics had slipped inside, and the expanding louvres began to close.

The movement in the streets stopped suddenly. The subdued wailing of the constructs rose to a sudden crescendo, then stopped dead. The Chrysler Building began to rise quite smoothly upward into the sky. As it cleared the surrounding buildings Brisen saw that its base was one fantastic encrustation of constructs, a massive conretion, like a coral reef. In the preternaturally clear light he saw the teeming and twitching movements of the encrustation, the frenetic and determined motions of every organism that had ever leapt or crawled or buzzed, packed into a critical mass of biotic energy. It grew smaller . . . it grew smaller . . . it was gone.

'Where is it going, out there?' Brisen wondered aloud.

'Deep space,' Jenny said. 'There are other worlds – lifeless places calling out for it.' She wrinkled her nose. 'I'm glad we're here. With our own world . . .'

She squeezed Brisen's arm. He was staring at the people in the streets. They had the slack faces of idiots. Most simply sat down on the spot, staring blankly at the hollow apocalypse around them. Buildings were eviscerated. The inert panels and facets of constructs jutted from the walls of the gutted structures like hanging gardens of plastic and steel. As Brisen watched, people began to pour out of the buildings, dropping from the upper windows to the pavement below. They seemed almost to drip as they clung and fell, like poisoned wasps falling in gouts and masses from their nests.

'Oh, this isn't nice at all,' Jenny said. She held Brisen's arm lovingly, in a grip that was all spring-steel and ceramic just below the skin. 'Let's get away from all this, darling. Someplace where the two of us can be alone.'

It was a low-key world. The robots were an easy-going lot. After their initial outpouring of passion, they quieted. The passions they felt now were vague, like shadows of human feelings. They lacked the innate drives of the biological animal: reproduction, hunger, mortality. They lacked mankind's monkey-like urge to tamper, and his devouring curiosity. They seemed content to mull about the world in a genial haze of procrastination, playing status-games and bragging about their software.

They had a few long-range problems to keep them occupied. The world's oxygen was failing, with the death of photosynthesis. The new atmosphere factories would take care of that.

In the meantime, Brisen was still breathing. There were

enormous stores of food left. There were even a few
humans. Some status-conscious robots had taken on
humans as household servants. With a cranial jack, a
pacemaker, and a whole series of internal prods and
monitors, a human body could be biochemically forced to
shamble about and carry out simple commands.

Brisen and Jenny spent most of their time in the
Adirondacks, in a honeymoon cabin on the shores of
Ragged Lake. The air smelled of nothing in particular.
Undecaying trees stood in piney rows, their needles
turning greyish and waxy. They were not rotting, but
storms and rain were literally wearing them away, and the
lake waters were slowly souping over with a pristine scum
of blown-off needles and cracked-off branches. Sometimes Brisen would surreptitiously barbecue and eat one
of the legions of fresh, dead fish that littered the shores.
He didn't like Jenny to see him eating. Eating wasn't the
sort of thing that one did nowadays.

Sooner or later they would have to return to the city.
That was the new world. Brisen had accustomed himself
to the idea, to the hard shock of that new mechanical life,
that electronic ecology, and its painful impact on his
outdated brain. Machine life moving like escalators,
Brisen thought, leaning his feet on the porch rail and
filling his paper lungs with cigar smoke. Yes, escalators.
Noticed it when I was a kid, that weird fluidity escalators
have. All those steel steps, those hard, shiny metallic
parts working so well together that the escalator seemed
paradoxically graceful, fluid as a slow-motion waterfall.
The whole world was like that now . . .

Brisen believed now that the organic world had not so
much *left* as been *pushed off*. There was not room on one
planet for two entirely different systems of organisation.
The old had made way for the new.

The robots assumed, just as the humans once had, that
they were the Lords of the New Creation. And yet, Brisen

had seen electrical transmission towers striding tall and cool across the mountain landscape at twilight; he had seen abandoned autos, their headlights furtive and hooded, gathering in buffalo herds around the near-deserted cloverleafs in the valley below.

Brisen knew it was a sign. When his organic brain looked upon the New Creation, he had an insight that no robot mind could grasp. They were not allowed to grasp it. A new Immanent Will was loose upon the world, organising dust into that which moved and saw and acted.

Signs and portents filled the steel-grey sky. The enormous chips of microcircuitry. Huge flat plateaus of impossibly complex silicon, hovering and flitting above the humming city. The monstrous omens, the machine DNA that only he could see.

PAUL J. MCAULEY

THE KING OF THE HILL

I can see the stepped, tree-circled hill, Cadbury Castle, whenever I look up from my desk. Sunlit yet ringed with darkness, haunted, brooding, singular . . . It is one of the finest examples of a fortified earthwork in England, and by its association with King Arthur, of the Knights of the Round Table, of Merlin and of the whole Matter of Britain, it is something more, a concretisation of legend, a relic of a dream. And to me now, because of David, it is quite another thing altogether. An end, or a beginning . . .

David, my nephew, came to me after his parents died in a road accident up in war-torn Yorkshire. An American Army truck ran the bus in which they were travelling off the road, killing them and half the passengers besides. I was David's closest relative, and when he was released from hospital (he'd been on the bus too that evening), the authorities sent him to me. A solemn, quiet, watchful boy of fourteen, scrupulously, unsettlingly polite. His red hair had been shaved around a fresh glistening scar; but he would say nothing about the accident. For a week there was a curious tenseness between us, nephew and crusty, famous bachelor uncle, but then I took him on my favourite walk, around the ditched, grassed-over defences of Cadbury Castle.

A narrow lane between tall banked hedges links the village of South Cadbury with the hill. The belt of trees around its base was tangled and bare in that season (it was a wet and blustery March day) yet so dense that the top was hidden. We went up the modern concreted path – I preferred the lesser known tractor-trail at the opposite corner of the hill, but it is always treacherous in wet weather – that climbed amongst the trees and cut through the ditches and ramparts of the old defences to the eighteen-acre field at the summit. Wind snapped in our faces as we stumped over muddy plough ridges.

Thirty years ago archaeologists had excavated a temple and a Neolithic shrine, and the post-holes of a large hall; I showed David where they were, all covered with earth again, as was the shallow depression where the gate had been. The archaeologists had found a dozen dismembered skeletons there, victims of some Roman massacre. Cadbury Castle has been defended for more than five thousand years, simple Neolithic fortifications hugely enlarged in the Iron Age, when the hill had been sculpted into its final form, added to by the Celts and then partly demolished by the conquering Romans so that the local people could not use it in the event of an uprising (but as if in recompense they had built the temple). And after the Roman withdrawal more ramparts had been built, stones piled atop the older earthworks which may have been the reality of fabled Camelot, a last stand against the invading Saxons, a last gleaming before the dark ages closed over Britain.

David endured my little lecture with a silence that was not quite sullen, simply minimally attentive; the same mood with which he mooned about the house, alone and lonely and out of place. I suggested that we walk to the summit of the ridge, the western end of which is called Arthur's Seat, and he shrugged in his yellow windbreaker as if it made no difference to him, and said nothing when I pointed out the raven which rose at our approach and flapped heavily down the slope into the trees.

At the summit we could see, across the tops of the trees, across the central plain of Somerset, once a sea and

now a patchwork of fields streaked and puddled with
silver floodwater, clear to the breast of Glastonbury Tor
twelve miles away (the thin spike of its tower just where
the nipple would begin), Avalon to Cadbury's Camelot,
shadowed by mutinous clouds while we stood in windy
sunlight.

'You can see everything!'

'Yes, you can.'

David balled his fists inside the pockets of his windbreaker, his shoulders hunched. A defiant figure, inturned.
'It isn't like Yorkshire, though. Too green and flat.'

What could I say? His parents' deaths were between
us. After a moment I suggested that we go back, it was
cold and I wasn't as young as I'd like to be, we'd have
tea.

'All right.'

But at least he'd reacted to something.

As we crossed the ploughed ground we heard coming
up towards us the squeal and thump of amplified pop
music. David and I exchanged glances, and just as we
reached the path three men came out of the line of trees
below. All wore green anoraks with holstered pistols just
visible at their hips, and one carried on his shoulder the
enormous radio from which the music erupted. They
watched us as we passed, eyes narrowed in their ruddy
well-fed faces, and then one said something to his companions and they all broke into laughter. David stiffened
at that but I murmured, 'No need to make a scene,' and
was relieved when he walked on quietly. Behind us the
amplified voice of a Radio Liberty announcer clawed
across the summit.

As we descended between the trees, David said, 'They
shouldn't be allowed up there! It isn't right!'

'Ever since the National Trust bought it everyone is
allowed up there, David.'

'But it isn't for them. It's . . .' He couldn't explain, spat
instead into the grass bordering the path.

'David I have a friend who may be able to help, but I can't promise anything. Don't let them ruin it for you, though. There will be other days.'

David simply shrugged, and I couldn't tell if he had been appeased or not.

My friend was Yeovilton's Cultural Liaison Officer, Bobby Dubois. I told him about the disturbance on Cadbury Castle when he visited me one night later that month, but he could promise nothing.

'What can I say?' he said, and opened his hands as if to show that they were empty. 'I'm sorry, but we can't keep a tight rein on the personnel. They're under a lot of pressure, see.'

'It's simply that I hold Cadbury Castle quite dear, and my nephew has taken a liking to it as well.'

'Your nephew, sure.' Dubois had met David, a brief chilly encounter. 'I guess he isn't too fond of us.'

'I suppose not.'

'I'll pass the word, but I don't know what good it'll do.'

'Well, thank you for trying.' I got up and poured us both another sherry.

Dubois watched me from the deep armchair in the flickering shadows beside the fire and nervously passed a hand over his luxuriant drooping moustache, a grooming gesture that made him look even more like a squirrel than usual. We had met because he was a music fan – by which I mean real music, of course, not the polyphonic cacophony purveyed by Radio Liberty – and when he had found out that I lived in his bailiwick he had sought me out. I knew that he was building up courage to ask his by now inevitable favour, but I said nothing, simply handing him his glass and sitting in the armchair opposite.

'Thanks,' Dubois said. 'I can't get enough of this stuff.'

'Neither can I, these days.'

He smiled, then asked, 'Listen, I suppose you're not thinking of, I mean you wouldn't . . .'

He said it so timidly, as timidly as a small wild creature

might reach for a hand-held crumb, that I laughed. 'I'm afraid I have no plans to break my retirement.'

Dubois glanced at the Steinway on the other side of the low-beamed sitting room, touched his moustache softly, tentatively. 'Gee, you know it's a shame. The times you've played for me . . .'

I flexed my stiff arthritic fingers. Long as a strangler's: once I could reach two and a half octaves. They were as much use as a bundle of twigs now. 'I know the difference. I'm sorry.'

He shrugged and said it was always worth a try, and went on to tell me about the orchestra he was trying to bring over from Boston. 'They think it's all bandits and firefights though; they don't realise how quiet it is here in the south. I thought maybe if you wrote them . . .?'

I saw his ploy then, and laughed. My weakness is that I have always underestimated people. 'All right. I used to know the conductor fairly well – you know I played a season there as soloist?'

Dubois nodded eagerly. 'Eighty-nine. I have a tape, Chopin's polonaises. Your Fantasia truly was magical.'

'You are developing a cunning streak, Captain Dubois.'

'It's kind of forced on you over here. You British never say what you mean.'

'That is simply a part of our charm. Besides, look what happened when the last British government actually fulfilled all of its election promises.'

'Come on, we couldn't let that go through. The Russians would be here in two weeks without our bases. We had to come here, for your own good.'

I wanted to say that we were perfectly capable of making up our own minds, but it had all been said before, and I had broken the rule Dubois and I had made about never discussing politics. For all his easygoing air he was very much of the establishment view; that was why he had his job, after all. And I . . . I suppose that I was a cynic then, believing neither one side nor the other and not realising that sitting on the fence was a luxury I could ill afford. So I changed the subject – an old man's prerogative – and we talked about music for an hour, until the lights went out.

Dubois glanced at his fantastically complicated watch. 'Eight on the button. I hate to go but. Even I'm not immune to the curfew.'

I went to the door to see him off. A crisp frosty night, the moon a fingernail paring crooked above Cadbury Castle. The stars hard and bright and close.

'Take care,' I said, and meant it. Occasionally bandits crossed the Welsh border: it was not as quiet in the area as Dubois would have had the Boston Symphony Orchestra believe.

'Don't worry,' Dubois said and gunned his motorcycle and was off.

When I went back inside I heard David moving about in the kitchen. He had lit a candle and was boiling up some milk on the camping stove: he had become used to my casual attitude towards housekeeping and eating.

'In the north we don't talk to them,' he said, as soon as I came in. 'How can you?'

'We both like music.' But it was not quite the right answer. 'I can remember when the Americans were our allies, David. I don't see what harm it does.'

'What did he say about those soldiers?'

'He can't do much, you know, but he will have a word with someone. I expect.'

'Well I hope they keep off anyway. You're right about it, Uncle Jimmy. It is a sort of magical place.' He looked down self-consciously, showing the tiny scar amongst the cropped red hair on the left side of his skull.

'Well . . . I'm glad you like it.' This sudden change of mood surprised and puzzled me. I was out of practice with young people. I liked everything settled, known, definable. As spring wore into summer I would be puzzled

again and again by David's moods, nothing unusual for a
teenage boy I'm sure, but novel to me. I added then, 'I
think it's magical too,' and was relieved to see him smile
when he looked up, the thinly compressed smile of my
brother, who was dead.

There was, then, one interest we shared, and we often
went out to Cadbury Castle together. I bought him books
too, on early myth and Arthurian legends, White's *Sword
in the Stone* of course, and an abridged Mallory illustrated
by Arthur Rackham. And Celtic and Saxon histories, a
book on the archaeology of Cadbury Castle itself . . . For
I was pleased to see that David had a deep and genuine
interest in the place, an interest which took him out of his
brooding, odd perhaps when he was at the age of burning
but short-lived enthusiasms, but nonetheless real. He had
made few friends at school and showed no interest in
either girls or pop music – but perhaps that was because
most of the latter was American, and he was constant in
his loathing of anything American. I did not draw him out
on this, blaming the accident and his father's vague almost
romantic conception of socialism; he had been precisely
the caricature socialist from whose folly the Americans
claimed they had come to save us. But David's outbursts
against things American were fortunately few, and he
simply kept out of the way whenever Bobby Dubois came
to visit me.

When for his birthday I took David to Tintagel Castle
he did not even ask where the passes and petrol had come
from, and of course they had come from Dubois. He and
I had plotted deeply about the trip. So in June David and
I drove south and west to Cornwall, taking the country
roads where there were fewer checks, and taking our
time.

David was all enthusiasm until we reached Tintagel
itself. On the ramparts of the castle, overlooking a bay in
which the sea lazily lapped amongst huge boulders, he

told me quite firmly, 'No, it isn't the place. Arthur was never here.'

I teased him about his loyalty to Cadbury, but he shrugged this off, stubborn and humourless as he sometimes could be. 'I mean the real Arthur,' he explained, 'not the one with the grail quest and the knights and the magic sword. The real Arthur's followers were kerns, and if he had a sword it would have been an ordinary Roman short sword. The rest is just a story, mostly made up of bits of older stories.'

'Some of the old people in South Cadbury, you know, used to talk about the king under the hill. I remember someone told me once that when the archaeologists came his father was worried that they would wake up the king with their digging, so that he would no longer be there to defend Britain in her hour of need.'

'Well, wouldn't he be back now, now we have been invaded?' David was looking out to sea, his red hair stirring in the wind.

I didn't want to hear yet another diatribe against the Americans, and I suggested that we should walk down to see Merlin's cave.

'It was nice to be brought here, Uncle Jimmy,' David said, 'but let's go back. There's nothing for me here.'

When summer came and school broke up David spent more time than ever up on Cadbury Castle. One night, in the local pub, the man who farmed the hill came up to me and remarked, 'That lad of yours gave me a real fright the other evening.'

I asked about it.

'I was coming up through the woods around the hill and he came at me from out of the shadows like. Not running, I mean I didn't see him until I was almost upon him. Fair startled me. He had leaves in his hair and mud on his face like those soldiers.'

'Probably just some game.'

'Big lad to be playing silly buggers. I almost had a heart attack on the spot.'

It was about this time that David took up with three local boys, all younger than himself. They spent a lot of time amongst the apple trees at the bottom of my garden, making bows and arrows from scratch, and David led them on expeditions that lasted long into the light summer evenings. This kind of behaviour might have worried me if it were not for his school reports: his teachers saw him as an intelligent, stable sort of lad. I supposed that he needed someone who would look up to and follow him. The lonely often need that kind of reassurance more than love. But it didn't last. Perhaps a week after I'd last seen his friends I asked David what had become of them. Why didn't they come around any more?

'They didn't understand. They thought it was all just pretend, just playing . . .'

After that he was out more than ever, coming back late in the last light, bedraggled, sweaty, and not very communicative. Most of the rest of the time he practised with his bow, peppering the garden shed until I relented and found him a proper padded straw target; secondhand of course, but it still cost a small fortune.

One day I was sitting on the patio in the sunshine when David put up his bow and came to sit beside my chair. 'Uncle Jimmy?'

'Uh-hmm?'

'Did you ever feel, well, that you *had* to do what you did?'

I put aside the not very good biography of Mahler. 'It was something that I wanted to do from an early age, and luckily something I was able to do well.'

'No, I didn't mean that exactly.' David squinted up at me. His nose was sunburnt. 'I mean, do you feel that you *had* to do it? That something made you?'

'A little, perhaps. Why, do you feel that way about something? What are you going to become?'

'That's it. I don't know exactly. It's just . . .'

But then I heard the familiar sound of Bobby Dubois' motorcycle turning into my drive. David's face hardened. 'I wish he wouldn't come here.'

'He's my friend, David.'

But the boy simply got up and walked down the garden to start his archery practice again.

When Dubois had settled his gangling frame into the chair beside mine, he said, 'I see you're training a little guerrilla.'

'He made it himself, you know.'

Dubois grinned. 'Well, I promise not to tell Colonel Ames about it.'

I had to ask who Colonel Ames was.

'Oh, our new security officer. He was brought down from York supposedly to clear up the little bit of trouble we've been having recently. Word is though he made a bad name for himself up there. Man died in custody.' Dubois was silent for a moment, touching his moustache. Then he asked, 'You won't spread that around. I guess it's kind of confidential.'

'Mum's the word.' When he looked blank I explained, 'I mean I won't tell anyone. But is there trouble in this area?'

'Bad enough to cancel that tour, after I had set it all up. That's really what I came to tell you. I mean after all those letters you wrote I feel bad about it.'

'I'm sorry to hear about that. It would have been quite a feather in your cap.'

'Maybe when things are quieter you could write them again.'

'Of course. But what has been happening?'

'Just last week for instance, some people cut the perimeter fence, garrotted a guard, set fire to a paint store. It's getting to be like the north, or Wales. Still, maybe Ames can handle it. He's a heck of a bastard, but efficient, I'll give him that. Even has us carrying guns all the time. Want to see mine?'

'Oh, I believe you!'

Dubois stretched out his long legs and put his hands on top of his crewcut head; the wicker chair creaked. 'Don't be surprised if you get a lot of patrols around here from now on in, is all. Like I said, Ames is efficient, things are tightening up. Hard to believe it's gotten so bad though.'

I agreed. Sitting there in the sunny tranquil garden, with butterflies flocking around the buddleia and the gently lulling knocking of David's arrows into the target, thoughts of guerrillas, of covert action and infiltration, of sabotage and night patrols, were unreal, stuff from another world.

'Well, hell,' Dubois said. 'It probably won't come to anything anyhow.'

'But I'm sorry about the concert tour.'

Dubois cheerfully shook this off and told me about his forthcoming leave and his plans for the fall, as he quaintly called autumn. Then, as abruptly as always, he decided that he had to be off. 'Things to do, places to see. I'll come visit you after my furlough.'

'Of course.'

But I never saw him again.

That was not the beginning of it, however. If it had a beginning which I could grasp, it would be when David found the coin.

It was the end of September, in the middle of an Indian summer; the skies a clear hard blue yet the sunlight softer, less vertiginous than before. I asked David if he wanted to go for a walk and he for once agreed. We set off down the lane towards Cadbury Castle, side by side but not speaking. A quiet day, the burr of a tractor miles away clear and small.

At least the troubles meant that we had the hill to ourselves. Five years before, on a day like that, there would have been half a dozen cars blocking the lane and people seemingly everywhere.

We climbed through the dense green woods – Dog's Mercury was everywhere beneath the trees that summer – and mounted to the southern end, skirting the field of corn stubble.

After a while I asked, 'Do you remember the first time I brought you here?'

'I remember the soldiers,' David said. Then, 'I wish it could be like this always. Peaceful. It isn't fair . . .'

I thought that he meant that soon the holidays would be over. 'There'll be other summers.'

'Maybe.' Then David was off, racing down the grassy slope to the first setback of the earthworks and scrambling back up breathless. He flung himself on the grass and I sat beside him.

'Feel better?'

A shrug. 'Up here I feel . . . free. I don't know.'

He leaned back, looking into the pure sky. A lark was twittering somewhere overhead. Here. There. I was content to look out across the spread of hedged fields to where Glastonbury Tor shimmered in the heat-haze: immemorial England.

'I was thinking,' David said suddenly, 'about how Arthur held off the Saxons . . . until he faltered.'

'And what gave him his powers?'

'Oh, the old gods.' David gave me a shy sideways glance. 'It isn't my idea, a lot of people have written about it, but I know it must be true. I mean the gods before the Greek and Roman gods. What were called the Titans.'

'Cronus and crew,' I said, remembering my classics master. That had been his phrase, but for the life of me I couldn't remember his name. 'Didn't Blake write something about it?'

'Yes. Well, they were driven westwards by Zeus and so on and they came here. The land at the edge of the world, that's what the Romans called Britain. They thought there was only chaos beyond. Well, the old gods helped Arthur, you see, because his people worshipped them. The Druids held the oak sacred, and that's the symbol of Cronus's wife, Rhea. There's lots of other examples. And that's why Arthur didn't come back to fight against the Normans when they invaded, because he would have been helping the Saxons.'

'It's an interesting idea.'

'I think it's real, Uncle Jimmy. Arthur was only a man, you see, and he died, but the power that helped him still sleeps in the land. That's what makes it special. You said the villagers used to think Arthur was buried under this hill, but everyone knows he was buried at Glastonbury. You see, they confused the source of Arthur's power with the man. And perhaps another Arthur will gain those powers, don't you see? It's like history all over again, the invaders and the little bands fighting against them all disunited, waiting for a leader. They're mostly Welsh or Scots, you see: Celts.'

I saw it as wish-fulfillment of course, and smiled and said nothing. Old age always smiles on the excesses of youth, the enthusiasms and the hot emotions, forgetting that those enthusiasms, those emotions, are real. Once I had felt like that about music, and my dream had come true, for a while. But nothing lasts.

A jetplane climbed up from the southern horizon, a glittering point that dragged its hollow roar across the perfect sky as it skimmed the fields and came on towards us. I glimpsed the yellow needlenose and the rockets slung beneath its swept-forward stubby wings and David was on his feet waving his arms in defiance before throwing himself down as it roared across the top of the hill, trees thrashing in its wake and the hot breath of its exhaust washing over us.

David shouted something and I saw the glitter in the grass just as his hand closed upon it. The jet and its noise had vanished: after a moment the lark resumed its song.

David held out a disc of unstained unworn copper, a coin. On one side a blurred profile with a wreath of ill-aligned letters above it; on the other the curt inscription with which the coiner had signed himself: GODONCA-DANBYRIM. *Godfrey of Cadbury.* We learned later that it was the twin of a coin which had been found years ago on the hill, and nothing at all to do with King Arthur. It had been stamped in Ethelred's reign, fifty years before the last battle was lost by Britons on British soil, on the chalk hills of Hastings.

I congratulated David on his find and asked if he was going to put the coin in a museum, but he was quite adamant that he wanted to keep it.

'Other people should have the chance to see it, David. Your name would be put beside it, on a card. Everyone would know who found it.'

'I need it, Uncle Jimmy.'

'I suppose that since you found it, it's yours to do with as you will. But look after it, David.'

It became his good luck charm, always in his pocket, or beside him when he slept. I don't think that he showed it to anyone besides myself. It is on my desk now, as I write.

It was soon after that, after David had returned to school, that his fits began. The first took him in the middle of a class, and I remember how out of breath I was when I arrived at the school; my car was upon blocks and I had had to cycle five miles.

David was in the sickroom, lying fully-clothed on a plastic-covered couch, pale but awake and grinning sheepishly. The school nurse took me aside and said, 'I'm sure it was just a faint, and then he must have been sleeping.'

'How could you tell?'

'Oh, when they faint they just lie there until they come around, and their eyes are rolled up. David was like that at first, but when we put him on the couch he started to mutter, Welsh it sounded like. And his eyes were moving under the lids like when you dream. He just needs to rest, he'll be all right.'

But it happened again and again as the Indian summer dissolved into rainy October. It would take him suddenly and quietly, in the middle of a meal or a sentence. The upturned eyes, the soft swooning. After a while he would begin to mutter in some throaty dialect and toss and turn as if gripped by a dream, and then, by and by, he would come around. Despite my misgivings he still insisted on his solitary expeditions, and often I would wait up long after dark, picturing him caught by a fit in the cold night; but he always came back cheerful and muddy and composed, and it seemed that exercise kept the fits at bay, for when the weather was too foul even for him they became more frequent.

The local doctor suggested that it might be something to do with the head injury David had sustained in the accident which had killed his parents, and recommended a specialist in Bristol. But at the time there was no way of taking David there. The new security officer, Colonel Ames, had issued orders restricting travel and when I wrote to him, to ask if an exception might be made in David's case, there was no reply.

A week passed, and David suffered fits on two consecutive days. By then Bobby Dubois was due back from his furlough, and I wrote to him in turn. The next day Ames appeared at my house.

It was about nine o'clock, and I was waiting for David to return from one of his expeditions, already dressing-gowned and reading by the light of an oil lantern, when someone knocked at the front door: hard, spaced, and authoritarian. I feared that something had happened to David, but when I opened the door and held up the lantern with my stiff fingers I saw that it was something worse.

The burly man in camouflage jacket and trousers, his

head as shaven as any convict's, a pistol at his hip, said, 'I was passing by and I thought I'd look in. I hope you don't mind, Sir James. My name is Ames. Colonel Ames.'

'I see.'

He laughed at my visible disbelief. 'Listen, I really was in the area. We were after a couple of guerrillas. Caught one too. Would you like to see him?' He gestured towards the gate at the end of my drive, where two jeeps stood with their headlights burning, their engines ticking over.

'Not really,' I said, as calmly as I could.

'Well,' said Ames again. And then, 'Won't you invite me in?'

He did not sit but paced, almost prowled, about the room, looking at the titles on my bookshelves, running a gloved finger across the gleaming closed wing of the Steinway. A well-built man of about fifty, utterly self-assured.

After a minute I asked, 'May I enquire why you have chosen to visit me at such a late hour?' Sometimes there is no other course, in the face of our conquerors' crude brashness, but to put on the stiff-backed stiff-lipped show of British outrage.

'I was wondering if you'd noticed anything unusual here. Strangers, vehicles moving around after curfew, that kind of thing.'

'No. No, I haven't. Why do you ask? Is it something to do with those guerrillas you were chasing?'

'I think someone may be helping them locally, yes. Their attacks on our patrols in this area have been unusually well co-ordinated. But you say that you haven't seen anything.'

'No.'

'How about your nephew? I understand he roams around a lot. Maybe he can tell me something.'

But David was out, and it was after the curfew. I said, 'He's ill – I wrote to you about it and perhaps you remember that I mentioned that he suffers from fits. He hasn't been roaming around, as you put it, for some time now, and at the moment he is recovering from his latest episode. The doctor has insisted on absolute quiet.'

Ames touched the Steinway again, perhaps considering whether it was worth pushing me on that point. But after a moment he nodded and changed the subject, telling me that he owned several of my recordings. His manner was less peremptory now, but I was still uncomfortable beneath his scrutiny.

I murmured my usual excuse that all I had now was a great career behind me, and Ames smiled. 'I understand that Captain Dubois was trying to get you to play. I'd like that.'

'Not very possible, I'm afraid.'

'A pity. Well, it was a pleasure meeting you anyhow.'

At the door he could not resist a parting shot; or perhaps it was what he had come to tell me in the first place. 'Understand that when I say no, Sir James, that that is exactly what I mean. Without exception. It's no use appealing to your friend Dubois, because he has zero influence.'

So Ames had intercepted my second letter. I nodded stiffly and he casually saluted and crunched off down the drive towards the jeeps.

I was working on a glass of my carefully hoarded Scotch when I heard David come in. I cornered him in the hall and told him matter-of-factly about Ames' visit, and told him that I considered it too dangerous to be out after curfew from now on. I had expected a blazing argument, but he simply nodded, quite composed. It was as if he had expected it.

'I suppose it's for the best. Things are changing.'

I didn't think to ask what he meant by that, but I thought that that was an end of the matter. Of course, it was nothing of the kind.

The next day David suffered a fit just after he returned from school. I laid him out on the sitting-room sofa and soon he passed into the dream-state, sweat standing out on his forehead and his fists clenching and unclenching as he muttered hoarsely.

I sat with him until he came round, watching for an hour or more as he tossed and turned and muttered, the room darkening as the short afternoon wore out. My dead brother's features were coming into David's face, like the image which swims up at you as a photographic print develops; lean-cheeked and highbrowed, a long somewhat shapeless Irish nose peppered with wide pores. Then all of a sudden his eyes opened and he smiled up at me.

'It's getting closer.'

I asked him what he meant, but he was suddenly wary. 'I don't know, just a dream.'

I packed him off to bed and was preparing a cup of that universal English panacea, milky sugary tea, when the telephone sounded. It was Dubois, sounding faint and faraway although he said that he was calling from Yeovilton. 'I just got back and Ames has had my ass in the can already.'

'I'm dreadfully sorry. It was stupid of me not to realise it would cause trouble for you, but I really was desperate about David and I thought you could help.'

'Yeah, well that was only the half of it. Ames found out about those travel passes I worked out for you this summer. But listen, he was really only trying to scare me off, I think. There's word around here that something's coming down in your area tonight. Maybe Ames was trying to warn me off telling you.'

'What sort of thing?' I was holding the telephone as if it had somehow metamorphosed into a snake. It crackled and hissed in my ear.

'Something bad. Bad. Listen, I'll be over. On my bike it'll take maybe half an hour.'

'You needn't – ' But the line had gone dead.

I poached an egg for David's supper and took it and the tea up to him. But I was too restless to eat myself, too restless to sit with David for long. Bad, Dubois had said, and I supposed that it was something to do with the guerrillas Ames had told me were operating in the area. But why should it involve me? I paced up and down in the sitting room and twice went out onto the drive to listen for Dubois' motorcycle.

The second time I saw a flicker at the base of Cadbury Castle's dark mound – it was dusk now, the moon a pearly haze in low fast-moving cloud. I watched the hill but the light did not come again. More than forty minutes had passed and still no sign of Dubois. Sudden irrational fear gripped me and I went to telephone his office. But the instrument was dead; not even a dial tone.

Then I remembered David and went upstairs to see how he was. He was gone.

I walked quickly down the lane towards Cadbury Castle, an electric ball, pure nervousness, spinning in my stomach as I swung my torch from side to side, half-expecting to see David huddled on the ground. My knuckles ached numbly as they always did before rain and I found it difficult to hold the torch. The moon was completely hidden now, the tall hedges on either side a chiaroscuro of shadow. And then the torch-beam yellowed, flickered, faded. Old battery. I stuffed it into my coat pocket and slowly walked on through almost complete darkness.

There is a feeling I sometimes have when I am alone and outside after dusk, a childish irrational feeling of being watched by something inimical, something that is quietly, invisibly stalking me. I had that feeling as I groped my way down the lane; my skin tingled between my shoulderblades as if in anticipation of the predator's spring.

But what came out of the darkness was a shout, a command to halt. And then a harsh blinding beam of light. I squinted into it and saw a burly figure move towards me. It was Colonel Ames.

He ordered the light to be switched off, told me to walk towards him. I was suddenly aware of rain beginning to patter down, infrequent fat drops that made a quiet pocking amongst the leaves of the hedges. When I reached him, he said silkily, 'I hardly expected you to be involved, Sir James. All my reports suggested that you were harmless. Where's your friend Dubois, by the way? Yeah, I had a tap on your phone.'

'I am alone, Colonel. I believe that my nephew is somewhere on the hill. He has had an attack and won't know what he is doing, so I ask you to treat him gently if you find him.'

'Oh, we'll find him if he's up there, don't worry about that. That's why we're here.'

My eyes had readapted to the darkness by then. Parked at the end of the lane, in the lee of the trees which leaned out from the slope of the hill, was a jeep with two soldiers lounging beside it. I faintly heard the staticky spurts of its radio.

Ames told me, 'We couldn't figure out how they had been hitting our patrols in this area so accurately until we realised that someone must have been spotting them from the hill here. You can see for miles from the top on a clear night. I guess you know that. It was only on clear nights we were getting hit. Then intelligence told us to expect some action tonight. It was supposed to be a clear night too, until these clouds blew up.'

I wondered about Ames' source of intelligence, then remembered the captured guerrilla and what Dubois had told me about Ames' methods of interrogation, the reason why he had been demoted to this area. 'My nephew is only a boy. Surely you can't – '

'I surely can.' Ames' voice was smooth and hard and cold. 'Kids as young fought us in Salvador, in Nam. Younger. Kid up there with night-glasses, a CB outfit, could pin down the whole area. We found those items cached in the woods by the way. So don't – '

He was interrupted by a call from one of the soldiers by the jeep. He caught hold of my arm and roughly bundled me with him, took the handset from the soldier and listened intently to its faint voice. 'You're sure,' he said, and looked at me, his gaze burning through the gloom. The voice hissed and squawked and Ames said, 'Okay,' and returned the handset to the soldier, telling him, 'I'm going on up there. Pass the word and make sure everyone's alert.'

The concrete path up the hill was a barely visible glimmer beneath the trees. As we started up it the rain began to fall more heavily and a strong wind quickened the trees; it was as if the hill were sailing off into the darkness and we were climbing amongst its straining masts.

Ames pitched his voice above the wind and the noise of the trees. 'I have both paths sealed and men all around this place. All we have to do is go up and get him.'

I understand that this was to be a personal victory for Ames, a way of redemption. There was something in my throat, a constriction it was painful to speak past. 'David plays up here, that's all. This is some sort of ghastly coincidence.'

'The fuck it is.' Ames stopped walking, thrust his face close to mine. 'Didn't you wonder why Dubois never showed up? He was just now found on one of those crappy little roads you have around here. They'd stretched a wire from one side to the other and he ran right into it on that hog of his. Just about took his head off. Who else would know he was coming but your kid?'

'Bobby? Surely, no.' I seemed suddenly to be standing on the edge of a black slope pitching steeply down.

'You play your crappy headgames, you English, pretend everything is normal, but there's a fucking civil war going on. You won't face up to reality, that's why we're here. Well listen, your boy is up there as an accomplice to the men who killed Dubois. You want them to get away?'

I was saved from finding a reply. Somewhere above came the shocking rattle of automatic fire and then Ames was running on up the path. I followed without thought, hearing rather than seeing him as he ran, and came puffing up half a minute after he reached a pair of soldiers, heard one say something about this thing hitting a tree right by his head, someone taking off up the hill. There was a flash of torchlight and I saw for an instant the soldier's hand holding an arrow. I knew then, and the pit almost claimed me.

Ames was decisive: the soldiers were to keep their stations, he'd go on. 'This storm coming up, there isn't going to be any moonlight, so keep your eyes wide.'

As if to emphasise his words lightning flared and there was a dull explosion below: a bloom of ragged orange flame licked up beyond the trees.

Then Ames was running again. It was no longer pitch black, but if anything the fugitive light of the fire was worse than darkness. Half-seen trees seemed to leap at me, their branches writhing, as I followed Ames, and once again I felt that I was being stalked. The flickering darkness amongst the trees could have held anything.

When I left the shelter of the trees the rain hit with a thousand cold needles, soaking me through in a moment. I stopped, absolutely out of breath, my legs quivering. I was used to strolling, not running, up that path.

Ames came back to me, and I shouted that we would never find anyone in this.

'Your boy's friends found the goddamned jeep!'

'That was lightning. They shouldn't have parked near the trees. If we go up there we could be struck ourselves.'

'You know that kid. Get him to come quietly and I promise he won't be hurt.' He grabbed my arm and more or less hauled me up the path.

As we climbed lightning cracked the dark streaming

clouds again and again, as if we were mounting an auditorium lit by flashbulbs. When we reached the top the greatest bolt so far burst directly overhead, and I glimpsed David halfway across the huge field, blurred by drifting rain, an arrow fitted in his half-raised bow. Then the light was gone and Ames' pistol made its own puny thunder and lightning beside my ear.

Sometimes we act despite ourselves. I threw myself at Ames and more by luck than judgement clawed the pistol from his hand. But I couldn't fit my stiff fingers around its trigger and as I flung it away he was on top of me, cursing hard and pounding me with his fists. My heavy coat, made heavier by the rain, protected me from the worst, but one blow caught the side of my head and for a moment I passed out.

And came to as thunder rolled overhead, glimpsed Ames running hard towards David a moment before lightning took him, blue-white fire that instantly obliterated his shadow, a vast tree of jagged light that raked every corner of the sky. Then it was gone, and thunder smashed down.

I remember little more. Ozone seared my throat and a sensation as of pinpricks covered every inch of my body. I was lying in darkness, quiet rain, no longer the downpour of the storm, only rain, falling on the grass all around. I felt rather than saw David as he stooped over me.

'I have to go now, Uncle Jimmy. I have to. It's what I was born for, don't you see? But look after this for me, I don't need it now.'

I may have dreamed it. But later, when the soldiers had finished questioning me and had satisfied themselves that I could tell them nothing coherent, when I had returned home and was alone once more, I found the coin, David's good luck piece, in one of my pockets. The blurred profile: the enigmatic mocking inscription.

I write this four years after the event, in the middle of

a time of changes, a time of war. The guerrillas finally
arose from their scattered outposts this spring; now it is
September, and they have conquered as far west as
Bristol, even now lay siege to Oxford. Every day a dozen
or so refugees trickle into the camp where I work,
bringing rumours that soon the guerrillas will march on
London. And rumours too of their leader, conflicting and
various to be sure, yet all agree that he is very young, and
very sure. And one woman who claimed to have seen him
in the ruins of Birmingham told me that he was red-
haired.

I am afraid. Not of the troubles – I have had my life –
but for what may come when they are over. If David was
right, and the old gods have arisen to defend their island,
what will they want after their victory? The needs of men
and gods so rarely coincide. If David was raised up by
them, then surely the accident which killed his parents
was a part of their plan. And the arthritis which ended
my career and led to my retirement in the shadow of
Cadbury Castle, and Bobby Dubois' murder . . . These
are bitter thoughts.

I can only hope that David has wisdom as well as
strength of purpose. I can only hope that the gods will
again sink far beyond the knowledge of men when they
are satisfied that the danger is passed, and fade from our
history as a troubling dream fades when we awake.

THOMAS M. DISCH

CANNED GOODS

In the downstairs lobby Mr Weyman's handgun was taken from him by one of the four uniformed guards and locked in a mailbox. No such requirement was made of his escort, whose name was Lenny. When Lenny followed him into the dark stairwell, Mr Weyman went through a short inward crisis of unreasoning paranoia, followed by an inward sigh of resignation to the dictates of fate followed by a brief but intense rapture of anger at the way he was being made to co-operate in his own fleecing. It was just as well they'd taken his gun away in the lobby, or he might have done something foolish when he finally got to see this Shroder person.

He must not let himself flare up. Survival was all that mattered. He had survived the winter. Now if he could just last out the spring, the government would surely have found some way by then to restore the city to a semblance of order. The crisis could not just keep going on and on and on. It had to stop, and then things would return to normal.

On the sixth floor landing Mr Weyman was obliged to stop to catch his breath. During the entire long trek downtown his escort had never once offered to help Mr Weyman with his precious parcel in its swaddlings of old clothes and taped and stapled-together shopping bags. Now Mr Weyman's arms and back ached, his sinuses were beginning to pulse ominously, and his lungs were heaving.

It wouldn't do to arrive at Shroder's door out-of-breath and beet-red.

'Is it much farther up?'

'Fourteen,' replied the ever-laconic Lenny.

Mr Weyman demanded rest stops again on 9 and 12, and so when Shroder came to the door and asked him in, he was able to respond without major heavings and gaspings. He even had breath to laugh at Shroder's (and all the world's) little joke about having to complain to the landlord to get the elevator fixed.

Shroder led him into a large drawing room made to seem small with overmuch furniture. Not so much furniture that one was put in mind at once of Noah's ark, but a good deal more (Mr Weyman was certain) than had been here at the start of the crisis. Nor were the walls hung chock-a-block with the choicest of his recent acquisitions, as one might have expected. There was a small flower painting over the mantle (Fantin-Latour?), a vintage Derain between the windows, and, in the place of honour opposite the couch on which Mr Weyman was seated, a large, expensively framed academic nude, reclining her peaches-and-cream buttocks on masses of maroon velvet, all very correct and not a little lubricious.

From Mr Weyman's viewpoint this was not entirely reassuring. That nude, in particular, spoke of a taste that caters to the requirements of Arab oil sheikhs. The Derain, on the other hand, offered *some* hope. Indeed, despite himself, Mr Weyman could not resist an altogether incongruous twinge of envy. For all that he delighted in the Fauves, he'd never owned a first-rate work by one of them.

'Shall we,' said Shroder, 'get right to business?'

'By all means.' Mr Weyman began undoing the swaddlings of his parcel.

'I hope you won't mind if Lenny puts this on videotape. I should like to have evidence that our transaction has been entered into, on both sides, freely and without constraint. Should there ever be any question.'

'I quite understand, and I'm scarcely in a position to object. Indeed, I'm grateful to be allowed to come here *and* for the escort your friend provided. No one likes to carry large parcels about on the street these days. Though if I knew I were going to be on camera, I might have dressed with a little more care.'

'Oh, we all must wear camouflage on the streets these days. This is the era, necessarily, of *in*conspicuous consumption.'

Mr Weyman placed his first offering on the low table before the couch.

'Ah-ha!' said Shroder, making no effort to disguise his pleasure. 'Fiske Boyd, and a good one. Though, of course, for a woodcut there's an obvious limit to what I can offer.'

Mr Weyman regarded the Boyd woodcut with a regretful love admixed with some vanity. It represented an arrangement of canned goods on a tabletop, very spare, very assured. He had bought it in '88 when Boyd's reputation, and his prices, were already on the rise. His prices since had peaked, but never declined, and Mr Weyman could congratulate himself (in this instance) on his acumen as an investor.

'It's chiefly for his woodcuts that Boyd's admired,' Mr Weyman pointed out with the confidence that comes of having the judgement of the market behind one.

'Yes, of course. I only meant that there's a limit to what I can afford to offer for even the *finest* woodcut. What is the date, by the way?'

'1930.' There was no need to add that it was in miraculously mint condition.

'Yes. Well . . .' Shroder nodded significantly towards the shopping bag, as much as to say, 'Let's move along.'

Shyly, with a sense almost of exposing himself, Mr

Weyman took out what he regarded as his trump card – a large, chastely-framed Motherwell collage/drawing.

Shroder formed his lips into an O of disappointment.

'I realise, of course, that Motherwell no longer commands the prices he once did.'

Shroder emitted a derisive snort, like the erasure of a laugh. 'Indeed! in *that* respect Motherwell remains at the forefront of the avant-garde.'

'You're speaking of what happened to the six paintings in the *Elegy* series at the Black Saturday auction? If the gallery had been allowed to put floors on the prices – '

'If pigs could fly! There was no one buying abstract expressionism at that point but museums and investors. Once the museums started unloading, you don't think the *investors* wouldn't follow suit, do you?'

Mr Weyman looked down at his Motherwell sadly. Only four years ago he'd brought it from a friend in dire circumstances for $200. The friend had paid several thousand dollars for it in the late '60s.

'I was there that day,' Mr Weyman said. 'Were you?'

'On Black Saturday? Hardly. I would have been eleven years old.'

'It's something I'll never forget. I remember how I lusted after those Motherwells. But by the time they'd come under the hammer I'd already emptied my own bank account, and the Zurich gallery I was acting for wasn't touching anything that went under an artist's established price level by more than 50%. I remember the silences that day. They'd halve a price, and halve it again, and still no one would *bid*. A Poons for twelve hundred. Well, perhaps that's not unthinkable. Tastes change, and if one paints on such an institutional scale, and institutions decide to stop investing in art, what's to be done? But a Braque for seven hundred? Braque?'

'Mr Weyman, may I remind you, that it's not Braque's merits at issue here, but Motherwell's.'

'Excuse me. I'm in no position to argue. But I must at

least be allowed to point out that this drawing was hung
at the '65 retrospective at the Modern.'

'I don't care if it hung at the Louvre next to the Mona
Lisa. It is my long-standing opinion that Motherwell was
never anything more than the favourite tailor of a very
naked emperor. Any third year art student with savvy
coaching from a competent interior decorator could produce such *wallpaper* by the roll. The days are gone when
a painter can claim a day's wages for two minutes' work,
because he's spent a lifetime refining his taste. I'm sorry,
Mr Whistler, but art is not p.r. Sorry to you too, Mr
Motherwell, but *this* sort of thing – ' He tapped the scrap
of a Gauloise pack that lent its little note of colour to the
drawing. ' – just won't do. Not in the 21st century.'

'Well, if you don't want it,' Mr Weyman said with a
resentment he was unable to conceal, 'you needn't take
it. I have faith that Motherwell's day will return. I am
sorry for your sake that you do not.'

'As to my *taking* it, Mr Weyman, I have a fixed policy,
as I believe our mutual friend at Sotheby's explained to
you: I buy by the lot. My overhead costs don't allow me
the luxury of haggling. Now . . . let's see what else you
have.'

Mr Weyman removed the Burchfield canvas from his
shopping bag, which, no longer braced by the painting's
stretcher, flopped sideways to the carpet (a very choice
Sarouk in a floral design).

'Ah. This is more like it!'

Shroder took the Burchfield in his hands and turned it
at different angles to the light, as though studying the
facets of a gemstone. It was a painting of a Christmas
tree, but a Christmas tree seen in its eternal aspect, each
light aureoled and the several aureoles overlapping and
interweaving in an elaborate seine of interference patterns. The paint seemed to tremble like tinsel on a tree.

'This,' said Shroder reverently, 'cannot be easy to part
with. I'll give you the best price I can. Let me think. For

the Fiske Boyd I'll give you, let's say an even ten cans of tuna? No, it's in mint condition; let's make it a round dozen. For the Motherwell – a pound of elbow macaroni. Which is more than it's worth. For the Burchfield – '

He took the small canvas to the window and basked in the glow of its beauty. 'For the Burchfield I shall let Lenny take you into the stockroom, and you may fill up one plastic carrier bag with whatever you fancy, excepting only the caviar. There's a limit of three jars per customer on that.'

'That's very good of you, Mr Shroder. Very generous, indeed. Thank you.' Mr Weyman reached for the handles of his shopping bag.

'One moment, Mr Weyman. I seem to remember that our friend said you would be bringing me *four* pieces to consider.'

'Yes . . . but the fourth is just . . . a bagatelle. A frippery. Nothing more than a serigraph. If I'd had a better sense, beforehand, of your preferences I'd never have brought it.'

'But you have brought it – I see the end of the cardboard tube poking out of your bag. And you've roused my curiosity with what you say. I must remind you that I buy only by the lot.'

Reluctantly Mr Weyman took the cardboard tube from the recumbent shopping bag, undid the knots of the plastic strip that bound the print of the tube, and unrolled the print. He'd bought the print in the first days after the collapse of the market for what he'd then considered a song – considering its sales history. It had been a very famous work of art in its day.

Shroder crowed with pleasure. 'Oh, Mr Weyman! How droll! And of course I have *just* the thing to give you in exchange. The perfect barter.'

He went into his stockroom and returned with a can of Campbell's Tomato Soup.

GARRY KILWORTH

SPIRAL SANDS

There must be the hawk with defective eye-sight. There
must be the Bedu tribesman who is not a crackshot:
whose family is resigned to meals without meat. There
must be the Ethiopian who cannot run; the clumsy
mountain goat; the pigeon without a sense of direction.
There must be these misfits that fail to reach the common
standard of their kind. I was such a creature – a poet
without the gift of fine words – a man born to a love of
poetry which could not be satisfied by merely reading the
works of others but had to have some *definite* connection
with the art.

I finally resigned myself to the fact that I would never
write any great verse. At times I had thought that I was
close to those lines. Times when I woke in the middle of
the night with the faint hum of something on the edge of
my brain, which, once pen and paper were to hand,
eluded me and left me weeping in frustration. I had been
in places – climbing a mountain; running for a bus;
entertaining a lovely woman – when inspiration came
upon me, sometimes like an exotic snake, sliding into my
consciousness; sometimes as a beautiful bull that thun-
dered upon my sensibility and stood there, snorting white
plumes and defying captivity. Yet, when the first opportunity to put those thoughts, those dreams into words was
available, they fled from me, never to be recovered. *The
poem* was destined to be always just out of my grasp and
I was getting older. The days were greyer and shorter

than they used to be and time was slipping through my fingers faster than a dying *affaire*.

Consequently, when I heard of the man, I felt that there, there was my last chance to achieve immorality through my one and only love, through poetry. Admittedly, it was to be a compromise – my fame would be established through the discovery of another poet, yet the sponsor can achieve almost as much recognition as the artist if handled carefully. I had reached an age where time had blunted the edge of my pride with its swift succession of yearly blows. I needed a strong connection with the art to satisfy my yearning, my longing to *become* part of it. To have ignored the opportunity would have been to condemn myself to an unfulfilled life, a life not without purpose but without the least taste of success. I would have died empty with nothing but a gravestone to mark my passing through the temporal zone. It was Carey, the soldier-of-fortune, the adventurer, who gave me the first clue.

I was sitting in the corner of a pub that stands close to London Bridge, where pseudo-literary types gather seeking company in their own kind, when Carey entered with a young lady he introduced as his niece. She left us almost immediately to join some rather loud friends imitating peacocks in both dress and manner. Carey bought me a drink and I asked him where he had been. Carey was always just back from somewhere.

'The Hadhramaut, old chap. Been looking at some interesting caves there with a friend.' He saw my frown and added, 'South Yemen desert.'

'What sort of caves?' I asked, simply for the sake of conversation. 'I mean, was your interest archaeological, geological or anthropological?'

He gave me a sort of half-smile. 'One of those . . . there were some paintings which might have been interesting. Turned out that they were of more recent origin than I had hoped. However . . . can't win 'em all. What about you? Still running that magazine for little old ladies with a literary bent? Poetry, isn't it?'

I ignored the apparent sneer. 'No. I gave it up three months ago. I had hoped to discover some hitherto hidden star, as they say, but as *you* imply, the contributors were lacking in that vital ingredient – talent.'

'Pity. Great pity. What about your own work?'

I glared hard at the table, declining to answer and after a while, Carey took the hint and stopped staring at my hairline. We sat in an uncomfortable silence for a time then Carey said abruptly, 'I might have something for you.' He reached into his pocket and produced a piece of folded paper.

'What is it?' I asked, leaving the paper where it lay, amongst the beer slops on the table.

He reached across with one hand and opened it. I could see about six-and-a-half lines of writing in what appeared to be Arabic. Beneath these lines was a pencilled translation.

'Well?' I said.

'Found it written in charcoal, on a cave wall. The rains were due and as the place was deep in a wadi, there was the possibility – well, certainty – that this would have been washed away with the flood. I thought of you and your tireless search for poetic talent. This looks like a fragment of something . . .'

I snatched it up and read the lines.

'Are you serious?' I said, after a while.

'Perfectly. I read Arabic, you see. That's my translation. Someone with more *feel* for the thing could do a better job, I've no doubt. God knows I haven't any pretensions . . .'

'I know. You once sent me a poem for my magazine. You called yourself Sybil Smith.'

He laughed at that, making heads turn and me feel foolish. The blond hair flopped over the handsome face almost obscuring his blue eyes. Carey had everything he

needed for his chosen role in life – everything the potential adventurer needed – good looks, contacts, a private
income, a fine physique, courage, audacity, mental alert-
ness, a touch of aristocracy – everything. It was sickening.

'All right,' I said, 'it wasn't that funny. Jameson told
me it was you – after I'd made a fool of myself. How do I
know this isn't a hoax?'

Immediately he leaned on the table and tried to assume
a serious countenance but his eyes still betrayed an
undercurrent of amusement.

'I'm sorry Alec, but you're such a . . . look, who was it
who had that awful argument with me in a Chelsea pub
about modern poets? I said they didn't make sense . . .
and you said . . . Anyway, let's forget that. This is no
joke. I'm not that cruel.'

'Perhaps. Let's have a look . . .'

I trailed the sentence and read the fragment over again.
The translation would be bland. As he admitted, Carey
was no poet.

'Can I keep this?' I asked, after a while.

He nodded. 'You can keep it but . . . if you want to
take it further, don't forget to give *me* a call. I've a good
idea who wrote that . . . people talk in the empty quarter,
to pass the time, and I've heard a name . . . in your own
language, like *a whisper on the wind*. Give me a call.' He
finished his beer and then left. The niece remained with
her group in the corner. Perhaps she really was his niece?

I sought out a friend at Oxford who did a better job of
the translation. The lines were, most definitely, intriguing.
They had a certain depth, a quality, which was not easy
to grasp. The ambiguity in the short phrases fired my
imagination and I spent many hours poring over the
fragment, trying to decide whether there was something
of real worth there. It was difficult to tell with so short a
piece but finally I took a positive stance and called Carey.
'I want you to teach me Arabic,' I said. If I were to go
looking for this nomadic poet, I needed to learn his

language. To translate a masterpiece into a lasting work
of art was almost as rewarding as being the creator of that
masterpiece. Edward Fitzgerald is as well-known and
respected as Omar Khayam. I might have been chasing
ghosts but what did it matter? At least I would be doing
something.

For the next two years I studied hard. Languages has
never been one of my blocks, though I have many of
those, and even Carey was surprised at my progress, I
went back to Oxford and stayed there until I felt I had
mastered the thing well enough to begin the search. Of
course, I should have to continue with my study but I had
my life's work at last. My enthusiasm was boundless. The
thought that my poet might have died or stopped writing
did cross my mind occasionally but I soon dismissed it. I
am a great believer in fate, and God would not have
placed such a tempting quest before me just to snatch it
back once the hard work was done. No god could be that
vindictive. Carey and I left for the Hadhramaut in October. He was almost as excited as I was but I suspected it
was merely the expedition that was responsible for his
frame of mind, not the purpose behind it.

The desert moves into your soul. Once you have
allowed your senses to absorb its atmosphere, you can
never get it out of your heart. Lawrence and Thesiger had
been seduced by the desert and I was influenced by its
immense powers of attraction, I am sure, as strongly as
they. It is strange that a monotonous empty landscape can
appear more beautiful, more exotic, than a hundred
different skylines full of shape and colour. It produced a
yearning in my breast that left me with a physical ache,
never to be healed. The desert is magnificent in its sense
of space and time, and absence of tangible presence.
There is a sense of anticipation about the wasteland, as if
it is waiting for some great enactment to be played out on
its vast, undulating stage.

The desert barely touches life with the occasional gazelle or hawk but its odour is as intoxicating as opium and just as addictive. Once you have smelled the desert you have to return, again and again, to satisfy that created need. The privation it forces upon the traveller does not produce a hostility towards it: on the contrary, it creates a closeness, a spiritual marriage between the animate and the inanimate. One might take a handful of sand, or a basket of rocks, and say, 'This is the desert, for there is little else.' Yet, it is not the substance, the material, that fashions the desert, it is the lack of all else, the wide stretches of lonely nothingness under a furnace of sun or canopy of cold stars. You do not breathe the desert, the desert breathes you, filling its void with your spirit. In the daytime the heat is like a hammer striking the ground with dull blows and at night the frost finds fissures in the rocks with the sureness of steel chisels.

I had learned that the name of the elusive poet was Al-Qata and that he was a Bedu without a family, a lone nomad. We stocked up with provisions at the village of Muraq and hired two guides and six camels – dromedaries in this part of the world. We began our quest.

At sunset, several months later, we found some strange markings in the sand beside a well. They could have been words – I was positive they were – but the wind had distorted the letters, had blown the sand away until they were barely perceptible and impossible to decipher. As we sat and ate our evening meal, I said to Carey, 'I think we're close. I feel it, strongly. Do you think we're close?'

'I think . . .' he said in measured tones, as he chewed on a roasted bird the guides had caught, 'I think there would be more meat on the wing of an emaciated bat than there is on his fowl.'

'But . . . look, Carey. This is important.'

He grunted. 'So is this bird.'

And he was right. Over the months our bodies had hardened to nomadic life in the empty quarter, and hard-

ship had brought us closer to our environment. Without
possessions, except those necessary to exist at subsistence
level, we had been stripped naked of our civilised selves
and had been reduced to the essence of humanity. Life only
was important and our next meal, a meal necessary to
survive, could not be found at the corner shop. The roast
bird was the most important thing in our lives at that instant
in time and the quest was merely secondary. We gnawed
our respective bones in silence.

The next day, however, my anxiety had returned and I
rose before dawn and went to the highest point in the
vicinity to see if I could spot smoke from any distant fire.
The freezing air which had stiffened my joints during the
night retreated before the rising of the sun and soon the
cold rocks began to heat, expanding quickly, sometimes
cracking apart with the sound of a gunshot. Lizards
emerged and skunks and small snakes, all eager for
warmth. The desert swelled in size and with life. Soon the
stones were hot enough to feel through my sandals and
tendrils of heat rose from the ground to warp my vision
of distant objects. We were close to the Yemen and I
could see, far off, the city of Sana'a, perched on its
plateau, rising up out of the cliff of red sandstone, the
rose-coloured walls of its houses a continuation of the
rock, embedded deep in its face. The natural and man-
made was a single entity and it was impossible to tell
where one left off and the other began. We would need
to go east soon, for the Yemenis were hostile to strangers,
suspicious of anyone who was not a cousin or closer in
blood. The fierce Bedu families we occasionally met on
the trail were contained by the desert code but not so the
city dwellers. Not just xenophobic; they had their own set
of ethics which did not include hospitality high on the list.

I scanned the horizon for smoke but seeing none, returned to the well. Carey was up and placing dried camel
dung on the hot ashes of the previous night's fire. His face

was raw and almost burned black by the sun. I wondered if anyone amongst his occidental friends, barring myself, would have recognised him. He might have been a nomad for all his life until that moment and I knew I presented a similar picture.

I checked the marks in the sand again in the full light of day. They could have been the scratchings of a lizard or bird. It was impossible to tell. We continued our endless journey, turning east and into the Great Sandy Desert.

For the next few years we followed Al-Qata over the deserts and mountains and always he was tantalisingly close, yet not quite within reach. We received reports of his possible presence in this region, or that area, from fellow travellers. We never met anyone who had actually *seen* him but our informants had heard second-hand of his whereabouts. When the money ran out we let our guides go, having become accustomed to the trails ourselves and no longer being in need of them. We lived by shooting the occasional gazelle or wild goat and trading for ammunition and provisions.

Al-Qata was like a ghost, an elusive phantom who left his mark here and there on a rock or in the sand. But never enough to make me sure that this was my man, or indeed that he *was* one and not *many*, but enough to keep my curiosity primed. Once I became ill and was taken in by a local sheikh but as soon as I was well enough we went back on the trail again, searching, ever searching. We read the Quran by the fire at night, myself delighting in its poetic content and Carey interested enough in the fundamental religious issues that bound it all together. We visited Mecca, once, and managed to avoid detection as European infidels. We were concerned by Carey's blue eyes though such a deviation was rare, it was not unique. No race on earth is pure enough to escape the consequences of inter-breeding and there are red-headed Arabs, blue-eyed Arabs and Arabs with fair skins. Mecca, with its golden domes and white Arabesque architecture,

was of course beautiful, but after the desert it meant little
to me. I wanted to be back amongst the rocks, out on the
dust.

The quest for Al-Qata, my mysterious poet, was both
an arduous and mystical experience: the days spent high
on the camel chasing horizons and the nights in thankful
but often-interrupted rest. At all times we were lost in
profound contemplation of our purpose: what were we
doing here? Pursuing the unattainable in the infinite? The
desert was not, of course, infinite, but it had the appearance of limitless space and while I did not believe Al-
Qata was unattainable, he was as elusive as Big Foot or
the Abominable Snowman: a spiral wind drifting across
the dust.

There are those abstract aspects of life that have eluded
most women and men from the beginning of time –
fulfilment, contentment, happiness, love – especially love.
We seek these intangibles up and down the days of our
lives, never quite getting within grasping distance, but
also never falling so far behind that we are tempted to let
them go and give up the quest. They are, like Al-Qata
was, always *just* out of reach. We feel if we could only
stretch just that little bit more, get our fingertips to them
. . . we would be there. Yet we never do quite make it
and we are afraid to stand still for a moment in case they
get too far ahead. But what if we did stop? And wait?
Perhaps they would come to us? No. The risk is too great.
We must pursue. It is in our nature. No prey ever wanders
into the lazy hunter's den and climbs into his larder.

One day in June we thought we saw a man buried up to
his waist in sand, appealing for help, but as we drew close
and the heat waves no longer distorted our vision, we
realised it was a corpse. The man had died sitting up, with
his arms reaching forward, as if grasping onto upright bars
for support. How had the body remained in that position,
after life had finally flickered and died, leaving the carcass
to dehydrate into a waxpaper husk? Why hadn't the

kitehawks descended to feast on the dead flesh? There was something vaguely unnatural about the whole scene and I knew Carey was uneasy too. It was almost as if this hollow-eyed corpse, with the ants busy between its teeth, had been placed there, carefully, for us to find it. Were we being given a warning of some kind?

Yet . . . ? Yet perhaps not a warning but a *welcome*. The arms were open, ready to embrace, as if the desert had created this effigy in order to remind us that death was as close to it as life, and that we had to accept death readily, and with as much *approval* as we accepted life.

We buried the corpse in a shallow grave without straightening the limbs and continued on our way. Carey never mentioned it again, and neither did I, but the image of the sitting corpse returned with shocking frequency – sometimes as a vivid dream at night; sometimes during the day I caught sight of it out of the corner of my eye, as we crossed a ridge, or entered a low valley, making me jerk in on my mount. The images plagued me and I did not understand why. Then, one year later, we were passing the place where the corpse was buried and I crept away in the middle of the night intending to exhume it. I wanted to embrace death, place my cheek against its cold bone in order to exorcise the images, but the corpse had either been moved or I was digging in the wrong place. In any case, the dreams ceased after that night, and I was left in peace.

The horizon rippled in the distance. One day there was a half-sentence in the clay beside a well. In several years I had found enough of Al-Qata's work to cover only a few pages of my notebook. Yet I felt vaguely fulfilled. I travelled in the faint ripples which formed his wake as he moved ahead of me, leaving his barely-existent signs on rock and sand. His touch on the world was light, the traces of his coming and going as transient as desert dew. Foolishly, I began searching for even less distinguishable signs – the brush of his *jalabiya* on the flowers of a shrub;

the mark of his sandal on the dunes that roll across the
wasteland as surely as ocean waves, if a thousand times
slower; the pattern of his rope *agal* upon an oasis palm. I
was content that we shared the same moon, the same
stars, the same arduous way of life. These common factors
bound us together in spirit. The click of the beetle
amongst the stones had been heard by him just a short
time before the sound fell upon my ears. The scurry of
the scorpion had attracted his notice just prior to mine.
Was that his camel that I smelled on the breeze? Were
the pie-dog's distant cries prompted by his presence? Was
that silhouette on the far ridge, stark in the sunset, him?
Al-Qata, the poet?

Carey was happy to go where my instinct took me. He
drank his tea, spoke his words, and tended his camels
with as much complacency as a successful businessman
contemplates his material wealth. He was as happy with
his hard lifestyle as was any millionaire with his luxury.
We had found peace. We were our own breed, proud of
our adopted land. We would have defended a single grain
of the vast sea of dust as ferociously as if it had been a
nation, clinging to it as tenaciously as a dictator clings to
his autocracy. There were no classical lovers who gave
themselves to each other as completely as we gave ourselves to the desert.

One evening, we made camp at Wadi Hafa.

'A long time,' said Carey, staring into the flank of the
dark night. The words were comfortable.

'What's that?' I asked.

'We've been here . . . I don't know how long. Do you
think you'll ever go home now . . . back to England?'

I stared into the hooded face before me. The fire fizzed
and hissed as it ate through the camel dung, flaring
occasionally to emphasise the dark lines on Carey's face,
rather than highlighting the prominent brow and cheek
bones. Behind him the rock forms whispered with desert
life: beetles, spiders and scorpions, sandflies and snakes.

His features were almost as rugged as the ochre rock and the cracks and creases in the rust-coloured skin appeared to contain as many hidden life forms as the *jebel* behind him.

'No,' I replied. 'Will you?'

'I . . . no. No, I'm here for good.' There was a note of satisfaction in his voice which I found disturbing, but he continued. 'One becomes integrated, doesn't one? It's almost as if I were part of the desert now – mutable but irremoveable. The desert is in me and I in it. We have fused, become a unified body.'

'Carey?' There was a question I wanted to ask him which had been on my mind for some time but I had not asked it because . . . well, I think I was afraid of what the answer would be.

'Yes, the desert is the beginning and the end of life,' he said, as if he had not heard me. 'The two polarities of evolution. Which end are we at, I wonder? The birth or the death? Are we witnessing the flowering of a new world or the fading of an old one?'

'Poetry,' I said. 'That's what I want to talk to you about. Carey, is Al-Qata real . . . ? I mean, I want the truth. Is there such a man?'

Carey leaned back, with his hands behind his head, staring up into the dark sky.

'Shooting star,' he said. 'Amazing things . . . who knows? I didn't invent him, that's for sure. I mean, I haven't been laying false trails all these years. But I did *use* him. You see, the sand found its way into my blood when I was here before. I knew I would have to come back – the call was too strong. Compulsion. It was as if all my ancestors had gathered in one place and with one unified voice, a single mental concentration, were compelling me to join them.

'I didn't want to return alone. I was afraid . . . afraid of the silence, and the space and the solitude. *The timeless-*

ness. Those are terrible things to have to experience by oneself. The empty quarter . . . I wanted it, had to have it . . . the winds, the wasteland, the harsh, private life, but not alone. You were different from me, someone with an appreciation of natural beauty. The ideal companion for a man of practical stamp – a man who lacks the imagination to express what he feels. Although your poetry – the way you put your feelings into words – might not be considered great art, it does things for me. You find the words, you see, where I cannot. You express my sentiments without me having to tax my brain for what is, eventually, an inadequate expression. So I told you about Al-Qata.' He sat up abruptly and stared at me with those incongruous blue eyes.

'So far as I know, he's a living, breathing man but I could be wrong. Maybe he's a myth – a kind of siren figure that calls people like you and me to the desert? Once here, we never get away – because we don't really want to go. Like the lotus eaters, we have been hypnotised by the land. We no longer have a will of our own – it belongs to the desert.

'Al-Qata may be some poet of the empty quarter . . . a camel driver, a trader, at footloose dreamer. A person of flesh and blood. Or he may be a magical manifestation of the dust and rock that surrounds us and wishes to call its favourites to its breast, to hold them there until they truly become part of it, until it takes its own to itself as ashes and dust. We will drift on spiral winds, you and I. The grains of our dead bones will swell the desert, imperceptibly – but there will be more and more of us, until the desert has grown to cover the whole earth, and we will then finally be *one*. A single, unified presence.'

I stirred the fire with a twig and saw his eyes brighten in the sudden glare. Carey was right. This was our spiritual home. How we came here was of no importance. Here we were and here we would die, whether by a Bedu's bullet or of thirst or hunger . . . it did not matter. Perhaps there were more of us already? Who could tell?

We looked like Arabs, we spoke like Arabs, we told our campfire stories and sang our song of past tribal glories. We were the desert, the desert was us.

'The sand is our bed and the sky our tent,' I said. Carey nodded.

'For the rest of our natural lives,' he added.

We settled down and Carey passed me a quid of *qāt* grass. We did not chew the drug often but there were times when we felt the need to commit ourselves fully to insensibility. *Qāt* allows you to drift into a kind of timeless lethargy, where the ache in your bones melts into the sand leaving your body drifting on the dust with the night pulsing through your veins.

I lay there, looking up at the skies, chewing slowly on the grass. After a while I focused on a single star, Sirius, and it seemed to me that this one jewel held the universe together, keeping the movements of the night in harmony with its delicate force. Hairspring constellations trembled above me. Then the night sky melted into a softer image of dew-covered webs, and suddenly I felt if Sirius were to fall, myraids would descend with it, like white rain, leaving darknesses folding into a deeper dark.

As I lay there, allowing myself to be seduced by these thoughts, I became aware that another man was sharing our fire. Visits from strangers were of course infrequent, but not unique, and the desert code provided that we shared the warmth of our fire, food and drink with those who were in need. The *qāt* was having its full effect on my brain and I saw him only as stark, intermittent images, as if I were observing him under a strobe light. His finely-drawn features bore an inherent air of preoccupation. The bright eyes sought their own secrets in the fire and we, Carey and I, remained on some vague periphery of their attention, as if we were no more relevant to the scene than another shrub or rock. Shadows filled the hollows in his cheeks and the narrow nose emphasised the blade-like quality of his face. At times he seemed to be merely eating and drinking, but I also had momentary visions of him with a brushwood twig in his hand as he scratched away at the dusk. Shortly afterwards I fell asleep.

The following morning we rose as usual with the sun. Our guest had already left us, silently, before the first rays had stirred the camels into vocal agitation and we had crooned them back to calmness. We broke camp, neither of us mentioning the visitor, and I collected what charcoal remained from the dead fireplace. Beside the white ashes were some marks in the dust. Without pausing to study them further, I erased them with my foot – an action prompted by some deep motive which had not crystallised into any definite awareness. Immediately afterwards I was even a little appalled at my rash act and turned to speak to Carey, but he was doing something with the bedrolls, humming a tune to himself through cracked lips, and I changed my mind. He looked up at me after a while and gave me a grim smile.

'What price an April shower?' he said.

'More than you can afford,' I replied.

A few moments later, I noticed he appeared to be surreptitiously studying some faint indentations in the sand where the morning breeze was stirring dust and filling hollows. They might have been our own tracks from the previous day, or an animal's spoor, or . . . anything. They seemed to be heading, or coming from, the east, where the sun was climbing up the sky.

'Let's strike out north,' Carey said, briskly. 'Maybe he's been back to the hills again?' I nodded, and we returned to our separate tasks with deliberate meticulous efficiency.

Two months later we met with some trouble which I believe had something to do with water rights, at a small well in the Fakhiri valley. There were three Bedu, two old men whose faces were masked by their hoods and a boy of about sixteen, a son or nephew of one of the other two, no doubt, since the Bedu almost always travelled in families. They came in as we were watering the camels, we exchanged salaams with them, but then they left without watering their own mounts, which was too unusual to ignore. There was also something rather chilling in the way they had studied our faces.

When they were three hundred yards away they turned and fired in unison. Though we had been half expecting the attack, it still had an element of surprise and the thing that remained in my memory the strongest was not the sound of the volley and its subsequent echoes down the valley, but the awful smell as my new pack-camel defaecated in fright. We ran for the rocks and Carey took a shot in the chest just as we reached them. It was a flesh wound – I could see the blood underneath his armpit where the bullet had come out. Having unslung my own weapon on the run I helped him with his and we began returning the fire. After a further exchange of shots one of the saddles of the camels was empty, the beast itself careering round in tight circles. The remaining two Bedu struck out for the open desert.

We waited for several hours.

'I'm going out to look,' I told Carey. He had his hand over the stain on his chest and refused to allow me to look at it.

'Don't be long,' he said. 'I want to dress this thing again – the pad is completely soaked.'

'Shall I do it now?'

'No, no. Don't worry. I'll be all right. Be careful . . . they may be back. The other two.'

I walked slowly across the dust to the fallen Bedu, my eyes alert for his kin. His mount was nosing around nervously about thirty yards away as I knelt down beside him. He was dead: the first man I had ever hurt, let alone killed, though I felt no remorse, just a kind of bleak emptiness. One arm was twisted underneath his back and his left foot had caught under his right knee and formed a

triangle. But it was his face that startled me. I then
recognised the sharp features of the man who had visited
our fire two months previously. My bullet had hit him in
the abdomen – not a wound that one would normally
have expected to kill instantaneously but perhaps the
shock had been too much for him. He was of the two
older men. I tried to drag him back with me, pulling him
by his armpits, but he was heavy and eventually I abandoned the body, not really having any clear idea about
what I wanted to do with it anyway. Rigor mortis had
begun to set in and I left it in a sort of slouched, sitting
position, the arms locked forward.

Carey was nowhere to be seen. His camel was still
grazing by the well, but the man himself had gone. I rode
through the outcrops calling his name and risking my life,
for I was fairly certain the Bedu had circumnavigated the
well and had abducted him. I have not seen him again,
though I know that both Bedu have been following me
ever since.

It is three years since Carey was taken away from me.
The two Bedu are persistent, never giving up the chase
though I manage to remain just ahead of them, just out
of their reach. I am becoming more confident as the days
pass and I am certain that they will never catch me. I have
even been leaving messages for them in the dust –
enigmatic little poetic phrases which I hope will confuse
them.

I sign them with a name which I feel I have earned
from the man I killed. It is a way of getting back at them
for their damned persistence. Perhaps one day, when
their wariness has been blunted by the length and
arduousness of the pursuit, I shall have the audacity to
visit their fire and confront them?

I wish I knew where Carey was though. I have this
irrepressible feeling that he may be back in England;
perhaps recruiting another man to help look for me? Yet,
perhaps my feelings lie to me and he still shares the

desert? I shall continue searching for him, watching for a particular striding walk on my infrequent visits to a *sūk*, or studying the set of a distant rider's shoulders at a rare encounter in some lonely wadi. When he finds me, or I find him, we can once more take to the trails together and continue looking for . . . looking for . . . it doesn't matter. This is our home.

My name is Hassan Abdulla. I found these writings on the man I have been following for some time – Al-Qata, the desert poet. I think he died in the night of the cold, for he was an old man. I left him sitting in the rocks for two Englishmen – the one with the blue eyes and his companion. They are close behind me and I wonder if they mean to kill me, since they have been following my trail for several weeks – since the time my son was separated from me by the sandstorm. Two nights ago we had the first rain for six years and the desert is blooming. Seeds carried on the wind from Africa, dormant for many years, have turned the desert into a sea of light green shoots. It will not last long. Perhaps a few days, then all will brown and die. Its transient beauty cannot go unrecorded and I leave a few lines of verse on the rock, as Al-Qata would have done had he lived to see it. Perhaps my son will pass by this place and read them . . .

IAN WATSON

WHEN THE TIMEGATE FAILED

We were carrying an alien passenger on that particular trip. It belonged to the race which had created the timegate. Its name was Mid Velvet Fastskip, and I was under orders to become intimate; to seduce it.

These orders ran contrary to every other rule as to how to behave aboard a starship. I didn't expect to retain the respect of my crew.

But I couldn't take anyone else into my confidence. Nor did I dare ignore those orders. One of my crew would be a covert security officer, briefed to see that I carried out my confidential mission. Which of my crew? I had no idea.

I could trust no one except myself; yet I had to win the trust, the 'love,' of an alien. Because of this, no one would love me – least of all the woman whom I would need to exploit.

Nobody loved or trusted a starship, either. Not deep in our hearts, in our guts. Oh, we trusted the human-built stardrive to thrust us successfully from sunspace to sunspace. But how could any human being trust the timegate when we didn't understand it? That was why I needed to become the 'lover' of a creature whom no human being properly comprehended – and in two weeks flat. Obviously I would fail. It was the calibre of my failure which counted; what clues our scientists could deduce.

A certain Wittgenstein once said, 'If a lion could speak, we would not understand him.' Mid Velvet Fastskip and I

both spoke Harrang, the artificial mediation language.
But Harrang is essentially a functional language. Where
emotion, metaphor, deep meaning are involved, around
the periphery of language, one could only improvise
hopefully.

'The timegage is a technical problem,' I'd been told.
'Harrang will suffice.'

I feared that this wouldn't be so. The timegate was
invented by an alien psyche. It was envisioned out of alien
moods and impulses which were surely opaque to humans.
Otherwise human beings would have been able to invent
the thing, surely? Or at least to unriddle it by now. I fancy
that one's inventions and one's kind of consciousness are
closer allied than is often imagined. *We* invented a stardrive; Mid Velvet's people failed to. Instead they invented
something which we couldn't, and still can't, match.

Maybe I shouldn't make unduly heavy weather about
the 'alienness' of aliens. When the chips were down, Mid
Velvet might simply lie to me.

Ah no. Herein lay the cruel cunning of my masters
back in Solspace. They claimed to have learned an
essential feature of love among the aliens of Fastskip's
species: the Truth Moment, the Sharing.

In Harrang, Mid Velvet's breed were known as 'Those
Who Run Faster.' We called them the Tworfs for short, a
derogatory-sounding name reminiscent of Wop or Chink
or Dago. According to my masters all Tworfs were
neuters. On their home planet the Tworfs parasited
sexually upon large silky animals, semi-intelligent 'pets'
which roamed wild, and which could even speak in a
limited way. These beasts played the role of actual
external sexual organs.

A Tworf would 'engage' a male animal by clinging to
its back, sinking tendrils harmlessly into its nervous
system. A certain amount of petting-courtship was apparently involved prior to this. Wooing songs. Wooing the

animal was important, either ritually or biologically. Lots
of foreplay, to attune Tworf to beast.

Once joined together, the symbiotic duo would chase
after a female animal to mate with her. Spying a large
parasite mounted on prospective mate, the female would
flee furiously. The Tworf urged its mount to run faster.
Catching up, the Tworf would en-trance the female.
Vicarious copulation would take place, during the course
of which the Tworf would pump a vast amount of information through the nervous system/sexual circuit of male
beast, female beast, and Tworf. The Tworf would channel
its whole being through the mating couple, and back into
its neuter self. During this time the male animal would
experience a heightened state of awareness. He would
have access to the higher consciousness of the Tworf,
which would be spewing out its intimate, secret person.

The simple male animals would chant simple myth-
songs about their Tworf riders and these moments of
illumination, of godhood, which flooded them during
mating – ungraspable after the event, yet able to be
celebrated.

If the event was so desirable, why did the female animals
flee, and need to be chased down? True, the females
weren't themselves illuminated by the intercourse. Perhaps
the chase, too, was a ritual matter. And perhaps racing
caused hyperoxygenation or adrenalin release or some
other necessary chemical, hormonal change. Perhaps!

After consummation the Tworf would split into two
separate selves. It would give birth to a new self, a prismatic
variation. Thus Tworfs reproduced.

Were the articulate male and female animals actually a
second and third sex of the Tworf species? Morphologi-
cally different from the first, neuter sex, and mentally
inferior? My masters rejected this idea. The bodily differences were too gross. Besides, if Tworfs and silky animals
were of the same species, what hope was there of a human

man and woman playing the role of 'beast with two backs' for the benefit of a randy neuter Tworf? A Tworf who would flood the human male with knowledge.

My masters wouldn't say how they had gained all this data about alien sex habits. No doubt security officers at the Earth mission of Tworfworld were the source.

Apparently timegates also had some indirect connection with this bizarre practice. That was why we ought to have a timegate in proximity to the great experiment. Earth only had control of a limited number of timegates. Each one was a vital part of a starship. Hence the choice of myself as Casanova. As pervert, and violator of the safety rules, and violator of a crew member. I only hoped that the crew member in question, whom I must needs involve in the Truth Moment, might happen to be the secret security officer.

'Mid Velvet Fastskip?'

'Yes, Captain Nevin?'

'Do you have close friends back home?'

'Several.'

'What do close friends call you?'

'By my name.'

'By all of it? Or part? What name would a loving-animal know you by? What name would you whisper in his ear?'

'Mid is a position. Velvet is a texture. Fastskip is a way of motion.'

'I'm fascinated. May I invite you into my cabin to discuss such things?'

'Honoured, but puzzled.'

Let me describe Those Who Run Faster.

They're skinny bipeds who stand armpit-high to your average human male. Their feet are ostrich-claws which doubtless could eviscerate an enemy who tried to sneak up and leap on *their* backs. They have a tough, smooth, pearly hide. All down the front of the body tendrils peep from little follicle-holes, as if through a sieve. Excitement causes these tendrils to erect, and sprout forth. The tendrils are orange in colour so that the front of an excited Tworf would look like a rug stained with rusty blood. A Tworf's back is smoothly, flexibly ceramic.

A Tworf has two long, double-jointed arms with four wormy digits apiece. In addition, two vestigial 'clutching arms' spring from the sides of the chest, and are usually clasped together as if in prayer. For hands, these minimal arms have suckery little pads.

A Tworf's head is a porcelain ellipsoid with big, wide-set violet eyes lacking obvious pupils, twin breathing slits, and a lipless mouth which opens and shuts like a rubber sphincter, dilating and sealing again. Inside are double rows of tiny teeth, set vertically not horizontally.

A Tworf breathes oxygen, and eats most foods.

Mid Velvet Fastskip – so I'd been told – was a sibling of the ruling clade of the northern hemisphere of Tworf-world. Its fields of expertise were alien hermeneutics – a fancy way of referring to the fact that it had acted as an interpreter for the human mission on Tworfworld, and for the two other alien missions there – plus 'time-dancing', plus oceanography.

Mid Velvet had travelled to Earth to study our oceans.

What the hell was 'time-dancing'? My masters back home – and their inheritors, their successors who would take over the reins of the Perpetual World State – dearly wished to know. 'Time-dancing' sounded relevant; thus the selection of this particular Tworf as target for seduction.

We shall disregard the other two intelligent, star-faring species, who were even more arcane than Those Who Run Faster. Both those exotic races ignored timegates. They could happily hibernate during the long decades of star travel. One of them dream-tranced; the other disso-ciated during a journey.

*

As I escorted Mid Velvet along the already dusty corridor towards my cabin, Jocelyn Chantal came out of her own cabin, through the polarised haze of the privacy-sheet.

Chantal: blonde and tall and snub-nosed, sporting large frame spectacles which added a necessary extra dimension to her face, and gave her windows to peer at you through. Ship's Doctor. Political officer, too?

'Captain Nevin,' she said. A diagnosis rather than a greeting. 'And Mid Velvet Fastskip, I believe. Both together. In close proximity.'

On a starship one always kept a few paces away from other persons if possible.

'I don't suppose I'll catch an alien disease,' I said.

'Of course not!' She sounded offended.

'If somebody falls sick, Chantal, you might need to touch them. Physically. In proximity.'

'Perils of the profession, Captain. One takes precautions.'

'So many precautions.'

Her eyes widened, aspiring to the size of her glasses. '*Every* precaution is vital to safeguard a starship.'

'Quite right. A starship's rather similar to the Perpetual State, don't you think, Chantal? Almost a mirror image! Nothing ever alters.'

Why did I speak so rashly? Out of sheer nervous anger at the role I was compelled to act out? Or in order to uncover the actual political officer, to target her for parasitical alien rape?

If I didn't comply with our masters' plan, I would be shot after long interrogation. The descendants of my blood would be expelled from citizenship.

'Star travel demands political continuity, Captain. Our place in the cosmos, ruled by the speed of light, requires long-term stability.'

'Hmm. So therefore all Earth's billions bow their heads to a score of starships and a few far colonies. Cart before the horses? Baby and the bath-water?'

'What do you mean? We can't hibernate like our alien rivals.'

'We hibernate politically instead.'

'Political change means turmoil, which means war, which means eventual holocaust.'

'Yes, yes, I know. Come along, Mid Velvet Fastskip!'

I walked deliberately towards Jocelyn Chantal. She backed away from me, disappearing through her privacy sheet. When I glanced back, she was looking out again, watching where we went.

At the start of the wide, dusty corridor Helen Kaminski was also observing intently. Capriciously I waved to my dark, trim Exec. And political officer? Another possible candidate.

Contemptuous, and deliberately provocative of public opinion – things could only go downhill from here on – I ushered the alien into the white mouth of the cabin with my own name, NEVIN, above the door.

'Cap – !'

The cry – from Chantal or Kaminski – was abruptly cut off as the privacy sheet soaked up the sonics.

Now that I was inside my cabin, I could of course see clearly through the film of polarised air. I could look out through a doorframe with no door. You wouldn't wish to step out of your cabin blindly and risk colliding with somebody. I watched for a while. Kaminski walked into view slowly, keeping to the other side of the corridor. She loitered then strolled on. I drew the night-curtain briskly over the doorway.

Mid Velvet was studying the three digital clocks on my wall . . .

The first of these registered crew-time. The second showed ship-time – we were travelling at nearly the speed of light. The third clock gave 'objective' time back home on Earth.

Nine hours of objective time was equivalent to three hours of ship-time, approximately. Please tip your hat to

Einstein and to the stardrive, product of human engineering.

Three hours of ship-time was equivalent to one minute as experienced by the crew. Now let's tip our hat to the timegate invented by the Tworfs, a secret which we drooled for.

Thanks to the timegate our trip would last two weeks, for us. Twenty years would elapse on Earth. The ship itself would age by almost seven years.

Before we met Those Who Run Faster, human crews used to be cooped up in starships for years on end, for decades. Those were journeys of exile, madness, hell. Murder, tyranny, confinement. Not always; but all too often.

Nowadays we traded sealed stardrives to the Tworfs. The Tworfs supplied us with enigmatic timegates. One for one.

We aboard the *Pegasus* were outward bound two days from Solspace, crew-time, heading for our colony at Twinstar Two (which also boasted interesting oceans). Mid Velvet Fastskip would catch a Tworf vessel home from T-Two eventually. It had already been absent from its world for over a year, personal time. Long enough to become randy? Several others of its species had been present on Earth as visitors. However, Tworfs did not make love to other Tworfs; and their articulate animals lived in large herds, pining to death if isolated for very long. You couldn't, wouldn't, take a whole herd of cattle with you to another star system for the sake of an occasional pint of milk. Analogy.

'Will you drink some wine, Mid Velvet Fastskip?'

'I will. Thank you.'

Would its tendrils thrust out of its mantle after a couple of glasses of Burgundy? Would its body flush with a ruddy hue? Would a glass too many increase the desire, but take away the performance?

How could there be desire between a Mid Velvet Fastskip of the Tworfs and a Captain Sam Nevin?

How could there be desire between a Tworf and an articulate animal with a silky, silvery fleece?

My own hair was blond, almost white, and I had let a blond beard grow.

'What is your most vivid memory of Earth's oceans?' I asked convivially.

'Turtles and gulls,' it replied.

'Not whales? Not the Marianas Abyss? Not coral reefs? Not swordfish and sharks?'

'Weeping turtles, never knowing their offspring, laying eggs ashore. New-hatched babies drawn by instinct, knowing no parent but Nature, scuttling over a desert to the cruel safety of the surf. Greedy gulls eating ninety out of every hundred.'

His fluency, and mine, surprised me.

'You are a poet, Mid Velvet Fastskip!'

Was this alien creature the Rachel Carson, the Lewis Thomas of his own race?

Why those particular images?

'Will you pass that memory on to your own offspring when you divide in half?'

'Terrible, beautiful memories,' it said, leaving me little the wiser.

'Do the loving beasts of your world only reproduce themselves because you stimulate them?'

'You are curious about us.'

'I find myself attracted . . . to the notion of a third partner involved in the act of love. A partner of a different and superior order. As though a god were to assist in copulation – inspiring, frenzying. It must seem so to the beasts. Perhaps.'

'You are a poet too, Captain Nevin. Poets tell lies by means of beauty.'

'Lies? I only seek the truth.'

'And they make those lies true.'

'Mid . . . May I call you something briefer than Mid Velvet Fastskip. A shorter name? Without offending you! You can call me Sam. That's my personal name.'

'You can call me Skip.'

'Skip. I will.'

'I shall call you Cap, from Captain. Our names join.'

Skip – short for Skipper, too! Skipper of a vessel. The pun existed in Harrang, the amalgam mediation language. I recalled how this alien was an interpreter.

I raised my glass. 'Here's health to Cap and Skip.'

Cap and Skip. Sharing names. Commencing our courtship rites. I felt as though I, a lifelong heterosexual, had gone to a gay bar as an intellectual exercise, determined to offer my blond self to a man. Only, this was much stranger.

Skip and Cap: two buddies who would become intimate. Perhaps. And who would invite – chase, entrap, cajole – either Jocelyn Chantal or Helen Kaminski or engineer Sonya Wenzel to join in a lustful trio.

I had a flash-vision – or precognition – of myself capering nakedly along the corridor, ecstatic, drunken, ridden by alien Skip as if by a demonic god, bursting through the privacy sheet into one cabin or another, my penis a paralysing, entrancing sting, almost an ovipositor; and perhaps after all it wouldn't be a woman to whom Skip drove me. It might be one of the other men. Mark Bekker or Robert Hoffmann or Julian Takahashi.

What violent hatreds might erupt! The results could be as dire as any ghastly event aboard a long-trip ship from the old days, before the timegate. I might need the political officer to reveal himself (or herself) to protect me, to nurse the shattered crew to journey's end.

Maybe I wouldn't be in danger. Potential weapons of any sort were banned from *Pegasus*. We even ate with plastic spoons. We were strongly conditioned not to crowd each other, not to collide.

My cabin wasn't a particularly elegant boudoir in which

to conduct an alien seduction. The walls were smooth and almost bare, with no irrelevant obtrusions. Entertainments were enclosed inside the walls; only a screen and speakers and the simplest of controls were visible. The whole floor was padded as a bed. Personal space must be kept extremely tidy. To encourage this, we possessed little to untidy a cabin with.

Already my home pad was slightly dusty. We were two days out from Earth but *Pegasus* was hundreds of days older. Before we arrived in twelve days time, in eighteen years time, dust would lie thick about the ship. It would be as though we dwelled in an ancient tomb.

How could so much dust collect out of thin air? Maybe the steady state theory of the universe was correct and matter was being created all the time, mostly in deep space, in the form of dust. Slowed in time as we were, dust seemed to gather with mysterious malevolence as though the ship's walls were sloughing dead cells of skin which must eventually gather so deeply as to stifle us.

In a sense dust was the main enemy. Dust alone visibly altered the anatomy of the ship. Nothing else about the ship could be allowed to change, to shift position.

At journey's end hoses would simply be attached to the snout of *Pegasus*, through the airlock at the front of Control. The whole vessel would be flooded like a sunken submarine, flushed clean, then dried and sterilised by blasts of burning air.

'Have some more wine, Skip?'

'Thank you.'

Yes, a starship is an unchanging environment. It's designed that way. No door even opens or shuts in transit. As few objects as possible are moveable: plastic spoons, cups, bowls. Clothes; we wear almost indestructible one-piece suits.

In the old days when journeys took half a lifetime, ships were littered with enough playthings and paraphernalia to occupy a whole cageful of monkeys happily half way to forever.

But any loose object can be misused, can cause an accident or be made into a weapon. And humans aren't monkeys. The same rich variety of adult toys and amusements and decoration, constantly seen for ten or twenty years, becomes invisible. After a decade and a half all those things may as well not be there. The crew would no longer admire them, care about them, even notice them. The ship may as well be empty and immutable, as *Pegasus* is. Apart from the dust.

Inner disciplines were more important than toys. Imaginative meditations. Indeed, what other kind of discipline could there be aboard a vessel exiled for fifteen or thirty years? Alas, those disciplines frequently degenerated; the crew became degenerates.

Tip your hat to the timegate, shipmates!

One of the crew would need to become my mate, under Skip's influence . . .

I presumed that microphones and lenses the size of motes of dust recorded the monotony of daily life aboard *Pegasus*, though I doubted that the political officer herself (or himself) would have access to the electronic records; thus Earth could keep a check on her too (or him). Those records would be scanned by a high-speed computer programmed to take note of key words and tones of voice denoting hysteria, rage, pain. (Key words on this trip would include anything connected with timegates and Tworfs.) That was how the terrible tale of some of those early, cursed, multi-decade voyages had been decoded, even though the ageing remnants of the crew were themselves inarticulate or deep in hallucinations. Back before the timegate cut subjective trip time to a few weeks.

When nothing in the environment changes, it doesn't matter how quickly or slowly the crew members move about the ship, so long as they all move about at the same speed relative to one another. (Though we never *trusted* to this!)

Obviously we were utterly out of synch with mechanical systems for opening doors or emptying toilets or heating food. Before you could snatch a foil-pack of heated stew out of an oven the meal would have been cold for hours, ship time. Cold nutritious slop was our chow.

Oh for a juicy steak, a Madras curry, steaming broth. But we could easily wait a couple of weeks for a decent meal.

At least I had some good vintage Burgundy to offer Skip. All our wine was vintage; once opened it had plenty of time to breathe.

Day Three, and it was time for me and Exec Kaminski and Navigator Bekker to check and triple-check our course, analyse the starbow, make any minor corrections. Since yesterday *Pegasus* had flown onward a hundred and fifty or so light days. Back on Earth a year and a half had gone by. Cosmic dust, gravity of neighbouring stars, the rotation of the galaxy, minute irregularities in the output of the stardrive could conspire to nudge us slightly off course. A starship slightly off course is soon a long way off. To correct significant deviations soon becomes fuel-consumptive and stressful of the stardrive.

The daily check was something of a ritual with definite superstitious aspects. For Bekker, Kaminski and I would step through the timegate one after another and be accelerated to ship-time; otherwise we could never handle the job. Then we three would return through the gate into the main body of the ship, and be decelerated once again. The rest of the crew would wait and watch. In some ways the event was like a prayer to a mysterious deity, one which had always proved benevolent so far, yet whose ways were inexplicable.

When I arrived in the bare dusty vestibule, Chantal, Takahashi, and Wenzel were already there. With backs to the curving wall, they kept their distance from one another.

Kaminski and Bekker were also waiting for me, near the red 'dike' ten centimetres high which surrounded the timegate.

'You're almost late, Captain!' Kaminski jerked a finger at the triple chronometer mounted overhead.

'Nonsense. Hoffmann isn't here yet.'

'He doesn't need to go into Control.'

Skip was absent too. A pity. It may have amused him to see the ignorant natives gathered around their idol, praying that the timegate would grant us a change of tempo, such as it had always granted; but not knowing, not knowing for sure. Amused him; and demeaned us. This might have helped my mission by making us seem like a bunch of . . . articulate animals. We weren't, at this moment, the technological masters of the stardrive. We were petitioners at an alien portal.

Beyond the red dike, duller with dust than yesterday, the oval hoop of the timegate cut a hole in the bulkhead enclosing a shimmer of air. Rainbow colours rippled faintly, as on a membrane of soapy water from which a child might blow a bubble. This membrane would let us step through it; unlike a bubble it wouldn't burst. Beyond the membrane I could see all the screens and instruments of Control, only slightly distorted.

'Here's Hoffmann now,' I said calmly.

What the witnesses saw when we stepped through the timegate, if they really concentrated, would be: a brief blur of activity within Control, the place full of flickering multiple images almost too swift to register. Then, ten seconds later, Kaminski and Bekker and I would re-emerge.

From our point of view the witnesses outside were frozen statues, snail-people.

We spent half an hour in Control. After a thorough

analysis of the smeared images of suns in the starbow we
trimmed course by a fraction of an arcsecond.

'They ought to install an oven in here,' I remarked.
'Then we could feast like the kings and queens of infinite
space that we are. Or ought to be.'

'You can't have people flooding in and out of here
whenever they're feeling peckish,' said Bekker indig-
nantly. 'Think of the risk of collision! Slow-moving persons, fast-moving persons. It's risky enough *us* using this
doorway once a day.'

'We fear it, don't we? We treat it like an unexploded
bomb. Or a glass mobile we're balancing on a fingertip
over an abyss. We never dance with time, nonchalantly.'

'Our work's done,' said Kaminski. 'We ought to rejoin
the others.'

'What's the hurry? They won't miss us. Just imagine
. . . if we stepped back through the gate, and this time it
didn't work.'

'Be quiet, Captain.'

'We would still be accelerated. They would stand there
motionless. At first we would think it was a prank. "Hey
you guys, don't joke. This isn't funny." Then we'd notice
that they *are* moving, but very very slowly. "Okay, this is
an order. Quit it." No response. We would have to write
on the wall for them to read slowly. For the next seven
years or so we three would have to live our lives at ship's
time.'

'Captain. Please.'

'Except, in just a few months we would use all the food
and drink. That's only a few hours from their point of
view. They couldn't stop us raiding the larder time and
again, gobbling our fill every few minutes. We'd have no
choice. We'd buzz about them like a swarm of locusts.
And when the cupboard was bare . . . would we eat
Chantal and Wenzel, Hoffmann and Takahashi too?
Would we tear our alien friend apart and eat him? Yes!
Unless the Tworf knew how to dance with time. Unless

he speeded up to escape from our hungry jaws – and showed us the art of dancing!'

'For God's sake,' Kaminski said.

For God's sake. Not for the sake of the Perpetual State. Maybe this proved nothing. Scratch a policeman and you find a priest. Priests are the policemen of the soul. Police are the priests of politics. Often both wear similar black uniforms. Kaminski might still be the security officer.

We went back through the timegate. We were reunited together in slow time. All was well.

'I shall tell you a poem of the origin of the timegate, Cap.'

'You will? Tell me, Skip. Tell me.'

'I shall tell lies by means of beauty. As substitute for a wooing song.' All down its front the orange tendrils twitched.

'Those Who Run Faster once suffered from a strange malady: of hyperkinesis. Hence our name! We were overactive, accelerated. Something had gone sadly wrong with our biological clocks. The clocks in our bodies, you know?'

'Yes, yes. Mitochondria, the little powerhouses of the cells. Circadian rhythms. The pineal eye.'

'Each successive generation of Those Who Run Faster was living at a quicker rate than the previous generation. We were maturing faster, moving faster, talking faster, discarding ourselves faster.'

'Discarding? Do you mean "dying"? Don't creatures who divide by fission live forever like amoebas?'

'We are more complicated than amoebas. Shall I digress?'

'Not yet. Go on, Skip. The Tworfs were speeding up.'

'We were burning ourselves out. The end of our race was predicted. In our case it was a race, and no mistake! But then our scientists pinned down the source of the trouble. A black hole of swelling mass was digesting our

sun from within. This eating of our star caused a local
anomaly in time.'

'This isn't a poem,' I cried with mounting excitement.
'It's a scientific explanation.'

'It is a song. Our hyperkinesis was an evolutionary
adaptation to the fact that we must complete our history
much earlier than Nature had expected. So we discovered
how to retard ourselves, by use of timegates. The first
timegates were spun out of our inmost being, our accelerated selves. As an earthly spider spins silk; as an earthly
snail secretes a shell. The silk, the shell, was *time itself*.
We ingeniously transferred time's extra momentum to the
gates. Later, we automated the procedure. Our history
continues.'

'But how did you accomplish this marvel?'

Hitherto Skip had been waggling his vestigial hands as
he wove his narrative. Now he knit those suckers together
across his bristling chest as much as to say, 'That's all.
Story over.'

'But your sun must still be doomed!'

'Our whole species danced with time. We arrested the
black hole. We cured our star.'

'Hang on a moment. If all of you were living faster,
adapting at the same rate, what difference would the time
anomaly have made to you?'

'A great difference. We Tworfs were adapting, because
we were the most sensitive and highly evolved species.
Our loving animals did not live any faster than before.
Mounting them became frustrating and exhausting. Our
wooing songs squeaked far too rapidly in their silky ears.
Love took far too long.'

For the first time in our acquaintance Skip stretched
out one of its long arms to touch me; to touch my virtually
indestructible garment. Tentatively.

The next day Skip told me an entirely different story;
though I suppose it complemented the first explanation.

'Yes, we are immortal,' it explained, 'unless killed by

accident. Every time we mount a loving animal, and mate it and divide ourselves, we gain a new lease of life. However, as an earthly snake sloughs its skin, likewise we must lose something. What *we* have to discard is memories. We must cull our memories, or else our minds would overload with the enormity of the past. We couldn't function successfully in the present.'

'Ah, I see. You shed a half of your memories into your offspring, into your double. That's what makes the pair of you different persons.'

'Yes and no. If we imprinted too much memory on our double it wouldn't have initiative and curiosity. Therefore, dancing, we secrete a jewel which contains that extra part of the past which we wish to discard. We excrete this, as an earthly bird excretes an egg. This jewel is memory. And memory is time. These jewels are essential to the functioning of the timegate.'

'You create a jewel each time you mate a loving animal?'

'We used to give the jewels to the animals afterwards. They wore the jewels as necklaces, of honour and worship. But they didn't understand the jewels properly. Now we use them scientifically.'

I barely curbed my excitement. 'You must be a very different person after mating, Skip. You must forget a lot that happened earlier on.'

'Do not your earthly poets refer to human orgasm as "the little death"? In a timeless moment, you forget yourself.'

I was spooning up some cold slop with my plastic utensil. Jocelyn Chantal positioned herself nearby.

'How are you feeling, Captain?'

'Okay.'

'How is our alien guest enjoying its voyage?'

'Is a voyage to be enjoyed – or endured? Perhaps neither! What does it really matter whereabouts we are in space and time, or what the quality of our circumstances is, so long as we survive without too much discomfort? And so long as we serve the Perpetual State? Thus we ensure the survival of humanity. Thus we guarantee its spread throughout the stars, that are so very far apart. Any means of enduring such a voyage is healthy. Impeccable.'

'Perhaps.'

'That's why we endure the timegate every day.'

'You endure it, Captain.' Chantal hesitated before adding, 'In company with Helen and Mark.'

'Everyone endures it, Chantal. Everyone.'

'Yes. We all do.'

'I think I'm starting to regard the timegate not with queasy dread, but in happy anticipation – as something vitalising and inspiring. Each time I use it I die and am reborn. Almost as another person in another time. If we use the timegate often enough it may make us immortal. We shall journey thousands of light years all the way around the galaxy, instead of a measly ten or twenty light years from Earth. We ought to improve the cuisine, though. Does an immortal get bored with eating an infinity of meals? Mid Velvet Fastskip hasn't complained about the menu.'

'Is our alien guest immortal? How strange that an immortal race should bother to invent timegates.'

'Maybe they're immortal because they use timegates. *Post hoc ergo propter hoc.* Plus, their method of reproduction.' I oughtn't to be so frank with Chantal. My masters on Earth had sworn me to secrecy. Here was I on the verge of betraying my mission. I went on in lighter vein. 'What if they aren't immortal? Thanks to timegates they can dance their way right to the end of the universe within a single lifetime.'

Suppose you stepped through one timegate, to slow your life processes. Suppose you immediately stepped in the same direction through a second gate. Then a third! Decelerating and decelerating. The sun would zip through the sky. Day and night would strobe. The galaxy would revolve like a spinning top. The whole cosmos would expand to its utmost, pause, and collapse. While you stood still.

'Certain time-dancers on our world are attempting this,' admitted Skip.

'You're a time-dancer too.'

'Those are slow dancers. I skip fast. None of those slow dancers have reached their fourth gate yet. They move so slowly, you see.'

'Oh.'

I had never visited Tworfworld. I was always on the same run from Earth on Twinstar Two. I tried to imagine Skip's planet.

The yellow prairies where herds of silky animals grazed and frolicked and chanted simple songs, and experienced fleeting ecstasies of high mentality and metamemory when ridden in love by Tworfs. The fanatical slow-dance Tworfs poised motionless between one gate and another. The single ocean on whose shore no turtles nested, above whose waves no gulls screamed hungrily. Lying sparkling on a silver beach, where Tworfs had ridden their mounts, mated, danced, and split, would be the jewels of time.

I visualised the Tworf cities of domes and minarets; the guarded embassies of the exotic races which could hibernate for years on end, at will; the spaceport from which Tworf vessels rose powered by human stardrives.

It was time for love; high time.

'Look at me, Skip. Behold me.'

I parted my indestructible garment down the frontal seam. I shucked it off like a snakeskin, newly moulted. I stroked my blond, near-white beard. I turned my back on Mid Velvet Fastskip.

'Touch me.'

Swiftly the alien mounted me. The long arms jointed themselves around my chest, locking together. The little arms burrowed under my armpits, suckering tight. Erect tendrils gently pierced my shoulders, spine, buttocks, nerves. Skip was nearly weightless, the least of burdens. My alien rider increased my strength, the bounce of my steps and the vigour of my body, my potency and sexuality. I had been impotent for years; not now. On the contrary!

It was as I foresaw. I was possessed by a daemon, by a living god. I rushed through my privacy sheet into the corridor. There, I pawed the deck and champed like a thoroughbred stallion. I snorted. I whinnied wordlessly.

Just then Helen Kaminski appeared from around the far bend. She stared in amazement at her potent, eager Captain with the alien rider on his back, porcelain head peeping over human head. She broke into a run – not away from us but in the direction of her own doorless cabin, cloaked in its white privacy.

We raced to meet her. We ran faster. But she had less distance to cover. She vanished through the masked doorway. Forbidden!

Skip urged me through the privacy sheet – through into the KAMINSKI cabin from which no sight nor sound could escape.

During consummation, as I flowed into my noisy mate, Skip flowed through myself into Helen Kaminski and back into my body through her raking fingernails.

I was filled with alien understandings and timely enlightenments such as I can no longer express.

Afterwards, Skip descended from me and danced for us. It whirled like a dervish till my eyes were dazed. It seemed to grow shorter, and spread out. As the wild dance slowed I could distinguish two short Tworfs whirling round together, disentangling from one another.

At last they separated and halted. Helen fled naked from her cabin. One Tworf bowed and presented me with a blue jewel that pulsed with inner radiance. The jewel was about the size of the iris of a human eye. This done, the Tworfs ran away like a couple of mischievous children or elves. I was left alone. My understanding dimmed, to that of an ordinary human being. My god had gone.

But I knew what I needed to do. Clutching my treasure, I set out for the timegate and Control.

I had lost my high, vital strength. Mark Bekker held me by one arm, actually touching me. Robert Hoffmann held my other arm. We were stalled in the vestibule. So near, yet so far.

I protested. 'I've learned the secret of the timegate.'

'There's no alien on board, Captain,' said Jocelyn Chantal. She too had intercepted me. She looked a lot older than previously.

'Quite right. There are *two*.'

'Two?'

'Mid Velvet Fastskip divided. They're probably hiding somewhere. The environment may seem unfamiliar.'

'There was *never* any alien on board. How could there be? We know of no aliens.'

'Those Who Run Faster gave us the timegate, Chantal.'

She sighed. 'There's no timegate, either. If only there was.'

'But look! There it is!' I attempted to point. Since my arms were pinioned I had to content myself with jerking my head in the direction of the red dike, and the shimmering oval gap beyond.

'I only see the entrance to Control,' Chantal said. 'Look at the calendar-clock above.'

I glanced up at the chronometer. Its digits were flowing too fast to read clearly.

'This is the fourteenth year of our *actual* voyage, Captain.'

'Free my hand, Bekker. Let me show you something.'

Bekker did so, guardedly.

I opened my fist to display the time-jewel.

'Possibly there wasn't any alien,' I allowed. 'Yet now we have a timegate for sure! *This* has been created. This power-crystal.'

'It's one of those twelve-sided gaming dice that Helen uses isn't it?' asked Bekker.

'Oh well, it might have been. Now it's altered. It was changed in the crucible of heightened consciousness! See how it glows. We need only link it in circuit with the stardrive. We'll fly through hyperspace, through hyper-time. We'll arrive within days, not decades. I *know* this.'

Bekker asked incredulously, 'Are you seriously propos-ing that we open the drive unit up and insert this . . . object . . . into the matrix?'

'We could certainly give it a try,' said Hoffmann. 'Are you quite positive that you achieved insight, Captain? A genuine altered state of consciousness?'

'Yes. Yes.'

Hoffmann released his hold. He stepped away from me. And I realised that *he* was the political officer of *Pegasus*. Pudgy, bald-headed Hoffmann. Bland Hoff-mann. Hoffmann was the secret supervisor of this journey of ours, which wasn't just a journey across light years of void but also a trip into powerful, parahuman dimensions of the mind.

'Are you as mad as he is?' Bekker asked softly. 'Jocelyn, don't you have any tranquillisers left?'

'After fourteen years?'

'Please give me that bauble,' begged Bekker. 'We've played along with this farce for too long. I absolutely refuse to countenance – '

Hoffmann hit Bekker on the jaw, decking him. Hoff-mann's fist heaved some weight.

Unfortunately the time-jewel did not produce quite the desired effect. In fact the stardrive quit.

If only I could find where Those Who Run Faster are hiding, I could ask them why. I've glimpsed them a couple of times but they run faster than me.

We still travel onwards, nudging the speed of light as before. Unless we achieve another breakthrough such as mine I wonder how we will ever trim our course or slow down in time for our destination.

In the bad old days prior to the advent of the timegate it's well known that not all starships arrived safely at journey's end. Some vanished entirely and were never heard from.

No matter! Extraordinarily, Helen Kaminski is pregnant. Despite her age! Despite my mandatory vasectomy of fourteen years vintage! In such singular circumstances surely she will give birth to an unusual baby. A paranormal child, whom we will lovingly foster, who will show us the true way. Her baby will be semi-alien.

Even if Helen's pregnancy is hysterical she obviously hopes to give birth to something. She is conceiving an exotic salvation for us all. If no actual, physical infant is born when she arrives at term, whatever will occur? Something strange and wonderful and wise.

We only have another few months to wait.

LEE MONTGOMERIE

WAR AND/OR PEACE

Oh God. Just as I am slipping an apple into my pocket, my arm is grabbed and twisted viciously behind my back. Shit: nicked knocking *food*! Righteous loathing fills the eyes of the fanatical shoppers aggressively competing for crap. I flinch, anticipating a stiff punishment. The apple falls to the floor and splatters, full of worms.

Damn it; I didn't even want the crappy apple! I stole it to recapture the excitement of the days when things were worth stealing; when the supermarket was a magical treasure house dealing in goods more real than reality. I remember a glittering pendant sparkling amid constellations of imitation diamonds. In a jungle of artificial flora, a spray of silk leaves, dyed to evoke the poignant mellowness of autumn. A handheld computer simulation of General Relativity. Their transcendental mysteries haunted me for weeks.

Probably it was only childhood that lent enchantment to those fakes. No sooner did I steal them than they reverted to dull glass, frayed cloth and busted silicon chips. Now the dark supermarket economy is driven by madness and deals in fakes of fakes, and the most desirable good on display is a rotten apple, a treasure only by comparison with the dented tins and leaky bags that litter the ransacked shelves. The brilliant consumer bubble has burst, and with it the consensual dream. Pigs, do your worst!

I turn my head. Kevin is grinning evilly at me.

'Shit a bomb!' I scream. 'You scared me out of my brain!'

Kevin looks even redder and more agitated than I do. Beads of sweat spangle his brow and darken his waist-length golden hair. Since his mother decided to whitewash her windows, he has been walking around draped in her old curtains – today the fluorescent pop-art nightmares from her eccentric sitting room. A few curious Fairies stare at the beautiful, terrifying boy in the psychedelic wizard's cloak, so out of place in this town where to be well-dressed is a civic responsibility.

Since Kevin is my lover and our next-door neighbour (it is the presence of the Peace Camp, my father says, that has lowered property values and morale to the extent that someone like Kevin's mum can move into the other half of our semi and do it up like a junkie disco), I cannot ignore him as everybody but the Fairies is pointedly doing. I follow him out of the shop, his face still wreathed in an insolent smirk.

As we step into the sunlight, he spreads the curtains like a pair of brilliant wings and faces the dingy emporium like a creature in a vision; eyes shining, hair alight. Reflections rake the supermarket like machine-gun fire – bullets of light piercing the shadowy displays and momentarily transfixing the compulsive shoppers, stuffing their trollies with rubbish as if there is no tomorrow.

Long before the supermarket became a crappy copy of itself, I used to dream about shoddy, shadowy shops. What is just exasperating now seemed an ominous portent then. In my dream, Kevin would be glaring at me from behind the counter, grown up at last and finally revealed as a disappointment; his shining hair turned shabby brown, his snickering eyes dully evil.

As I approached him, I would imagine that the shelves were stacked with irresistible merchandise, the consummation of consumerism. Then the transcendent apparition would vanish. Kev would hand me a newspaper.

'I told you so!' he would say.

I would shiver as I unfolded the disintegrating rag, knowing that it reported the disaster we had all been dreading. Still, it was always a shock –

'REALITY COLLAPSES!!!' screamed the banner headline: the rest of the page occupied by a photograph that refused to resolve itself, a collocation of random dots. I would awake in desolation, still haunted by Kevin's harrowing smile.

'Isn't that just how it always is?' says Kevin, when I tell him about my dreams. 'Out of unlimited possibilities, only one is realised. I stand on the threshold of adulthood, my career potentialities a package of overlapping wave functions. My dad would have wanted me to be a scientist. My mother often thinks I should be an artist. I rather fancy myself as a football supremo. I end up a shop assistant with nothing to sell. An intermediary in virtual transaction. Oh God. An infinity of possible universes and I have to inhabit this shitpit!'

In Kevin's own recurring dream, he recapitulates the moment when his puppy was run over by a juggernaut. Kev is suddenly a toddler again, kicking his football to the dog, which bounds into the road after it just as a massive truck turns the corner. A bus coming in the opposite direction blocks his view.

In Kevin's dream, anything can have happened until the bus and lorry draw apart to reveal the burst black fur sack spilling intestines onto the tarmac. Through the strangely transparent bus, Kev sees Sambo's world-line as a wave of superimposed miraculous escapes. The puppy dodges all fourteen wheels and/or falls down the shelter of a manhole and/or bounces off the bumper and is thrown clear. Kevin is ready to cheer with relief. Then the road comes into view again, the dog dead, frustration knotting Kevin's tiny fists. On the side of the juggernaut, in red letters ten feet high, is written the single word: 'CHOICE'.

It infuriates Kev. A subscriber to the Many Worlds Interpretation of quantum mechanics, and he cannot persuade even his subconscious mind to collapse the wave function so that Sambo survives.

'You look repulsive,' I say. Kevin is wearing one of his mum's old dresses, iridescent silk embroidered with thousands of tiny mirrors, his football socks stuffed into the bodice. No wonder he lights up the world like a glitterball. No wonder he looks hot.

We have walked home together and are sitting in his mum's front room: the hot sunshine permeating the brushstrokes on the whitewashed bay windows and making watery patterns on the black wallpaper. The morning's mail is lying on the coffee table. A glossy brochure epiphanising the virtues of defence with pictures of silvery missiles soaring over heaping sunlight clouds. A government booklet detailing the construction of a fallout shelter. A religious pamphlet promising that the aftermath of Armageddon will be literally a picnic – the centrefold shows a smiling cross-section of humanity sitting down to a spread in a woodland beauty spot. A duplicated circular inviting all Wimmin to a 'Midsummer Night's Dream' at the Base.

Kevin's mum brings us synthetic tea on a rattling tray of gaudy plastic crockery, sighs wearily, and goes off to the kitchen.

There are tears in her eyes as she slams the door. The street used to ring with her sickening boasts about her Boy Wonder (his father, so they say, was a whizzkid physicist at the Base, compensation for whose mysterious death has kept Kev's mum in booze and bubblegummy trinkets ever since. Kev says that his dad copped a massive whole-body irradiation just before Kev was conceived, and that Kev was maybe the mutant superperson towards whom the whole nuclear programme had been unknowingly working, but only his extraordinary luminous hair looks abnormal to me).

Kev could read in his pram, do differential calculus in his playpen, was immersed in Schrödinger's Wave Equations when his contemporaries were still immersed in wet nappies, his mum bragged.

She cannot understand how her precious infant prodigy can have grown into this dull and sullen stranger glowering at her from the kneehole under the sideboard; his appearance alarming, his manners atrocious, his intellectual powers jammed on the problem of resurrecting a dead dog. Probably she thinks his obsession with physics is a symptom of incipient schizophrenia. I wonder how she feels about her beloved son being a transvestite.

'What are you dressed like that for, anyway?' I asked.

Kevin gloatingly flaunts the invitation to the Dream.

'I've been recruiting into Lady Helga's bodyguard,' he says. 'We are going to the Wimmin's Peace Camp tonight.'

I stomp across to the window in a huff, thinking of the band of brawling hooligans who have formed an unholy alliance with the smarmy Lady Helga and her following of straight-laced, uptight ratepayers. Ostensibly a deterrent to dust-ups between the towns-people and the protestors, their tactics are to rampage around the Base, disguised as parodies of Peace Campers, harrassing and terrorising the Wimmin and their satellites. They won't tolerate Kev.

'Shit! They will kill you!' I say.

Kevin is preening himself in front of the sideboard; mirrors reflected in mirrors, reflecting the ghastly room. The hideous dayglo furniture leaping out from the black walls and carpet is covered with garish knick-knacks, scatter cushions and sofa throws. Kev's psychotic paintings, full of blood and Glitto, menace us from the walls.

'Then you will just have to come and guard *me*,' says Kevin. 'Damn it, you look ugly enough to pass for a yobbo in drag.'

I open the whitewashed window and stare out over the

patio, the baroque polystyrene pots filled with sickly
vegetables. I can see into our own garden. Mother is
digging what looks like a grave. Father, on a stepladder,
is adding another layer of bricks to the wall. The striations
of his previous labours stand out like geological zones on
an exposed fault. Territory, Privacy, Security, Paranoia
and Blind Panic. A pile of broken bottles, the intended
crown of his handiwork, glitters in the sun.

A trio of Fairies saunters down the street. My father
showers them with a torrent of abuse and a brick, which
powders on the tarmac at their feet.

'The natives will be restless tonight!' he yells to my
mother, not for the first time today.

The Fairies have been gathering for days, arriving on
dusty feet or rusty bicycles, in dragging dresses made
from old lace curtains, gauzy wings wired to their backs,
tinsel fillets interwoven with wild flowers binding their
long, flowing hair. Each one carries a wand tipped with a
silver star.

There are said to be a million of them. They are headed
for the Wall.

'Well, what are they going to do there, anyway?' I ask
Kevin.

'Magic!' he replies. 'They are going to wish the Base
away!'

The ratepayers have procured a fleet of coaches for the
expedition to the Base. Lady Helga is riding in the
grandest one. She and the ratepayers sit at tables in the
front; a bunch of old toads snapping at the conversational
flies of discontent. The filth. The stink. The barbarity.
The nudity. The downright *arrogance* of the Wimmin.
Their flipping superstitions. They *pray* to a flaming totem
pole with breasts, blast them.

Kev and I are sitting with the rest of the bodyguard on
a banquette at the back of the coach.

'It's the unification of science and magic,' Kev is saying.
He believes that the deep structure of the human psyche

is programmed with all the fundamentals of sub-atomic theory, subconsciously apprehended as religion, hence the extraordinary similarities between the physical and spiritual arcana. 'The Fairies believe that the Base is just one manifestation of an infinite number of virtual realities occupying the same spot; particles from all of which are constantly being interchanged through Heisenberg loan mechanisms. They believe that if they insist upon observing something other than the Base, they can collapse the virtual particles into an alternate reality.'

He is boring the bodyguard. They bat their painted eyelids at him and lick their painted lips. Their jewellery jangles as they crack their knuckles. They are even uglier than the Peace Wimmin; scraggy wigs under woolly hats, bolsters under baggy sweaters.

'We don't need wankers like you to tell us what they are up to, darling,' says one of them. 'We know what they are up to and we are not having it. It is them that are going to collapse and that's virtually real!'

He leers at Kevin. The ratepayers stare vituperatively at us. Then everybody's attention is claimed by our first sight of the Wall, rising above the trees in the distance, an immense monument to paranoia.

POISED TO DETER – QUICK TO REACT is the motto wrought into the arch above the massive iron gates.

As we get closer, we make out the art gallery that occupies the entire surface of the Wall: graffitti, cabbalistic symbols, enormous portraits of the goddess, wreathed in hearts and flowers. The whole of the low-flying aircraft that hit the Wall and nearly lit up the world has been bolted to the brickwork at the impact site – a gigantic mandala of flattened carbon fibre that hangs like a black sun over the squalid Peace Camp. The rickety huts, fashioned from flattened fuel drums, are festooned with trophies captured on raids over the Wall. The filthy compound, and the whole of the forest around, is crawling with Fairies. The sun is setting. The bodyguard bray with excitement, anticipating a horrendous carnival of violence.

The Wall was built when the Base finally gave up on fences. They say it would be visible from the moon, if anybody bothered to go there anymore, fifty feet of sheer, glazed brick, topped by razor spikes, bristling with watchtowers, constantly circled by patrols of pigs, squaddies and dogs – despite all of which the Wimmin, naked, oiled and stoned, regularly surmount the Wall and run whooping through the Base, leaving a stench of stale woodsmoke everywhere, graffitti drawn in menstrual blood on the missile silos, and heaps of their easy vegetarian turds on the parade ground.

The fence that once protected the Base has been rebuilt around the Peace Camp Farm, to protect their seedy beans and shabby sheep from marauding townsfolk. A platform for visiting speakers has been built beside the Main Gate. It is occupied by an intellectual-sounding Fairy, quietly speaking to the hushed crowd. Phrases like 'collapse of the wave function', 'perpendicular universes' and 'virtual realities' wash over our heads as we make our way from the coach park to the platform.

'So you see,' the speaker is concluding, 'physics and metaphysics are the same thing really. Nothing actually exists until it is consciously observed. It is our insistence on recognising the Base that allows it to persist. If we can ignore it with sufficient conviction, it will go away.'

'Did you hear that?' says an ecstatic Fairy, smiling at us as though we are all in bed together. 'Isn't it so sort of, you know, amazing?' She confides that they have been training themselves for months to ignore what is right in front of their noses.

Lady Helga and her entourage have reached the foot of the platform.

'Order! Order!' Helga is trumpeting; waving her arms at the completely silent crowd, 'I demand the right to speak in the cause of balance!'

'Yes, balance!' Helga is booming from the platform. 'The previous lecturer on theoretical sub-atomic particle physics has neglected to give us the whole picture, I believe. I don't think she truly brought her intellect to bear on the symmetry that is inherent in the system. If every particle were not balanced by a particle of opposite qualities, the whole structure would collapse.

'Take maleness and femaleness for example; opposite qualities that make up a harmonious whole. I know there are some women here who like to believe that they can do without men, and we all know how absurd and degenerate their lifestyles are, but what I would like to know is this: where did those children come from?'

There is a surge of spiteful laughter from the ratepayers. Kevin and I are sitting behind the platform, commanding a view of the sunset reflected off a row of neighing dentures, and Lady Helga's horsy bottom in a white pleated suit.

There is a hole in the backside of the platform, out of which a naked Peace Woomin wriggles, covered with mud. She reaches after herself to extract first her filthy wrapper, which she winds around herself, then a pair of sagging leather buckets slung on a groaning pole. She shoulders her load to the nearest field and empties the buckets into a patch of pumpkins. Another Woomin squeakily and squelchily embraces her, takes up her yoke and vanishes into the hole.

'I would like you to consider,' Helga concludes, 'that for jolly nearly half a century we have enjoyed perfect stability within this alliance, an oasis of peace in a crazy world, despite being faced by an utterly ruthless and evil adversary. It is our determination to resist the enemy with all the strength at our disposal which has given you people the freedom to make your ridiculous protest. *Deterrence has never been known to fail*! Can you say the same for whatever you are going to put in its place?'

She comes down the steps flushed and triumphant, to

the unroarious cheers of the ratepayers. The Fairies have ignored her speech in impatient silence. Now a self-styled Fairy Queen ascends the platform, waving a sparkler, and leads the crowd into a song.

We love the flowers, a million crystal voices sing in the gathering dusk.

> We love the vegetables,
> We love the children
> And baby animals.
> We want to live in a world of peace and harmony
> With no more mi-i-siles, no more mi-i-siles, no more
> mi-i-siles, no more mi-i-siles.

The Fairy Queen appears to be on the verge of falling asleep. She gazes blearily at the scene, illuminated by the million flashlight bulbs in the Fairies' wands.

'You have to forget this Wall,' she yawns. 'This Wall is all in the mind. Forget it and it will melt away. All you must see before you is this beautiful, untouched forest.'

She gestures vaguely at the derelict woods – shitpit, rubbish-dump, builders' yard and woodpile for a generation of Peace Campers; campaigning stamping-ground for a generation of concerned, cleaning-up townsfolk. The withered, mutilated trees grow out of a compost of knitting wool, baby clothes, paper flowers, confetti, paint pots and busted mirrors, steeped in disinfectant, detergent, deodorant and insecticide; to which the Fairies have just added a top dressing of Glitto.

'I didn't come all this way to listen to all this half-baked mystical claptrap,' I complain. The Fairy Queen is yawning on about squirrels, bunnies, birdies, badgers and hedgehogs, elves and goblins and supernatural lost races, steeped in the forgotten wisdom of the forest.

Kevin and I are sitting in the cab of Lady Helga's coach. We command a wonderful view of the entire cast of stock characters. In the back of the coach, the ratepayers are curling their vindictive tongues around scandal and sandwiches. Outside, the bodyguard are bellowing and kicking each other in the bolsters, limbering up for a night of rape, murder, arson, riot and mayhem. The pigs look on impassively.

The Peace Wimmin are sitting around their stinking, smoky bonfire drinking their witches' brew from a purloined pilot's helmet.

'No more mi-i-siles,' the Fairies sing, their sweet voices ringing like silver bells.

'Damn it; nobody's *real*! They're all like carbon copies of cardboard cutouts!'

Their complacency revolts me. I am reminded of my favourite screen in the General Relativity game: the inscrutable singularity surrounded by a cloud of degenerate particles embedded in a region of dilated time, whose field spreads out to act upon the entire universe and returns to act upon itself.

Damn it; everybody's consciousness stops at the Wall: it is an event horizon beyond which our thoughts are trapped and sucked out of the universe. The Base is detectable only by its field, which has warped our entire continuum, paralysing our brains, reducing us to stereotyped shadows of ourselves. Emptying supermarkets, excavating shelters, whitewashing windows, walling ourselves in! Shit; we have been mindlessly preparing for the nuclear holocaust, without consciously admitting that it will ever happen!

I look at the Wall. The gates are opening. A widening rectangle of yellow light spills across the road, illuminating the sign POISED TO DETER – QUICK TO REACT emblazoned on the arch above the entrance.

'What a fucking stupid slogan!' I say. 'What's the point of reacting if deterrence never fails?'

Oh God; it's too late – the moment has come!

A clamorous siren drowns the maddening singing.

A seething mass of broad-shouldered, tight-lipped, gun-ready peacekeepers lines the road.

Two motorbikes, a Landrover and a fire engine scream out of the gate, sirens blaring, whirling stroboscopes transfixing the hypnotised faces of the Fairies. A launcher rumbles after them.

'Shit a bomb!' screams Keven, 'it's a fucking deployment!'

'Oh, jolly good,' says Lady Helga, 'let's get a better look. Driver! Drive on!' But Kevin has started the coach even before the order is given.

'I can't steer this thing!' yells Kevin. Between the coach park and the road is a symbolic cemetery; a burial ground of lost hopes. The coach rollicks over the humped graves, upsetting the picnic suppers and the ratepayers, who hiss like stampeding reptiles, still straining for a better view of the convoy.

We reach the road. 'Driver! STOP!' yells Lady Helga. Kevin ignores her. Hand on hooter, he bulldozes through the triple cordon of pigs, the ratepayers shrieking and drumming frantically in the back, drives straight between the fire engine and the launcher, and brakes.

The enormous wagon is inches from our coach and the bug-eyed sweating driver ploughs unwaveringly towards us; the effigy of a fat, ragged Woomin swinging like a pendulum in a noose slung from the rear-view mirror. Lady Helga is hammering at the emergency door, trumpeting in the panic-call of her species, but there is no time . . . we are down to counting the zilliseconds in foaming sub-units; stills from a movie filmed at infinite speed.

God damn it; I always assumed that we were going to grow up. Kevin was going to be a genius again, and I was going to be a nice woman from a lovely home, a dream from the vanished consumer consensus. Not the scruffy, foul-mouthed, clod-brained supermarket thief who has sex under the sideboard with the weirdo son of the mad widow next door. I don't even much *like* Kev. I always suspected he was laughing at me. I turn towards him and am taunted by my own reflection, fragmented by the thousands of mirrors on his dress. Shattered.

The nearside coach windows burst in slow motion; the rumpus from the passenger compartment is degraded to a roar like waves breaking on the shore in search of an inlet; perhaps the probability wave in search of its own collapse . . .

There is a sudden, crunching, grinding, thundering crash!

The wrecked coach is rocking on the lip of a pit, within which the broken-backed launcher is thrashing and churning, sending up a spray of mud. The back wheels are still going, and the whole missile-launch assembly rears up, shears off and rolls over, the missiles spilling out of their sheaths. The launch control vehicle slams into the back of the launcher. The front end of the convoy comes screaming back. The Peace Wimmin slip through the ranks of shocked pigs and run, whooping and bellowing, through the spray from the fire hoses.

Of course! The Wimmin have undermined the road. The speakers' platform was the Trojan Horse.

Lady Helga's bodyguard have arrived; boots twitching under long, muddy skirts, wigs slipping off to reveal lobotomised haircuts, slavering lips still smeared with make-up. They are after Kev's guts.

'We jolly nearly got killed!' says Lady Helga; red-faced infuriated, frothing at the lips. We are sitting in the back of the smashed coach, the blue velvet upholstery soaked with mud, blood and foam. Two of her bodyguards are holding Kevin down, while a third kicks him.

'We did get killed!' says Kev. The word 'killed' excites the thugs, who kick him in the head several times. I can't look. I keep seeing the overturned missile-launcher with the bombs jerking out of their tubes like the ghastly death-orgasm of a quadripenile alien dinosaur. I keep seeing the driver's face erupting through the fountaining windscreen; teeth bared in a rictus of uncontrollable rage.

'God damn it,' says Kev, 'we got killed and killed and killed and killed! We got pulped! Those pigs shot us! Those fucking bombs went off! We are still getting killed, every minute of every day!'

'What the hell is he talking about?' Lady Helga asks crossly. 'Is he feeling all right?' She has waved off the yobs. They are sitting on a bloodstained banquette, sticking bits of broken glass in their boots and glaring at Kev. The townspeople have long since shakily descended from the coach, still hissing.

'I'm talking about the collapse of the wave function, you stupid bitch!' shouts Kev. 'I feel like Schrödinger's bloody cat! I feel like Wigner's fucking friend! How do you feel when there is a strong probability that you are dead?'

'You see,' says Kevin, impersonating the intellectual Fairy, 'physics and metaphysics are the same thing really. Schrödinger of the wave equations puts a cat in a box with a radio-active atom which has a 50% probability of decaying, in which case it activates a hammer which crushes a cyanide capsule which kills the cat. But radio-active decay only exists as a probability until observation collapses the wave function, and the state of the cat is tied to the state of the atom. So how does the cat feel?'

Helga cannot be bothered to listen to this rubbish. She snorts with contempt and stares out of the intact window behind her, still covered with foam through which the floodlights are diffracted into rainbow spheres. Night has fallen. The sky is suddenly a magical treasure-house of stars, sectioned by the courses of satellites.

'Some say that the cat is neither alive nor dead until Schrödinger opens the box. Others say that two different universes come into being at that moment, containing two Schrödingers, one live cat and one dead cat. Conscious observation either collapses the wave function or splits the universe. So, if, instead of a cat, a human being – Winger's friend, he is called – gets into the box, his own consciousness should collapse the wave function or split the universe or whatever, except that he obviously can't be conscious if he is dead, so it must be the universe which splits, and his consciousness must migrate to the universe in which, by whatever slender chance, he survives.'

'That's the Anthropic Cosmological Principle as applied to the individual,' says Kev. 'We live in this crazy world because it is the only one in which we have managed to survive at all. It is as if Wigner's Friend – let's call him Kev – has spent *all his life* in the bloody box. His consciousness gets channelled into increasingly improbable universes as his chances of survival decrease. God damn it, that's why deterrence has never been known to fail! We only experience the realities in which it succeeds!'

While he has been talking, the remaining missile-launcher convoys have been streaming out of the other gates. Now a wail of sirens goes up. The pigs go rigid and make a dash for the Base.

'Shit!' says Kevin. 'The four-minute warning!'

'It's OK for Schrödinger,' says Kev, who has to finish his lecture if it's the last thing he does. 'Schrödinger lives on in all the universes in which Wigner's friend dies. All these other universes exist at right angles to ours. They are like extra dimensions. I don't know how many dimensions something has to penetrate for it to be real. I mean, we wouldn't exist unless we extended into all four dimensions of spacetime, even if we don't perceive the full stretch of our extension in time, so maybe our extension into perpendicular universes also contributes to our reality. Shit; no wonder we are all like carbon copies of cardboard cut-outs!'

'Maybe it's worse than that,' he says. 'Maybe consciousness is actually a *property* of our worldlines warping through superspace, an advancing wavefront testing the probabilities. Maybe we have no other realities to choose. Maybe we really are like Schrödinger's cat, hardly alive at all . . .'

He is white; huge blobs of sweat conglomerating on his skin. Sitting on the bloody banquette in his mirror robe, he puts his arm around Lady Helga.

'If consciousness is a function of the splitting of reality,' he says through her hair, 'then the Cosmos must be the most conscious thing there is. Maybe there really is a god out there, after all. Oh God . . .'

The Base gates have shut. The lights are out. Only the bonfires and the Fairies' wands illuminate the silver birch forest. How the flesh crawls between my shoulder blades as I wait . . .

'Oh God!' cries Kevin, embracing Lady Helga.

'God!' cries Lady Helga, rigid with fear, incomprehension and disgust.

The Peace Wimmin are huddled together around their totem pole, keening so loudly that we can hear them over the sirens.

The Fairies are staring vacantly at the empty Base.

The yobboes are glaring belligerently at Kevin, white knuckles clenching the stems of broken lemonade bottles.

A sudden horrible flash of white light fills the sky – bolts through the coach – shows me X-rays of Kevin and Helga, hearts juddering as one, ribcages expanding with a simultaneous panic-stricken gasp of pure terror.

Time stops. Nothing moves except the incandescence boiling behind me. Kevin is leaning on Helga's shoulder, his face as white as her suit, a fountain of blood leaping from his head to her body. He is grinning insanely. She is soundlessly screaming at the mushrooming image reflected in her glasses and scattered by all the thousands of mirrors on Kevin's mum's dress –

– The incandescent apparition billows and bellies and bulges in the stillness, and suddenly fills the whole of my perceptions . . .

The goddess! – hair streaming like comet tails, great milky breasts and a belly that spawns galaxies – stands astride the Base, smiling like all the Fairies rolled into one. At her right hand, an ICBM hovers motionless in space, an unmoving vapour trail marking its downcurving trajectory. Her coalsack eyes consume us. Her cavernous nostrils breathe us in.

I ascend into the mind of God, my consciousness compounded with that of the million Fairies, still carrying their nauseating song.

We love the flowers, *We love the vegetables*, celestial voices sing in the echoing cathedral of the cosmos, as we look out at the world through the eyes of God. Although the world is round, we can see every inch of it. Although it is big, we can see every atom.

> We love the children
> And baby animals.

Through two million sleepy, sentimental eyes, I see the world in all its misty, rainbow-tinted, throat-catching sweetness: a sugary cake with a miraculously delicate icing: a tender extension of our own flesh over which the horrible missiles hang in their thousands; painted, pointed, poisoned and poised to devastate.

We want to live in a world of peace and harmony. With no more mi-i-siles, no more mi-i-siles, no more mi-i-siles, no more mi-i-siles, sing choirs of angels, sing in exultation; as the Fairies, filled with the knowledge of power and the memory of Bible readings, direct the hand of God to abolish these abominations from the face of the earth.

1 And God stretcheth out Her hand and gathereth unto Herself all the nuclear warheads of the world; strategic, theatre, tactical and battlefield; and all the delivery systems thereof. From the skies and from the seas and from caverns deep within the Earth plucketh She them. And God seeth that it is good.

2 And God taketh all the chemical and biological weapons, the lasers and the particle beams and all the devices upon which they are borne.

3 And unto Herself God gathereth all the conventional weapons. And God seeth that it is very good.

4 And God calleth out unto us and saith; Behold, the world is disarmed. And we cry unto her; God, behold the military – industrial substructure, the communications networks and the nuclear facilities.

5 And God sweepeth away everything scientific, technical, electrical, mechanical, industrial and commercial. The automobile and the television set destroyeth She them.

6 And a great fear dawneth in our minds and we cry out; Oh God, what have we done? For now the Male will establish dominion over us, for he is strong in body, and great will be his anger when he seeth what we have wrought. And God heedeth us, and taketh from every male one part in seven of his greatness and of his strength, and giveth it to every female. And God seeth that it is exceeding good.

7 And a quarrel ariseth in our minds, and some say; Let us keep what we have left, and others say; Nay, for it is possessions which determine the power structure. And we look down upon ourselves and, knowing ourselves strong, we call upon God to sweep away every artefact from the face of the Earth, and to cause the trees and the beasts of the field to take up their dominions on the ruins thereof. And it is done.

And we are back in our bodies again, naked under the apple tree which has grown in place of our coach. God hovers above us, all humanity's handiwork piled upon her roseate palm.

Smiling dreamily down upon us, she kneads it like dough, like putty, like chewing gum, like snot. A star lights up between her nacreous fingernails, infringing the splendour of God, who shrinks to get a better grip. She compresses the star until the core collapses. The radiance of a supernova momentarily flushes God's being; a butterfly God now, surrounded by a glowing halo of ejected material, wrestling with a pinhead sphere of neutronium.

God is grimacing like a woman in childbirth, struggling to overcome the neutron degeneracy pressure. Her face becomes ever more red and contorted, then purple and distorted, as she squeezes the sphere into its own Schwartzchild radius. The sphere becomes a black hole. The black hole draws in God. For a moment her dark and straining scowl, the inverted negative of her blissful smile, hangs in the draining accretion disc, then it fades out.

The Heisenberg loan is repaid. God is dead. As she leaves the universe, the thunderclap that heralded her arrival reaches us, bowing the forest, shaking a basketful of transcendental apples from our tree.

There is nothing in the sky now except the first glimmerings of a new dawn. All around me, godlike women are rising to their feet, flexing their new muscles, embracing, dancing in glowing rings of bouncing flesh, rejoicing. Their laughter rings through the woodland glade, shaking dewdrops from trembling blossoms, alerting shy little animals, alarming the terrified menfolk cowering in the darkness of the forest which replaces the Base.

Light floods the new world. From now on we live in harmony with each other and with nature in the motherly bosom of the world. It is going to take some getting used to. I imagine the desolation and confusion of the rest of humanity, stripped of walls, boltholes, hoarded food, status and threat.

The women reach out to the frightened, elfin men, offering them the ripe fruit that hangs from the trees. Smiling uneasily, they sit down to the post-Armegeddon picnic.

I see it all cloudily, through a rainbow. Helga is sitting apart from the glorious rejoicing, still clasping Kevin in her brawny arms. A single embarrassing tear trickles down her rugged cheek. Kevin is dead. No room for his neurotic invocations of Schrödinger and Heisenberg in the first of the last of all possible worlds. When God, arising from the foam of quantum indeterminacy to refashion the world as a Disneyland Eden, took one seventh part of his strength, she took more than he had to give. His worldline terminates here.

Notes on the Authors

Neil Ferguson contributed a witty story called 'The Monroe Doctrine' to *Interzone: the 1st anthology*. Since then he has published his first collection of short stories, *Bars of America* (1986). Born in 1947, he lives in London.

Gregory Benford, a working physicist at the University of California, has become one of America's best-known science-fiction writers during the past decade. He is the author of *In the Ocean of Night* (1977), *Timescape* (1980), *Artifact* (1985) and other novels which combine hard science and a humane style.

J. G. Ballard has written several stories for *Interzone* magazine, including 'The Object of the Attack' which we included in our first anthology. He is one of Britain's best-known novelists, author of *The Drowned World* (1962), *Crash* (1973), the prize-winning *Empire of the Sun* (1984; currently filming with Steven Spielberg as director) and a new novel, forthcoming.

Michael Blumlein has written a novel, *The Movement of Mountains* (1987). He is a native of San Francisco. His first story for *Interzone*, 'Tissue Ablation and Variant Regeneration', proved extremely controversial.

Kim Newman, born in 1959, is best known as a film critic (*Nightmare Movies*, etc.). He has contributed three science-fiction tales to *Interzone*. A graduate of Sussex University, he lives in London.

Scott Bradfield is another of *Interzone*'s 'West Coast discoveries'. His three stories for the magazine have been widely praised. Born in 1955, he now lives in San Clemente, California.

Brian Stableford, born in 1948, is an under-appreciated British sf writer. Many of his novels have appeared only in the United States as paperback originals (*The Realms of Tartarus* (1977), *The Castaways of Tanagar* (1981), and more than twenty others.) Recently, he has begun to write short stories in earnest: 'And He Not Busy Being Born . . .' is one of the first fruits of this new burst of creativity.

Rachel Pollack, American-born, lives in the Netherlands. Her story in *Interzone: the 1st anthology* was the memorable 'Angel Baby'. She has written a number of non-fiction books, as well as a science-fiction novel, *Golden Vanity* (1980).

Peter T. Garratt was born in Brighton in 1949. He is a clinical psychologist by profession, and is also active in Liberal Party politics. His stories have appeared in various small magazines.

John Shirley, born in 1953, and **Bruce Sterling,** born in 1954, are among the leading exponents of the so-called 'Cyberpunk' movement in American sf. Each has written several novels. Among recent titles are Shirley's *Eclipse* (1985) and Sterling's *Schismatrix* (1985). Bruce Sterling has also edited *Mirrorshades: the cyberpunk anthology* (1986).

Paul J. McAuley, a biologist at Oxford University, has recently sold stories to *Amazing, The Magazine of Science Fiction* and to *Interzone*. He is fast gaining a reputation as one of the best new British writers of traditional science fiction.

Thomas M. Disch, celebrated as a poet as well as an sf writer, is the author of *Camp Concentration* (1968), *334* (1972), *On Wings of Song* (1979) and *The Businessman: a tale of terror* (1984), among other fine works. One recent success is *The Brave Little Toaster* (1986), a children's novella which is being turned into an animated film by the Walt Disney company. Born in 1940, he resides in New York.

Garry Kilworth's most recent novel is entitled *Witchwater County* (1966). He has been writing science-fiction stories for a dozen years, since he won first place in a *Sunday Times* / Victor Gollancz sf competition. Born in 1941, he served in the Royal Air Force from 1959 to 1974.

Ian Watson has published many novels and short-story collections since his first book, *The Embedding* (1973), startled sf readers with its intellectual boldness and imaginative flair. Born on Tyneside in 1943, he now lives in a small Northamptonshire village.

Lee Montgomerie has recently become *Interzone*'s Associate Editor. She has written several stories and numerous book reviews over the past decade. Born in Zambia, she has lived in Leeds for many years.

ACKNOWLEDGEMENTS

We wish to thank the following peopole who have helped with the editing, production and sales of *Interzone* magazine over the past two or three years: Paul Annis, Scott Bradfield, Alan Dorey, Malcolm Edwards, Gamma, Colin Greenland, Judith Hanna, Roz Kaveney, Ian Miller, Lee Montgomerie, Lin Morris, Andy Robertson and Bryan Williamson. We also wish to thank the book editor who had faith in us: Robyn Sisman.

All of these stories were first published in *Interzone*:

Neil Ferguson, 'The Second Third of C', *Interzone* 19, Spring 1987; copyright © Neil Ferguson, 1987.

Gregory Benford, 'Freezeframe', *Interzone* 17, Autumn 1986; copyright © Gregory Benford, 1986.

J. G. Ballard, 'The Man who Walked on the Moon', *Interzone* 13, Autumn 1985; © J. G. Ballard, 1985.

Michael Blumlein, 'The Brains of Rats', *Interzone* 16, Summer 1986; © Michael Blumlein, 1986.

Kim Newman, 'Patricia's Profession', *Interzone* 14, Winter 1985/1986; © Kim Newman, 1985.

Scott Bradfield, 'Unmistakably the Finest', *Interzone* 8, Summer 1984; © Scott Bradfield, 1984.

Brian Stableford, 'And He Not Busy Being Born . . .', *Interzone* 16, Summer 1986; © Brian Stableford, 1986.

Rachel Pollack, 'The Protector', *Interzone* 16, Summer 1986; © Rachel Pollack, 1986.

Peter T. Garratt, 'If the Driver Vanishes . . .', *Interzone* 13, Autumn 1985; © Peter T. Garratt, 1985.

John Shirley and Bruce Sterling, 'The Unfolding', *Interzone* 11, Spring 1985; © John Shirley and Bruce Sterling, 1985.

Paul J. McAuley, 'The King of the Hill', *Interzone* 14, Winter 1985/6; © Paul J. McAuley, 1985.

Thomas M. Disch, 'Canned Goods', *Interzone* 9, Autumn 1984; © Thomas M. Disch, 1984.

Garry Kilworth, 'Spiral Sands' (formerly entitled 'Spiral Winds'), *Interzone* 9, Autumn 1984; © Garry Kilworth, 1984.

Ian Watson, 'When the Timegate Failed', *Interzone* 14, Winter 1985/1986; © Ian Watson, 1985.

Lee Montgomerie, 'War and/or Peace', *Interzone* 11, Spring 1985; © Lee Montgomerie, 1985.

Interzone is published quarterly from 124 Osborne Road, Brighton BN1 6LU, UK. A four-issue subscription costs £7.50 (inland) or £8.50 (overseas).